"A riveting story that will hook you from page one. A terrific read. Unputdownable!"

—Deborah Crombie,
New York Times bestselling author

"The thrills are also abundant, and the plot takes a left turn when the reader is sure it's going right. Ryan has a gift for writing superb thrillers, and this one is sure to be a big hit with her growing fan base."

—*Library Journal*

"Ryan's trademark breathless storytelling and an almost unthinkable premise that will give every reader a chill. A terrific, fast-paced read spiced with just the right amount of romance."

—William Landay,
New York Times bestselling author of
Defending Jacob

Praise for *The Other Woman*

"Ryan raises the bar sky-high—I knew she was good, but I had no idea she was this good."

—Lee Child,
New York Times bestselling author

"Nonstop action . . . Ryan grabbed me on page one."

—Sandra Brown,
New York Times bestselling author

THE
WRONG
GIRL

HANK PHILLIPPI RYAN

To Mane
maybe so
need y! B
ham B

FORGE®

A TOM DOHERTY ASSOCIATES BOOK • NEW YORK

THE WRONG GIRL

A Forge Book
Published by Tom Doherty Associates, LLC
175 Fifth Avenue
New York, NY 10010

www.tor-forge.com

Forge is a registered trademark of Tom Doherty Associates, LLC.

ISBN 978-0-7653-6914-7

Forge books may be purchased for educational, business, or promotional use. For information on bulk purchases, please contact Macmillan Corporate and Premium Sales Department at 1-800-221-7945, extension 5442, or write specialmarkets@macmillan.com.

First Edition: September 2013
First Mass Market Edition: August 2014

Printed in the United States of America

0 9 8 7 6 5 4 3 2 1

Curiosity is lying in wait for every secret.

—RALPH WALDO EMERSON

THE
WRONG
GIRL

1

"Listen, Jane. I don't think she's my real mother."

Jane Ryland took the phone from her ear, peering at it as if it could somehow help Tuck's incomprehensible tale make sense. *Real mother?* She didn't know Tuck was adopted, let alone looking for her birth mother. Why would Tuck call *her*? And spill this soul-baring saga of abandonment, adoption agencies, then meeting some woman in Connecticut? Jane and Tuck were barely friends, let alone confidantes, especially after Tuck had—

The doorbell?

"I'm in your front lobby." Tuck's voice buzzed over the intercom at the same time it came through the phone. "Sorry to show up at your apartment on a Sunday, you know, but I couldn't come to the *Register,* of course."

Of course. It'd be humiliating for Tuck to visit Jane at the newspaper where they'd shared a cubicle as "news roomies" only months ago. Once a hotshot reporter, Tucker Cameron had been fired from the *Register* for sleeping with a source. The Boston Police public relations officer, of all dumb choices. In the months since, according to the nonstop newsroom gossip, the two pariahs, Tuck and Laney, had dropped off the map. Until now. But that was Tuck. *Never a dull . . .*

Jane pushed the red button in the intercom box, retied

the drawstring on her fraying weekend sweatpants, and opened her front door, making sure Coda didn't streak through her legs. The calico—a kitten, really—had arrived on the downstairs stoop a few weeks before, tiny paws icy with snow. All Humane Society intentions disappeared after the shivering fluff nuzzled into Jane's shoulder, but neither of them was quite used to the other yet.

Jane heard the entry door click open, three flights down, and Tuck's footsteps climbing the hardwood steps as she talked into her cell. "So what am I supposed to do now, roomie? I'm not a reporter anymore. No one will talk to me. Laney's looking for a job. I'm like a—well, you're the only one who can help me. The only one who was even nice to me. After."

Tuck's head appeared around the landing, a black knit cap over her dark ponytail. A puffy snow-flecked black parka emerged, then her black jeans. She paused, one leather glove grazing the mahogany banister, the other raised in tentative greeting. Tuck's trademark swagger—her outta-my-way confidence—was missing.

"Tuck? You okay?" Just another February at Jane's. First a stray kitten, and now—was Tuck crying? *Tuck?*

"I guess so." Tuck stomped the last of the snow from her salt-stained boots, punched off her phone, stuffed it into her parka pocket. "I'm trying to be angry instead of miserable. But I can't let this go."

She swiped under her eyes with two gloved fingers, wiping away what could have been snow. "It's my whole life, you know?"

"Tell me inside. Get warm. Dump your boots by the door." Jane took Tuck's soggy parka and cap, draped them over the banister, then ushered her visitor into the living room, pointing her to the taupe-striped wing chair by the bay window. Slushy snow pelted the glass, the wind clattering bare branches, the last of the afternoon's feeble gray light struggling through. Coda slept on the couch, almost invisible, curled on a chocolate-and-cream paisley cushion.

"Tea? Beer? Wine?"

"Wine. Thanks. This has really kicked my ass." Tuck plopped into the chair, then twisted one leg around the other. "The lawyer I contacted at first was worthless, then the agency got my hopes up, but now, well, this is worse than not knowing. Which is why I'm here."

Which made no sense whatsoever.

They'd been office mates for only about two weeks. Jane was dayside, covering politics. Tuck worked the night shift, seemed to care only about her sensational front-page Bridge Killer stories. Their paths crossed only when their stories did. Now for some reason Tuck seemed to think she needed Jane's help, so here she was. That was Tuck.

"Hang on a sec, let me get you a glass." Jane padded to the kitchen, grabbed the wine from the fridge, twisted it open. *What would it feel like, not to know your own mother?* As a kid, she'd thrown around adoption like a threat. "When my REAL mother comes to get me, you'll be sorry," a petulant eight-year-old Jane taunted her parents. She and BFF Laurie, slumber-party faces smeared in beauty goo, speculated in late-night whispers whether Jane's chestnut hair and hazel eyes meant she might really be adopted, might really be royalty or Bono's girlfriend's abandoned daughter.

Jane *did* know what being fired felt like. It happened to her last summer and the sting hadn't quite gone away. So if Tuck needed her for something? She held out the glass and sat cross-legged on the couch. Least she could do was pour some wine and listen. "Okay, all ears."

With Coda's purr a rumbling underscore, Tuck spilled the details.

Jane's reporter training switched into gear, assessing what could be wrong, or a coincidence, or a mistake.

She ticked off her questions, finger to finger, as she did with every story she covered.

"So back at the beginning. You called the agency. Your mother told you which one?"

"Yes. 'The Brannigan,' they call it. Brannigan Family and Children Services. Ten years ago, when I *first* called, they told me all the records were sealed until my birth mother gave the okay to open them. A closed adoption, you know? Then I guess I tried to forget about it. I mean, I was eighteen, she might have been dead. Plus, I knew my mom—adoptive mother—wouldn't love that I was looking."

Tuck paused, rolled her eyes. "She'd have said, in that snarky voice she uses, 'Why do you need *another* mother, Tucker dear? Am I not enough for you?'" She shrugged. "She'd probably still say that, even in her . . . condition. But she lives in Florida, she stayed in their condo thing after Dad died. So she'll never know."

"Condition? She's . . . ?" Jane searched for a way to ask. She missed her own mother every day. *Poor Tuck*.

"Yeah. Doctors say it won't be long, and ah, I don't know. I'm trying to deal with that, too. It's hard." She puffed out a breath, shook her head. "*Anyway*. Last week, after all that time, the Brannigan called to say they'd found my birth mother. It felt perfect, you know? With me and Laney serious, thinking of kids, and the last of my adoptive family almost gone? But now . . ." Tuck pulled the stretchy band from her ponytail, then twisted it back on. Took a sip of wine, carefully replaced her glass on the coaster.

She looked at Jane. "But now, even though I'm not at the paper anymore, I think I may be on to the story of my life."

2

"**Kurtz got here** first. She's got the two of 'em in her cruiser. See 'em? Parked out on the street?" The beat cop, a grizzled veteran Jake didn't recognize, cocked his head toward the Roslindale triple-decker's inside stairway. "Lucky my new partner likes kids. Looks pretty bad upstairs, gotta warn you, Detective Brogan. DeLuca's already up there. Back room on the left, second floor. Crime Scene's on the way. The ME. And family services. Snow enough for you?"

"It's Boston, right?" Jake's words puffed in the chill. He brushed now-melting flakes from his police-issue leather jacket, pulled out his BlackBerry for taking notes. He looked to the top of the stairs, scanning. Sniffed. Nothing. The entry door behind him was open, letting in the cold. Any smell was long frozen away.

"Door open when you got here, Officer Hennessey?" That's what the cop's badge said, R. Hennessey. Looked old enough to be a lifer, still on the beat.

Hennessey nodded. "They're canvassing, seeing if anyone saw anybody leaving. So far, no."

"And there are two kids? Whoever called nine-one-one wasn't clear. We know who that is yet? I have the kids as last name—" Jake checked his BlackBerry shorthand.

His phone always ridiculously auto-corrected. "Is it Lussier?"

"So says the nine-one-one caller." Hennessey, a stocky fire hydrant zipped into foul-weather gear, flapped his leather gloves against his BPD navy parka. "Wish we could close the damn door."

At least Hennessey knew enough not to touch the scarred wooden doorknob of 56 Callaberry Street. There was barely room for the two of them in the cramped square of dark-paneled foyer. The dusty bare lightbulb overhead didn't cut it, and the one on the first landing was out.

"So, the kids? Don't they know their mother's name?"

"We asked. 'Mama,' the boy said. Their own names, he knew. Phillip and Phoebe. What kind of a name is Phoebe?"

"Hennessey?" Commentary, he didn't need. "How many kids? The nine-one-one call indicated—"

"Apparently two. Maybe the caller meant three people resided here, ya know?" Hennessey shrugged. "We found a boy and a girl, approximately one and three years of age. Weren't crying or anything when Kurtz brought them down. Guess maybe they don't know. Victim's their mother, looks like, white female, age approximately thirty. Checking her ID now. Cause of death, looks like blunt trauma. No weapon so far. Like I said. Ugly. Frying pan, something like that."

"So says—?" Jake raised an eyebrow. It wouldn't have been Kurtz, the officer who had the kids in her cruiser. She was new on the street, just promoted from cadet, now evidently partnered with Hennessey. The ME was still on the way.

"So says your partner, DeLuca." Hennessey lifted his plastic-covered cap with one hand, propping it while he scratched a bristle of gray hair. "Guess he'd know. You two the big-time detectives and all."

Here we go. All he needed. Yes, his grandfather, Grandpa Brogan, had been police commissioner. Yes, Jake got his gold badge at thirty, three years ago. Jake had aced the academy, probably gotten higher scores than this guy. Still, even cracking last fall's Bridge Killer case, getting the commendation from Superintendent Rivera, hadn't stopped the sneers from the old-timers. "The Supe's fair-haired boy," they called him. Whatever.

Jake ignored the bait. "So the nine-one-one caller? Any ID? I know we'll have it on tape, but anything else I should know?"

"Yo, Harvard, that you?" Paul DeLuca's voice boomed down the stairwell. "You planning on coming up here anytime soon?"

"Chill," Jake yelled back. Jake's college history and Brahmin mother were a constant source of amused derision for his partner, though after a few close calls together and a couple of massacres on the basketball court, their relationship had matured into respect and good-natured banter. Jake held two thumbs over his phone keyboard. "So, Officer Hennessey? Anything? Sign of forced entry? Anyone else live in the apartment? Husband, boyfriend, the nine-one-one caller?"

"Nope. Nobody's owning up. Neighbors all say it wasn't them. Mighta been a blocked cell, ya know?"

Calling from a cell phone, Jake knew, didn't give dispatchers a GPS location. Enhanced 911 often worked only from a landline.

"Cell phone nine-one-ones are a bitch," Jake said. "Keep at the canvass, though, right?"

Hennessey's eyes went past him and out to Callaberry Street, where a gray-and-blue cruiser idled, plumes of exhaust darker gray than the darkening afternoon.

"Poor kids," the beat cop said. "They're screwed."

3

"The woman from the agency said my name is Audrey Rose Beerman, can you believe it?" Tuck laced her fingers together, clamped them on top of her head. "It's an okay name. But I don't feel like an Audrey Rose Beerman."

Jane took a sip of her Diet Coke, not quite sure how to react. What did Tuck want *her* to do?

"Maybe it's all about what we're used to. How we see ourselves." Plain Jane, Jane the Pain—the nicknames Jane'd been saddled with as a bookish kid in the relentless social hierarchy of Oak Park Junior High had sent her to name-fantasy world. *Anything but Jane.* For a while she'd wished to be Evangeline, courageous girl of the forest. Then Hyacinth, all flowy skirts and poetry. Her mother chose "Janey" when affectionate, "Jane Elizabeth" when making one of her pronouncements. As in "Jane Elizabeth Ryland is a perfectly good name. Evangeline is ridiculous."

Hey, Mom, Jane sent a message upward. *You were right. Miss you.*

But today was about Tuck. "So you didn't know your real name? Before?"

"Well, yeah. I did. That's one of the weird things, and tell you about it in a minute. But anyway, my—adoptive mother, I guess I'm supposed to call her—told me the agency always said my birth mother—" Tuck stopped mid-sentence, slumped her shoulders. "It's impossible. 'Real' mother? 'Birth' mother? 'Adoptive' mother? I mean, the woman I called my mother took care of me and changed my diapers and let me stay left-handed and yelled until the softball coach let me be the pitcher. She's kind of a whack job, at times, but what mom isn't, right? My biological mother, who conceived me, carried me for nine months, gave birth to me—she left me at the Brannigan."

Jane's eyes widened, she couldn't help it. How would it feel to take something from yourself, a helpless new human, and give it away? That child was now twenty-eight. Twenty-eight, bitter and confused. And, somewhere, was a woman grieving the loss?

"I'm so sorry," Jane almost whispered. "But your poor mother. It must have been horrible."

"Not so horrible she couldn't dump me at—well, whatever. My life has turned out fine. Even after the shit hit the fan, Laney and I are okay. He insists everything will work out." Tuck fiddled with the fringe on the chocolate-and-cream afghan draped over the chair. Jane's mother had crocheted it in her hospital bed, the last afghan she made. "Not feelin' it so much today, you know?"

Today was turning out to be quite the Sunday. Jane needed to get this talk back on track. Whatever that track was.

"So, Tuck. What is it you want me to do? You got a call from the Brannigan. They said they found your birth mother. You drove to Connecticut, and then what?"

"Long story short." Tuck folded the afghan over the arm of the chair. "I go to Connecticut. We meet at Starbucks. She's great, she's terrific, I'm in a Hallmark card or a Lifetime movie. I've never been so happy. I'm crying, she's crying. We each order a triple venti nonfat latte—exactly the same thing!—and we start crying again."

Tuck pressed her lips together, closed her eyes briefly.

"'Audrey Rose. You're so beautiful,' she says. 'I knew you'd be a knockout.' She said that, 'knockout.' 'You have my dark eyes,' she says, 'so skinny, and my crazy hair.' We spend two days together. I'm thinking—I have a biological family. I have a history. I have a story."

"Well, that sounds wonderful, Tuck. It sounds like—"

"No." Tuck slugged down the last of her wine. The timer behind the couch clicked on the bulbs of the brass lamp beside her. Jane was shocked to realize it was almost dark outside. February in Boston. It wasn't even five.

"I'm telling you, Jane. She's not my mother. She expected her long-lost daughter. But I'm . . . I'm not her."

"You're not—why would you think that? Come on, Tuck, why would they—?"

"I don't *know*. That's why I'm here. You're the reporter. My only—you've got to find out for me."

Tuck stood, tears welling, tumbling a throw pillow to the floor. Coda opened her tiny green eyes at the sound, looked up, then dropped her head back into her paws.

"Imagine how she'll feel? When she finds out?" One tear rolled down Tuck's cheek, and she swiped it away. "After all the plans? The calls? She looked so happy. But I know it. I *do*. They sent that poor woman the wrong girl."

4

The crime scene cleanup people would have quite a job on their hands. Not as bad as some Jake had seen, but murder was never good. They'd arrive soon enough, whoever the landlord hired, see it for themselves. Jake closed his eyes briefly, making a promise to the woman on the linoleum floor. "We'll find this asshole," he muttered. *Hennessey was right. Poor kids. Poor woman.*

There'd been nothing on the stairway. He'd kept his gloved hands off the banisters and walls, hugging the wall to avoid possible suspect footprints, was careful walking up the three flights to the top floor. The wooden front door of apartment C stood open, leading to a threadbare living room, cheap couch with haphazard pillows, then a dining room with an oval table, white tablecloth, three twisty metal candlesticks in the center, no candles. Clean. No family photos, no keepsakes. No sign of forced entry, exactly as Hennessey had reported.

"Yo, D. What you got?" he called toward what must be the kitchen, but DeLuca had gone out a back door. Left it open. A spotlight glared from one outside corner of the minuscule back balcony, and Jake saw his partner's lanky silhouette leaning over the wooden railing.

Three floors up. No escape that way, probably. Unless the bad guy could fly.

It was four steps across the living room to an archway into the kitchen. Jake paused, getting a read on the place. Sniffed, as he always did. No gas, nothing burning, a sweet fragrance of—maybe some cleaning thing. He surveyed left to right, cataloging the elements, typing notes without looking at the keyboard. Dented white refrigerator, seen better days, but clean, no grubby smudges around the handle. He'd have to check inside it. Two saucepans on a gas stove. Open box of Quaker Oats on the drain board. An open box of Cheerios, on its side, a few pieces spilled on the floor. *Cereal.* Jake looked at his watch. Five in the afternoon. *Huh.*

No dishes in the sink, a stack of multicolored sponges in a plastic dish, some generic green soap on the side. Kitchen table. A high chair, aluminum and plastic, not new, the molded pink serving tray wiped clean. A little pink bowl with a rabbit decal.

And that body on the floor. One side of her face against the once-ivory linoleum, the other revealing an angry red welt. More than a welt. The skin had already turned purple. Her eyes were open. A trickle of blood made a jagged seam across the yellowed floor, the dark seeping into the cracks between the tiles. *Blunt trauma?* Jake typed. *Weapon?*

White female, approx 30, eyes brown, hair blond, he typed. It spilled across her back, clean, shiny, cared for. Arms splayed. Hooded sweatshirt. Levis, bare feet. If you ignored what seemed the cause of death, it looked like the woman simply decided she needed a nap. Or been dropped from the ceiling. Had she—tripped? Hit her head on the stove? Or floor?

Jake stood, assessing. A siren wailed in the distance, the sound keening through the open back door. All the streetlights had popped on, and the interior lights in neighboring triple-deckers. People would be gathering below, the neighborhood disaster irresistible. Photog should get snaps. Sometimes the bad guys did return. Yellow crime scene tape should be up. Where the hell was the new ME? Maybe she was the siren.

It wasn't suicide, anyway. If the woman had been clonked with a frying pan, like Hennessey said, it wasn't in sight. No sign at all of a murder weapon. The woman looked poor. Had a family. But the place was—same as her hair—cared for. She'd be sad to see her kitchen messed up this way. Blood and Cheerios.

Jake never got used to that first moment. The first glimpse of the victim. Murder was the consequence of greed or fear or drugs or anger or frustration or money or whatever made someone explode and decide their needs were more important than whoever was in their way. Jake and DeLuca had seen their share. Solved their share, too. Plenty of bad guys owed their current long-term residency in MCI Cedar Junction to the work of Brogan and DeLuca.

Her ID was somewhere in the shabby little apartment. They'd find it, then find who she knew, then figure out who had a problem with her. This was a domestic, Jake predicted. They'd close it fast.

"Yo, Harvard." DeLuca stood at the back door, his sport coat open, black hoodie underneath, no hat. His hatchet nose red from the cold, he swiped the back of his gloved hand across it. "You ready to join us on this planet?"

"Yo, D," Jake said. Jane always said D looked like he'd gotten thinner every time they saw each other. DeLuca lived on black coffee and roast beef subs—maybe that was it. Right now Jake had a bigger question. Besides the murder weapon, another important thing was missing from this crime scene.

"We've got a dead woman." Jake zipped up his jacket, zipped it down, then up again, like he always did when thinking. "No apparent murder weapon. An empty apartment. Two little kids who can't talk. So who the hell called nine-one-one?"

5

Niall Brannigan strode up the front walk of Brannigan Family and Children Services, cataloging mistakes. No one had deadheaded the decorative mums along the garden path. Now some were rotting and brown. *Such* a waste of money. *Such* a poor public image. No one left tomorrow until those were gone. A fine mist lifted from the snowy grass, the last of the afternoon's light disappearing. Still light enough to see a litany of annoyances.

Fallen twigs and branches, pine needles strewn across the flagstones, patches of ice on the cobbles. What, the whole grounds crew was surprised it was winter? His polished wing tips, protected by stretchy rubbers, marched through the slush.

"Ridiculous." He said it aloud, swiping his plastic pass card through the new gadget mounted beside the front door. His father would have cringed, someone screwing holes in the wood Mother told him had come over on the *Mayflower*. Brannigan allowed himself the day's first smile. *Doubtful.* But a useful and effective story.

A bell pinged, a green light appeared, and he clicked open the door. Inside, only the night lights lit the dusky hallway. The place was closed Sundays—he'd come here after afternoon mass—but as executive director, he liked to confirm all was well. Organize a few files, the mail, the upcoming schedule. See what new children were arriving. And departing. Ardith wasn't waiting at home, but probably at her precious yoga, as always. Thank heaven for liberated spouses.

He wiped his feet on the bristly reed doormat, loosened his striped muffler, and began to unbutton his overcoat.

An office light shone down the hall. *On?*

Yes. On. A dull glow came through the narrow pane of one of the admin offices. *Someone was here?* He reached for his cell phone. Should he call 911? The second smile of the day curved his lips. Unnecessary.

The front door had been locked. So had the back, since no alarms clanged. Not a break-in. All he had to do was check the fancy computer scan on his fancy new lock machine, and he'd instantly know who was here, when they got here, and which door they used. No one had cleared overtime with him. Whoever was working today was doing it on their own time. And without pay.

He folded his gloves into a pocket, then crossed his arms, contemplating the closed office doors lining the carpeted hallway. One wall was all photographs, a calculatedly impressive gallery of silver-framed infants and toddlers and the occasional preteen. Their "wall of fame," they explained to first-time visitors. Privately the staff called it their "family jewels." Children were the Brannigan's profit center, even though the service was a properly registered non-profit. Their "profit" was making families, he often explained, not only the money. Although the money was lovely.

Brannigan sniffed, cleared his head of random thoughts. At sixty-seven some thought he should retire, turn the place over to—whoever. *Not going to happen.* But who was here? Door number one, admin, closed, no light. The second door, bursar, closed, no light. The third door, History and Records, Munson's office, no light there, either. His own office door, at the end, was still bathed in darkness, as it should be, a single pin spot illuminating his brass nameplate.

The fourth door. Closed as well, but a spill of orange glowed through the window and under the door. Lillian Finch's office.

Brannigan sniffed again. He might have predicted as much.

What had Mother always said? *You can't know too much about your employees.*

He knew enough about Lillian Finch to know exactly where she was. And as a result, he could predict exactly who was poaching Lillian's office on an illicit Sunday afternoon. Did she think he wouldn't find out? And now, he had a decision to make.

6

Maybe there was nothing to find.

Hush, Ella, she shushed herself, propping one elbow on Ms. Finch's desk and tucking a stray lock of hair back into the bobby pin. She'd been Lillian's eyes and ears for the past however many years, not that she'd ever call her Lillian to her face. Even those times when she'd been invited for tea at Ms. Finch's beautiful home.

Anyway. Lillian always kept every piece of paper, and had told Ella, again and again, that documentation was the key to everything. If there was something to find, Lillian would have it.

Ella turned another page in the thick manila folder she'd pulled from the bank of wooden file cabinets along the back wall. Birth certificate for baby girl Beerman, a certified copy. Father's name, not listed. Audrey Rose Beerman, dark eyes, dark hair, deemed healthy, all her shots. Letter from the birth mother. Court order. A revision. A few photos in an envelope—swaddled infant, toddler in a pinafore and floppy hat. Nothing odd, nothing strange, nothing she hadn't seen dozens of times in dozens of family folders.

Was that a noise in the hallway? She looked up from her paperwork, fingering the loop of one earring, her heart twisting for a beat or two. She wasn't supposed to be here on a Sunday afternoon. She'd get in trouble if anyone found out.

A noise? No. Only the creaking of the old building. Chilly, too, with the heat down. She buttoned her thin cardigan, wished she'd worn jeans instead of her corduroy skirt.

The call from that Tucker Cameron woman was, well, upsetting. She'd taken it the day before yesterday, Friday, last call of the afternoon. She'd already had her coat and muffler on, almost hadn't picked up the receiver.

She sighed. She never could resist the phone. What if it was a match? Wouldn't want to miss that. She'd answered, then tried to understand what the woman was saying, her words coming too fast to comprehend.

The wrong girl?

Impossible. The Brannigan was in the business of making families. Nothing "wrong" about that. Ella reassured the woman, as best she could, there was no mistake. Someone would call her back.

Should she have reported it? At five on a Friday? What good would that have done? Monday would be soon enough. Lillian wouldn't be angry with her.

She hoped.

Ella eyed Lillian's desk, the silver container of massed white roses next to a silver-framed photo collection of the families she'd created. Lillian was a saint, no question. Still, she was pushing fifty, fifty-five, maybe, and someday she'd retire. Ella would be ready to take the big desk.

She turned another page of the Beerman file. There was the R and R request from the mother, Carlyn Parker Beerman, asking the Brannigan to rescind her initial stop order of the closed adoption and release information requested by the birth daughter. Date of issue . . . Ella squinted at the page. Smudged. But clear enough, three months ago. She'd heard Ms. Finch phone the daughter herself.

She leaned back in Ms. Finch's puffy chair. Getting to make the Call was one of the things she loved most. They both did, she and Lillian. The call where you know you are changing someone's life. Two peoples' lives. Two strangers, two people who probably thought about each other every day, maybe missed each other every day, would finally be together. After all those years, a mother meets her daughter. A mother meets her grown-up son. A father sees his child for the first time. They recognize themselves in each other's eyes. They realize they're not alone.

A sacred moment. That's how Ella thought of it. Maybe it would even happen to her, someday. If she never found her own mother, she'd at least spend her life putting families back together.

There wasn't always a happy ending, *that* she knew. You can't choose your family, and sometimes people regretted reality. Even wished they'd never known the truth. That wasn't her responsibility. At the Brannigan, all they did was answer requests. After that, families were on their own.

But this Audrey Rose Beerman thing. Ella stared at the call log she'd filled out two days ago. Audrey Rose Beerman, because that's who she most certainly was, insisting she wasn't Audrey Rose Beerman.

Why would she say that? It was impossible.

Ella stood almost before she realized it. Her fingertips brushed the slick desk, the manila file sliding to the carpet, papers inside fanning out on the floor. That *was* a sound. It *was.*

7

"**Call from . . .**" The caller ID's disembodied voice came from the wall phone in Jane's kitchen. She winced, hoping it wasn't about to announce a call from Jake. Tuck already suspected their relationship, half-teased Jane about it when they worked together. That would be a real Dear Miss Manners moment, having Jane's "pal" in the Boston Police detective squad call her on a Sunday afternoon while Tuck sat in her living room. Unlike Tuck, Jane still had her job. Unlike Tuck, it was because Jane hadn't gotten caught. Jane and Jake realized their careers were safe only as long as their relationship wasn't discovered.

Not that there *was* a relationship. There couldn't be, not while Jane was a reporter and Jake a cop. They'd skidded their passion to a halt one night last summer, after a little too much wine and almost too little clothing. What if someone found out? Was it worth their careers? Sleeping with a source was forbidden, according to the *Register*'s ethics protocol. The Police Department's, too. It wasn't as if she was one bit in love with the sandy-haired twinkly-eyed hilariously funny and brilliantly—

". . . Alex Wyatt," the caller ID voice finished. "Call from Alex Wyatt."

"I know you have to get that." Tuck clamped her arms across her chest, propping her feet on the coffee table. "Tell that jerk I said—well, no, don't. Probably better for your career if you don't let on I'm here. Right?"

"Gotcha." Alex wasn't a jerk, though. Tuck was bitter since he'd been the one who fired her. But as brand-new city editor, Alex had gotten word from on high. He'd had no choice. "Although he's actually not—well, whatever."

Jane uncurled from the couch, scrabbling her fingers through her finally growing-out but still too-short hair, speculating. Why would her boss call on a Sunday? The *Register* newsroom staff was barebones—increasingly worrisome budget cuts hit the weekend staff especially hard. A front-page story could happen at any time, any day. Problem was, news doesn't know what day it is.

"Call from Alex Wyatt." If there was a big story, she'd be lucky to get it. Especially since she was the new kid and even veteran reporters were getting laid off. Jane tipped one hand in a pouring "more wine?" motion to Tuck, who handed over her empty glass as Jane dashed to the kitchen, sliding around the corner in her bare feet.

"Hey Alex, what's up?" She clamped the phone between her shoulder and cheek as she opened the fridge. Pretty bleak territory: weary celery, string cheese, a couple of Diet Cokes, and lemon yogurt. Last night's pizza. She pulled out the last of the Pinot Grigio and hip-checked the door closed.

"Sorry to call you on a Sunday. I'm swamped with snow coverage. Boston's fine, but half of Newton still has no power, National Grid is freaking, the governor's having another news conference, the Star Markets are outta milk. I mean—it's snowing, right? In New England? In February? You'd think—"

Damn. Snow? She'd just lost at news roulette. *Snow?* Freezing, boring, and bleak. How many weather clichés would she be forced to use? White stuff, winter wonderland, no business like snow business? But there was this pesky job thing. As in, she needed hers.

Jane eyed the wine bottle. Lucky she'd stuck with Diet Coke. She was a team player. She'd yank on her storm gear and take the T into town.

"There's a body in Roslindale," Alex was saying. "Cops telling us they suspect homicide. Got a pencil? I'll give you the deets. I know it's a mess out there—so I'll have the fotog pick you up in the newsroom Explorer. He lives close to you, it'll be no problem."

A murder? In Roslindale? *Okay, better than the snow assignment.* She winced at her cynical assessment. *That's what being a reporter does to you, turns human suffering into a calculation of potential column inches.*

"Yeah, I know. Better than snow." Alex was reading her mind, as usual. He'd been a reporter, too, her competition, until his promotion last summer. As a result, another promising romance prospect—Hot Alex, as her best friend, Amy, had dubbed him—bit the dust.

"This one's different," Alex continued. "Two little kids left alone, Family Services has them. 'Tragic,' our stringer says. There's no one else to send. I'll hand it off to another reporter tomorrow, so only this one story. I'll need your piece for the earlies, so chop chop. And Jane?"

"Yeah?" She'd better take food. Jane stretched the spiral phone cord so she could reach to open a cabinet. She pulled out a plastic sandwich bag, twisted open a half-full jar of salted almonds, and dumped in the entire contents. Opening the fridge, she added the string cheese to the bag. In the car it'd stay cold.

"Detective Jake Brogan's the primary," Alex said. "Think you can get us some exclusive stuff?"

"I—you—why would—" Jane's stomach clenched and the taut phone cord knocked the empty almond jar from the counter. It hit the floor, cracking into three pieces on the tiles. Coda, eyes wide, appeared in the doorway.

Jane shooed her away, fearful of the glass. *Jake?* Alex knew they were friends, but what if he now suspected—? Or was he—

"Kidding," Alex said. "Keep me posted, Jane. Fotog's on the way. Like I said, he lives near you, so, all the better. We go to press in three hours."

8

"**Friggin' media. Looks** like a headlight circus down there. TV live trucks, the whole nine yards." DeLuca plastered himself against the living room wall, using one hand to pull back the lace curtains covering the windows, craning his neck to peer outside without being seen. "How the hell do they find out so fast? They're here before the friggin' ME. You seen the ME yet? Squad says she's hot."

Jake ignored him. Though he'd heard the same thing about the new medical examiner, now was hardly the time.

"Where the hell is Family Services?" Jake said. "Radio down to Kurtz, D. Tell her to get out of here, no sirens, take the kids to headquarters, someplace safe."

This was turning into a shit show. Jake eyed the open front door of apartment C. "All we need is a bunch of cameras blasting in those kids' faces. Whoever they are. And whoever their mother is."

"Was." DeLuca let the curtains go.

"Was." Jake looked toward the kitchen, where the woman's splayed body seemed to soak up all the light in the room. They could do nothing until the medical examiner arrived to clear the scene. Then they could focus on finding whatever would close the case. Jake predicted two hours, max, they'd have a suspect. Boyfriend, ex-husband, jealous lover. Certainly a man. *Probably.*

A squawk from DeLuca's radio interrupted his thoughts.

"Kurtz is outta here, she says. The kids'll be at HQ. My take?" D cocked his head toward the body. "This one's textbook. Domestic. I give it a couple hours. We'll be booking some sleazeball ex-husband."

Hearing from DeLuca exactly what he'd been thinking made Jake wince. Cops' number one mistake, jumping to conclusions. Meant trying to mold the clues to fit the story they'd created instead of waiting for the real story to reveal itself.

"Could be," Jake said. He yanked the zipper on his jacket, then caught himself in the silly habit. Jane always gave him grief about it. "Or not. Where the hell is the damn ME? We're screwed until she—"

"Until she what?"

Katharine Bradley McMahan, MD. Jake had only seen photos, but this was definitely her. The puffy black parka, glistening with snow and with MCMAHAN embroidered in red on the chest, looked two sizes too big for her. She lugged a battered square black leather bag, white-stenciled MEDICAL EXAMINER.

Jake had skipped the governor's welcome reception for the second female ME in Massachusetts, figuring he'd meet her soon enough on the job. The papers had called her predecessor FrankenDoc, and he was now awaiting trial for trafficking in human organs. Scuttlebutt was Dr. McMahan, with her Ivy League degree and hot-shot pedigree, had been shipped in from L.A. to erase that grisly image.

"I'm looking for Detective Brogan?" The woman glanced at Jake, then DeLuca, then decided on Jake. Her dark hair was coated with snow, her ears pink with the cold. The dripping leather laces of her snow-stained boots dangled to the floor, untied, tongues flapping open, revealing blue scrub pants tucked into thick wool socks. She stayed on the hallway side of the threshold.

"I'd shake your hand, Detective, but my mittens are soggy. Before I come inside, I've got to—you're Detective DeLuca, right? I'm Doctor McMahan. Call me Kat, okay? Whatcha got?"

"I'm Paul—," DeLuca began.

"White, female, thirty-something," Jake said at the same time. *How old was McMahan, anyway? Twenty?* She barely came up to his shoulder. About to drip all over his crime scene. "Appears to be blunt trauma. No murder weapon yet. You ready to take a look?"

"Let me get this stuff off, my boots at least. We don't have snow in L.A. How do you guys manage? I'm a disaster." She put her medical bag on the hallway floor, clicked it open, pulled out a clear plastic ziplock bag, stuffed her mittens inside, and put the plastic bag on the hallway floor. She kicked off her boots, toe to heel, then stood in the doorway, dangling one dripping boot in each hand. "Ah. Situation."

Jake watched in disbelief as D reached out as if to—take her boots?

"Paul DeLuca," he said. "Maybe I can—"

"Oh, I'm fine, thank you so much, Detective." The ME gave him a quick smile, then tucked both boots under one arm, drew out another plastic bag, bigger, and stuffed them inside. She placed the boot bag on the hallway floor next to her mitten bag, pushing it with one toe when it tipped over.

This has to be a joke. DeLuca was shifting his feet, fidgeting as if he'd just met the prom queen. And this bag-toting California Girl was about to pronounce the cause of death? *Jane will not believe it.*

Jake pointed toward the kitchen. "Dr. McMahan?"

"Kat, remember?" She hung her parka over the newel post and picked up her medical bag. "Bring it on."

* * *

"Bring it on." Jane pulled down her fleece cap, tucked in her plaid muffler, clicked off her seat belt. So what if the TV stations were here already? Not her problem anymore. She didn't miss TV. *Not at all.* "Got my snow boots, got my trusty notebook, got a pencil."

Alex had sent fotog Hector Underhill, who'd arrived at her apartment almost before she could throw on her thick-soled snow boots and down-filled parka. He'd started complaining before they'd driven half a block. Newer at the paper than she was, "call me Hec" was one of the *Register*'s new crop of "budget-saving freelancers." With thirty-two days and counting, he griped, left in his freelance gig.

Jane had not been eager to hear yet another life story from a bitter journalist she barely knew. But she was a team player. "Any big plans for what's next?"

"Nope. I've got some other stuff going, though. Here and down south. With my nephew. I'll concentrate on that, I guess." They turned off the main drag, headlights battling the gray afternoon, windshield wipers clacking away the snow. "Sucks to be a freelancer at fifty-five. Sucks to be old."

They'd hit the jackpot on parking, even found a semi-legal spot. Smoky exhaust plumed from three TV live trucks double-parked along Callaberry Street, their rear doors open, news crews huddling inside. Jane remembered those cramped quarters, never enough room, the flickering monitors and squawking radios and snaking cables, empty coffee cups and discarded potato chip bags, the editing panic to crash a story on the air before deadline. She'd always made it. Always.

"You miss video?" Hec slung a battered leather camera case across one shoulder and opened the car door, then turned back to her, brows furrowing under his green Celtics cap. "Hope that's not stepping on toes."

"All good," Jane said. Everyone knew she'd been fired from Channel 11 last year for protecting a source. Truth be told, she wasn't completely over it. *Jerks.* But no reason to dwell. She knew how Tuck felt, though, with the rug being pulled out from under her. She hoped Tuck was okay.

She sure didn't seem okay.

Jane had promised to call her tomorrow. *No time to think about that.* "It's all in my rearview. I'm all about the *Register.* Now I don't have to worry about my hair, right?"

"I hear ya." Hec slapped a laminated press placard onto the dashboard and pointed to a gray triple-decker across the street. "I'm betting it's that house."

"That's why you get the big bucks." Jane dug out her notebook and cell phone, stashed them in her parka pockets. "Leaving my purse in here, okay?"

She checked the digital clock on the dashboard, then joined the media crush on Callaberry Street. Two and a half hours till deadline. Piece of cake.

9

Jane's voice. **Downstairs.** Though Jake couldn't make out the words, he recognized it. Arguing with Hennessey—that much he could make out through the open apartment door, probably trying to convince him to let her upstairs to the crime scene. Which she knew, and Hennessey knew she knew, wouldn't happen. Though that would never stop Jane from giving it her best shot.

Jake smiled, imagining that tilt of her hips in those ratty jeans she loved, the way she planted her fists on her waist when she was trying to make a point, how she was just the right amount shorter than he was. How terrific she smelled. *What was she doing here?* He yanked on his jacket zipper, then tried to focus on what Kat McMahan was saying.

"In summary, preliminary findings pending autopsy indicate subdural hematoma, suggesting intracranial bleeding, severe concentric damage to the right occipital cranium originating in a stellate fracture." McMahan held a tiny silver recorder to her lips. She'd unbuttoned her white lab coat, revealing a black I HEART L.A. T-shirt underneath. "Suspected massive blunt trauma. Severe lacerations to the upper right forehead, evidence of protracted external bleeding. Why? No obvious defensive wounds, fingers are . . ."

McMahan stopped, crouched, then encircled one of the woman's wrists with a gloved thumb and forefinger, leaving the victim's pale hand dangling. ". . . undamaged. No bleeding of the cuticles, no broken fingernails. Place of death, kitchen, is heated and all windows are closed."

She looked up at DeLuca, narrowing her eyes. "Hey. You guys didn't close the . . ."

"No, sir. Ma'am. Doctor," DeLuca said.

"Kat," she said.

"We didn't touch a thing," DeLuca continued. "It's exactly like it was when we arrived. Kat."

Jake couldn't believe it. Jane downstairs. DeLuca up here. Never a dull moment. He should have gone into finance with his dad, or law school, like his mother always pressured him to. *Did Jane know he was here?* Jake half-listened for her footsteps on the stairs.

"Time of death approximately one P.M." McMahan sniffed, nostrils flaring. "Odor of—unknown. No signs of other injury, no broken bones, no external sign of drug use, no . . ." She hesitated, tilting her head, staring. She seemed to forget anyone was in the room except for her and the dead woman.

DeLuca, on the other hand, seemed to forget about the dead woman, his eyes only on the ME.

"You two see anything? Find anything?" McMahan stood, holding her latex-gloved thumb over a red button on the recorder, pausing it and her examination. "Murder weapon, I mean? Like a . . ." Using the recorder like a pointer, she traced the shape of the wound, as if reminding herself. "Maybe a . . ."

DeLuca cleared his throat. "Oh, no, ma'am. Not SOP. We were waiting for you before we—"

"Like maybe a what?" Jake interrupted. *Jeez. A dead woman on the floor and DeLuca was sucking up.*

McMahan shrugged and buttoned the recorder into a

side pocket of her lab coat. "I want to say . . . frying pan, but that's too cliché. No one has a rolling pin anymore, right? I mean, for what?"

"Detectives?" A voice from the hallway. Not Hennessey. Not Jane.

"Headquarters to Brogan, do you copy?" Jake's beeping radio interrupted whoever spoke from the hall. He gestured DeLuca to the door, *check it out,* then thumbed the talk button. "Dispatch? This is Brogan, I copy."

"Supe requesting a call, please, Detective," the dispatcher said.

Kat McMahan crouched again, examining the woman's bare feet.

"Jake?" DeLuca was already back. "Afterwards is here."

McMahan looked up from the feet. "Afterwards?"

"Crime scene cleanup company," Jake explained.

"Detective Brogan, do you copy?" The dispatcher's voice crackled through the room. "Superintendent Rivera is standing by for your call."

"That's efficient," McMahan said. "*Too* efficient. They always show up like this? Kinda soon. Kinda crowded in here about now."

"Copy," Jake said into his radio. "Will do. And—"

"They're telling me the landlord called, Jake," DeLuca said. "Says he told 'em to start with—"

"Negative. Big time," McMahan interrupted, talking over him. "My crime scene guys aren't even here yet."

Jake held up a hand. "Tell Afterwards to go the frick away. Someone will alert them when they're needed. And tell them—wait a sec. They say the landlord gave them the go-ahead? Great. Ask the Afterwards people who the hell the landlord is. Get his number, then call and find out who this tenant is. Mystery solved, right?"

* * *

That had been a pitiful waste of time. The cop, Hennessey, hadn't given Jane the time of day, no matter what she tried. Worse, she already *knew* the time of day, which grew later and later as she learned less and less about whatever happened upstairs.

She trudged toward the Explorer, feet freezing, fingers freezing, regrouping. Jake was upstairs. With numbing fingers, she found the cell phone in the pocket of her black parka, flipping it over and over in the silky lining. She was a reporter, he was a cop. Should she text him?

If they weren't trying to keep up appearances she'd have called him, probably a couple of times by now, as she would any other source. But now, she couldn't. The wages of deception.

Now, she had nothing. Usually there were neighbors, onlookers, sniffing around, some spotlight-seekers hoping to be interviewed. At this point, she'd be happy with a victim's name and a couple of those generic "seemed like a quiet family" or "they loved their kids" pseudocomments. Today all the easy pickings were probably peering out their front windows, curious, but staying warm. Inside.

Jane sighed. Time to knock on some doors. Never the best idea, especially not after dark in an unfamiliar neighborhood. Sure, knocking on the right door could get her some info. Knocking on the wrong door could get her in trouble. But a deadline was a deadline, and hers was a quickly evaporating one hour away.

"Whatcha got?" Hec leaned against the car, waiting for her, arms crossed over his array of cameras. "I shot a couple exteriors, nothing exciting. That cop at the door, wide, medium. Nothing that'll win us a Pulitzer. Or get us a front page. Any ideas?"

The ME's white van was parked in front of a fire hydrant a few yards away. That at least confirmed there was a victim, one who was probably dead. Someone had cleared the snow from the hydrant, but whoever got out of the van on the passenger side had stepped right into a knee-high pile of slush.

"Let's look for a person with wet shoes," Jane said. "Hey. Check out the vans."

One after the other, the side doors of the multicolored news vans clanged open, the vans looking like circus clown cars as they disgorged neon-jacketed reporters, photographers lugging cameras with unwieldy tripods, and engineers with clackety metal light stands tucked under their arms and rolls of cable coiled over their shoulders.

"Grab your stuff, Hec." Jane pointed to the vans, all doors now flapping open, their glaring spotlights aimed at 56 Callaberry. "They're raising their microwave antennas. Reporters are actually coming outside. Damn. Something's up. Why didn't *we* know whatever this is?"

Her cell phone trilled. Was it Jake? Maybe that Hennessey cop had ratted her out, not knowing he'd actually be telling Jake *she* was here. She dug for the phone. Not Jake. *Alex.* He'd better be giving her info, not asking what was going on. Because she had no idea. This would have been a good day to stay home.

Too late now. "Hey, Alex. What's up? We're—"

"You set for the news conference?" Alex was talking before she finished. "You probably got this, but the BPD flack called. Says the body's on the third floor, cops are coming outside with a statement. That'll be a new top for your story."

A silhouette appeared behind the crime scene tape at the open front door of the murder house.

She'd recognize that shape anywhere.

"On it, Alex," she said.

10

Kellianne Sessions wished for the billionth time for some way to avoid looking like the Pillsbury Doughboy. It was completely freezing out, so she'd layered tights and a long-sleeved leotard under her jeans and T-shirt, zipped herself into the required white Tyvek, then put her white puffer jacket over that. Why she had to wear the moon suit now, before they even started, was totally ridiculous. But Kevin said the clients bought into it, said it made their Afterwards crew look "professional." Her brother, the big shot.

If Kev was such a big shot, how come they always, always, got to the murder scenes too early? She was sick of it, sick of waiting, sick of this stupid job and sick of the whole gross idea.

But that's what the Sessions family did. Kevin, Keefer, and Kellianne. And their mother, Karen, who kept the books and made the appointments and got their hazmat certifications and made sure their dad ordered enough cleaning stuff. *If it was good enough for your father . . .* Her brain gagged at her mother's perpetual chant. If she never heard it again, it'd be too soon. Talk about soon. Soon she'd finish her classes, pay off her tuition bills, buy a one-way ticket to someplace warm with palm trees and water and no freaking snow and no freaking dead people to clean up after.

Someday.

Right now, she was cramped into the incredibly hot back seat of the Afterwards truck, Keefer in the front seat zoned out with his ear buds, Kevin inside the triple-decker. She'd bet ten billion dollars they were too early again. She wiped a place on the car window with her fingers to see out. The news people were still here, for crap sake, she recognized that hooker-looking girl from Channel 5. And that was absolutely the ME's white van parked by the hydrant. Long as the ME was still here, they couldn't go in and start. Even she knew that.

"Yo, team." Kevin opened the driver's side door, blasting her with cold air.

Team. What a full-blown moron. *Who died and put him in charge?* She winced, remembering the morning's visit to the hospital. Well, their father hadn't died *yet.*

Keefer looked up, his head still moving in time to whatever played on his iPod.

"We're in, we're golden." Kevin cranked the heat up even higher. "Gotta wait till the news conference ends, then the ME's guys are coming to take the body. Maybe an hour or two. Then us. So we'll stand by. Ten-four?"

Kellianne rested her forehead against the chilly glass, staring at nothing. *Ten-four?* What a *moron.* They were *so* screwed. And Keefer and Kevin never seemed to care.

She was counting the days.

Ella stood, motionless, waiting. Listening. That *had* been a sound, she was sure. But now, standing with fingertips barely touching her boss's desk, she had second thoughts. Maybe she was a little jumpy. Well, okay, guilty, because how could she explain why she was going through papers in her boss's office?

Well, she *could*, but the explanation would not be a good one. She was supposed to go through channels, Mr. Brannigan always said. Snooping through files on a Sunday was *not* channels.

She counted to ten, silently, then to ten again. Listening.

Ella, you're losing it, girl. She tried a tiny smile, wondering if she could smile her fear away. Whistling a happy tune would make noise. The silly thought made her smile again.

She nodded, convincing herself. She was alone. There was no one outside.

Should she go look?

Easing herself back into Lillian's leather chair, she leaned down and gathered the spilled papers back into the manila file. What she could also do, of course, was copy it all. Then, from home, she could call this not-Audrey-Rose-Beerman, this (she checked the file) Tucker Cameron. See what she could find out.

Who would know?

Niall Brannigan stood, silent, in the muted light of the carpeted hallway, watching the glow of light under Lillian Finch's office door. He'd checked the parking lot. No cars. A few taps on his office computer confirmed Ella Gavin's pass card had been swiped two hours before. Naturally, he hadn't announced to the staff that he could monitor their pass card use. Why offer his employees knowledge they didn't need?

Never one to rush a decision, he imagined—in fact savored—what would happen if he simply opened the door of Lillian's office and confronted the girl. She was a girl to him, no matter what he was supposed to call her.

One other option was to do nothing. Give her enough rope to hang herself. She'd have to walk out at some point, use her pass card to leave. He could check the time remotely from his home. On Monday, he could ask this young lady exactly what she thought she was doing.

Enough rope, he decided.

He spun the gold links of his watchband around his wrist, feeling their slickly solid weight, remembering the same watch on his father's wrist. What would his father have done with such an impertinent employee? One who disregarded protocol and thumbed her nose at procedure? One who was clearly snooping where she didn't belong?

His smile broadened. Who cared what his father would've done?

Niall was in charge at the Brannigan now.

11

"**I'm Detective Jake** Brogan, this is my partner, Detective Paul DeLuca, and with us is Dr. Katharine McMahan, medical examiner."

Standing on the wood-slatted front porch of 56 Callaberry, Officer Hennessey's uniformed bulk blocking the open door of the triple-decker behind him, Jake spoke into the bouquet of microphones TV crews had duct-taped to a metal light stand. He squinted into the battery of too-bright lights, wondering yet again what was so damn newsworthy about a poor woman's death. Crime Scene was inside, getting photos and fingerprints, so at least the investigation was underway. He put a shading hand above his eyes, pretending to scan the clump of reporters and photographers organizing themselves five steps below on the scraggly snow-patched front lawn. A couple of neighborhood types, lookies, lurked on the fringe. He was actually scouting for Jane.

"You guys ready?"

There. Black parka, that little stretchy hat. Some photographer stood beside her, snapping away. Still weird to see Jane without a TV camera.

"Jake!" a woman's voice called from the pack. "Lynne Squires, Channel Five. Can you give us an identification of the victim?"

"Can you confirm there's a victim?" came another voice.

"We hear there are kids." A man's voice. "This is Reuben Seltzer, from Channel Two. We're broadcasting live now, Detective, so can you confirm—"

"I have a brief statement," Jake interrupted, "we'll take a few questions, then we're done. It's late, it's cold, we're still investigating. You want more, you know to call Tom O'Day at headquarters." He paused. They were doing their jobs. Like he was trying to. "I'm here so you'll all go away and leave the neighbors in peace."

"Detective Brogan? Jane Ryland from the *Register*." Jane's voice. From the back. "The medical examiner doesn't usually come in person. Can you tell us—"

Katharine McMahan stepped forward, leading with her chin toward the bank of microphones, but Jake put out a hand, stopping her. "Ms. Ryland, as I said, I have a statement, it will come directly from me, and only from me."

"But Jake, she's got a point," another voice piped up. "Why is Dr. McMahan—"

"You guys want the statement?" Jake wasn't happy with this. It wasn't SOP for him to be in front of the microphones. But the new PR flack, Tom O'Day, was out-of-pocket somewhere, the Supe said. So Jake was "volunteered" for the short straw. *Sundays*. He should be inside with the crime scene techs, checking evidence, not out here babysitting the media.

"Ready? At approximately four forty-seven this afternoon Boston Police nine-one-one dispatch received a call reporting an incident at fifty-six Callaberry Street, Roslindale."

"It's a triple-decker, what floor?"

Jake ignored the question. They'd already checked the usual resources—registry records, resident list, even the phone book and Google. So far, nothing was showing for a resident at 56 Callaberry, apartment C. Interesting. As soon as he wrapped up this circus, he could go back to looking for answers.

"Units from Area B responded to the address in question, found the body of a deceased white female, approximately thirty years old, in a third-floor kitchen. Police also found two juveniles, both now in police protective custody awaiting results of our investigation. We are asking the public for help in this matter, and hope that anyone who saw or heard anything, or who may have some evidence or information about what happened or may have happened, or who is acquainted with the victim, please call the Boston Police tip line at . . ."

"We know the tip line number, Jake," a reporter's voice called out. "So is this a homicide? A domestic? Give us something, okay?"

"Do you have any suspects? Jake, should people in this neighborhood be afraid? Take extra precautions?"

Jake should have known this was coming. The no-win question. If he said people *shouldn't* be afraid, reporters would assume it meant they had a suspect and a motive, but weren't making it public. That would be the headline. If he said people *should* be afraid, reporters would decide a crazed unknown mother-killer was on the loose, and *that'd* be the headline.

As well as the end of his career as a cop.

"Our team is doing knock-and-talks now," Jake said, floating a non-answer, "to assess—"

"Any witnesses?" a voice interrupted.

"Is this the victim's home? Or whose?"

Porch lights flicked on at the house across the street, then the one next to it, and then the one next to that one. The Channel 2 guy had said they were broadcasting live. Talk about a ghoul magnet. People watching TV were now seeing their own neighborhood, live, on the air. They'd *all* be coming outside now, unable to resist the lure of disaster. Get their faces on the air, participate in tragedy, maybe record it all inside so they could watch the whole thing again later over a beer. *Time to get this thing over with*.

"The incident is now under investigation," Jake read the final line of the statement the Supe had e-mailed to his phone. "And we're done."

"Jake, Jake, one more question!"

Another reason why television sucked.

Jane hid a smile, remembering the not-so-old days when this frigid deadline-pushing news conference would have been a stress-inducing nightmare. "Going live" meant you had to ask the first question, make sure your news director saw you were the front-line big gun. Working for the *Register*, though, Jane kind of enjoyed watching it all play out, especially the TV types fighting for the spotlight. She'd make her deadline, piece of cake, and not have to worry about whether her hair frizzed in the misty snow. Leaving TV felt terrific. It *did*.

She watched Jake, squinting against the lights, field the barrage of questions. Dr. McMahan looked like a slinky version of one of those little Russian dolls-in-a-doll, all big eyes and dark hair and red lips. Franken-Doc's replacement was even hotter than the gossip that already surrounded her. Dr. McMahan whispered close to Jake's ear, then went back into the apartment.

So why *was* the ME here? Jake hadn't answered that.

Or much of anything else, for that matter. Jane had already used her phone to check resident listings for number 56, top floor, but nothing. No names. The cops had no ID. She didn't, either.

Jane listened with half an ear, suspecting Jake wouldn't reveal much more, and composed her story, scrawling it in pencil on her snow-dampened notebook. *Police are soliciting the public's help in finding the identity of a young woman found dead in her Roslindale triple-decker apartment Sunday afternoon. Officials revealed there are two children . . .*

Jane paused, mid-sentence. Poor things. Jake hadn't said their ages. But, really, there were three victims here, not only the mother. Life as those kids knew it—whatever it was—was certainly over. What would happen to them? Would relatives swoop them up? Maybe this marked their entrance into the bureaucratic morass of the foster care system. *Maybe that's a good follow-up?* Maybe she could talk with Alex about—but that was for later. She had less than an hour to bang out today's story.

Police admit they have no leads on the possible homicide at 56 Callaberry St., but say they were called to the scene by a—

Huh.

"Detective Brogan!" All the other reporters called him Jake in public. She didn't. They had to be careful. But she had one more question.

"Detective Brogan, Jane Ryland with a follow-up. You said you have no witnesses and no information. So who called nine-one-one?"

"Miss Ryland, any further information will have to come from Tom O'Day, media relations, at headquarters." Jake was answering Jane's question, hiding a smile, *of course she would pick up on the crux of this thing,* but suddenly Jane wasn't listening to him. She'd picked up a cell phone call in the middle of a news conference? Who'd be so important? "That's it, folks. Thank you."

He turned away from the mics and the lights and the still-clamoring reporters. That was over, at least. With no exploding land mines. It'd be worth some brownie points with the Supe, too, who'd probably monitored the whole thing on that ancient TV in his office. Now on to—he turned to check, couldn't help it. Jane still had her back to the house, hand cupped over her phone. Who was she talking to so intently?

"Leonard Perl," DeLuca interrupted his thoughts.

"Huh?" Jake said, turning back to him. "Pearl?"

"P-E-R-L. He's the landlord, according to the Afterwards dude," DeLuca said. "Lives in Florida. 'Fort Something,' the genius told me. So, case closed. We find this Leonard Perl, get the four-one-one on his tenant, track down her ex-husband or whatever, read 'im his rights, go home, and watch *Law and Order*. DeLuca and Brogan score again."

"Detectives?" Kat McMahan trotted across the first-floor landing and down the stairway, white lab coat flapping over her T-shirt and scrubs, her latex gloves not touching the walls or the banister. "Can you come upstairs again? I need to show you something."

12

"Can we go now? Please?" Kellianne Sessions gripped both hands over the back of the front seat, pleading with her older brother as he got into their van. Kev had joined the group of neighbors who arrived to check out the reporters while Keefer had stayed in the front seat, obliv, glued to his iPod. She'd sat through the whole news conference, sulking, sinking into her parka. Trapped, totally, by this whole thing. People had to die for them to get paid. How sick was that?

She'd probably wind up with some disease from all the junk they had to use to clean up after somebody who died. Whatever got rid of the stench and the crud, had to, like, eat away at your lungs and blood when you breathed it in. Sometimes the death smell stuck in her nose no matter what she did. She knew people looked at her funny. The smell was always part of her.

"What's the prob, Kel?" Kevin slammed the driver's side door. "You got a big date or something? He can wait. Then you can tell him all about your latest cleanup job. Bet the guys go nuts over that. You're the queen-a-death."

Jerk. She kicked the front seat with her boot for punctuation.

"Huh?" Keefer turned around, eyes wide, yanking out one earbud.

"Ignore her," Kevin told him. "Here's the drill. We'll wait till the cops leave, then go in and scope out the place. The landlord's guy got a key for us. We gotta see what there is, what we need to bring. We gotta call the landlord and give him the estimate—he's got insurance, so we're golden."

"Oh, right." Kellianne rolled her eyes. The estimate. Like that was reality.

"Then we'll book. And you can head off to meet Prince Charming."

Kellianne ignored him, counting the minutes. All the reporters were leaving, the news trucks pulling out of their parking spaces and heading off to their cool jobs at the TV stations. Funny, though, they had to show up for death, too. The cops, the really cute one in the leather jacket and the geeky tall one, were going back inside. Weird, now that she thought about it. Cops also had to show up for dead people.

She pulled out her phone, punched up her favorite game app, Killerwatt. Fun with death, right? That was her whole life.

Ella Gavin stared at the phone she'd dropped beside her on her living room couch. She had to think. She'd already called Miss Cameron, no taking that back. They'd arranged a meeting for tomorrow morning, Monday, before work. What could she do now? Probably stay up the whole night worrying. But it would be okay. Whatever was true was good.

She'd moved her knitting bag off the coffee table to make room for the stack of paperwork. It made her stomach twist to look at the sort-of-stolen documents. Was there a way the Brannigan people could discover who'd made copies?

Whiskers chose that moment to jump onto her lap, purring and nudging.

"I know, kitty. Maybe I shouldn't have done it. But it's my responsibility to help make sure things are all in order. These are people's lives, after all. And if Miss Finch made a mistake, somehow, and sent . . . poof."

The cat had brushed her tail across Ella's mouth. She plucked the cat hair from her lips, then cuddled her pet closer, comforted by the rumbling purr. "We're happy, right, Whiskey-roo? Everyone should be happy, and with those they love. That's what we do. And . . . and . . ."

A peculiar beep from the phone beside her startled them both. The cat jumped off Ella's lap onto the twisty brown throw rug.

"It's only out of batteries," Ella reassured herself as much as the cat. Why did this whole Brannigan thing make her such a scaredy? She was barely thirty years old, good at her job. She paid her rent, paid her bills, went to church, and someday would find the One.

"I'm not a wimp, kitty." She picked up the first page of her copied files. Easy to tell she'd been in a hurry—each page was skewed and off center. But the facts were clear. An infant called Audrey Rose Beerman had been left in Brannigan custody, then adopted by Brian and Deirdre Cameron. More than twenty years later, a grown-up Tucker Cameron had been informed that "Audrey Rose Beerman" was her first identity and Carlyn Parker Beerman her biological mother.

The paperwork looked perfectly in order. Lillian Finch did not make mistakes. But Tucker Cameron insisted it was wrong. Why?

Maybe she didn't get along with Carlyn Beerman? Maybe her adoptive mother was pressuring her? Ella had seen *that* often enough. Adoptive mothers got possessive, demanding, jealous. Wanted to keep up the illusion.

Being someone's "mother" could be defined in a lot of different ways.

"You can't choose your family, Whiskers. We are who we are."

Had she missed something? Should she look at the records again? She was tired. Confused. And she had to admit—frightened a little bit. She wasn't used to taking matters into her own hands. Too late now.

Beyond her living room curtains a frosty twinkle of stars emerged behind wisps of gathering clouds. Was Tucker Cameron the same person as Audrey Rose Beerman? If not—well, if not, what?

Tomorrow morning, she'd find out. Whatever was true was good.

13

"See?" **Kat McMahan** pointed to the kitchen floor. A once-shiny web of red had dried to crusting brown lines outlining each square tile.

"Blood on the floor? Yeah, I see it," Jake said.

"Well, I think—"

"They're gone downstairs." DeLuca appeared in the doorway. He held a stack of numbered orange plastic tents to mark the crime scene.

Jake took yet another look around. *Not much to mark.* No bullet casings or bloody gloves. He had to get on this. Look around the apartment for himself. *There had to be something.*

"Hennessey's holding down the fort," D was saying. "And I told Afterwards to hit the road. Call in tomorrow. Bloodsuckers." He shrugged off his bad joke, placed the markers in a stack on the floor, and pulled a digital camera from an inside jacket pocket. "Kat? Okay if I get some extra photos in here? Crime Scene's doing the back rooms, prints and evidence collection, but I want my own stuff."

Jake cocked his head toward the ME. "Dr. McMahan was telling me about the—"

"Blood on the floor," Kat interrupted. "And yes, Paul, please get a shot of that. From this angle." She pointed.

"And this one. In gauging the potential blood flow of the victim's head wound, two things. First, it shows this is the primary scene of the murder. This is where she was killed. She wasn't moved. But the amount of blood, the volume, is more than one would expect from a wound of this type. In other words . . ." She paused, one eyebrow raised.

"It's someone else's blood," Jake finished.

"Could be," Kat said.

"The bad guy," DeLuca added.

"Could be," Kat said. "So before this gets cleaned up, we'll need to have photos taken in situ, then—"

Since when was an ME telling him how to do his job?

"Gotcha, Doc," Jake said. "DeLuca will get our shots, *as usual,* then we'll have Crime Scene pull up the tiles, send them to the lab. See if the blood matches the victim, or if we have ourselves a giant lead."

He had to give her credit, though. He might not have figured that out. "Thanks," he added. "DNA could take weeks. But could be big."

"So who was the hot babe at the news conference?" Kat asked. "The pushy one in the tight jeans and Burberry muffler? The one who asked why I was here."

Jake shot her a look. *Hot babe?* "Ah—she's . . ."

"Jane Ryland from the *Register* newspaper," DeLuca finished Jake's sentence.

"You know her? Tell her she should stick to questions about the crime," Kat said. "I'm here because I'm a hands-on kinda gal. But our in-house practices and procedures should stay in-house."

Tell Jane what to ask? *Like that was gonna happen.* "Well, I don't—"

"Now. If you two have no objections," Kat went on, ignoring him, snapping the wrist of one lavender latex glove, "as soon as you're finished with your photographs, I'm gonna alert my guys to come take this poor woman to the morgue. Back in my examination room, we'll see what else we can find."

So this newbie ME wanted to make it clear she was in charge. Not his problem. What *was* his problem—identifying this woman on the floor.

There'd be a purse, somewhere, with ID. Insurance files. Rent stuff. Financial records and checkbooks and all the other items that defined each person's history. In some drawer? A box in a closet? They'd find it. Now that the news conference was over, and this ME was finally wrapping up, they could start looking.

But where were the worried relatives? Calls from frantic neighbors and friends? Two beat cops were out canvassing, Hennessey reported, so he'd see what they dug up. But not one person had knocked on this apartment door—according to Hennessey—to see what happened to the victim and her kids.

Her kids. Two kids.

"Gonna take a look around the place while you shoot, D," Jake said.

No answer. DeLuca focused on his photography, Kat directing each shot. Jake shook his head. D was a big boy.

The rest of the apartment lay only a few steps down the dingy hallway, no pictures on any walls. To his left, a tiny bathroom, pink plastic shower curtain, three wet washcloths dangling over a metal rack. Three toothbrushes, two short, one taller, in a clear plastic Mickey Mouse cup. Wastebasket with crumpled tissues, empty toothpaste tube, dental floss. Jake took a pen from his pocket, lifted the lid of a white plastic clothes hamper. Sniffed.

And winced. It reeked. But no smears of red, no signs of a murderer's hurried cleanup, no stash of bloody towels. On top, at least. Someone'd have to bag what was inside, then go through it. He hoped not him.

"Hey, Brogan. Hello and good-bye. We got what we

need, photo-wise." Photo Joe wore his equipment like a SWAT guy, cameras on bandolier straps across his chunky shoulders. Other crime scene techs used tiny digitals. Not Photo Joe Marcella. "Domestic, I'd say. We're outta here."

Lee Nguyen followed him, as usual, toting a bulky black suitcase marked PRINTS. She wore purple gloves and her BPD-issued navy nylon jacket over a white turtleneck.

"Domestic, yeah, mos' def," she said. "We're done. Later, Jake."

"Later?" he said. *Done?* Not on his watch. "Joe and Co.," some cops called the two of them. Their evidence collection sometimes left much to be desired. "Hold it. You guys wanna take the bathroom now?"

"Not particularly," Nguyen said.

"It's why you two get the big bucks." He hated when the old-timers, hell, when anyone, tried to cut corners. No way was he going to let Joe and Co. do a half-assed job. "I'll head for the bedrooms if you're done back there."

"Ten-four," Joe said. "Will do."

"Good," Jake said. Now he could scope out the rest of the place. Find those personal belongings. Across the hall, an open door to a bedroom. One window, lace curtains, view curtailed by a too-close brick wall.

Four-drawer veneer dresser with mirror, no photos tucked into the corners. He'd check the drawers. It smelled of—Jake sniffed again. That pink baby stuff. Lotion.

One twin-sized bed, pristinely made, Jake catalogued. Bedspread white. Two pillows. A stack of diapers. Cookie-cutter stuff. Nothing. Beside it, two little—well, not cots, but almost mini-beds with white Pooh comforters and a stuffed bear in a yellow-striped T-shirt perched on each little pillow.

He stood in the doorway to the bedroom, staring. Assessing.

"There we go," Jake whispered. Then pulled out his BlackBerry.

Where's the baby? he typed. Because next to the twin bed, next to the two toddler beds, sat a delicately white-slatted wooden cradle.

14

"Alex, no one said they knew her. At all. It was almost bizarre." Jane stuffed her hands into her jeans pockets, leaned against the doorjamb to Alex's office. She'd raced to her cubicle in the *Register* newsroom and banged out her story in plenty of time, copying it from her still-soggy notebook. Tuck had texted, but no time to text back. Alex ought to be psyched she'd gotten anything at all, not criticizing her for her lack of pithy and meaning-ful quotes.

"We went door to door, knocked on all we could. I gave everyone my card. No one had anything majorly interesting to say, only the usual 'who'd-a thought' and 'didn't know her' type of thing," Jane said. "I got all their names. But people don't always talk in sound bites."

She'd gotten all there was to get in the time she had. No question.

"I couldn't miss the deadline. Hec shot exteriors and the news conference. Sometimes it happens that way, right? At least I got the info on the two kids. Phoebe and Phillip, the cop told me. Their last name is Lussier, I eaves-read that on his notes. So, Phillip and Phoebe Lus-sier. I bet they're at Youth Services. You know, maybe I should . . ."

Alex wasn't listening anymore. He'd plopped his elbows on his desk, propped his face in his hands, and stared at his desktop computer monitor. Jane's draft of the story showed on the screen.

"Police sources reveal the unknown woman was killed at her home in . . ." He was proofreading her copy, out loud.

She fidgeted with her black turtleneck as he read.

"Wait a second," Jane said. "*Is* it her home? The cops didn't actually confirm that. Jake—I mean, Detective Brogan—said in the news conference she was found in the kitchen. So let's change that."

"Good catch." Alex wiped the lenses of his wire-rims on his plaid shirt, then typed a few words. Then a few more. "Let's also change 'snow-dappled front lawn' to 'snow-covered front lawn,' and move Jake's plea for assistance to the top."

Jane made a face, knowing Alex wasn't looking at her. Anyone who *could* change something you wrote *would* change it. Rule one of editing. *Fine,* snow-covered, if that really made the story better. He knew they were pushing the deadline.

"Because that's what this is really about, right?" Alex nodded, agreeing with himself as he typed. "Cops don't know who the victim is, neither do we. *There.* Done. Sent. Front page of the Metro section. And you're outta here."

He spun his chair to face her, gave her a thumbs-up. "Nice job, Ryland. And thanks for being available. I had others who bagged, let my call go to voice mail, you know? Because they didn't want to do snow. You stepped up. I appreciate it."

Okay. Even if he always changed her copy, he was a cool guy. And he'd hired her at the *Register,* trusted her, saved her, when she was sure her career was imploding. She'd never stop owing him.

If she had any sense, she'd accept his praise and go home. But she felt so sad. There were loose ends. She hated loose ends.

She parked herself on the arm of Alex's file-covered couch, thinking. The tweedy beige cushions were, as usual, covered with piles of manila folders and spiral notebooks. Alex still kept files on paper. For him every place was storage.

"Thing is, Alex. You said you were gonna hand off this story to another reporter, but I can't stop thinking about those kids. Whoever their mother is—was—what happens to them? If it turns out they're alone now? There'd be three victims, you know? The mother—and her orphaned children."

Alex blinked, spinning a pencil on his desk between two fingers. They both watched the yellow blur as it slowed, then stopped.

"Can you move over a little?" Alex said. "I need to look at something." He wheeled his swivel chair to the couch, started moving stacks of papers.

Jane hopped aside, watching with amusement. "The piles of files system, huh? You know, if you scanned all that into your computer—"

"Trust me." Alex didn't look up. "I know I have it."

Damn it. Jane's cell phone vibrated against her thigh. Alex was deep into his treasure hunt, so she sneaked a peek at the screen. Tuck. *Damn.* Jane had cut her off in midsentence when she'd called during the news conference. She let it go to voice mail and slid the phone back into her pocket.

"Here. *Ha.* I knew it." Alex handed her a stack of papers held together with a black metal clamp. "The most recent Health and Human Services Inspector General report on the Massachusetts foster care system. Might be some leads here. I printed it after the thing with the Hyde

Park kid—remember, the one who got put in that disgusting basement? Thought we might do a foster story someday."

"You kill me," Jane said, taking the report. "How do you always—?"

"And Ryland?"

Jane's phone buzzed again. She tried to ignore it. "Yeah?"

"You might be on to something. If Phillip and Phoebe are about to enter the foster care bureaucracy? Maybe you can try to protect them."

"*Now?* We're going in *now?*" Kellianne whispered, even though no one else could hear except her brothers— Kevin, on his billionth cigarette, and Keef, so out of it his head lolled against the car window. One earbud had popped out, and she heard the pounding bass of some heavy metal crap. "Did we get the okay from the cops? I never heard anything."

"'Did we get the okay from the cops?'" Kevin used that mocking voice, like she was some four-year-old. "Ooh, let me check my special notebook."

"You're such an asshole." She was honestly going to k—

"What's it to you?" Kevin shot back.

"Huh?" Keefer sat up, blinking. "What time is it?"

"Showtime." Kevin twisted around in the front seat, narrowing his eyes at her. "Listen, sister. If it makes you feel any better? Keefer and I'll do it. By ourselves. We're not gonna clean till later, but we've gotta go scope."

Kellianne puffed out a breath. It was the middle of the freaking night. Almost. The clock on the van's dash said 11:15. The cops had gone about half an hour before. The cute one by himself in the cruiser, the tall one in the white van with that woman. And the whole time, for freaking ever, they'd been rotting here in the Afterwards van. "What can you do tonight that you can't do tomorrow?"

"Who died and put you in charge?" Kevin said. "Keefer, you set?"

"Rock and roll," Keef said.

15

"Listen, Tuck, I gotta interrupt you." Jane turned off the ignition. All the way to the Riverside train station this morning, Tuck insisted Jane was "the only one" who could help her. No wonder Tuck had been such a kick-ass reporter. She made it impossible to say no. "This Ella Gavin is going to freak if I walk in with you."

Jane draped her arms across the steering wheel of her Audi, staring through the windshield at the front window of the Dunkin' Donuts. The wipers flapped against the tentative snow, the defroster blasted on the highest setting, the radio muttered the news. Coffee-toting commuters, heads down and in full Monday back-to-work mode, hustled through the flakes to their buses and trains.

"What if she recognizes me from when I was on Channel Eleven?" Jane continued. "Even if she doesn't, who are we going to say I am?"

"You worry too much, Jane." Tuck unclicked her passenger-side seat belt, then flipped the sun visor down, checking her glossy pale lipstick in the mirror. "I'm pissed off now. Truly. I'm getting to the bottom of this. And I'm so grateful for your help."

"*She'll* be the pissed off one," Jane said. "The last thing Ella Gavin wants is a reporter sniffing around. That's the last thing anyone wants. I'll wait for you here."

Tuck tugged the black cap from her head, revealing a cascade of newly auburned curls.

"Whoa," Jane said.

"Told you I was pissed," Tuck said. "I had to do *something*. Anyway, why don't you wear this hat, stick your hair underneath, and here, wear my sunglasses. I'll say you're my friend. Can you do a Southern accent?"

"It'll never work."

"It'll work."

Jane watched a stocky young woman in a toggle-front wool jacket and lace-up snow boots appear from between a row of cars, pause, and draw a fringed black-and-white woolen scarf closer around her neck. The sun glared off the hoods of the rows of cars, and scarf lady shielded her eyes with a mittened hand.

"I bet that's her." *Fine.* Maybe Tuck would finally explain why she thought the Brannigan had made a mistake. Fine. As a favor to a former colleague, she'd go in, find out, get it over with, leave. "She's looking at her watch, but not running for a train."

"Fab," Tuck said. "We'll let her go first, then we'll—"

Jane closed her eyes, changed her mind, turned on the ignition. "Tuck. Wait. This is so . . . personal. I feel like I'm intruding. You go in and get the scoop. I'll go to the paper, work on my own stuff like I'm supposed to, and meet you for lunch. Then you can tell me everything. If you want."

"Hey, turn that thing off, Jane. I *want* you to come. And what if this is a huge story?" Tuck said. "I mean, Ella Gavin called *me* back, right? She's gotta know something. Or be guilty about something. Maybe she discovered the woman I met in Connecticut is a . . . a . . . some kind of con artist. Who pretends to be people's mothers and then rips them off. That'd be a story, wouldn't it?"

Jane faced Tuck, looking at her from under her lashes,

skeptical. This was Tuck's life, not a news story. "You're kidding, right?"

The woman in the muffler had scurried into the coffee shop, disappeared through the revolving door. Their appointment was for 8:15. The dashboard clock said 8:15.

"Okay, so no." Tuck dismissed the idea with a flick of her palm. Then she touched Jane on her sleeve, entreating. "But Jane. Seriously. I have to find out. I *do*. What if . . ."

This had the potential for disaster. Tuck should be prepared for a truth she didn't expect.

"Tuck? 'What if' this Ella Gavin has confirmed Carlyn Beerman *is* your birth mother? And that's what she's about to tell you?"

Jane worried she was crossing some line. But Tuck had put her there. "What if you really *are* Audrey Rose?"

Ella Gavin wished she'd brought a hat, wished her feet weren't so cold, wished she were anywhere but here in the parking lot of the Riverside T station. And this was all her idea. She squinted against the sun—how could it be so bright and be snowing at the same time? It was like everything was happening at once.

Which it was.

All she had to do was turn around, hop back on the T, show up at the Brannigan, and if anyone asked, say she'd gotten the all-clear from the dentist. She'd e-mailed Ms. Finch about her "early morning appointment," reassuring her supervisor she'd be in by 9:30. The folder of paperwork—in her Target shopping bag in case she had to take it back to the Brannigan—would be well-camouflaged. She could throw it away, or shred it, or, heck, toss it in a trash can here at the station. Done and done.

She was leaving.

But what would she tell Tucker Cameron? It was Ella's suggestion they meet. If she canceled, or didn't show up—that didn't mean the inquisitive Miss Cameron would go away. It meant she'd persist. Certainly call the Brannigan, and probably reveal Ella had called *her,* bad enough, then, even worse, tell how she'd bailed on their appointment. After that, Ms. Finch—even Mr. Brannigan—would get involved. And probably lawyers.

She was staying.

Will I never learn to keep out of people's lives? She took a deep breath, her nose wrinkling from the cold—but that *was* her life, wasn't it? Everything she did changed people's futures, whether it was saying yes, or saying no, or saying . . . *guess who called us?* And then, life went on. The dominoes would fall.

This time, though, the dominoes could end up falling on her.

Ardella Morgan Gavin, she scolded herself. You are a grown-up with an important and responsible job. *Get a life.*

She turned and marched through the slush, heading toward the door of the Dunkin' Donuts, whatever was about to happen.

"I'm only trying to help," she whispered. "That's always a good thing."

16

"**I think I** understand this," Jake said.

"Alert the media," DeLuca said. "And it's only Monday."

Jake ignored him, nosing the cruiser into the parking space in front of the once-bright-yellow clapboard house. When they first showed up this morning, every shoveled space on Hinshaw Street had been taken. Not by cars, but by metal trash cans, webbed lawn chairs, and in one parking space, an orange plastic playpen. Neighborhood rules said once you cleared the snow from your parking spot, it was yours. Ignoring the rules would get you a punctured tire, or the gash of a key along the paint. D had lugged two battered aluminum folding chairs to the sidewalk so they could park. Aware of the social contract, they would put the chairs back in place when they'd finished their visit.

"It's to save their spot, Harvard," DeLuca said, palming the snow off his leather gloves. "Not just here in Southie. Probably in Wellesley and Dover, too. Or, ya know, they have their servants do it."

Jake shifted into reverse, then park. "Not 'I understand' the parking, D, I grew up in Boston, remember?" He grabbed his second-of-the-morning coffee from the cup holder and slugged down the last dregs. "'I understand' about this woman. About this case. The nine-one-one call tape was a bust, came from a cell, no ID. That means someone heard something—but why aren't they owning up to it? The victim was dead when the call came in, if you go by what your Dr. McMahan is estimating the TOD."

"So either it was a witness who's spooked for some reason, or the killer himself. Huh," D said. "But the longer we weren't on it, the longer the killer'd have to get away. So why call?"

Jake cocked his head at the yellow house. "Because of them, I figure. The kids. Whoever killed our vic knew the kids were there. Must have. Knew they were going to discover their murdered mother sooner or later. So. Someone might have hated her enough, or been mad at her enough, or whatever the motive, to kill her. But even then. He still cared about those kids."

D nodded, scratching his nose with one finger. "And if he knew the kids—"

"The kids knew him. Exactly." And was there another child? That cradle haunted him. Jake patted his jacket for his cell, then opened his car door. He looked at De-Luca. "You ready?"

D joined Jake at the bottom of the shoveled front walk, gesturing go *ahead*. The front door was only a few steps away. Cast-iron window boxes were filled with snow, a wood-burned sign over the door read CEAD MILE FAILTE. "So, you're thinkin' the kids might tell us who he is?"

"Yup. If we're lucky. And sometimes we are." Jake pulled out his badge wallet for ID, in case someone demanded to see the gold, even though he knew the court-appointed guardian who lived here was expecting them. Jake had a good record of talking to kids, but a text message from the brass reminded him that this Bethany Sibbach, a child therapist, was required to be their conduit, since the not-quite-witnesses were juveniles. About as

juvenile as they come. If there was a baby somewhere—
well, someone knew. And Jake would soon find out.

He lifted a fist to knock on the gray front door, then
opted for the black button of a doorbell. He heard the
bing-bong, hollow, inside. "If we're lucky, Phillip and
Phoebe might be able to tell us who the bad guy is. Or,
almost as good? Tell us who their mother is."

"Poor kids," DeLuca said.

"Detective Brogan? This is dispatch, do you read?"
Jake's radio crackled from his belt. "Superintendent Rivera requesting a landline, stat, please."

DeLuca puffed out a breath. "Now what?"

Jake took the radio mic from its holder. "Brogan, I
copy. Can you—"

The door opened.

A forty-something woman in a nubby sweater vest,
leggings, and an oversized heather green turtleneck balanced a squirming little girl on one hip. From somewhere
behind her came the beeps of a video game.

The woman, smiling, pointed at Jake's radio with the
cell phone in her hand.

"I know. I'm Dr. Sibbach, hello and good-bye. Someone from your headquarters called to warn me you've
got another assignment." Her voice had a soft burr, and
she placed a quick kiss on top of the little girl's wispy
brown hair. "No worries. Phoebe and I will be dandy
until you get back."

Tuck's stupid hat was incredibly itchy, but Jane had to
admit this Ella girl—woman—hadn't given her a second glance. Tuck introduced her as "my friend Jane,"
then Jane had been dispatched to stand in line for three
regulars, one with Splenda, and six chocolate doughnut
middles.

When Jane arrived at the table in the corner balancing

the flimsy cardboard tray, Ella was holding up a piece of paper. Pointing at something. Tuck leaned in, peering at whatever it was. A thickly stuffed manila folder took up half the table in front of them, and a red Target bag took up all the room in Ella's lap. They both looked up as Jane approached.

"Here's the coffee," she said. There was utterly no reason for her to be here. This was as nuts as it gets. "And the middles."

The two women muttered their thank-yous and went back to focusing on the paper, their heads almost touching.

Weird, they both have the same color hair, now that Tuck's gone auburn crazy, Jane thought. Whole thing is crazy. Tuck had still not told her exactly why she felt she wasn't Carlyn's daughter. She'd kept repeating, "Let's go hear what this Ella Gavin has to say." Well, she was hearing it now.

Jane grabbed a molded plastic chair to sit across from them, wincing as it scraped across the tiles. She didn't have to check in with the city desk until ten. She'd already e-mailed Family Services with her request for info about the foster child system. For now, she could sit here. Drink her coffee. Then this would be over.

"So, Jane?" Tuck pronounced her name carefully, as if to create the illusion that somehow "Jane" was an alias. "Miss Gavin seems to think—"

"Ella," the girl interrupted.

Well, she's acting like a girl, Jane defended her own assessment. High little voice. Bitten nails and fidgeting. A bobby pin holding obviously growing-out bangs.

"Ella." Tuck offered the briefest of smiles. "Seems to think the Brannigan doesn't make mistakes."

Ella nodded, her curls bouncing with her certainty. "The Brannigan has a fifty-six-year history of reuniting families. We would never—"

She looked around, seemed to remember they were

in a bustling coffee shop. "Are you okay talking here?" Her voice dropped to a whisper. "I mean, it's not very private."

"I'm fine, Ella," Tuck said. Not whispering. She flipped up the plastic lid of her coffee, took a sip, flapped the lid back down. "Go on. Tell my friend what you said."

"We put families together, that's what we do." Ella looked at Jane, her eyes wide and sincere. "These are the documents in Miss Cameron's—I mean Tuck's—file. I can't give them to her, of course, but I wanted to show her at least a few of them. So she could understand how carefully her history is documented. It's not paperwork. It's reality. Lillian Finch—I explained who she is, right, Miss Cameron?"

Tuck nodded. "Go on."

"Ms. Finch puts together the files, confirms with the History and Records department, of course, and then, when Mr. Munson from H and R says go, she makes the Call." Ella made finger quotes around the words. "That's what we call it. The Call."

Jane could almost hear the capital letter. She risked a look at Tuck. *The Call?*

Tuck raised an eyebrow, so quickly Jane almost missed it.

"If you get the Call from Ms. Finch," Ella continued, "there's no question about it. It's—a big step. Sometimes people aren't ready to hear it. But Miss Cameron? Tucker? Trust me. You're Audrey Rose Beerman."

Ella paused, as if waiting for a response from Tuck.

Jane couldn't read Tuck's face. Posture perfect, arms folded on the table, Tuck was staring at Ella, silent.

"What I guess I wonder," Ella finally said, "is—why don't *you* think so?"

17

The entire place *was going to hell*. Niall Brannigan tapped one finger on the mahogany expanse of his desk. This Monday morning certainly seemed to prove it. Something would have to be done.

He leaned across his paperwork and punched his phone to speaker, almost knocking into his ceramic mug of Irish Breakfast. Grace had delivered it with exactly the right amount of cream and sugar, accompanied by a chocolate cruller served on his mother's favorite fluted crystal plate. Monday mornings were supposed to begin another week of Brannigan success. But not *this* Monday. Nine forty-five, and already—

"Miss O'Connor? Have we heard from her yet?"

"No, Mr. Brannigan." At least Grace had picked up the phone.

"Or the girl, Ella?"

"No, sir."

Brannigan's fingers drummed on the desk, the only sound in the room. Outside he could hear the snowblower, *about time*, and down the hall, phones ringing. Unanswered. Things were about to change. He'd see to that.

"Sir?"

"That's all, Miss O'Connor. Ring me when you hear from either of them."

"Sir?"

What was wrong with this girl? Could she not hear?

"Sir?"

He paused, calculating. "Is it Lillian Finch?"

"Sir? They say—it's the police."

"Come. Freaking. *On.*" Kellianne Sessions could not believe it. Could. Not. Believe it. Kev and Keefer were lolled on the couch of the dead woman's apartment, watching the freaking *Simpsons* on a junky TV. Was that show *always* on? Her moron brothers had assigned her to the back of the place as soon as they'd arrived this morning, told *her* to pack up the bedrooms and check for any residue or externals, vac the rugs and bag the contents. Now it was pretty darn obvious they were trying to get rid of her while they goofed off.

"You guys billing for this? That's pretty freakin' bold."

"You hear that?" Kev didn't take his eyes off the screen. "Miss Priss here is worried about *bill*ing."

"Who's Bill Ling?" Keefer jabbed his brother with an elbow. "Good one, huh?"

Kellianne saw they'd at least baffled up the kitchen with plastic, rolling out clear sheets of it, overlapped and tacked them from ceiling to floor, so the solvents from the kitchen area didn't contaminate the rest of the place. It was strong stuff. She'd had her first whiff in the hazmat class practicums, now she was kinda used to it. Which was disgusting. She didn't want to be used to it.

Someone had died in this very place. Well, not died, been murdered. Creepy. She'd seen it all on the news, every channel. The reporters, the cops, and the freaky onlookers. She never watched cop shows on TV, or any of that serial killer stuff, but all her friends geeked out on it. "Did you see the dead person?" they always asked. "What's it like?"

It was like, horrible, that's what it was.

She stamped a foot, though its intended drama was muffled by the cotton-then-plastic boot thingies she had to wear over her shoes. Her Tyvek moon suit was about four sizes too big, it was hot, and it was grotesque. Flipping burgers—even babysitting—would be better than this. How could she get enough money to bail on this whole nightmare?

Kev and Keefer were annoying. The laugh track from the show was *incredibly* annoying. How could they sit there and watch a dead woman's TV? Sit on her couch? Shove over her stuff so they could put their moron feet on her coffee table?

Just then, Kellianne had an idea.

A really, really good idea.

"No, sir, the officers didn't tell me what it was about." Niall Brannigan's receptionist was clearly having a hard time trying to give her boss information without giving Jake any. She'd been pleasant enough, introducing herself with a polite "Good morning, may I help you?" when he and DeLuca arrived at the executive director's well-appointed outer office, maybe figuring they were potential clients. After they'd shown their badges, though, Jake saw call-me-Grace go a little white under her careful makeup. Now, "helping" them did not seem to be her first priority.

Jake couldn't hear Brannigan's questions on the other end of the phone, but even with the woman's guarded answers, what he was asking was obvious. It was also obvious the young woman was intimidated by the man in the closed-door office behind her.

"Yes, Mr. Brannigan. I *did*," Grace insisted. "But apparently they need to talk to *you*. No, they wouldn't give me any further . . ."

She looked at Jake, eyes wide, silently pleading for assistance. Jake smiled, but shook his head. *No way.* He and D were here at Brannigan Family and Children Services to talk to the executive director, end of story. If Grace was having a hard day? Welcome to the club.

"Yes, sir. Yes, sir. Yes, sir. I will." Grace hung up, then glanced at the closed door behind her. She looked at Jake with an expression he'd seen a million times. "Mr. Brannigan is in a meeting, I'm afraid. And he wonders if—"

Jake interrupted. "I see." Which was true. "Detective?"

"After you," D said. He gestured toward the closed door.

"Wait, you can't just—" Grace stood, her chair swiveling, both hands up as if to push them away.

Jake was faster. He was already at the inner door, hand on the knob, pushing it open. "I'll explain to your boss, ma'am," he said, "but we—"

"I'm so sorry, Mr. Brannigan." Grace squeezed past the two of them, trying to get into his office first. "They're—"

"I'm Detective Jake Brogan, Boston Police." Jake flipped his badge wallet closed. The guy, tight-ass in a gold-buttoned navy blazer and prissy pocket square, was already standing, barricaded behind his big desk. One finger tapped the shiny wood.

Jake suppressed a smile, as well as his instant dislike. "My partner, Detective Paul DeLuca."

DeLuca followed Jake into the room. "Sorry to interrupt your . . . meeting."

Brannigan touched the shiny clip on his tie, narrowed his eyes for an instant. "That'll do, Miss O'Connor," he said, as the door closed behind her. "Gentlemen? What can I do for you?"

"You have an employee, Lillian Finch." Jake kept his voice noncommittal, aware of their tightrope. This was always one of the crucial moments. Jake and D had information. Maybe Brannigan had it, too. Maybe even more. Or maybe he didn't know.

"Yes." Brannigan frowned. "But she's not in yet this morning."

Then Brannigan switched on a smile, Mr. Helpful. "I'd call her assistant for you, but she hasn't arrived this morning, either."

Jake exchanged a glance with his partner.

"What's the assistant's name, sir? Did she call to say she wouldn't be in? Is she usually late?" DeLuca had taken out his spiral notebook, pen poised over a page.

"Ella Gavin is her assistant's name. And no, she's not usually late." Back at Jake. "Detectives? Is there something wrong?"

"Ah, there is, Mr. Brannigan. I'm sorry to have to tell you. Lillian Finch is dead."

18

"**Why don't I** think she's my birth mother?" Tuck spun her coffee cup between her thumb and forefinger, seemed fascinated by the sound of it scraping on the plastic tabletop. The coffee shop's morning crush and bustle had dwindled, and the three women were the only customers still at a table. The place smelled of fresh coffee and something cinnamon. A TV, mounted in the corner above the cash register, flickered a muted CNN. Jane read the screen crawl: "Severe weather on the way for New England. Officials warn residents may have to . . ."

"Well, here's why." Tuck stopped her cup-spinning, took a sip, then grimaced.

Remembering something? Jane wondered. Or maybe Tuck's coffee was cold. They'd been here a good hour, maybe more, looking at documents and listening to Ella explain how foolproof the Brannigan's system was. That alone was enough to make Jane skeptical. Nothing was foolproof, any reporter could tell you that.

Tuck propped her chin on her intertwined fingers, elbows on the table, seemed to weigh what she was about to say.

"Listen. There were two things from my—birth mother. One, a handwritten note from her that was tucked into my blanket when the Brannigan took me in."

"A note?" Ella tilted her head, frowning. She opened the manila folder, flipping documents, one by one, quickly, shaking her head as the pages rustled by. "No. That can't be. If there *was* a note, it would be in here, definitely, a copy of it at least. I mean, I know I copied the whole file. What's more, I know History and Records is required to keep any and all . . ."

Her voice trailed off, one hand still turning pages as she stared at them. "I mean . . ."

"A note?" Jane couldn't resist interrupting. Why hadn't Tuck told her that right off the bat? She'd certainly buried the lede of this story. "What did it say?"

"Exactly." Tuck pointed a finger at Ella. "And Carlyn Beerman, lovely a person as she was when we met, did not say a word about a note. I gave her every opportunity. Since you say there's also no copy of the note in your file, that means your infallible Ms. Finch got it wrong this time."

"Ms. Cameron, that's not—"

"But Tuck, how'd you know there was a note?" Jane had to interrupt again. This didn't make sense. Tuck had explained she'd been left at the Brannigan in a closed adoption, which meant all the papers are sealed until the child is an adult, and opened only if both parties ask to see them. The whole point was to keep everything secret and private. Had a remorseful birth mother tried to leave Tuck a clue about her first identity? "Forgive me, but are you sure it's real? Do you have it? What does it say?"

"How do I know it's real? My adoptive mother told me. And my adoptive father," Tuck said. She peeled back the plastic lid of her coffee cup, then tore the lid into pieces, dropping each shard, one by one, into the dregs left in the cup.

"Told me about it from the moment I could remember. I've seen the note, of course, a million times, but

Mom has it. It was my birth mother's way of saying good-bye, but it's also my way to prove ... well, I know it by heart. 'We each travel our own road,' it says. 'Always choose the future over the past.'"

Jane stared at her, trying to comprehend. To get a message like that from your mother? The message she left as she was walking out of your life? This one pretty much implied—*don't try to find me*. Poor Tuck. The two little kids from Callaberry Street, too. There hadn't been a note for them, of course, when *their* mom left. How could they possibly learn to accept the story *they'd* hear, someday?

"Of course we could do a DNA test, Miss Gavin." Tuck tossed her head, pushed the ruined coffee cup away. "If your agency agrees to pay for it. But why bother? That note is my proof. And so is this."

Tuck plunged a hand into her parka pocket, and came out with a black velvet bag. Pulling apart the thin black drawstrings, she drew out a delicate gold bracelet, one circular charm dangling from the chain. She held it between two fingers, and it glinted in the too-bright fluorescent lights of the coffee shop.

Jane leaned in, trying to get a better look.

Ella leaned in too, frowning, touching her fingers to her lips.

"Again, you're perplexed," Tuck continued. The gold charm twisted slightly with the motion of her sigh. "Which answers my next question. This baby bracelet was also attached to my blanket. But there's nothing about it in your file, correct?"

"I—we—well—," Ella stammered. "Ms. Finch will have to look at ... we can call her and—"

"I see. And here's another question for you and Ms. Finch. If I'm Audrey Rose Beerman, how come this charm bracelet is engraved with my birthday—and the name 'Tucker'?"

19

Jake watched Brannigan settle on an attitude. His face had registered surprise, certainly, then anger, maybe even a little fear. He had apparently decided on sorrow, which, in Jake's assessment, wasn't a comfortable choice for him. Jake and DeLuca remained standing near the doorway. Apparently this Brannigan had no interest in making *them* comfortable, either.

"Mr. Brannigan?" Jake pulled out his BlackBerry, ready to take notes. DeLuca still razzed him about his habit, but it was easier than trying to read his pitiful handwriting. Plus, this way the info was already transcribed, and he could zap himself an e-mail and send it to his files. Jake saw the green 2 on his message icon. He'd have to call whoever it was later. The Supe knew he was here; he'd assigned them this notification, even though they hadn't yet inspected the crime scene.

"May I ask, did Ms. Finch seem worried about anything? Depressed? Had she mentioned any reason she might be under unusual stress? And may we sit down? This may take a few minutes."

"How did she die?" Brannigan waved them to the club chairs in front of his desk.

"Well, that's under investigation, Mr. Brannigan."

That was true. The Supe had told Jake that Crime Scene reported Lillian Finch was a possible suicide—plastic bag over the head. Or possible homicide—pillows had been duct-taped over her face.

Question was, how much did Brannigan know?

"That's why we're here." DeLuca took the chair on the left. He propped one ankle on the other knee and tapped his notepad with his Bic pen. "Investigating."

Brannigan lowered himself into his leather swivel, steepled his hands on the desk.

"Could you . . . give me some time, gentlemen? This news is very distressing. I'll need to compose myself. I'm sure you understand." He stood up again, barricaded behind his desk, fingertips grazing the mahogany. "And in the meantime? I'm calling my lawyer. I'll instruct my secretary to give you his number."

This guy watched too many cop shows. Might have been smarter for Mr. Bigshot to suss out what Jake was going to ask, instead of kicking them out.

Still, not necessarily a bad thing. Calling a lawyer? Put Brannigan square on the guilty list.

"We'll be in touch," Jake said.

"Soon," DeLuca said.

"Jane Ryland to see Margaret Gunnison?" She was late. She'd barely gotten to the twenty-third floor in time, risking her car in an iffy parking spot outside the bleak brick facade of the state's Department of Family Services building. The text from the DFS public relations person arrived soon after Tuck had pulled out that charm bracelet, and Jane raced away, leaving Tuck to her own devices to get wherever.

"Now, or after next week," the PR flak had warned. Margaret Gunnison, apparently knower of all knowledge about the state's foster care system, was about to spend the second week in February in Anguilla, eager to take off from Logan this afternoon before the snow hit.

Jane untied her coat and stuffed her gloves into the pockets. *I better not miss this meeting because of Tuck.* She leaned closer to the barrier separating her from the elaborately coiffed woman commanding the blinking phone console. "Ms. Gunnison is expecting me."

The receptionist assessed her through tarry eyelashes, then pushed a button on the intercom, setting columns of red and green lights flashing.

"DFS. May I help you?" she said into the phone. "No, he's not here, but I'll patch you through to his cell."

Her necklace announced—in rhinestones—her name was Vee. On the wall behind Vee, a chronologically arranged row of eight-by-ten framed and dated portraits labeled DFS COMMISSIONERS showed prune-mouthed white men in increasingly contemporary suits and haircuts, one after the other—until the last picture in the row, a black woman in a carefully tied scarf.

"You're the one from TV, right?" Vee said. Two more green lines began to ring. Then another. Vee ignored them.

Jane kept up her smile. She was tired of explaining why she'd been fired, and even more tired of accepting sympathy and support because she had protected a source. It was over, she had a new job, she was happy happy happy. And as she so often heard, nobody watched local TV anymore. Which, truth be told, made her even happier.

"I'm with the *Register* now." Jane looked at her watch. Cutting it *so* close. She had to get the scoop about the victim's children, learn what would happen to them and how this system worked, and she absolutely could not wait until someone got back from a Caribbean vacation to get those answers. "Like I said, Ms. Gunnison is expecting me, and—"

A buzzer interrupted, and a thick metal door clicked open.

"Thanks, Vee. Jane? I'm Maggie." Maggie Gunnison had poked two yellow pencils through her dark ponytail, misbuttoned her navy cardigan, and was now battling an unwieldy stack of paperwork. As she adjusted the pile in her arms, trying to keep the door open with one hip, one of the pencils clattered onto the floor. She rolled her eyes behind her wire-rimmed glasses. "*Perfect*. That's what happens when you try to rush, right? I only have about fifty million cases to handle before I go. They told you I don't have much time, right?"

"Right." Jane tried to look sympathetic as she picked up the pencil. "The day before vacation is always a bear. You're very kind to see me."

Maggie was already through the door, motioning Jane to follow her down a dingy hallway warrened with modular office cubbies and cartons of copy paper stacked shoulder high. It smelled of aging drywall and stale coffee.

"What do you want to know? They told me you wondered about the Callaberry Street kids. The police notified us of the . . . incident." Maggie stopped in the middle of the hallway, took a breath, turned to Jane with a frown.

"Look. I can't discuss any specifics. I've seen your stuff on TV. You know the drill. They're juveniles, it's private, it's protected, it's confidential, there's no way under any circumstances I can—"

"I completely understand." This was not the moment for a hard sell. But Maggie looked crazed with paperwork, about to be sprung from this fluorescent sweatshop into a sun-filled week on the beach. Jane should certainly be able to convince her to spill the beans. On s*omething*. She pulled out her reporter's spiral notebook and twisted open a ballpoint, realizing Maggie had already revealed some big info.

The police had called DFS. Why? Were the Callaberry Street kids about to go into foster care? That gave her story a perfect news peg. She'd keep it vague, like she was only getting background.

"I'm researching a consumer education story on foster kids. Foster care. Why the children get placed, and what happens to them later. How foster parents are chosen. Are there enough DFS people—"

"Caseworkers?"

"Caseworkers. To get to know each child and family individually? To make sure the kids are in a good place?" She eyed the files in Maggie's arms. "What if it doesn't work out?"

Maggie tightened her stranglehold on the paperwork, as if shielding it from the marauding reporter. Made no move to lead Jane to her office. "I'm not sure why they directed me to speak to you."

"Oh, don't worry, I'm not asking specifically about Phillip and Phoebe. But kids *like* Phillip and Phoebe." She paused, wondering if Maggie would correct her, or ask how she knew the names. But—nothing. "What their future holds. Generally. That's all."

"Listen." Maggie looked at the floor, institutional carpeting battered and flattened by decades of trudging civil servants, then back up at Jane. "It's not like a private adoption agency, where, I don't know. It's difficult, and often heartbreaking, but it's all civilized. It usually follows . . . a choice. Foster care almost always follows tragedy. Kids whose parents abuse them, or abandon them, or get arrested and leave them with no one. The kids stay in state custody, fostered, until they're adopted. Sometimes the short-term parents fall in love and that's a relief. But it doesn't always happen. So there's a cycle. A stupid, relentless, impossible cycle."

Jane could see the tension around the young woman's

mouth, the beginning of dark shadows under the rims of her glasses. "Cycle?"

"Yup. Like Callaberry Street. That's why you're here, right? When something goes wrong, those children go back on the foster list, and we try to find another approved family for them. Emphasis on *try*. Sometimes a relative will show up, and offer to take them in, but even those homes have to be approved. That takes time. Even infants have to wait. The longer they wait, the more difficult it gets. Yes, the families get a state-funded stipend for each child they take in. Is this the kind of thing you want to know? I don't have much more time. Five minutes."

Maggie pointed toward a closed office door, and Jane followed her down the corridor, processing the surprise Maggie had revealed. Phillip and Phoebe were *already* foster kids?

That would mean the victim was their *foster* mother, not their biological mother. Maybe they weren't even brother and sister.

What if an overburdened state system had actually put them into danger? Placed them with exactly the wrong woman? That could be a big story. If Maggie was aware of that? An even bigger story.

Jane would behave as if Phillip and Phoebe's past was something she already knew. Now she had to learn whether a foster father existed. Who the birth parents were. Those people would be instant suspects. *Did Jake know this? He had to.*

If she got the scoop, Alex would have to let her take over the Callaberry murder story. And that would be the good news. Every big headline equaled job security. This one could be her biggest headline yet.

20

"So, Phillip? Do you have a little baby at your house?"
Jake sat cross-legged on the floor of Dr. Bethany Sibbach's toy-strewn living room, running a bright blue Batmobile across the carpet. Jake and DeLuca had purchased the toy at a CVS after leaving the Brannigan. The Supe assigned another team to the Finch case, agreeing Jake needed to focus on Callaberry. Jake couldn't help but think the kids were the key.

That empty cradle. Bugged the hell out of him. Dr. Sibbach insisted she'd been given no paperwork about a third child. Insisted there were only two kids. But that didn't add up. Nothing added up. They still hadn't found ID for the victim, no files, no paperwork of any kind. That bugged him, too. More than bugged.

Was there a baby somewhere? In trouble? Though everyone said no, little Phillip would know for sure. Question was, could he tell Jake?

Leonard Perl, the Florida landlord, hadn't called back. Seemed like time to notify the Ft. Lauderdale PD. Get them to put some fear into the guy. DeLuca stood in the hall, talking on his cell to Kat McMahan, insisting he needed to check on the medical examiner's progress. D had never been so fascinated by the morgue.

"Baby at youah house!" the little boy said.

Jake looked at the therapist, who sat on the flowered couch, Phoebe in her lap. The little girl clutched some kind of thick toasted cracker, crumbs from it dribbling down the front of her dress. There was more cracker on the pink cotton than in Phoebe's mouth.

"Is that a yes?" Jake asked. "Would you say he's confirming—?"

Bethany shook her head. "Phillip's in a repeating phase, Detective Brogan. He's two, I'd estimate. He'll try to echo whatever you say. Repeating is how they learn. It'll be unlikely he'll be able to tell us anything. Feel free to try, though—Phoebe, honey, shush—I suppose it can't hurt. He's quite taken with you, it seems. He only stopped crying when you arrived."

"Everybody likes a Batmobile," Jake said. The little boy had snatched the car, trying to balance it on his head. "Phillip? Are you making the car into a hat?"

"Hat!" the little boy crowed. He showed Jake the car. "Cah!"

"Car," Jake reached for it. "Thank you, Phillip. Batcar."

"Bahcah!" the little boy pulled it back, hugging it to his chest.

"Batcar." *What they don't teach you at the police academy.* "Phillip? Do you know your mommy's name?"

"Mommy name!" Phillip replied, still clutching the toy. Then his forehead seemed to crumble, and his lower lip quivered. "Mama?"

Phillip let the car drop to the floor. It landed, upside down, one wheel spinning, forgotten. "Mama?"

"Oh, dear." Bethany glanced at Jake, mouth tightening, shaking her head. She brushed the crumbs from Phoebe's dress, then handed the little girl to Jake. "Can you hold her for a second? I'm afraid Phillip's about to—Come here, sweetheart."

Jake smelled the sweet shampoo in Phoebe's hair, felt his two suddenly huge hands almost encircle the white sash on her waist as he reached out to take her. He propped her on his lap, then adjusted the white cotton sock drooping precariously from one foot. He felt her little body settle into the crook of his elbow. With a gurgle and a coo, she grasped his forefinger with her hand. "Gah," she said.

Jane, he thought. And then dragged his attention back to where it should be.

"So much for that idea," Jake said. "Would have been much easier if Phillip here could have pointed us in the right direction."

"Probably better though, for him at least, Detective, that he couldn't." The boy had buried his face in Bethany's sweater, glued his wiry body to hers, and planted his sneakers on her leggings. "His brain function hasn't developed enough to comprehend what happened. He clearly has a memory of a 'Mama'—that's okay, honey, everything will be fine—but we hope that will fade and be replaced by some new and kinder memories. Ms. Lussier is deceased, I'm told. And Phoebe, at this age, she should be completely free of—well, one step at a time. Detective? Seems like you're done here. Unless you'd like to babysit a while."

Jake realized he was jiggling his leg, bouncing Phoebe, and she was still hanging on to his finger. Where would she be, a year from now? Ten years? She was at the mercy of the system, thanks to a killer Jake had no idea where to even begin looking for.

"Hard to tell which would be more difficult, Doctor," Jake said. "Taking care of these two, or finding out who killed their mother. Guess I'll handle the one I'm trained to do. I think we can clear these two from our suspect list. Should I—?" He looked at Phoebe, straining toward the floor.

"You can put her down, Detective. She's not going anywhere."

Exactly like this case, Jake thought. Not going anywhere.

Jake stood, his knees complaining. He shook out a leg and reached for his jacket. Where was DeLuca? "Thanks, Bethany. Let us know if they spill the beans."

"Will do, Detective. At this age, spilling is what they do best. And you know—"

"Excuse me, ma'am." DeLuca appeared in the entryway to the dining room, cell phone in hand.

Phillip turned at the sound of male voice, then snuggled closer to Bethany. Phoebe, clattering multicolored wooden blocks into a cardboard box, didn't look up.

"Hey D." Next on their agenda, tracking down Leonard Perl and hitting up the Callaberry Street neighbors with a few more knock-and-talks. Now they'd turn the heat up a notch or two. Not even a day since they found the body, but already this case worried him. Doors were not opening the way he'd so optimistically predicted yesterday. "The kids are a dead end, it appears. They don't have a clue about their mother's name."

"They don't, huh?" DeLuca stashed his cell into his jacket pocket. "That's okay. Because I do."

21

Jane watched Maggie Gunnison tap a pass code on a number pad, heard the office door click. Maggie put a hand on the doorknob, but seemed reluctant to turn it.

Jane had to keep her talking. And she'd just thought of how. "Do you allow single parents to be fosters?"

"Well, sometimes we—"

"Hey, Maggie." A young man approached, wearing pressed jeans, earbuds plugged into his ears and a white cord dangling down his fashionably untucked plaid shirt. He pushed a rickety metal cart stacked with file folders. A shock of dark hair curled under the bright green Celtics cap he wore backward, its plastic band making a green stripe across his forehead.

"Sorry, ladies. Comin' through. Cool that we're getting out at three for the snowstorm, right? Makes me proud to be nonessential." His voice was too loud, as if he'd forgotten no one else could hear his music. He put a steadying hand on the files, then narrowed his eyes at Jane. "Hey. You're Jane Ryland! I'm a big—"

"Hey, Finn." Maggie shot him a look, then pointed down the hall. "Let's go into my office, such as it is, Miss Ryland."

Jane followed as she entered, turning to give the guy

an apologetic what-can-you-do wave. *Always nice to have fans.*

"Sorry," Maggie was saying. "Finn Eberhardt's one of our newer caseworkers. He can be a bit of an oversharer. Forgive him. Anyway, you asked about caseworkers before—we've got five full-times. Me, Finn, three others. *Five!* And two thousand seven hundred fifty-eight children. The math stinks. It's not that there aren't families who might want them, it's that we can't do the home visit assessment paperwork fast enough to assure the kids are in safe places. So they wait. Even infants wait. You asked about parents. Yes, sometimes we use single mothers. It's not ideal, I suppose, but what can we do? Too many kids need help."

"And now there are two more." Jane risked it. "What will happen to them?"

Maggie closed her office door behind her, pushing it shut with the flat of one running shoe. The windowless room was a nest of file folders, stacked against the walls, tipping next to a green four-drawer file cabinet, piled chest high on a wooden desk. A seemingly endless philodendron carefully coiled on plastic hooks garlanded the walls, glossy heart-shaped leaves snaking up to one corner, edging along the ceiling, then down the other side.

Maggie dumped her paperwork on top of an already precarious mountain of manila, a tiny cloud of dust puffing from the bottom.

"All these are children who need foster homes." She patted the files. "Their parents are dead, or crackheads, or sick or crazy or basically defeated. Parental rights terminated. The children did nothing wrong, but they got dumped. One flutter of a butterfly wing—you know?—they could have been a Kennedy or a Saltonstall. But, little Phillip and Phoebe? They got dealt the shit hand. Sorry."

Jane shrugged, *Got it,* eyed the one visitor's chair. Stacked with files.

"So Phillip and Phoebe?" Jane began.

"Look. Eventually the two kids will be sent to another foster home. I'm hoping they can stay together. But there's no guarantee."

"But that's . . ."

"Yeah. I know. I've only been in charge here a year. And I cry every night."

"Your job is so difficult," Jane said.

Maggie adjusted the leaves of the philodendron, carefully draping a loop across a beige metal bookshelf. "Well, we do what we can. I'll be better after a week off, right?"

"Absolutely. But, um, their foster mother," Jane kept her voice oh-so-casual, as if this were something that just crossed her mind. "Were these the first children she'd taken in? How do you spell her name again? I'm not sure I have it right."

"Good try." Maggie shook her head. "That, I can't tell."

With a rasp like an insistent wasp, the intercom on Maggie's desk broke the silence.

"I told Vee to tell me when twenty minutes was up. Thanks, Vee," Maggie said into the speaker. "I'm okay. We're done."

"It's not the time," Vee said. "I forgot about that, actually. It's the police. They're on their way here. To see you. They're asking about Brie—"

Maggie lunged for the phone on her desk, grabbed the receiver, punched off the speaker button.

Brie? Jane didn't want to write it down, but she'd remember it, because it was past lunchtime and she was starving. Brie? Maybe it was Bree. Part of a name. Part of a name Maggie definitely did not want her to hear.

Maggie turned her back, whispering into the phone. Maybe "Bree" had nothing to do with the Callaberry

Street kids. But judging by Maggie's demeanor, and if the police were on the way, then Jane had overheard a pretty tantalizing tidbit.

Jane pretended interest in the framed photos of children on the office wall until she heard the click of Maggie hanging up. She waited a beat before turning around, so it wouldn't look like she'd been listening.

"I should never have come in to the office today," Maggie said.

"The police?" *Might as well go for it.* "Anything you can tell me?"

"Yes," Maggie said. "Good-bye."

22

Alone in the echoing faux marble elevator lobby of the Department of Family Services building, Jake punched the "up" button, then watched the number twenty-three go green above the only car that seemed in working order. The door of one elevator was propped open with a couple of two-by-fours and zigzagged with duct tape. The other had an orange sawhorse barricading it, a hand-scrawled sign proclaiming OUT-A-ORDAH.

Our tax dollars at work, he thought.

But the good news was he had the victim's name. Brianna Tillson. According to DeLuca, Kat McMahan ran the fingerprints, standard operating procedure. Not much hope the prints would be on file, unless the victim had been in the armed forces, or arrested, or had some kind of high-level security clearance, so Jake had put no eggs in that basket. But there they were. Because—

Jake checked the elevator lights again. Sixteen. The lone elevator was moving, but seemed to stop at every floor. Probably picking up all the state employees heading for lunch.

Because Brianna Tillson was a foster parent. She'd been printed, per Massachusetts regulations, when she applied for the state-supported program. And that, he and D agreed, was a huge break. Huge.

D had called the DFS before he'd even told Jake. So DFS now knew they had a foster parent as victim. And Jake knew he had a hell of a lead.

Not only did they have a name, but soon a whole history would unfold. Upstairs in the files there'd be a dossier on those two kids. Who, it now seemed, were not Brianna Tillson's, but biologically someone else's. Question was, whose.

That person was suspect number one.

Maybe the files would reveal Brianna Tillson also had a baby.

D insisted he needed coffee and would meet Jake in Maggie Gunnison's office. Then they'd get some answers.

The clunk of the elevator's mechanism announced its arrival. It rumbled to a stop, and as the brushed silver doors slid open, Jake had to step back to avoid being trampled by the lunch crowd. Mufflers, hats, parkas, talking, everyone with earbuds or a cell phone clamped to their face. Everyone striving to be first, they jostled through the opening, gloved hands banging the black rubber strip to keep the doors open. And then in the back—*Jane*.

Jake. Jane saw him, visible in flash-frame glimpses through the hats and scarves and shoulder bags of the ten million people who crammed themselves into the stifling elevator, floor after floor, after she got on. He hadn't noticed her yet. Savoring a moment of secret surveillance, she watched him in that leather jacket she loved, his hair all mussed the way she loved. She wanted to smooth it, touch him, unzip that jacket and tell him that she'd decided they should—*Wait a minute*.

He was on his way to see Maggie Gunnison. Had to be. Why?

* * *

What was she doing here? If it *wasn't* to see Maggie Gunnison, that was too much of a coincidence. If it *was* to see Maggie, it was a bad coincidence. What's more, Jane had gotten here before him. That meant his life was about to become even more of a mess. Exactly why they'd decided to remain uninvolved. Even though—

"Hey, Jane," he said. The elevator was empty now, except for her. The lunch crowd had scattered. They were alone.

"Hey, Jake." She had crossed her arms, and was leaning back against the chrome railing, that Jane-smile on her face. "We have to stop meeting like this."

She looked terrific.

"Going up?" she asked. "What floor?"

The doors began to slide closed. Jane didn't budge. Jake jumped forward, almost not thinking about it, slamming one hand on the door, forcing it to stay open. The closing mechanism battled back, rumbling its impatience, as he stood on the threshold.

"What're you doing here?" he said. "You came down. Aren't you getting off?"

The elevator door seemed frantic to close, shoving against his hand. He leaned into it, waiting, still not stepping inside the car.

"Oh, I want a lawyer," Jane said. "Because I don't have to answer that. Unless you want to come in here and try to convince me."

"Going up?" A guy in a puffy green jacket covered with snowflakes and lugging a unwieldy pizza box also covered with snowflakes strode past Jake and parked himself in front of Jane. "Could you push ten for me?" He turned to Jake with the beginnings of a frown. "Snowing like a son-of-a. And I got hot pizza. You going up?"

"Smells fabulous," Jane said. "Pizza's my favorite. Especially hot. You coming, *Detective* Brogan?"

Jake took a step into the car, the doors swishing closed behind him. He pushed the button for ten. But not for twenty-three.

"You'll pay for this, Ryland," he muttered. Somehow, his hand twined into hers. And hers curled back into his. He felt her lean in closer to him, pressing her arm against his jacket, her head briefly touching his shoulder. He could smell the perfume in her hair. Even over the cheese and tomatoes.

"That might be fun," she whispered. "But do you think these things have surveillance cameras?"

23

"It is with deep regret that I call you all together."

Regret? Regret about what, Ella wondered. *Could Mr. Brannigan know what happened to Miss Cameron? Or what Ella had told her in the coffee shop?*

Ella tried to shrink behind the other employees, edging into a corner of Mr. Brannigan's outer office, gauging whether he was looking at her. *Was he?* Why had he called everyone here?

The others murmured, filling the silence with soft speculation as Mr. Brannigan surveyed the room.

He narrowed his eyes at her. He did.

She was late, that had been bad enough. She'd arrived at the Brannigan just before ten, counting her blessings that Ms. Finch was out, reassured she'd never know how late Ella arrived. She stashed her bag of copies under her desk, having decided, in a flash of defiance on the subway, not to shred them, but to take them home. They were evidence, of something, and who knew what might happen to the real paperwork?

But then on her desk, a scrawled note from someone, almost illegible, the words tumbling to the edge of the page.

Meeting. Mr. B's office. *NOW*. Hurry.

Now Ella stood behind Collins Munson, trying to make herself invisible. A dozen staffers were crowded into the ornate room, maybe more, so maybe no one noticed when she came in. She pressed her back against a lofty bookshelf, feeling the spines of the leather volumes against hers.

"As you might be aware, the police visited us at the Brannigan this morning," Brannigan continued.

Ella felt the blood drain from her face, she really did, and her knees went so jelly she almost fell against a big upholstered chair. Catching herself, she knocked into Collins Munson's navy blazer and pointy elbows.

"Sorry," she whispered. Mr. Munson glared down at her, frowning even more than usual behind his horned-rims before turning his attention back to the front of the room.

"It is with much sadness that I tell you . . ." Brannigan paused, looked at the floor, then looked up at them. ". . . the police informed me that sometime last night, our dear Lillian Finch passed away."

Oh sweet mother of . . . What could have happened? She couldn't breathe. She couldn't. Maybe this was her payback. Maybe God telling her she should not have interfered in what was not her business. Ella felt the fear and the guilt creep up the back of her neck and tighten her throat.

Ms. Finch was dead? Ella felt the scream, threatening, but knew she had to stay silent, had to think. *Not now,* she thought. *Hail Mary, full of grace. . . .*

"I don't have many answers for you, my dear colleagues, but if you have any questions," Brannigan finished, "I shall try to answer."

Yes, I have questions, Ella yearned to say. Why had

Ms. Finch made the Call to the wrong woman? Did she know what she'd done? But now was not the time to ask. Maybe that time would never come.

Collins Munson cleared his throat. Ella looked up at him. So did everyone else. Munson, who "had the keys" as Lillian always put it, to the History and Records department, might be the only one who dared ask the first question. Or any question at all. He'd been around forever, since before Ella arrived three years ago. He had a parking space of his own. He'd placed hundreds of children, Ella knew. Reunited hundreds of families. Kind of a legend.

"Mr. Brannigan? Do the police know"—Munson cleared his throat again, his words catching in grief— "how she died?"

"Ah, Collins. This is difficult for all of us." Brannigan shook his head. "The authorities may know. I asked, of course. But they did not choose to inform me, and insisted they had to end our conversation and continue their investigation. Please cooperate with them, all of you, as they do. And please keep me informed if they contact you."

How she died? *How she died?* Ella's mind raced, calculating. Of course, well, of course, that was the question. The police? Came *here*? If Ms. Finch had died of natural causes, that's what they called it on her TV shows, it wouldn't have been the police who came. Would it?

What if Ms. Finch knew she'd . . . made a terrible mistake? What if she couldn't live with it? Would the police have come to tell them that? If she'd . . . killed herself? But that was a mortal sin. Lillian would never—

"In closing, let me acknowledge, we shall all miss her," Brannigan was saying. "But we must continue our good work, and know she would have wanted it that way."

Ella stared at the rug, its colors blurring with her tears of sorrow and confusion and panic and fear.

* * *

"Tacos," Keefer said.

Her brothers hadn't budged from the couch. Kelli-anne stood in the hallway, hands on hips. Beyond mad. Now the two were watching a music video, blasting the speakers, something with stuff blowing up. She'd like to blow *them* up, the morons. Her fingers were raw from the stupid duct tape, and she'd lugged about fifty plastic bags of carpeting squares—okay, maybe five—to the barrel at the front door. Why Kev insisted she yank up the carpet from the bedroom when the body was in the kitchen seemed ridiculous. But she was too—whatever—to argue. *Get it done,* right? Then it would be over.

Besides, now that she'd figured things out, now that she'd had her good idea, the more they left her alone the better.

"No way, asshole." Kevin sprawled on the couch, his white-bootied feet still plonked on the dead woman's coffee table. "I'm not eating one more frickin' taco. I could go for a meatball sub, though. The ones from down the street. I'll buy if you fly."

"Let's get the princess to fly," Keefer said. "She's always whining for food."

She?

"I'm right here, assholes. And I'm not hungry." Kelli-anne was dying in the Tyvek suit. But now it didn't matter. She smoothed a sleeve, then the zippered front, making sure it looked flat enough. "You go. I've gotta finish in the back."

"But you gotta bill for lunch," Kevin said. "Or it makes us look bad."

"Put down that I got a sub and a soda, big shot," she said. "Dad's gonna kill you if you get caught padding the bill, though, ya know."

"Caught by you and what army?" Keefer said. He

jabbed his brother with an elbow. "Pretty funny, huh? And like we're afraid of Dad."

"Shut up about Dad," Kevin said. "We going for the frickin' subs or what?"

Leave leave *leave. They have to leave. Or this will never work*. The landlord was an out-of-state, according to the Afterwards paperwork, so that was good. The insurance company knew the drill, they were cool with whatever up to the policy limits. No annoying relatives had called or showed up demanding to take stuff, like sometimes happened. The cops had cleared the scene. So seemed like no one would be snooping in here.

All good for Kellianne. All very, very good.

24

"I'll tell if you will," Jane whispered. They'd almost arrived at pizza guy's floor, and Jane didn't want to let go of Jake's hand. But Jake had to be going *somewhere*. In about two seconds, he'd have to declare a floor. After that she'd know whether he was headed for Maggie Gunnison. Whether he knew about "Brie."

"Tell what?" Jake's voice went into her hair.

He smelled like citrus, and cinnamon, and coffee. "Why you're here," Jane said. "You first."

The elevator stopped at ten, the doors sliding open. The pizza guy got out, leaving them alone. Jane didn't move.

Jake didn't, either.

The door closed, and they were alone.

"Wonder what'll happen if no one presses a button?" Jane turned, slowly, looking up into Jake's eyes and not letting go of his hand. She remembered his touch from that one night last summer. The night of Jake's apartment and his hands on her skin and their clothes on the floor and—the night she said no. They'd done the math—reporter plus source equals disaster. They thought they'd nipped this in the bud. In reality, it was way past the bud.

She dropped her tote bag to the floor, and stepped so close to him she could feel his chest rise, then fall. The elevator beeped, signaling its impatience. *You're in an elevator, Jane Elizabeth.*

"Is this your idea of sharing a room? Hmm?" Jake touched a gloved finger to her face, gave that smile she missed every day. "Want me to push the stop button? Or maybe . . . stopping isn't what you had in mind."

She felt the sleek leather slide down the side of her cheek. Almost couldn't breathe. And then she burst out laughing.

"Jacob Dellacort Brogan." She batted his hand away. The elevator's beep grew more insistent. "I could have you arrested. For like, incorrigibleness or something."

"You started it," he said.

"Did not." Although she had. And she deeply wished they could continue. "But listen, aren't you on your way somewhere? Hadn't you better push a button?"

Push a button, huh? She'd kill him if *he'd* said that.

"You were already on the elevator, Ryland, in the lobby," Jake said instead. "But you didn't get off, so I know you're trying your sneaky reporter tricks on me. Good luck with that, sister."

He stabbed the elevator button marked L. The beeping stopped. "You're going down." He saw her reaction, and nudged her with an elbow. "Shut up. You know what I mean. And I'm going back up. Alone. I'm working, and so are you. You're the one who insisted we make work stuff off-limits, right? If you'd like to chat about anything on your list of acceptable topics, feel free. We have ten whole floors to do so. And then we say *adiós*. *Your* idea, remember."

She picked up her bag, slung it over her shoulder, made that pouty little face at him. "Jerk."

"As I often hear," he said.

The elevator shuddered, then began to move.

"Okay, fine. Anyway, listen to this," Jane said. "I did have kind of a weird morning. Tuck, you know?"

"Yeah, sure. Have she and Laney—?"

"I only have eight more floors," Jane said. "You want to hear this?"

He raised both palms, defeated. *Tuck, huh?* She'd driven him nuts when she was covering the police beat for the *Register*. She was hot, sure. But relentless. Manipulative. Also unreliable, unscrupulous, and a problem waiting to happen. What's more, Jake had found, not always honest. After the Laney debacle, Jane admitted she felt sorry for Tuck. He'd never understand why. *Women.*

"So Tuck's adopted, it turns out," Jane was saying. "Who knew? She showed up at my apartment, yesterday— yeah, bizarre, I know—and told me she'd gotten a call from this adoption place, the Brannigan. Ever heard of it?"

The Brannigan? What did Jane know about the Brannigan? Did Tuck have a connection with Lillian Finch? Jake checked the flashing lights across the top of the elevator. Almost at two. In ten seconds, the doors would open, and he'd have no way to find out what Jane was talking about without letting her know why he cared. The Brannigan? Was that where this Tuck story was leading?

"It's like a, a child placement agency, right?" He'd answer what she'd asked, then take it one step at a time. "They do private—"

"Yeah, adoptions," Jane interrupted. "Let me get through this, okay? Because we're almost to the lobby. So Tuck says they called her, and—"

"Who? When?"

"When what?"

The bell pinged, and the elevator doors rumbled, ready to slide open.

"Oh, never mind," Jane said. "I know you're working. It's probably nothing. You know how Tuck is. See you soon, okay?"

She stepped out of the elevator, fluttering a wave over her shoulder. "Later, gator. Stay warm."

Was she teasing him? Knowing she had information he'd want to hear? Jake held back the door with one hand. He had only seconds to make a decision.

Margaret Gunnison had told him she had to catch a plane at Logan, and she'd be in her office only another hour. She wasn't a suspect, not a flight risk, so he couldn't justify making her cancel her trip to the Caribbean. Which meant he had to get upstairs. Still, Gunnison couldn't be the only DFS staffer who had access to the Brianna Tillson files. And those files—including whatever there was about whoever was supposed to sleep in that empty cradle—were not headed to Anguilla. They'd be available whenever he got there.

On the other hand, Lillian Finch. Clearly she had not suffocated *herself*, unless she'd taken a bunch of sleeping pills and taped a pillow over her own face to make it look like murder. Possible, he supposed. But pretty damn unlikely. Kat McMahan would soon have the final say. But way more likely someone killed her.

Now it seemed possible Jane knew something about Lillian Finch's death—or, at least, something unusual about the Brannigan. Had the dead woman called Tuck? Why?

Tuck as suspect? He dismissed that thought as quickly as it arrived. *No. Not Tuck. But what does she know? The moment I ask Jane about it, she'll smell a story. And that'll be another mess.*

Tuck, Jane, Brannigan, murder. All too close for coincidence.

In a murder investigation there were no coincidences. There was only luck and timing. Time to talk to Jane.

He stepped out of the elevator. The doors swished behind him. "Hey, hang on, I at least have time to hear the rest of—"

"Well, well, looks like I shoulda brought coffee for three." DeLuca sauntered toward them, carrying a four-pocketed cardboard tray with two Mickey D extra-larges. His black knit cap was dotted with snow. "Hey, Jane. What brings you here?"

"Hey, yourself, Detective," Jane said. "Might ask you the same thing."

Four women bundled in mufflers and heavy coats strolled in, all talking at once. One punched the up button, and the elevator doors opened. They piled in, leaving wet boot prints on the now-damp floor, then one held the door with a mittened hand.

"Going up?" she asked.

"Nope," Jake said. "Thanks."

The elevator doors closed again. Leaving the three of them.

"Jane was asking me about the Brannigan." Jake had to warn D that she was on to something. He needed to hear the rest of the story.

"You get the bad guy?" DeLuca said. "That'd sure make our lives easier."

"What bad guy?" Jane looked at D, planting her hands on her hips. Looked at Jake. Decided on D. "For what?"

"Callaberry Street," Jake answered.

"Right. Didn't we see you there yesterday?" D added.

"Well, Callaberry Street is why you guys are here, correct?" Jane said. "To see Margaret Gunnison?"

"Detective Brogan, this is dispatch," Jake's radio crackled, the dispatcher's voice bouncing off the marble walls and plate glass windows. "You copy?"

He tried not to roll his eyes. "Brogan. I copy."

"We have a call from a Margaret Gunnison? She's

the assistant commissioner of the Division of Family Services?"

"Copy."

"Apparently you're supposed to be in her office now? The Supe is wondering—"

DeLuca punched the up button, and the light went on. The car was at fifteen. So much for talking to Jane. But Jane wasn't going to Anguilla. She was on to something. And he needed to find out what.

25

No way was she letting them go upstairs. Jake seemed way more interested in the Brannigan thing—or maybe in Tuck?—than Jane had expected. He'd gotten *off* the elevator. And clearly been annoyed with D for mentioning "the bad guy." These two stories were connected, somehow, whatever happened at the Brannigan and the Callaberry death, and they were going to ensure her continued employment at the *Register*. *Thank you, journalism gods.*

"Does Margaret Gunnison have something to do with the Brannigan?" she asked. Might as well try to get the rest of the story. The elevator pinged. On its way down.

She watched the two cops exchange glances.

No answer, huh? Okay, then.

"Is it"—she was taking a chance here, but why not?—"something about Bree?"

Jake took a coffee from D's tray, flipped the lid, took a sip. Not answering. D grabbed his own cup, then pushed the tray into a metal waste bin. Not answering.

Jane almost burst out laughing at their studied evasion. She must be on the trail of something, because they were not-answering like mad. Often a very good sign that the question was worth asking.

"Guys?" Jane said. "If you're finished with your coffee

break? Something's going on, and you're doing a pretty stinko job of covering it up. What does Brannigan have to do with Maggie Gunnison? What's the deal with Bree? I'm a reporter, remember?"

"I sure do." Jake jabbed the up button. The floor indicator blinked 4, and coming down fast. "But duty calls. So if you have questions, you'll have to contact PR. That's how we do it downtown. You want the number?"

"Gimme a break." Jane grabbed his jacket, then took her hand away. The silver doors slid open. "Off the record. Tell me."

DeLuca stepped into the elevator. "I'll leave you two kids alone," he said.

Jake stared at her, but she couldn't read him. He seemed to think for a minute, his back to DeLuca. Jane could see D's boot was keeping the elevator doors open.

"What?" Jane asked, wishing for telepathy. Jake wanted something from her, she knew him well enough to see that. And she sure did want something from him.

"Like I said. Call PR, Jane," he said. But with his thumbs he was clearly sending her a different message. *Text me.*

I have to get out of Mr. Brannigan's office. I have to go home. Ella tried to hold back her tears, tried to remember to breathe, knowing it was not proper to cry in front of the entire Brannigan staff, yet she couldn't help it, not at all, no matter how hard she clenched her fists. She was upset about Ms. Finch. And she was upset about that bag of copied documents that festered, like the Tell-Tale Heart, under her desk.

What should she do with those now?

"Then that concludes our meeting," Mr. Brannigan was saying. "Again, I thank you all for your patience and compassion. I will have more information as it becomes available."

The office door opened, and Grace gestured the down-cast staffers into the hallway. Ella turned, following them out, head bowed. Her fingernails bit into her palms. *I have to go home. I'll take the documents with me. I'll burn them. Or something.*

She stood a little straighter, reconsidering. Trying to regroup. Whatever someone did wrong, it really *wasn't* her fault. She was the good guy. She was trying to help. She was—

"Miss Gavin?" Mr. Brannigan's voice lassoed her from behind. "May I ask you to stay a moment?"

Ella's stomach hit the floor.

"Close the door, please, will you?"

The girl was an idiot, no doubt about that. Crying? Well, of course she was upset that her supervisor was dead—he supposed. But Brannigan had long harbored the suspicion that Ella's deer-in-the-headlights act was only that, an act, and that she actually had her eye on the big desk in Lillian's office. Not that she'd have the temerity to say anything to him about it. He stopped, remembering the new reality. Now he'd never be able to ask Lillian.

Funny how things worked. Or didn't.

"Miss Gavin?" Brannigan circled behind his desk, waving her to a visitor's chair, careful to keep a sympathetic expression. Make sure she knew she wasn't . . . in trouble. He had her, certainly for being late today. Also for her unauthorized visit to Lillian's office last evening. Why was she there? What's more, it would be helpful to know how much Lillian had told her, if anything. He'd had perfect confidence in Lillian, but then one never knew with women.

"I'm so sorry for your loss, for all of our loss. Ms. Finch was a particular fan of yours, always spoke highly of you, and . . ."

"Oh, Mr. Brannigan, what happened to her?" The girl had tears running down her cheeks, her nose going all red. She twisted her hands, worrying the edges of her cardigan sweater between her fingers.

"Well, we don't know, Ella," he said. "But I'm wondering if there's any way you can help us help the authorities in this matter. Did she ever, say, divulge to you any reason why she was, perhaps, upset? Worried?"

Brannigan worked to keep his own face blank as he tried to read Ella's expression. Fear, certainly. Knowledge, possibly.

"No, nothing," Ella wiped her eyes with the back of one hand, then cleared her throat, as if the words didn't want to come out. Gulped. "Nothing. I mean, what do you mean?"

"Was she—happy in her work? Did she have, shall we say, any stresses in her personal life?"

"Her—well, no, Mr. Brannigan—we never—I mean, she wouldn't have—I mean, I never thought—"

Ella didn't seem able to finish a sentence.

"You're upset," he said. *And doing an unsuccessful job of hiding something.* "But we must persevere. If you'd like to, perhaps, take the rest of the day off, go home?"

She leaned forward, eyes widening, like a child longing for a sweet. "Yes, I—"

"But first," Brannigan said, "could you bring me Ms. Finch's current files? I'd like the dossiers on the next clients designated to get the Call, as well as those from the last month or so."

Ella stood, as if straining toward the door. "Okay—I mean, yes, I'll find them."

Seemed as if her voice still wasn't working properly. Interesting.

"Ella? Is there something—"

The girl blinked at him. "No, I was only thinking . . .

it's actually Mr. Munson in History and Records who'd have the archived files. Should I ask his office for them?"

"Don't bother them now," Brannigan said. "We'll talk about Ms. Finch's clients tomorrow."

Now. *That* expression was worrisome. How much did this girl know?

26

Jane watched the elevator doors close, wiping away the last glimpse of Jake—he might have winked, but she couldn't be sure. He'd acted out *text me,* though. Of that she was certain.

Still.

"Grrr." She said it aloud. Jake was upstairs getting all those confidential files from Maggie, exactly the ones Jane needed, exactly the ones Jane would never have access to. Even if she made a formal public records request, Family Services legally had ten days to answer her. Even then, they'd deny the request. Kids were kids, foster care was confidential, and the privacy exemption to the Public Records Law ensured the records were beyond sealed. To her. Not to the cops. Not to Jake. *Grr.*

She should call Alex. Give him an update. Jane scrabbled in her tote bag for her phone, resolving, again, to return it to the special phone pocket so it didn't *always* get swallowed in the black hole.

One message, the green indicator said: 1:04 P.M. No wonder she was starving again. No wonder the lobby was full. *Lunch hour must be over.* A clump of slush-covered workers waited in the ragged security line, peeling off dripping parkas and snow-flecked mufflers, stuffing them into beige bins on a puddled conveyor belt.

She pressed play, held the phone to her ear, clamping it between her cheek and shoulder while she tied her belted coat. The ceiling-high plate glass windows in the front lobby of the DFS building misted with damp, and in the swirl of snowflakes outside on the concrete plaza, a bronze statue of Alexander Graham Bell wore a blanket of Boston white. Grim, gray, and brutally cold. *Gloves.* She yanked one from each coat pocket.

The message clicked on.

"Jane? It's me, Tuck. Call me. Right now. I'm serious."

Tuck. She felt guilty, sort of, about running out on their meeting. Holding one glove, she pulled on the other with her teeth so she could still hold her cell and hit "call back" with her bare thumb. Tuck answered before the phone even finished ringing.

"Listen, Jane. I got a call from Ella Gavin. She's completely freaking out. She says the police were at the Brannigan today, because—"

Jane stopped in her tracks, the other glove dropping to the floor. A businessman in a soggy trench coat almost ran into her, banging his heavy black briefcase against her leg.

"Oh, sorry," she said. *Ow.* She picked up the now water-stained glove from the damp stone. *The police? Were at the Brannigan?* "But what do—?"

Tuck interrupted. "Listen, okay? Ella says the police were at the Brannigan because someone there died."

"Died?" Was this why Jake looked so dumbfounded when she mentioned the Brannigan? Only one thing "died" meant in Jake's world. "What do you mean, died?"

"Ella Gavin says her boss, Lillian Fitch, I think, turned up dead. And here's the thing. She's the one who told Ella I was Audrey Rose Beerman. She's the one who told Ella to send me to Carlyn Beerman. She's the one who wrecked my life."

Jane stared at the floor. Trying to process. Tuck only cared about Tuck, *what else is new.* But *Jake* cared about . . .

"So now we're never gonna know what happened," Tuck was saying. "Ella was going to help me try to figure it all out, but this Fitch person is the only one who—"

"Tuck, what do you mean, died? Did she have a heart attack? A car accident?"

Tuck was silent for a beat. "Well, shit. I don't know," she said. "Ella didn't say, and I didn't ask. Some reporter I am. Was."

"Was Detective Brogan one of the cops who came to the Brannigan?"

"Why would Jake go to the—?" Tuck stopped, mid-question. "Oh."

"Yeah," Jane said.

A murder at the Brannigan. *At* the Brannigan? Well, at least of a Brannigan employee. The one who'd possibly made a potentially embarrassing and reputation-ruining mistake. Still, who would commit murder over that?

"Tuck? Does Carlyn Beerman know they sent her the wrong girl?"

DeLuca, on maybe the day's fifth cup of coffee, leaned against the pitted concrete wall of the courthouse lobby while Jake punched in numbers on his cell phone. The closed double doors to Courtroom 1 towered on one side of them, on the other were doors marked Courtroom 2, propped open with a phone book. A couple of guys, witnesses awaiting call probably, fidgeted in their new-looking suits on a pockmarked wooden bench. The rent-a-cop manning the metal detector leaned against a stack of black plastic bins, reading a magazine.

"Curtis James Ricker?" Jake said into the phone.

He'd gotten Brianna Tillson's sleazeball ex-husband's address easily enough from his probation officer here at Dorchester District Court, a dismal scumbag magnet known as the Dot. The Dot's offices were closing early on account of snow. But Jake and D still had time to make the call before the place went dark.

"This is the state unemployment office, sir," Jake lied. It was poetic justice to be conning a con artist. "We're calling about your unclaimed benefits?"

Guys like Ricker were always on the take. The kind who'd buy lottery tickets, convinced each time it was their turn to win. Convinced the world *owed* them. Jake hoped Ricker's greed would trump any potential suspicion about this call.

"We have to confirm your status, sir, from your file. You are no longer married to a Bry-anna," Jake intentionally mispronounced the name, "Tillson? Divorced, let's see, nine years ago? Okay, correct, that's what our records show. And—what?"

Jake smiled as Ricker fished for details about his "benefits." This guy was hook and line already. According to Maggie at DFS, Tillson had dumped her no-account husband years ago. The state had cleared Brianna to be a foster parent, Maggie explained, as long as he was out of the picture. Sadly—for Brianna and her foster kids—it seemed Ricker hadn't been clear on the rules.

"Sir, your benefits are retroactive according to the regulations recently promulgated by the state legislature, as I am sure you are aware." He read aloud Ricker's Social Security number. "If that is your correct social, you are potentially due a considerable reimbursement resulting from the state's miscalculations about your history. Can you describe your current employment situation?"

Ricker was buying the phony benefits story even more

easily than Jake had hoped. He began a whining recitation of his "situation," with himself as the put-upon victim of bureaucracy and mismanagement. By this time tomorrow, if he had half a brain, Ricker would be talking only to his lawyer.

It was gonna be a domestic, after all. After they collared this guy, they could refocus on Lillian Finch, whose body was now in Kat McMahan's custody.

Officers Hennessey and Kurtz had reported no valuables had been stolen from Tillson's or Finch's house. They agreed no crazed killer or burglary thing was going on. Each case was individual. That meant in each case it was all about motive.

What a bitch being assigned two murders at the same time. Budget cuts, the Supe had explained. As if that made it doable.

Luckily, it was looking like Tillson would be easy.

Finch was tougher. Jake needed to get to her files, check out her house. Who'd hate a middle-aged middle-income adoption agency employee enough to kill her like that? A financial advisor, playing fast and loose with her investments? Maybe Ms. Finch had discovered it? But then Jake and D would, too. A relative disappointed with a change in the victim's will? In that case, all the suspects' names would be conveniently listed in probate court. Maybe it was someone unhappy about an adoption.

Tuck?

Sleeping pills pointed to a female killer. Smothering, not so much.

Not Tuck.

Shit. If the Supe wanted quicker answers, he'd have to hire more cops.

Ricker's whine seemed to be winding down.

Jake interrupted, impatient to reel this guy in.

"Now, finally, sir? For security purposes, to prevent the possible exposure of your Social Security number and potential theft from your mailbox, we cannot use the U.S. Mail to deliver your reimbursement. You must be at home to receive it in person. You understand it's for your security and your protection."

Ricker knew about theft from mailboxes, since that's what he'd been nailed for ten years ago. *Gotta love it.* Mr. Ricker was about to enter the criminal justice system once again. He wouldn't get out so fast this time. First degree premeditated murder carried life without parole.

"Well, as it happens, sir, yes, we do have a courier." Jake gave D a thumbs-up. "If you're home, we can have the money delivered to you today. Yes? Let me double-check your address? Excellent. Mr. Emerson and Mr. Hawthorne will be at your home shortly. You'll need to show them a photo ID. Happy to be of service."

He clicked off the cell phone, tucked it into his pocket.

"You were a lit major, right?" DeLuca tossed his coffee cup into an overflowing metal basket. It teetered, then stayed. "Guess Mr. Ricker missed that day."

"Yup," Jake said.

"Moron."

"We going there now?" DeLuca buttoned his navy pea jacket and slammed a knit cap on his head. "Snowing like a—"

"You know . . ." Jake started to run his jacket zipper up and down, then stopped. "Maybe Ricker called nine-one-one."

DeLuca nodded, heading toward the front door. "Good thought."

"Maybe he's the one who took the baby." Jake fell into step beside him.

DeLuca scowled. "Geez Louise. The baby thing again.

I keep telling you. A person could have a cradle, a million reasons why. There's no report of a baby, Harvard. You watch too much TV. There's no missing baby."

"No, I don't. And there could be." Jake held the heavy glass door open, gesturing his partner though. Wet snow pelted them as they headed down the broad courthouse steps, the steep concrete already accumulating a layer of slush. "And if there is, where's that baby now?"

27

Two problems. And, Jane realized, there was really no one to talk to about them.

She pushed open the prism-glassed door of the Kinsale Pub, a dark-paneled fern-draped hangout favored by local pols and civil servants, managed by the legendary bartender Jimmy the B. She needed food.

That made it three problems.

She scanned the room. Deserted, this late in the afternoon. She headed for the bar, happy to be alone. She needed to think.

First problem. Tuck insisted Carlyn Beerman did not know of the Brannigan's mistake. Tuck was planning to confront the Brannigan people about it first, she'd said, after she "figured out what the hell to do and how to do it and whether we need a lawyer." As a result, Jane couldn't say anything to anyone. Not that she'd know what to say or who to say it to.

Second problem. Jake had pantomimed *text me*, and that's exactly what Jane had done. But no text came back. She swiveled onto the black vinyl stool at the end of the zinc-topped bar, draping her coat over the seat, lining up.

Trying to focus on her story, Jane had battled through the city's ancient property tax computers in the chilly basement of City Hall and found the owner of 56 Callaberry was a Leonard Perl of Fort Myers, Florida. The bad news, Boston's perpetually outdated Residents List showed Perl as the only tenant. Clearly wrong. Since his address was Florida.

"Talkta the Mayah," the clerk had growled when Jane pushed him for more current data. "Budgit cuts."

Still, she'd reassured herself, Perl would know who *did* live there. Jane checked for his phone number but nothing was listed. *Damn.* Cell phones were ruining reporters' lives. No way to find anyone's number quickly anymore. Perl was a dead end.

Nothing was working. The Tuck thing. The Callaberry thing. Her life.

"What'll it be, Brenda Starr?" Jimmy the B emerged from the kitchen, a bear in a white apron. "Working on a big headline?"

"Hey, Jimmy. Could be. A hamburger, medium-ish. No bun. A Diet Coke and, uh, just this once, French fries."

"The usual," Jimmy said. "In five."

Jane swiveled, back and forth, hand on the bar, replaying her conversation with Maggie Gunnison. One critical tidbit, at least, came from that. The victim's name was Bree Something.

Bree Something. Not much to go on. She couldn't find more about those poor kids if she didn't get the rest of the name. Jake probably knew it by now, of course, and she *could* wait until the cops released it. But that was no way to get a scoop.

She stared out the front window, an expanse of plate glass framing a colorless landscape of the snow-whitened concrete of City Hall Plaza, a flat urban tundra crisscrossed by briefcase-toting pedestrians. Three o'clock. Apparently these were the nonessential workers let out early to beat the inevitable snarls of snow traffic on the Mass Pike and the Southeast Expressway. The nonessentials scurried from the unwelcoming complex of gray stone and redbrick buildings, heading to the T or to the overpriced parking lots. "Nonessential" workers. *There* was a dilemma. Better to be nonessential and go home early? Or essential but work late and be stuck in traffic? Jane always picked essential. Especially now the *Register* bean counters were rumored to be plotting layoffs.

She sipped her Diet Coke, stomach growling as the fragrance of deep-fat frying wafted from the kitchen, watching the commuter show, everyone wearing a hat, some losing their battles with umbrellas. If nothing had consequences, she'd race back to the office, find Alex, and chat with the city editor about what she'd learned. She'd tell him Jake had mimed "text me." That would make her queen of the May, since having a police source was hot stuff in the news biz. Alex would be impressed, her job future would solidify, and everyone would live happily ever after.

But everything *did* have consequences. Especially with the barbed wire separating a professional relationship and a personal one. Crossing that ethical boundary could topple her career. And Jake's. To protect them both, she'd only tell Alex about her visit with Maggie Gunnison, and figure out what to do about the Jake part when the time came.

She picked up a fork, twirling it in her fingers, focused on the front window. Luckily Alex didn't expect her to file a story today. Another reason she didn't miss TV.

The double doors of the DFS building disgorged another pack of nonessentials, one of them wheeling a black suitcase, another using one hand to hold on to his—

Her fork clattered to the zinc-topped bar. "Jimmy!" she shouted toward the kitchen. "Don't trash my food, okay? I'll be right back."

A bright green Celtics cap. A green plastic band like a gash across the forehead. Jet-black hair peeking out from underneath. Heading for the Government Center T stop. She had to get to him before he got underground.

"I'm leaving my coat," she yelled over her shoulder, grabbing her tote bag. No time. She had on boots and a heavy sweater. "Two minutes!"

She powered out the front door and sloshed through the curbside slush, checking Cambridge Street both ways for frazzled drivers who'd be so distracted by the snow and the slickening streets they'd fail to see a jaywalker playing Frogger in the suddenly rush-hour traffic.

"Sorry! Sorry!" she muttered, holding up a hand, as if that would stop anything, and tried not to slip as she picked her way, fast as she could risk it, across the icy pavement.

Finn, right? Finn . . . Egleston. Everly. Eberhardt. Finn Eberhardt. Her fan. The oversharer.

"Finn!" she called. This was exactly what she needed. She couldn't let him get away.

Kellianne stared at the teddy bear. It sat on her bed, like an alien visitor, making a dent in one of her puffy pillows. Why did it feel so creepy having the stupid bear touching her stuff? It was only fuzzy tan fabric and a couple of black button eyes. A stupid yellow-striped T-shirt. Not even that cute. But it might be worth—something. To someone. Along with the rest of the stuff. She'd figure that out.

It'd been easy, once she'd gotten the brilliant idea. Her Tyvek suit was so ridiculously big, no one would notice she'd stuffed two bears down one floppy leg, and the rest of the—what would she call them, *souvenirs?*—in the other. She hadn't quite planned the whole deal in advance, so it worked nicely when Dumb and Dumber told her they'd change clothes in the truck and she could use the vic's bathroom. *Adiós, suckers.* She stashed her treasures in her tote bag and walked out like it was any other day. And it was. Except for her, it wasn't. It was the first day of the rest of her life. She'd heard that somewhere. It seemed right.

The stupid bear stared back at her. Like he knew she had the candlestick, and the little plastic rabbit bowl, and another of the fuzzy brown bears, all in her tote bag. Hidden under the bed. Which, come to think of it, was kind of where *she* wanted to be. She touched a hand to her stomach. She felt a little weird inside.

Maybe this wasn't a good idea.

No. It was. Staring down the bear, she lifted her mop of hair onto the top of her head with both hands, then, with a sigh, let it fall back onto her shoulders. She didn't have to decide right now. She'd left these things off the inventory, so the family, if they existed, or the state, if they didn't, would never know they were gone. If you looked at the paperwork, this stuff never existed. And finally, *finally*, she'd be the one who got to make a decision.

Then, *ta-da*, she'd be on her own. Not cleaning up the disgusting aftermath of other people's lives. She looked at herself in the dresser mirror. Today was the first day of the rest—

"Princess!" Kev's voice grated on her, it always did. Like he was king of the—

"What?" Her voice came out all twisty. She'd have to chill.

"What?" she said again, working on what normal sounded like. Not like brother Kev would notice. She could always tell him she was having a "bad day." He hated her to talk girl stuff.

"Gotta hit the road again," he yelled through the door. He pounded a couple of times.

What a moron.

"Why you telling *me*?" Good deal. They'd be gone, and she'd have some real privacy. "Adi-*fricking*-ós."

"Adi-fricking give me a break," Kev said. "I'm saying, we got a call from the cops. Another job. So we gotta go make nice on the landlord. Get this puppy in the bag."

"Another . . . ?"

"Some rich old lady got killed," Kev said. "But fine. We'll go, we'll check it out, we'll make a killing of our own. You don't have to come. Whatever. We're outta here."

Rich. The magic word. And you know what it meant? It meant she'd had a *great* idea.

"Hang on, asshole. I didn't say I wasn't coming. Dad says I have to, remember?" Kellianne reached under her bed, grabbed the canvas handles of her empty tote bag, and pulled it to her. She picked up the bear, not really looking at those beady little eyes, and shoved it back into the tote bag.

"Two seconds!" she yelled. She jammed the bag back under the bed and adjusted the flowery dust ruffle to look like nothing had been disturbed.

She checked her image in the mirror. Her skin would clear up, once this was all over, and she'd get a real haircut instead of one of those student things, have an actual colorist make it blond, instead of doing it herself at the bathroom sink, like, every month. She actually had a pretty good body. That's what she'd been told. She smoothed her jeans over her hips, imagining. Everything she thought she hated turned into exactly the opportunity she needed to make her life happen.

She checked the dust ruffle. Perfect. Plenty of room under the bed for whatever she was about to find at the rich lady's house.

28

"Finn!" No use. The wind and the honking cars and the hiss of the traffic carried her voice away from him. Jane plowed across the plaza, grateful for her chunky black turtleneck, even though it was quickly becoming a wet black turtleneck.

"Finn!" Her ankle twisted under her, the heel of her boot stuck in a now-invisible crack in the uneven concrete. She caught herself, one-handed, on the freezing metal of a bright blue mailbox. She paused, throat dry from the cold.

"Finn!"

He turned her way—*yes*—but didn't seem to see her. She pushed off the mailbox and sprinted, as carefully as she could, toward the retreating figure. He was almost to the T entrance. *Now or never.* She stopped, made her hands into a megaphone, and gathered her voice. "Finn!"

He stopped. He turned.

She waved and trotted toward him, like it was perfectly natural for her to be outside at City Hall Plaza at three in the afternoon in a gathering snowstorm with no coat.

"I thought that was you." She dragged in a ragged breath. "I was in the Kinsale, saw you through the window."

"Jane Ryland?" Finn's eyebrows approached his hat's plastic band. "Whoa. I told everyone you were in our office today, talking to Maggie, so cool. They all wished they could have seen you in person. They said you work at the paper now, cool. Hey. Where's your coat?"

"Oh, Finn. You are a lifesaver." She hated to lie to him, or to anyone, but she needed this info. This was going to be a total seat-of-the-pants fast-talking fabrication. "I was calling my story in to the paper, the Callaberry Street incident? I was sitting at the counter, dictating to the news desk, and I realized—I never got the correct spelling of Bree's last name. Maggie's long gone to Anguilla, lucky girl, but that meant I had no one to call. I was going to be in *so* much trouble with my boss! Then I saw you, and I was so psyched to see you, I forgot my coat."

She paused, wrapping her arms around herself, feeling the snow stacking up on her hair and shoulders. Her nose was probably bright red, and she could no longer feel the tips of her fingers.

"I bet you're on your way to the train, Finn, I'm so sorry. But you're the only one I can turn to. Is it B-r-e-e or B-r-i-e? And how do you spell her last name?"

"This oughta be good." Jake and D tramped up the snow-sodden wooden steps of the Allston duplex. A narrow front porch displayed a collection of soggy newspapers, some still in their plastic bags, and a teetering stack of abandoned yellow phone books. Two battered metal mailboxes, open and empty, one with a peeling label that said CKER. Left side, 343A Edgeworth Street, was vacant, according to Sergeant Hirahara in Records. Right side, 343B Edgeworth Street, was occupied by a Curtis James Ricker. Who was right now expecting the prize patrol. Not realizing that he was the prize.

"Almost feel sorry for the guy." DeLuca poked the grimy doorbell with one finger. "Almost."

A muffled thumping came from inside, like feet hurrying down the steps from a second floor. Someone was playing music, loud.

"Almost," Jake said. "Be great to get his cell phone, you know? We could find out if he used it to call 911."

"I'll snatch it," D said. "You distract him."

"Good plan. Then we'll figure out who's gonna distract the judge from the Fourth Amendment."

The inside door, white, pockmarked, pulled open, and a lug of a guy appeared behind the cracked glass of the storm door. Flannel shirt, worn jeans, face creased and puffy, like an aging pale walnut wearing a baseball cap. No shoes.

Sex offender, Jake thought. Though he knew the guy wasn't.

"Curtis James Ricker?" Jake used the voice he'd perfected in the phone call. He raised his voice over the music.

"Who's asking?" The guy looked him up and down, assessing. "You Mr. Emerson?"

"Mr. Ricker?" Jake said, avoiding the question. *Greed. The great convincer.* "We do have something for you."

"But we can't hear you that well," DeLuca said. "May we come in? Maybe turn down the, uh, Allmans?"

The living room smelled like beer and cat piss. This guy probably wouldn't open a window till spring. An open can of Mountain Dew balanced on a stack of magazines next to a full ashtray. The biggest flat-screen TV Jake had seen in a long time flickered a muted hockey game. Ricker aimed a remote at a box of blinking lights and the decibel level went down, marginally. *No place like home.*

"So?" Ricker held out a wide flat palm, then stuffed his hand into the back pocket of his jeans and pulled out a thin leather wallet. He extracted a plastic card, held it in Jake's direction. "I mean, here's the photo ID you asked for. Take a seat, if you want."

"No, thanks." Jake took the ID, confirming that DOB and vital stats matched those in the probation records. Then he got an idea. *Shit.* A good idea.

"Mr. Ricker. One more question," Jake said. "You have any . . . dependents? Or children?"

Ricker's face hardened, assessing. "Why?"

"You do or you don't," DeLuca said.

"Forgive my colleague," Jake said. "He's binary."

"Bi-?" Ricker looked at DeLuca.

DeLuca shrugged.

"Anyway, Mr. Ricker, I should have mentioned on the phone. If you have dependents, and we can locate them, your benefits might be increased."

Could Phoebe and Phillip be Ricker's children? Could he know about the baby? The Lussier name was a snag, but one step at a time. There had been no father's name on the foster paperwork, but Gunnison had explained that was often murky.

Jake envisioned a boozy quarrel, or some beef about money. Whatever it was wound up with one dead wife on the kitchen floor and two kids in another room playing with teddy bears. And maybe a third kid.

"Dependents?" Ricker said.

Jake imagined the rest of the Callaberry scenario. In one ironic burst of fatherly instinct, Ricker had used his cell phone to call nine-one-one, anonymously reporting his own crime but protecting his children. Had he also grabbed Brianna's purse and paperwork? Only someone familiar with her would know where she kept it.

Everything fit. If they could link Ricker to Brianna through the children, they'd have their domestic, exactly as he and DeLuca predicted. Ricker's fingerprints were in the probation records. If the medical examiner or the crime scene techs came up with latents, they could compare them. They could order a paternity test and subpoena the cell phone, easy enough. They could compare Ricker's blood with what Kat McMahan found on the kitchen floor. When they got it, this guy could go away for a long time.

But first they'd need probable cause. Jake checked Ricker for Band-Aids. None visible. They needed more evidence before they could call in the lab techs and order the noose-tightening tests.

"Yeah, dependents," Jake said. "Children who might rely on you for support."

Ricker seemed to be contemplating.

"Not that tough a question," DeLuca said.

"No," Ricker said. "No dependents."

"Ah," DeLuca said, sounding as disappointed as Jake felt.

Finding the truth is never easy, his Grandpa Brogan had warned him. *But a good cop doesn't need easy.*

"One more thing, sir," Jake said. "We have you as previously married to a Brianna Tillson. Who at one point filed a 209a against you?"

"Restraining order," DeLuca said.

"Old news," Ricker said. "Does that make a difference in—?"

"Last time you saw her was?" Jake risked pushing him a bit.

"Man, I don't even remember. Listen, I gotta take a leak," Ricker said, cocking his head toward the back. "Mind? You guys want some water or something?"

"No, thanks," Jake said. "We'll wait right here." This guy was still expecting a windfall. He wasn't going to bolt. Even though he'd made a quick exit after the mention of Brianna Tillson. As he left the room, Jake saw the outline of the cell phone in Ricker's back pocket.

DeLuca jerked a thumb at it. "Bummer," he muttered.

"You're not half as bummed as this guy's gonna be," Jake said.

Curtis Ricker's day was about to crash and burn.

Jane's fingers were ice. But things were definitely looking up. Her hamburger had still been hot when she'd returned to the pub, and now, down the block, she could see there was no ticket on her car. Best of all, starstruck Finn had given Jane the victim's name, Brianna Tillson. Of course he thought she already knew it. With that knowledge, any good reporter could dig up background, come up with a revealing personal profile and a headline story. *Take that, layoffs.*

Her cell buzzed somewhere deep in her purse.

Tuck?

Or Alex, wondering where she was. Giving him the scoop on Tillson would be fun.

She paused on the sidewalk, hunching her shoulders in the cold, rooted for her buzzing phone. Caller ID was blocked. She punched the green square with a bare finger.

"Hello?"

"Don't even think about Brianna Tillson," the voice said. "Let alone put her name in the paper. You saw what happened to her? You see the blood on the floor? Pretty terrible, huh? She didn't know enough to shut up. You? I bet you do."

"Who is this?" This was a pretty stupid move. The caller's number would be right in her cell now. Findable. Traceable. Unless he—*he?*—had a burner phone. "Who are you calling?"

"Right." The voice—a man? *Finn?* But he didn't have her cell phone number—was hollow, muffled. "Forget about the murder. Got me? Say yes, and we're done."

A chill went up Jane's back, colder than the darkening

afternoon. She looked around, up into the fogged office windows, across the street at a silhouette in the front seat of an idling car, over at the straggle of pedestrians hurrying down Cambridge Street.

Every person she saw was on a cell phone.

Was one of them talking to her? Was there a way to tell? Here she had a—killer, maybe—on the phone. Area A-1 police station a block away. A slew of cops almost within yelling distance. Yet it didn't make a bit of difference. The guy hangs up, the guy disappears.

"You know you're talking to a reporter, right?" Her voice came out more confident than she felt. "Is there something you can tell me? I can keep it confidential. You know I can."

"Confidential I don't need. Quiet's what I need. You. Keeping quiet."

"Listen, I can help you make a deal." *Dammit*. This was someone who knew about Brianna Tillson's murder. How would he know to call *her*? Well, she'd written the bylined story for this morning's paper. That narrowed it down to everyone who read the newspaper. *Wonderful*. "I know people in the po—"

"Police department?" A derisive laugh. "I. Don't. Think. So. This is call number one, *Jane*. You don't want me to call you twice."

29

Kellianne stopped in the doorway, her Tyvek suit snapped up to her neck, her blue mask dangling around her neck, gloves on, taking it all in. Kevin always made them suit up for the first entrance—she supposed that was logical, in case the person had died of, like, swine flu or something and was still contagious. Or if there was still a lot of . . . whatever . . . all over everything. Dead bodies had a kind of smell, she couldn't really describe it. If there was blood and stuff, it was really hard to clean up. But that's why they were here.

And easy to see, this house or condo or whatever was a complete gold mine. Enough stuff in this lady's living room alone to—

"You coming, princess?" Kevin took a ring of keys from an envelope in the mailbox and jangled it at her like he was trying to wake her up. "Or are you going to stand there like a doof while we check this place out?"

Kevin looked like a snowman, wearing his white suit and booties in the middle of the plushy living room. Talk about a doof. Keefer, too. Doofs from Doof City. She couldn't wait until . . . Funny how what was bad sometimes turned into what was good.

"Coming, jerk." She snapped the blue mask over her mouth and nose and followed her brothers into the apartment, tried to remember to breathe the right way so her glasses wouldn't fog up. She'd get contacts, too, when this was over. Green ones, maybe.

They padded down a thickly carpeted hallway, Kellianne checking out the floor-to-ceiling rows of baby pictures on the white walls. Kevin, nonstop talking, halted in an open doorway.

"Suffocated, with a pillow." Kevin read from his stupid clipboard. Talking to Keefer, not to her. Per usual. Why didn't *he* have to wear his stupid mask? "Somebody used tape and stuff to hold the pillow on. Or, maybe she did it herself."

"Sick," Keef said.

"Dead, right? Either way?" Kevin pointed his clipboard toward a big four-poster bed, the kind that seemed like it should have a canopy thing on top. But it didn't. The bare mattress was showing, one of the shiny blue ones with silver stripes. "Happened in that bed, I guess. According to this, the cops took the sheets, and the pillow. Big time smell of death, right? So I say we're gonna need—"

Kevin droned on as she surveyed the room. The dresser had a big mirror with a bunch of curling photos tucked around the edges. Baby pictures, all looked alike. A million little cat figurines, all colors, crowded onto the dresser. Little cats on the nightstand, too.

Kevin, still ignoring her, made check marks on his list of supplies. He always told customers they needed to clean the "death room," and other rooms that touched it, and the bathrooms, including all the ceilings. They always ripped up all the carpeting, cut it up, and hauled it away. It was pretty expensive, and Kellianne always thought a lot of it was kind of not necessary. People didn't seem to notice. Once Kev started talking about the "smell of death," seemed like people began to smell it everywhere.

Looking at the little cat statues again, Kellianne smiled and smoothed her Tyvek suit. "You want me to . . ." She paused, reconsidering.

"Huh?" Kevin looked at her, eyes mocking. "You saying something?"

"I'm not gonna do the inventory," she said. She flipped up her mask and planted her hands on her hips to make sure he knew she was totally serious. "Look at all this. There's way too much stuff. It'll take for freakin' ever. I'll start in the other room."

Kevin pulled his mask off his face, stretching the white elastic way up over his head, then letting it snap back down so it landed like a hat. "Look who's giving orders, Keef."

"Gotta salute," Keefer said, demonstrating. "Guess she knows who's boss."

"Abso-freaking-lutely," Kev said. "*I* am. So, Miss Princess, *we'll* be taking the other room. And you'll be doing the inventory here."

"No way." Kellianne pouted, big time. She knew he hated when she did that. "You always tell me you have to—"

"Ah, life sucks, doesn't it, sister?"

"But—" He was such an idiot.

"See ya, sucker," Kev said. He snapped open his clipboard and handed her some sheets of lined inventory paper. "You should have a pen, right? Come on, Keef, you and me can check out the medicine cabinets."

"Someday you're gonna get caught." Kellianne couldn't resist it, although she was happy to be rid of them. Talk about a sucker. She'd read some story in grade school about a rabbit and a briar patch. She was the rabbit. She looked at the blank inventory pages, trying not to smile.

Whatever she wrote down was all there was. Kellianne could make reality.

"Someday, you're gonna get a brain." Kevin shot the

words over his shoulder as he strutted out the bedroom door.

Someday? Kellianne no longer needed to hide her victory smile. *That someday, dear brother, has already come. It has al-freakin'-ready come.*

"All set?" Jake had dragged DeLuca away from the temptation of Curtis Ricker's desk drawers. D was placidly "reading" Ricker's tattered issue of *Maxim* when the guy shambled back into the living room. The music had flipped to some insistent bass-thumping anthem, still so loud maybe it meant Ricker had a hearing problem. But what he was about to hear would be crystal clear.

Ricker was shoving his cell phone back into his pocket, carrying a huge glass of ice water in the other hand. *Take a leak, huh? Wonder who he'd called on that phone.* It wouldn't be long before Jake found out.

"Thanks, needed that." Ricker hefted his water. "Sure you don't want—"

Jake reached into his inside jacket pocket, nodded to DeLuca to do the same. "Mr. Ricker? I'm Detective Jake Brogan, Boston PD."

Jake watched Ricker's brain struggle with this new reality.

"This is my partner, Detective Paul DeLuca." They flopped open their badge wallets. Jake held his up a bit longer than necessary. Sometimes this part was fun.

"But you said you were—"

"We didn't, actually," Jake said.

"*You* did," DeLuca said.

"We're here to talk to you about the death of Brianna Tillson," Jake said, stashing his badge. "Want to take a seat?"

"She's dead?" Ricker lowered himself onto the plaid

couch, clanking his ice water onto the coffee table. He pulled out his phone, licked his lips. "How did—?"

If he called a lawyer, they were done. Jake talked fast. "So my first question. Where were you on the night of—?"

Ricker, in one swift motion, took his cell phone, and plopped it into his ice water. And put his hand over the top.

"Dammit," Ricker said, shaking his head. "Lookit that. Musta dropped it."

"That's gonna ruin—" Jake reached for the phone, but Ricker stood, hand still clamped over the top of his phone on the rocks.

"Yeah, I guess it is," Ricker said. "That puppy's toast. Now I'm gonna have to call my lawyer from the kitchen landline. And you two? Are gonna have to leave."

"That's destruction of evidence," Jake said.

"Evidence of what?" Ricker said.

It was tempting to push him on it. They'd asked him about "dependents." But you could have children without them being dependents. Maybe Jake's clever questioning had actually lost them info.

Whatever Ricker said now would get thrown out in court, now he'd mentioned his lawyer. Jake would save his questions for later.

He pulled out his own cell phone, pretended to dial. Pretended to be pissed, which wasn't that tough. "Guess we're done here," he said to DeLuca. "I'll let our friend in the probation department know about the extravagant sound system and entertainment center Mr. Ricker is enjoying. He'll wonder where that came from, you know? Mr. Ricker being unemployed and all. I wouldn't leave town, Mr. Ricker. Your probation officer is about to be very concerned with your well-being. Hello? Probation? This is Detective Brogan from the . . ."

"You done?" Ricker yanked open his front door. Waved an arm, showing them out. Slammed it behind them.

"What was that all about?" DeLuca muttered as they walked toward the cruiser. "His sound system?"

A curtain moved in a window across the street. A face appeared briefly in the glass, then vanished. The streetlights had come on, the ones that still had bulbs making splotches of yellow in the graying snow.

"It was about bullshit." Jake tucked his cell back into a side pocket. "Needed him to think I was making a call while I snapped a photo of that cell in the ice water. Who'd do that if they're not hiding something? It's consciousness of guilt, no question. Mr. Ricker has given us some fine ammunition for our search warrant application."

30

"Do people really talk like that, Alex? Except in the movies?"

Jane sat on the city editor's bumpy old couch, stacks of manila file folders crowding her into one corner. She'd parked her car in the *Register*'s dank basement garage, looking over her shoulder, wondering why no one replaced the broken bulbs, imagining footsteps in the shadows and picturing bad guys behind every row of cars. By the time the molasses-slow elevator finally arrived in the corridor outside Alex's office, she'd invented a whole spectrum of explanations for her threatening phone call. None of which was reassuring.

Should she be freaked out? Or dismiss it? She could make a good case either way. She'd gotten her share of nasty calls as investigative reporter at Channel 11, but none before at the *Register*. She could hear Professor Kindell back in Ethics 101, telling her j-school class "a good reporter comes to town and stays until everyone hates them." If you weren't making people angry, he'd said, you weren't doing your job.

Still, she had to tell Alex. Now. She'd trudged to his office, frowning. Following another j-school rule, she'd keep no secrets from her editor. Except for the Jake thing. Which wasn't really a thing.

Alex had stayed behind his desk, listening, as she demonstrated how she'd tried and failed to scope out whether the caller was someone she could identify.

"It seems so Hollywood cliché," she went on. "Talking like they'd think a bad guy would talk. It sounded so phony I almost didn't tell you. On the other hand, it wasn't random. So, here I am."

Alex started spinning his iPhone on the flat of his battered old desk, watching the black case pinwheel on the polished wood. It stopped, and Alex pointed it at her. "I'm supposed to call Tay Reidy, you know, when these things happen. And he'll certainly call the cops. No question about that. But this close to deadline, I've also got to think about another question: Do we go with the story?"

"Well, of *course* we do." Was he kidding? Kill her scoop? Jane dragged her voice back to a lower register.

"What if we make the phone call part of the story? You have to admit it's compelling, someone threatening us. Now it's not just a—Well, I don't mean *just* a murder. But it's possible that the *killer* called me. And I'm not sure that's ever happened to me. Has it happened to you?"

"It could be some nutcase, Jane." Alex spun his phone again like a toy top, the plastic case clicking against the wood. "Someone with an agenda we know nothing about. It'll be impossible to characterize it in a story."

"Then we won't characterize. We'll write the facts." Jane stood, then turned toward Alex's power wall. Yale diploma. One from Columbia J-School. A couple of Polk Awards. A blank place where she remembered seeing his wife's photo. Ex-wife now.

Deep breath. "We can say I got a call, the caller said x, y, z, we let our readers draw their own conclusions. I'll try to confirm the victim's name with the police.

Then we'll go with what we got. That's what they taught you at Columbia, right?"

Alex took off his glasses, polished them on the tail of his flannel shirt. He seemed very interested in the glasses.

She had him. She knew it. One more push should clinch it.

"How long do you want the story?" She'd assume her victory. Ten column inches would be a nice chunk, guarantee good placement on the front of the Metro section. She stood, ticking off her points on her fingers. "After I call the cop shop, I'll start with the news about the victim's name, then see what else I can come up with. I have a whole hour or so to write it. I have the info on the foster care system. We can use some of that, a tease of what's to come. Once we break this, the other newsrooms won't touch it. We'll own the story."

Alex, glasses back in place, swiveled his chair toward her.

She didn't like his expression. What did Jake say his Grandpa Brogan always told him? *A good cop doesn't need easy?* A good reporter didn't, either. But it looked like this was about to get tough.

"Ah, it's a no," Alex said, shaking his head. "Sorry, Jane. Good job, good hustle. I like your perseverance. But it's only a murder victim's name, you know? Not worth the risk. We can afford to back off this time. Okay?"

"You're kidding me," Jane said. She leaned over his desk, palms flat, trying to keep her tone light. She took a step back, semiretreating. He was still her boss, even though he was wrong. "If you were still on the street you'd have pushed your editor to run with it. You know that."

"And he'd have told me the same thing, Ryland. I've got to go by the book, and that means talk to the publisher first. If Mr. Reidy wants us to report that phone call to the cops, we'll do that. If he wants us to run the story, I'll let you know that, too."

Alex stood. In two steps, he was next to her. He touched her, briefly, on one shoulder, then leaned on his desk, his dark eyes level with hers. "But Jane . . ."

Hot Alex, her brain said. She took a step back, out of his force field.

"Jane," Alex said again, his voice softening. "What's important is—whoever it was, whatever the motive, he threatened you. Flat-out threatened you. No story is worth that. You see what I'm saying?"

She tore her eyes away from his gaze. She *did* see what he was saying. And she didn't like it. He was spiking her scoop.

"What if he's calling everyone? What if it's not only me? What if he called all the TV stations? And said the same thing? What if *they* go with it? Listen, all we have to do is bang it out for the online edition, and we win."

Ha. She got him with that one. Holding a story was one thing. Getting scooped was another. Especially when the *Register*'s circulation was verging on abysmal. Breaking big news was the paper's only ammunition.

"But you're the only reporter who knows the name Brianna Tillson, right? That's how you sold me the story, remember?" Alex raised one eyebrow, his eyes almost twinkling behind his wire rims. He had laugh lines, too. The beginnings.

Her shoulders sagged. Alex was right.

"So that's that," Alex said. "But I do have one question. How'd the caller know your cell phone number?"

Jane blinked at him, silent for a moment. She hadn't thought about that. She plopped back down on the couch, considering the possibilities. *Oh.*

Her eyes widened as she talked, realizing the implication of what might have happened. "I handed out my business card to all the neighbors I interviewed yesterday.

Remember?" She looked at her watch. Pushing seven. Outside Alex's window, the night sky bloomed with snow-filled clouds, making it seem much later.

"It must have been someone on Callaberry Street. Someone I already talked to. One of them lied to me. Someone I interviewed knows what happened to Brianna Tillson. Whoa. Now I have to go figure out who."

"No. Jane. Do not even *think* about going there." Alex made the time-out sign. "It's dark, and it's dangerous. Go home. Be careful. I'm sure Mr. Reidy will want to call the police. You and I will talk about this tomorrow."

"Hec," Jane said.

"Heck?" Alex smiled, looking perplexed. "Is that expression left over from your on-air TV days? I mean, saying 'hell' is okay. It's just us."

"Not h-e-c-k. H-e-c. Hec Underhill." This day was becoming a lot more interesting. "Remember, Alex. Hec got photos of everyone we interviewed. I have their names. That means we may have an actual, identifiable photo of the murderer. Right downstairs in our very own photo lab. All we have to do is get Hec to show us his pictures and figure out which one is the bad guy."

Alex narrowed his eyes, considering. "But I need to call—"

"But nothing." Jane opened her tote bag. "I've got my notebook right here. All the names. Calling Tay Reidy can wait. You coming with me?"

Niall Brannigan didn't care about the crime scene tape draped over Lillian's front walk. That was for outsiders, and he was the opposite of an outsider. The key Lillian had given him at the beginning of what she insisted on calling their "relationship" gave him the right to be here. Now it was necessary that he get inside.

His gloved hands clenched his steering wheel. Poor Lillian. He hoped her death had not been painful. He hoped—*Oh well*.

He unclicked his seat belt, flipped up the collar of his heavy coat. Dark out. The green numbers of the dashboard clock read 7:32. Eventually, Ardith would wonder where he was. But not quite yet. Tonight was her book club night, if he remembered correctly. Or perhaps yoga again. There was always something these days. He'd be home soon enough to suit his dear wife.

The yellow plastic tape looped around the dimly glowing cast-iron lanterns at each side of the walkway, then stretched across the flagstone path. There was no police tape sealing the door. It would take him all of two minutes. He'd go in, get what he needed, come out.

If anyone saw him, he'd claim he needed records Lillian had taken home from her office. Better, from *his* office.

He pushed open the car door, avoided the slush by the curb, and clicked the automatic lock. He heard the sharp beep of a car horn. His heart jumped, twisting in fear. *What was that?* He caught his breath, surprised at the clench of his chest. Then he smiled. *My car door. Perhaps I'm a bit jumpier than I thought.*

He clicked his keys again, to make sure. Another beep. *Yes, that's what it was.*

The gray van parked on the street could belong to any neighbor. Happily, there were no police cars. He looked across the tree-lined street to Lillian's house. Some lights were on, he could see that through the bay window curtains, but the police had probably left them on to fool intruders. Lillian lived alone and now everyone knew she was . . . gone.

He was across the street before he knew it, lifted one leg carefully over the tape, then the other, marched up the flagstones. His heart was pounding, so silly, since there was no need to hesitate. He belonged. In and out. He felt his chest flutter in anticipation as he fingered his coat pocket for the gold knob of his keychain. Saw his breath plume white in the chill.

Ready. And go.

31

This has to be it. The proof. The key. But why did Lillian—?
Ella picked up the piece of paper, a skewed copy with one
edge blurred and the other edge off the page. She turned
it over, then looked at the front again. Her living room
TV was showing a cooking show, usually her Monday
night favorite, but tonight she'd muted the sound. The
empty Target bag, her now-tattered document camou-
flage, lay beside her on the couch. The files now covered
her glass coffee table. Whiskers jumped onto her lap,
nosing into the paper.

"Shoo, Whisk," Ella whispered, and for once she
obeyed. The words on this RR 103 were baffling. She'd
seen a million report release forms since she started at
the Brannigan, but never one as potentially life-changing
as this one.

The top copy, the white original, always went to the
birth mother. The blue page went to admin, the green to
finance, the yellow to the state. The pink page was the
last one of the multipage form. The photocopy she was
holding would have been of the pink one, since on the
bottom it said: "for agency files." The forms were notoriously blurry, from being typed through so many carbons
back then. Now the forms were completed by computer,

but the older files still contained the old-fashioned pull-apart kind.

Female Baby Beerman, the fuzzy heading read. Mother: Carlyn Parker Beerman. These RR 103s had been sealed along with the rest of the files. When Carlyn called to release them, that's when Lillian—*Lillian!* Ella pressed her lips together, holding back tears, trying to focus. That's when Lillian had opened the manila envelope and started the search for Carlyn's little girl.

Ella ran a finger down the paper again. Addresses, phone numbers, a social. Date of birth. She skipped to the important part, rereading the typed answers.

Line 17. Identifying marks. *None.*

Line 18. Identifying indicators. *None.*

Line 19. Identifying clothing, tags, or jewelry. *None.*

None. No glittering charm bracelet. She could almost feel the weight of Tuck's evidence in her hand, see it sparkle in the harsh light of the coffee shop. Tucker Cameron's birth mother had left her with a bracelet. A bracelet that proved her name and proved her identity and proved, yes it did, that she was not Audrey Rose Beerman.

Identifying jewelry. *None.* And nothing about a note.

Ella leaned her head against the back of the couch, staring, unseeing, at the flickering screen of her television. Stretched out behind her, Whiskers lowered a comforting paw onto Ella's shoulder.

"I know, Whisk," Ella said. "Seems like Lillian Finch really did send Carlyn Beerman the wrong girl. Now what do I do?"

Her mind spun with possibilities. Lillian had either known, or she hadn't known. If she *had* known—was that why she was dead? Or was it a mistake? If so, was it her only mistake? Had she taken her own life in anguish and guilt?

Or maybe Lillian was dead because she *didn't* know—

and someone else did. Someone who wanted to make sure Lillian never found out. Or maybe because she *did* find out, maybe *that's* why Lillian was dead. Someone killed her to keep her quiet.

And now, she, Ella Gavin, single, alone, and only trying to help, had discovered the same thing. What would happen to her when whoever killed Lillian discovered what Ella knew?

Jake twisted open his second IPA, tossing the cap into the white plastic wastebasket by his kitchen door. The files about Phoebe and Phillip's past he'd gotten from Margaret Gunnison—such as they were—lay open on the round table by the kitchen's tiny window. She'd told him she'd assigned the staffer who copied them to also "dig up" Brianna's records from the archives. Those he'd have in a day. "Or two." Gunnison obviously wanted to get to the airport. Skittering branches on the old silver maple outside his condo battled with the new Paul Simon CD he'd finally downloaded. Diva, as usual, curled into a golden retriever ball at his feet. She'd eaten dinner. Jake hadn't. The beer would hold him until he got through the files.

He turned the last pages of the caseworker's sketchy and unrevealing notes, then started over. *There must be something here about what happened. Or about a baby. Sure haven't seen it yet.*

DeLuca had bailed the second their shift ended, elaborately insisting that medical examiner Kat McMahan was not on his social calendar. D was a shitty liar, but Jake didn't push his partner on it. Could be it was better if Jake didn't know the full score. DeLuca certainly suspected his relationship with Jane, but didn't bug Jake about it. Least he could do was give his partner the same respect.

Jake's cell phone vibrated on the table. The number came up: blocked. Time: 8:15 P.M. Maybe it was Judge Gallagher? She'd be "out," her clerk had said, until eight, unavailable to hear their pitch for the warrant on the Ricker residence. They'd e-mailed her their warrant application, but could be he was screwed on that, anyway. Ricker could have dumped everything incriminating by now. The "money for you" ruse had seemed like such a good idea at the time. Still, he reassured himself, the ruse had elicited valuable info from the guy. If they'd arrived *chez* Ricker as cops, the guy would have clammed up instantly. Roll of the dice.

The phone vibrated again.

"Brogan." He took a fast swig of his beer.

"Brianna Tillson, right?"

It was Jane.

"No, this is Jake Brogan." *Situation.* If she was calling about the Tillson name—who the hell had leaked *that?*—it was a potential mess. That didn't mean he wasn't pleased to hear her voice. He only wished she was saying something else. Something soft. And promising. "You must have the wrong number."

"Jerk." Jane's voice had that smile in it.

"So you always say." He knew he was smiling, too.

"Anyway, this is a professional call, *Detective* Brogan," Jane told him. "I'm calling from the *Register* to confirm the identity of the victim of the Callaberry Street murder. Brianna Tillson. Correct? And to confirm the identities of her foster children, Phillip and Phoebe Lussier. Correct?"

"Professional, huh? Professional reporters understand protocol, which is that only public relations spokespeople can comment on ongoing investigations. Correct, *Ms. Ryland*?" If Jane ran with those names, he was screwed. The Supe demanded they inform the victim's next of kin before the names were released. So far, they hadn't informed next of kin, because so far no one knew if there *were* any. For now, the identities were not public.

Still, somehow, Jane had discovered them. That left Jake holding the bag not only on a potentially botched Ricker arrest but also on a potentially blown identity. Not the best way to impress the brass.

"I left a message in the cop shop PR office, I really did," she said, "but my deadline is like, *now.* I know I'm pushing, Jake, but—"

"Ms. Ryland?" He hardened his voice, letting her off the hook in case her city editor or some bigwig was in earshot. Anyone else, he'd hang up the phone. Reporters were used to it. But Jane had confided she was spooked about layoffs. Maybe Alex was giving her a hard time.

This exact situation was what they'd always struggled with. It put him in an impossible position. He couldn't give her special treatment. But he couldn't *not.* She *was* special. To him. That's why the whole thing was impossible. "I'm sure you understand that I cannot confirm or deny identities of homicide victims until the next of kin have been properly notified. Tell your city editor—"

"Jake? Hang on, okay?"

Jake finished his beer, listening to the fuzzy silence on the phone. Diva looked up, one ear flopped, inquiring. He gave her a reassuring pat and a half-shrug, as if she'd understand. "Women," he said.

"I tried to text you, Jake." Jane's voice had lowered to a whisper. "Is that what you were signaling by the elevator this afternoon? Were you going to tell me the name? But I really need to ask you. Did you tell anyone that *I*—"

The call-waiting chirp on Jake's phone interrupted, silencing whatever Jane was saying. The ID came up. RIVERA.

Why was the Supe calling him? Maybe Judge Gallagher had agreed to the warrant.

"Hang on, Jane. One second." He clicked the button. "Brogan."

"Brogan? What the hell is she doing?" The Supe's hollow voice meant he had Jake on speakerphone. Was someone else in the office? And *she*? How'd the Supe know Jane was on the phone?

Or Rivera could be talking about Judge Gallagher. "Sir, we applied for a search warrant for the—"

"Search warrant? What search warrant?" Rivera cut him off. "Hell, no. I've got some newspaper guy on the other line who's telling me—"

Jake heard a murmur in the background, someone else talking.

"Alex Wyatt," the Supe said. "From the *Register*? On the other speaker. Says some asshole called one of his reporters, Jane Ryland? And semi-threatened her if she pursued the Brianna Tillson case. How the hell does she know the name of—"

"Sir?" Jake interrupted. *Threatened Jane?* "I hear you. Let me check. I'll let you know."

He clicked the button on his phone, hoping the Supe didn't notice he'd about cut him off, and stood so quickly two documents slid from the pile, landing on Diva's back. Spooked, she nipped at them, then leaped up and scurried away.

"Jane?" Something was wrong with his voice. He cleared his throat, then tried again. "Jane? Is there something you'd like to tell me?"

32

Lots of things, Jane thought. But nothing she could tell Jake if there was a chance anyone would hear. She swiveled in her office chair, staring at the fraying fabric of her cubicle walls, hearing the muffled clicking of computer keyboards, a few phones ringing. Judging by the acrid odor of burning dark roast, someone had again left the communal coffeepot on too long.

"Tell you about what?" she asked. Jake's voice sounded funny. Seemed like he was talking about something specific. *Now what?*

Already this evening hadn't gone the way she'd hoped. When she and Alex arrived at the *Register*'s basement photo archives, Hec Underhill had already gone. Archive Gus pinged him on the Nextel, but the photographer didn't answer. Alex, impatient to begin with, went back to the newsroom to oversee the early edition. Jane hung around the photo lab, crossing her fingers Hec would return.

As she waited at Hec's desk, she'd jiggled one foot. Picked the hem of her jeans. Pulled a speck of lint from her black turtleneck. Looked at her watch. Maybe he'd tried to contact her? She dug in her bag, found her cell phone on the first try. But nothing from Hec. No text from Jake, either. Not even Tuck had called.

"Damn." She'd said it out loud.

"Huh?" Gus looked up from his computer.

"Nothing. Sorry."

One good thing, at least—no more anonymous calls.

She'd puffed out a breath. Impatient. "Gus? Can you try Hec again?"

Gus, perched on a high stool in front of a multiscreened monitor, was mousing through an array of photos from the snowstorm.

"Sure." He clicked the Nextel. "Hec? This is base. Do you copy?"

He paused, and they both listened to silence.

"Sorry, Jane." Gus had shrugged, then parked the Nextel into the charger. "He's out-a-pocket. You know Hec. Freelancers. Always somewhere. Feel free to hang out, ya know? Have one of those cookies. I have to make this deadline."

"Thanks, Gus." It should have been *her* deadline, too. Maybe she could still get the Brianna scoop in the last edition? All she had to do was call Jake. She'd broken off one little morsel of a chocolate chip, nibbled at it as she worked on convincing herself.

It would be perfectly okay to call him, even expected. No matter what was up, or not, in their personal life, she was a reporter working a story. It was her job to call a police source if the goal was to get to the truth. And to a balanced story. Alex would agree.

Right. *Great idea.*

But she couldn't call Jake in front of Gus.

"Ask Hec to come find me, ASAP, okay?" Ignoring the elevator, she ran up the three flights to the newsroom and around the corner to her cubicle. Punched in Jake's number. But now that she was actually talking to him on the phone—well, if she interpreted the disapproval in his voice correctly, her "great idea" was more of a disaster.

"Earth to Jane?" Jake was saying. "About a threatening phone call. Might you have thought that could be a bit of information I'd be interested in?"

"How did you know I got a phone call?" She frowned, propping her elbows on her desk, holding the receiver against her cheek. It could only be Alex who told the police. Would he do that?

"'How'? 'How' is not the point," Jake said. "The point is, someone—"

"Jane?" Alex stood in the opening of her cubicle, cell phone in hand. "I'm on the phone with the—"

Her brain was going to explode. No room for one more thing to fit inside. But she couldn't let Alex know she was talking to Jake.

"Who's there?" Jake said. "Is someone in your office?"

"—the police." Alex finished his sentence. "And the publisher."

"Call ya back." Jane looked up at Alex, still holding the phone to his ear. Smiled her best innocent smile. "What's up?"

"Yes, I'll tell her," Alex said into the cell. He clicked off and leaned against the side of her cubicle. A picture of a beach in Nantucket, souvenir of the last big story she'd push-pinned to the wall, floated to the floor. Alex picked up the green plastic pin, then the photograph.

"Sorry." He stabbed the photo back onto the fabric divider.

"Oh, no problem," Jane said.

"Not about the photo, Jane."

Not a good sign.

"That was Tay Reidy on the phone. I told him about the call you got, and he and I called the cops. Superintendent Rivera. He is not happy. No one is happy."

"Alex, it's—Listen, all we have to do is look at the glass as half full." She could tell from Alex's frown he wasn't buying her pitch. But she had to try. "Tomorrow, I'll go downstairs again and find Hec, and we can—"

"Yeah. About tomorrow. Mr. Reidy is of the mind that your situation has potentially put you, and all of us, in danger. I disagree, I admit, but nevertheless. If you come into the building tomorrow, he fears, the caller may, well, who knows. So Mr. Reidy has 'suggested'— you're not going to like this, Jane, but remember I'm only the messenger—that you stay away from the *Register* for a few days. Get out of town, even. Back off. Until the police can investigate."

"Get out of *town*?" She stood up, then sat down again. "Back *off*?"

"Tonight the cops are going to keep an eye on your apartment. Anyone suspicious shows up, anything looks off, call nine-one-one. No sleuthy stuff."

"Are you kidding me?" Maybe he *was* kidding. He didn't look like it, but she'd give it one more try. "We're about to break some pretty big news, and he says back off?"

"Jane." Alex raked a hand though his hair. "What the publisher says is what we do. End of story."

Got that right, Jane didn't say.

Niall Brannigan leaned against Lillian's front door, half-hearing it click shut behind him. *Warm in here.* What was wrong with his shirt? Tight. *Take off the tie, loosen it.* He clutched his set of keys. His nerves were getting to him. *Take a deep breath,* he instructed himself. He tried, then had to try again. *Why is it so difficult?* He wanted to smile, but that wasn't working, either.

He put a hand to his chest, feeling . . . *tight,* like a wrenching, as if an elephant were sitting on his chest. If he could only make it to the couch. A few steps across the room.

"Who the hell are you? Keefer! Get in here! Lookit this!"

Who was shouting? Was someone in the room? Brannigan narrowed his eyes, trying to make them work. Someone in a white coat and a mask. A doctor? But not a doctor. Only one step to Lillian's soft couch. He needed to get—in the other room—the photo of—

"Holy shit, Kev, who the hell is this?"

Now someone else was talking, another man in white.

"Hey. Buster. Who the freaking hell are you?"

"He's like a million years old. How'd he get in here? Hey, Grampa. What the hell are you doing here? Who the frick *are* you?"

He knew this. He knew his name. He just couldn't think of it at the moment. "It's—I'm—"

"Call the cops," one man said. "Call nine-one-one."

"Yes, call—" Brannigan tried to make the words come out, but he knew somehow, it didn't sound like yes. The room grew darker, then lighter, and the elephant still sat there, and he needed—

"No. No freaking way. We're not supposed to be in here till like tomorrow, you know that. How would we explain—"

The white suits kept talking, arguing, ignoring him. He needed to interrupt.

"In the bedroom drawer, there's a—," he said. Ah. Better. *Better.* He dropped onto the soft welcoming cushions of Lillian's couch, her faint scent of muguet and roses lingering on one silky pillow. The lights were bright now, exactly as they should be, and the elephant was gone. His fear was gone. The ceiling was white, so white, so fascinatingly white, why hadn't he noticed that before? He needed a moment to—But now the voices were yelling at each other, arguing, incessant but somehow hazy around the edges.

"I said, get him outta here!"

"But how are we supposed to do that? He's a—"

Someone—screamed? But not one of the white suits, it sounded like a girl, someone who worked for him at the Brannigan? But why was she screaming? So silly. It would all be fine.

33

She was going to die.

Right here, right now, and it wouldn't matter because her stupid brothers would be arrested for her murder, and she wouldn't care. It might even be worth it to be dead to have those two idiots in handcuffs and behind bars.

How can someone this old weigh this much? A million pounds, Kellianne calculated, seething. He weighs a million freaking pounds.

Kevin had draped one of the old man's arms over her shoulders and the other over Keefer's. Kev walked in front of them, "scouting," he said, as the two stumbled along the front walkway toward the street, holding the guy up between them.

After the man collapsed inside, Kev had made her take off her white suit, right when she had everything in place. Demanding privacy, she'd stashed her loot in the dead woman's bathroom. They'd never come in the bathroom when she was in there. So that was okay.

But now, if any of the neighbors looked out their windows, wouldn't they see them? Her and Keefer lugging some sick old man down the front walkway of the dead woman's house? *I mean, how is that gonna work?*

She took a deep breath, her nose wrinkling at the

scent of mothballs and old man smell. Her white nylon parka was gonna smell like—*Shit*. Now she had to grab one of his hands and give it a yank to keep him from slipping off her shoulder. She hoisted the stupid guy and took another step or two, then stumbled, barely catching herself.

"*Shit*." She should drop the guy, right on the wet brown grass. The brother brain trust could just deal with it. Without her.

She wasn't going another step.

"Pssst, Kevin," she whispered, needing to get his attention without making noise. No lights were on in the nearby houses, but someone could be calling the cops right now. "This is the dumbest, beyond dumb-ass thing you've ever—"

"Move it, princess," Keefer hissed at her. He was holding up the guy's other side. But Keefer was so much taller than her, the guy was all tilty. Which made him even heavier. He was still breathing. She knew that, at least.

"But—"

"It is what it is, right? Keep walking."

No way. "Kevin!" she whispered, loud as she could, the sound tensing in her throat. "Stop, you asshole!"

Kevin stopped, pivoted, and strode two steps toward them, glaring at her, his face all lines and shadows. His silver down vest was hanging open, unsnapped, and he wore his stupid baseball cap, strap in the front, and precious sunglasses balanced on top.

"Listen to me, sister. You don't have any say in this, right?"

She didn't like the sound of his voice.

"You keep walking," he said. "That's gotta be his car across the street, the Lexus. Where'd he come from, otherwise, right? You keep your freaking arm around him, like I told you. And this will all be copacetic."

"But what if—"

"There is no 'what if.'" Kevin leaned forward, his eyes drilling into hers.

She hated that. What an idiot.

"Besides, he looks like some kind of drunk, ya know? If anyone's looking?" Kevin waved a hand at the neighborhood. "So let's all look sad for the neighbors, oh, no, Grampa had a little too much booze, must have been so upset over poor what's her name. We're helping him to his car. O-frigging-kay? Keep. Going."

Lucky it was dark. Lucky the neighborhood streetlights were kinda dim. Dim. Like Kev, who kept acting like he was the boss of her.

Headlights.

Coming around the corner.

Kellianne felt her heart totally hammering in her chest. She tried to imagine what they would say if—

Kev stopped, backed up close until he was right in front of them, as if to hide the unlikely trio from the road.

The guy got even heavier. His head lolled to one side, his bristly white hair grazing her mouth. She. Was going. To *die*.

The car was headed right toward them.

No one said a word.

The car whooshed past. Its piercing blue headlights grazed the surface of the walk, but no light touched them. The driver didn't even slow down. Kellianne held her breath as it pulled away, leaving them in the dark.

It wasn't dark enough to keep her from seeing the guy's mouth hanging open, eyeglasses about to fall off. She looked down at the flagstone path, trying to keep his image out of her brain. Her boots were muddy, glistening with slush. *His* feet were twisted, shoes coming unlaced, now his feet were facing in, no one's feet could ever naturally do that. She remembered to breathe, then looked up, at the road, at the disappearing taillights, at Kev. Anywhere but at *him*.

"Toldja." Kevin was waving them forward with a "hurry-up" spiral of one gloved hand. "Make it look like you've got to get him to the car. He's not dead, you know? He just had a stroke or something."

"And then what?" Keefer, lugging his half of the load, turned to her in the murky pool of the streetlight, muttering, as they crossed the road, step by ridiculous step. "We're gonna put him—"

Kevin got to the curb, then faced them, hands on hips. "Look. If we call the cops, and they find him in her house, they're gonna know we were inside early. If they know we were inside early, we are ska-rooed. You know the deal."

"Yeah, but—" Keefer was frowning.

"Yeah, but nothing. Who's to know where he had his heart attack or whatever? Right?" Kevin kept talking, his voice low and persuasive. "Right? So, listen. It's all good. He had keys, remember? We've gotta find them to get him back into the car."

"I'm not looking in his freakin'—"

"Shut up, princess. I'll hold him up while you—"

Kevin took the last three steps to the car, and tried the driver's side door. "Hey, no way. The door's already open. How great is that?"

He still wore his gloves, Kellianne saw.

She frowned the whole time as she helped Keefer slide the guy behind the wheel. Keef had picked him up like a baby, plopped him in the front seat. She'd stuffed his legs into place, wincing as she saw his head bonk against the steering wheel.

She stood up, took one step away from the car, keeping her hand on the door handle.

"He's in. We done? I'm closing this door."

"Shit." Keefer was pushing her aside, leaning in over the guy. "Holy . . ."

"What?" Kev whispered.

"What?" Kellianne whispered.

"He's not breathing anymore." Keef's voice was weird, all freaked out. "Look. See that?"

"You sure?" This sucked, Kellianne thought. Sucked bad.

"You wanna check up close, little sis?" Keefer twisted around, cocking his head toward the body.

"Close the door," Kev ordered. He pointed at Keef. "*Now.* If he's dead, he's dead."

Keef reached for the door handle.

"Softly!" Kevin hissed.

The door clicked shut with a muffled thud. Kellianne looked around, eyes darting from house to house. Nothing. No lights flipped on. No sirens screamed down the street, not even a dog barked. Only the wind twisting through the bare rustling branches of the trees, and the three Sessions, standing by a dead guy.

"Don't you morons see? This is *better.*" Kevin widened his eyes and held out both hands, like he was trying to convince a little kid. "Now he can't talk about seeing us. Right? Or tell what happened. He can't—jeez. Come on, we need to get back inside."

Kellianne trotted after her brothers, across the street and back up the flagstone walk, considering. *Better?* It could work either way, she supposed.

If they got into trouble, like the cops started asking questions, well, none of it was her idea and nobody could say it was. And if it actually worked, if, like, the cops thought this guy had his heart attack behind the wheel, maybe, felt bad, pulled over, then died, well, that wasn't her fault, either. Shit happens.

Then she thought of something. Something not good at all. She had to tell Kevin. He was about to open the door, and she'd better stop him.

"Hey. Kev."

Kevin had left everything unlocked. He was pulling

open the white-trimmed storm door but turned to her, his stupid cap all sideways but his stupid sunglasses still in place.

"What, for godsake? We need to get inside." He turned the brass knob of the front door, and pushed it open.

"I'm just saying." Kellianne, the last one in, closed the storm door behind her. They stood in the entryway, looking into the living room. Only the puffy couch pillows that had fallen, haphazard, onto the dead woman's expensive-looking rug betrayed anything unusual happening inside. "You're so smart and all, but this guy had a key to the house, right? So it seems like he had to know the dead woman. So aren't the police gonna connect—"

"If they do, Miss Buzzkill," Kev interrupted her, she hated that, "they're gonna think he was on his *way* to see her, right? Maybe he didn't know she was dead. I mean, obviously he didn't. Why would you come visit a dead person?"

Kevin was sneering again. She hated that, too. He kept talking, his eyes all sneery, like she was so dumb.

"Right, princess? But he never made it inside. Because the door was sealed with crime tape. And we're gonna do that right now. Capisce?"

"Yeah, capisce?" Keefer echoed. He stabbed two forefingers at her, poking the air. "We got nothing to do with that guy. Okay? And we're gonna seal the door when we leave."

Keef turned and looked back through the storm door. Kev did, too. So did Kellianne. The three remained silent for a moment. Staring across the street.

In the glow of the streetlight, Kellianne could make out the glow's body, head down, sitting behind the steering wheel. Kind of, she guessed, like he'd just parked there. Maybe getting ready to open his door. Which, come to think of it, was exactly what he *had* done about twenty minutes earlier.

Maybe this would work.

"Okay," Kellianne said.

34

"Why would you think she'd be home, Tuck? Shouldn't you call?" Jane watched the numbers on the gas pump fly by as she filled her Audi with unleaded. Not exactly how she'd planned to spend her Tuesday morning, but then, nothing in her life was going as planned. Frankly, that was becoming a pattern.

Her hand nearly froze to the pump handle, but self-serve was cheaper. If it turned out her job was in the *Register*'s budgetary gun sights, she'd be wise to keep expenses down. And she should have worn a hat. She wrapped the end of her plaid muffler around her other hand. Freezing.

Freezing and banished.

Tuck had her passenger-side window open and was pecking at the keys on the car's GPS. "She lives there, that's why," Tuck said. "It's not where we met, remember, but I know . . . hang on a second, I can't talk to you and enter the address at the same time."

Banished from the *Register*. *So ridiculous.*

"I know, Mom, glass half full," Jane muttered at the flashing numbers. Come to think of it, she *should* remember that. She wasn't banished from journalism. She could work on a different story, and she didn't need to go into some building to do it. Eventually, Alex would love it and Tay Reidy would unbanish her and all would be well.

It could happen. Might as well believe it.

But truth be told, she didn't. As the gas pump numbers racked up more dollars, Jane's worries spun even faster, imagining what would happen if she got fired again. Her father would—well, he'd probably pull out his favorite phrase, "I told you so." Then remind her he'd have preferred her going to law school, and remind her that Lissa had followed his advice, then point out how happy her sister was now. How engaged Lissa was. All that Jane wasn't. She'd have to sell her condo, move somewhere, find another new job. *As what?* And Jake—

The gas pump bell dinged. Jane jammed the hose back on the hook.

Jake was so angry last night. She had to admit she wasn't thrilled with the nasty phone call, either, who would be? But it was the cost of doing reporter business, and she couldn't live her life spooked every time some goon felt unhappy with her story. She promised Jake she'd be careful and made it home fine. No bad guys or boogey men. No repeat phone call. Fine, okay, she'd checked the street outside her front window a time or two. She hadn't noticed any police cruisers—so much for "keeping an eye on her"—but who knew?

She swiped her credit card through the payment thing again with a little more drama than warranted.

Get out of town. Ridiculous. She should be basking in glory over the Brianna Tillson scoop and working on her take-out on foster care. She should be studying Hec Underhill's photos to see if any of the Callaberry Street neighbors she'd interviewed looked like someone who would make a malevolent phone call. Or kill someone. Instead, she was embarking on a wild-goose chase with Tuck. Still, if she hit pay dirt, she'd be back in control of her life.

"Got it," Tuck said. "The GPS says it'll take, like, two hours to get there. A straight shot west, then down eighty-four. Hang on, I'm hitting the bathroom."

Tuck slammed the car door, heading toward a battered tin sign that said LADY'S. She glanced up at the whitening sky, then swirled an orange cashmere muffler around her neck.

Jane slid into the driver's seat, yanking the seat belt across her parka. Jake was fuming because she hadn't informed him instantly about the call. Alex was fuming because they had a perfectly good scoop about Brianna Tillson but couldn't use it.

Everyone angry at Jane. Lovely.

Her story was killed, her exclusive out the window. All that cultivation of Maggie Gunnison and her serendipitous sighting of Finn Eberhardt—not to mention her frostbitten arm-twisting to weasel information from him—had resulted in absolute zero. Which is about as cold as it was at this Mobil station in the Framingham service plaza of the Mass Turnpike.

"Glass half full," Jane muttered.

Tuck was back in her seat. "Glass of what? Full of what?"

"It's an expression. Listen, where were you anyway, yesterday? I texted you a couple times."

Jane turned the ignition, pulled forward, and waited for a break in the highway traffic. Cars hissed by, tires spitting sleet, some tailgating the municipal salt-spreader trucks working to keep ahead of the always-icy turnpike. Lopsided mountains of graying snow, piled shoulder-high by the public works plows, lined the access ramp. This stuff wouldn't melt until March, maybe April. It would only get dirtier. At least there was no snow in the forecast. Around here, anyway.

"I was—" Tuck leaned forward, peering through the windshield. "Okay, you can go."

Jane ignored her, flipped on her turn signal. It didn't matter why Tuck hadn't called her, she guessed. What *did* matter—

"Did Ella tell you she was keeping those copies of the documents?" Jane inched forward, eyes on the traffic, ready to bang the gas when there was an opening. "Sure would be good to have them, you know?"

"Nope," Tuck said. "She told me at Dunkin' she had to get rid of them, in case—well, I guess she wasn't supposed to copy them. So she certainly doesn't have them anymore. We're screwed on that end. *Go.* There's plenty of space."

There wasn't. Good thing Tuck wasn't driving. "Well, wait. The Brannigan people, Ms. Finch, contacted you. Didn't they give you copies?"

"'The child'—that's what they call me—'the child' doesn't have access. It's all sealed." Tuck waved a hand at the cars whizzing by. "Sheesh. We're never gonna—"

Jane hit the accelerator, sneaking her Audi in behind a salt-spattered red SUV filled with kids. An Irish setter barked at her, silently, through the rear window, as the SUV pulled away. The traffic had thinned out, as always happened on the Pike. Crowded as hell for a mile, then next to nothing for reasons known only to highway engineers.

The green mile-marker signs flashed by, the concrete barriers along the side of the highway a blur of jagged cracks and mismatched plaster patches. They were on their way to find out what Carlyn Beerman could tell them. Tuck insisted the woman-who-was-not-her-mother must be key to the whole thing.

The "thing": that Carlyn's biological daughter was out there somewhere. As was Tuck's real birth mother. Waiting for their long-lost family to find them.

Maybe Jane could make things right. After all, that was her job, as a reporter, to make the system work.

To hold the bad guys accountable. To make happy endings.

When she was growing up, Jane's mother had eventually gotten used to her rescuing baby birds, adopting stray animals, and marching for better food in the school cafeteria. Even back then, preteen Jane needed to find out who caused the problems and figure out how to fix them. *Not your responsibility,* her father would instruct her. Jane could never understand that. *Then whose?* she would ask. Now, being a reporter meant fixing things was her *job. That* he couldn't criticize.

"We can't get the info from the Brannigan now, that's for sure." Jane adjusted her rearview mirror and gooshed wiper fluid across her windshield. "I can see us, sashaying in there, asking about your birth-mother concerns in the middle of a potential murder investigation. Speaking of which. Did Ella call you with any update on Lillian Finch? Did the cops visit Ella's?"

"Nope, she didn't call." Tuck rummaged in her purse. "Gum?"

"Don't you think that's strange?" Jane shook her head at the gum offer, eased into the fast lane, and passed the SUV. Now that the road opened up, everyone pushed the speed limit. *Massachusetts drivers.* But seventy seemed safe enough. No staties with radar guns lurked by the side of the highway, ready to nab her for speeding. "Ella was freaking, remember, when she left us? And now Ms. Finch, the woman who she says made the big mistake, is—"

"Dead," Tuck said. "Yeah."

"Remain on the current road for one hundred five miles," the plummy GPS voice instructed.

"Yeah," Jane said. "Not that her death has anything to do with . . ."

She paused, staring as the highway unspooled ahead.

What if it did? What if Lillian Finch's death was connected to Tuck?

"Hey. Tuck?" A black pickup seemed to be closing in on them. Was it? Jane watched it in the rearview. It was. Getting closer by the second, verging on tailgating, flashing its double-tall headlights at them. "I've got to watch the road, but check behind us, okay?"

Jane risked another look in her rearview as Tuck twisted around to peer through the back window. The truck was definitely closer. Definitely picking up speed.

"See that truck?" Jane said. "The black one? Isn't he getting kind of close?"

35

"Did you touch anything, Mrs. Richards?" Jake knew he
sounded like a TV detective, but at least those crime
dramas got people to understand what was important.
Law & Order as a vehicle for citizen education was
pushing it, maybe, but if Dolly Richards had been savvy
enough to keep her mitts off the Lexus, he and DeLuca
might catch a break. This guy was dead, that was for
sure. Question was, who was it? And why?

"Did you open the car door? Recognize who was
inside?"

Jake had peered through the ice-covered passenger-
side car window when he and DeLuca arrived at Margolin Street, happy to see no smudges or swipes from
curious fingers, knowing he had to keep the crime scene
pristine until the techs arrived. Jake could see the man's
face was turned toward the passenger side, his plaid
muffler obscuring his features. Gray hair, navy overcoat,
no gloves. Not breathing, motionless, skin on his hands
blanched. The dead man's hands were in his lap, not on
the steering wheel. The windows were not fogged. No
one was breathing inside.

No bullet holes in the car, no blood that Jake could
see, no signs of a struggle or violence. But it was still

early, and he was still collecting puzzle pieces. Guessing was a waste of time.

Crime Scene would be here momentarily, and DeLuca was running the license plate. This poor guy clearly wasn't going anywhere.

"Touch anything? Of course not, Detective." Mrs. Richards shook one finger at him, exactly like his Grandmother Brogan used to do. "I see all the shows. I know what to do. I called nine-one-one. I saw the car out my front window when I went for the morning paper, on the porch. Then I started thinking, had I seen the car last night? There was another car parked out there, a grayish van, but it went away. With all that's been going on around here, I knew I should, well, call the 'cops,' as they say. But I couldn't really remember about the car, so I thought, well, I—"

Jake hid a smile. Dolly Richards was clearly relishing her moment as potential witness to real-life human drama. Her gray curls peeked out from under a crocheted white hat that sported a crocheted flower over one ear. She'd gone a little overboard with the rouge. If he didn't interrupt, she'd just keep talking.

"Ma'am?" Jake narrowed his eyes at the obviously lifeless man behind the wheel of the Lexus, searching for something he might have missed.

"I get up early these days. Don't want to waste any of the time I have left! The paper boy hadn't arrived when I first looked, but I did notice this car. Not so much the *car,* but a person inside. Now, makes sense there'd be a person if they were driving, and I didn't think a thing of it, maybe he was leaving. But when I went back for the paper, it seemed to me that he hadn't moved. *That's* when I started to smell trouble. So I wrote down the license number, like I always do, I write them all down. I called nine-one-one, and said, I'd like to report—"

"Ma'am?" Jake tried again. "So this green car had been parked here all night?"

"Well, that's what I told the girl on the phone, the nine-one-one girl. Like I said, I'm not sure." Three frown lines appeared across her forehead. "Of course, the police were here the other day, so I figured they'd be—well, I think I'd recognize all the usual cars, and there are always cabs, of course, there was one earlier that night. I don't want to make a mistake, you know? But I think . . ."

Jake let her talk as he pieced the story together. He pulled out his cell phone, opened a new file for Margolin Street. *Does that sound familiar?* If the green Lexus had been here all night, the already-iced morning dew would be a problem enough for the print guys. Another homicide. *Christ.* That was going to push their unit to the max. Still, any luck, this was a heart attack. They wouldn't know until the ME got hold of the case. DeLuca had magnanimously volunteered to watch for Kat McMahan's van.

Wait. What had Mrs. Richards said? "Police were here the other day? For what?"

Mrs. Richards looked up at him, both hands landed on her hips. "Well, for heaven's sake, Detective, that's Lillian Finch's house. Right there. Across the street. See the yellow tape across the front door?"

Holy shit. Margolin Street. He clicked open his notes from the meeting at the Brannigan. Did he even have Lillian Finch's address? He scrolled through his typed-in bullet points. No. It was certainly in the master case files, but not in his cell phone notes. He wasn't the initial primary on Finch. *Damn.*

Mrs. Richards leaned toward him, conspiratorial. One white-gloved hand clutched his jacket sleeve. "Detective, do you think you have *two* murders to solve? Now I'm really going to keep my doors locked. We all think someone killed poor Lillian, of course—do you think whoever that was also killed *this* poor man?"

Tuck turned in her seat again, looking out the back window at the Mass Pike behind them. "*Idiot,*" she said. "Move over, Jane. Let the frat boy pass you."

Jane flipped her blinker, checked for traffic, eased her Audi into the middle lane. She could hear the hiss of salt and slush under her wheels, the lane markings barely visible through the road's thin veneer of almost-snow. She clicked on her windshield wipers, clearing a half-moon slash of glass framed with spackled gray.

"Pass me, you jerk," she said. Instead, the black truck swerved in behind her, seeming like inches from her rear bumper.

"'Objects in the mirror are closer than they appear,'" Jane read on her side mirror. Not good.

"Come *on,*" Jane said. *Call nine-one-one if there's anything strange,* Alex had told her. He'd also told her to get out of town. Was someone following her? Seemed unlikely. What would be the point?

All the cars on the Mass Pike were following someone, if you looked at it that way. Plus, Massachusetts drivers were notoriously aggressive. Maybe this one was giving two women a hard time for the absurd "fun" of it. Probably had a case of beer in the front seat.

"Can you see him now? What's he doing?"

"Driving." Tuck snaked around, her arm braced over the black leather seat back, looking out the rear window. "Has a hat, so I can't see his face. Maybe you should—"

Jane put on her blinker again, moved into the slow lane. *If they want to pass, now's the time.* The truck stayed on her tail. Matching her slower speed.

Should she turn off? Take the next exit?

The exit was half a mile ahead, according to the green

sign on the metal stanchion above them. What if the truck was actually following her, not randomly tormenting them? The exit might lead to civilization, fast food places and shopping centers, the protection of other people and other cars. If they weren't so lucky it would lead to twisty back roads and deserted stretches of nowhere. The truck could pull right up to her and if he had a gun—oh, *ridiculous. Ridiculous.* She was getting herself spooked.

She'd get mad instead. This jerk was a menace to everyone on the highway. And Jane could make it right.

"Can you get the license plate? Can you describe the guy?" Jane's leather gloves clenched around the little steering wheel, and she trained her focus on the road stretching ahead. "We'll call the cops and report it."

"There's no license plate on the front," Tuck said. "Weird. It's a Dodge RAM, some kind of decal on the windshield, but I can't read it. Wait, now I see the guy has on a—Well, never mind, that's not gonna help us."

"What?" Jane said. "Has on a what?"

"A green Celtics cap. Like that narrows it d—"

"Hang on," Jane said. She twisted the wheel, banged the accelerator, then swerved across two lanes, all the way to the left, into the fast lane, leaning on the horn. A couple of cars in front of her sped away, probably wondering what the hell she was doing.

"Holy shit, Jane, what the hell are you—?"

"I *said,* hang on. Get ready. I'm not kidding." Jane flicked a look into the rearview. The truck was behind her. She couldn't make out the driver's face. All she could think about was Finn Eberhardt, that's how she'd recognized him at City Hall Plaza in the snow. His backwards Celtics hat. Could he have followed her? What if he'd put two and two together about—*Hey.* Had she given Maggie Gunnison her cell phone number? She had. *She had.*

She'd thought she was conning Finn into giving her information, but what if she'd actually been revealing her motives to exactly the wrong person? He might have figured she'd find out Brianna Tillson's name eventually, and played along to see what she'd spill. And now Eberhardt knew she was interested in the case.

Was something going on at DFS? And how was he involved? What if Finn Eberhardt had gotten her phone number from Maggie's files, and called her, threatening? Maybe he'd followed her all the way from home. Had the truck been at the gas station? She squinted her eyes, struggling to remember. The Dodge behind them was either driven by a random jerk with a twisted idea of fun, or a mid-level caseworker involved in some sort of scheme. A scheme she couldn't begin to imagine.

NEXT EXIT, 8 MILES, the sign said.

"The truck's getting closer," Tuck began. "And—"

"I know." *Now or never.* With one motion, she banged the gas, yanked the wheel, and crossed four lanes of snow-slick highway, leaning into the turn as if her weight could keep the car on an even keel. They rumbled over the slush-covered chevrons of yellow paint at the edge of the exit, rear tires jouncing over the raised pavement, and veered into the exit lane, landing almost on the opposite side of the pavement, flirting dangerously with the corrugated aluminum barriers.

"You're crazy!" Tuck was bracing one hand on the dashboard, the other flat on the side window.

"Maybe. Possibly." Jane's voice wasn't quite right. She realized she didn't need to keep such a death grip on the steering wheel.

She took her foot off the gas, resisting the urge to hit the brakes, and downshifted, shaping her body along with the turn, letting the car settle into the elongated curve of the exit. No one appeared behind them. No way for the truck to exit for the next eight miles.

Easing the car into the left lane, she saw the highway markers pointing one way to a Taco Bell and a Mobil, the other to a Holiday Inn. Food, gas, lodging. Civilization. A few hundred yards away. She'd have a moment to think. Then make a phone call or two.

"Well? Tuck? Anything?"

Tuck twisted around again, scouting behind them. "Nope. Nothing. No one." She poked one finger into the upholstery of Jane's seat back. "So hey, Speed Racer. Care to tell me what *that* was all about?"

36

"Jake?" DeLuca approached the green Lexus, his black watch cap pulled over his hair, black turtleneck under his battered leather jacket, his Sorels salt-stained and edged with damp. ME Kat McMahan, in a bright blue parka, white moon boots and black briefcase, tramped in the freezing slush beside him. Jake noticed they carried matching Store 24 paper cups, hot coffee steaming from the flipped-open plastic lids.

"Detective DeLuca, this is Mrs. Richards, who called nine-one-one," Jake said. DeLuca wasn't going to believe this. "She's the house on the corner, and she was telling me—"

"Yes, I was saying—," Mrs. Richards piped up.

"Thank you," DeLuca said. "But, ma'am, can you give me and Detective Brogan a few minutes? Go inside and get warm, maybe, then we'll both come follow up."

"But—" Mrs. Richards, almost pouting, turned to Jake for support. "You should let him know what I told you."

"Ma'am? Detective?" Jake figured D was going to tell him about Lillian Finch's house. He'd probably checked the address when he got the radio call. Jake held up a hand, trying to put Mrs. Richards on hold, and also signal DeLuca he had things under control. Which was somewhat true.

"What we need to do first is—," Jake began.

The black van marked CRIME SCENE pulled up in the center of Margolin Street and the driver's side window rolled down.

"Yo, Jake? Yo, D. Hey, Doc." Photo Joe gestured at them with a paper cup, sloshing coffee on the pavement. The milky sun that had worked its way through the clouds briefly glared on the side mirror, sending a burst of light onto Joe's doughy face. He shaded his eyes with the coffee cup hand, sloshing more liquid onto the street. "It's me and Nguyen. Where do you want us?"

"May we use your driveway, Mrs. Richards?" That'd solve two problems—parking Joe's van and dismissing the hovering neighbor. "For Officer Marcella? He's here to get photographs. Then we'll be right over to see you."

"Well, certainly. Follow me, officers." The woman padded off, focused on her new assignment.

Jake turned to DeLuca and McMahan. The two were standing side by side, coats touching, the medical examiner closer to D than Jake himself would have stood.

"Can you freaking believe it?" Jake said. "Quite the coincidence, huh?"

"Hell no, it's not a coincidence." DeLuca swiped off his wool cap, wiped his forehead with it, stuffed it into his jacket pocket. Took a slug of coffee. "We see this guy yesterday morning in connection with a mysteriously dead employee, and now, here he is? On her street? Dead as hell and probably frozen stiff? You think *that's* coincidence. Are you shitting me? Sorry, Kat."

"I've heard worse, *Detective* DeLuca." Kat McMahan nudged D with an elbow. "Excuse me, Detectives. Might I have access to the—"

"What are you talking about, D?" Jake interrupted the ME, frowning. "What guy?"

"The guy in the front seat," DeLuca said. "According to the license plate? This fine set of wheels belongs to one Niall Brannigan. Late of the Brannigan Agency. Boss to the late Lillian Finch. And from the looks of it—"

"Late himself," Jake added. *Niall Brannigan?* What the hell was going on at that agency? And on Margolin Street? Two dead coworkers, zero explanations. "Not only late, but I'd say, very unlucky. Or very much in trouble."

"Yeah. In trouble, dude." DeLuca nodded. "Exactly like—"

"—we are," Jake finished his sentence. "Exactly like we are."

Ella had never seen Grace cry before. Crying was a daily occurrence at the Brannigan, for sure. In a wrenching moment of decision. When papers were signed. When people said good-bye. Sometimes, there were tears of joy. Finding the family they'd dreamed of. Tears of realization that life's puzzle, missing a piece for so long, might finally be whole.

But sitting at her desk in front of Mr. Brannigan's closed door, Grace could not be sharing tears of joy with a reunited family. Ella paused outside the open doorway. Mr. Brannigan's secretary sat, head in hands, at her desk. Her sleek dark hair had come loose from its stylish little bun, random strands of escaped curls touching one shoulder of her tight black sweater. Touching her other shoulder, Ella was perplexed to see, was the hand of Collins Munson. He leaned close to her, speaking words Ella couldn't make out.

Ella's determination began to evaporate. She'd planned to tell—she'd *decided* to tell—Mr. Brannigan everything. It was the right thing to do. She'd even called him this morning on his private line, but no answer. Ella took two steps back into the empty hallway, reconsidering. Her parka was suffocating, her muffler was scratchy, and her one-strap backpack, documents burning a hole inside, was way, way too heavy.

She should go to her office, take all this off, and think things through again. *Where was everyone, anyway?* It was Tuesday, a workday. Usually, phones were ringing, copy machines whirring, and computers clattering. People waiting in the lobby. Not today. The hallway was deserted. Office doors closed. She looked at her watch. Nine thirty. It was probably everyone sad over Lillian. She'd go to her office, and then . . . *oh*. Lillian was gone.

Her shoulders sagged and the backpack fell to the carpeting. In an instant, Grace and Mr. Munson looked up. Saw her. Munson leaped away from Grace, his tortoiseshell glasses twisting on his nose, his tie catching on the back of her chair.

"Miss Gavin?" Munson adjusted his glasses.

Grace pulled a tissue from a flowered box on her desk and dabbed her eyes. She fussed with her hair, blinking at Ella as if trying to remember who she was.

Ella had to say something. "I'd like to make an appointment with Mr. Brannigan," she began. "At his convenience, of course, but—"

"Miss Gavin?" Munson interrupted her. "Step in, please. Did you talk to Mr. Brannigan last night?"

What was this all about?

"No. Does he need something?" Ella decided not to say she'd tried to call him this morning. She entered the office, assessing the closed inner office door, the distraught secretary, the hovering executive. A coffeepot hissed from a shelf in the corner. Grace had a cup of steaming tea on her desk, the tea bag's string dangling down one side of the flowered china.

"Ah. No. Miss Gavin? The police. Found a car." Munson adjusted his glasses, which were not out of place. "Mr. Brannigan's car. And it appears something must have happened to Mr. Brannigan."

"A car accident?" Ella could not believe it. "Is he all right?"

"No." Munson adjusted his glasses again, eyeing Brannigan's closed office door. "We—Miss O'Connor, actually—was contacted by the police a few moments ago. And I fear the police think—"

"Now *I* have to call his wife," Grace said. "And tell her Mr. Brannigan is *dead*."

"What?" Ella heard her own voice crack. The floor seemed not quite steady. She put a hand to her throat, as if she could feel the scream. He was *dead*?

"No, Grace," Munson said. "It's not necessary that you call Mrs. Brannigan. The police do that. And Miss Gavin?"

"Yes?" Her voice had come out a croaking whisper, her heart clenched. Ella dug her fingernails into her palms. If the police checked Mr. Brannigan's private line, would they discover she'd called him?

Her fingers tightened around her backpack's webbed strap. She had to hang on to these documents. *No.* She had to get rid of these documents. *No.* How would she decide? She cleared her throat, tried again. "Yes?"

"The police say no one is to leave," Munson instructed her. "Go to your office, Miss Gavin. Talk to no one. And wait."

Oh, dear God, Ella thought. *No one can protect me now.*

Jane stirred three packs of sugar into her extra-large coffee with skim milk, balancing the paper coffee cup on the edge of the steering wheel. As soon as she and Tuck caught their breath a little, they'd pull out of the

Taco Bell parking lot, head back to the Mass Pike, and continue their journey. No way could whoever drove the black truck find them again. Not this morning, at least. And really, looking at it in the cold (and safe) light of this suburban parking lot, the black truck probably had nothing to do with the DFS case, nothing to do with the threatening call about Brianna Tillson. How would whoever it was even know where she was? If he really *was* following her, no way he could know where she and Tuck were headed.

In the passenger seat, Tuck was texting someone, her husband, Laney, probably, who Tuck reported was job hunting in Philadelphia.

Jane took a deep breath, smelling the dark roast of her coffee and a faint fragrance of fried something from Tuck's side of the car. She felt a little shaky, no denying that. Was Alex right to get her out of town? Or was that the worst possible thing?

She pulled her cell phone from her jacket pocket, propped it on the dashboard. She should call him. Tell him. Then see if anything was developing with Tillson. Maybe Hec could bring his photos somewhere, away from the *Register*. She could work on the Tillson story and still obey the publisher's orders.

A sip of coffee. *That truck.*

"Tuck? Can you do me a favor?" she said.

"Sure. All done." Tuck stashed her phone, and started peeling the flimsy waxed paper from her breakfast-a-rito. Shards of orange cheese dripped onto her parka. She picked them up, one by one, and popped them into her mouth. "Five second rule, right? What favor?"

Jane's phone trilled, interrupting, and a photo popped onto the screen of a young woman in a Springsteen T-shirt, baby propped on one hip and holding hands with a little boy dressed as Spider-Man.

"Ah, yeah, wait a sec, this is my building super." Jane

grabbed her cell phone from the dashboard. "Hey, Neena. What's up? Oh, hi Eli."

Her building super's nine-year-old son loved to use the phone. And especially loved to call Jane. Eli had a crush on her, as only a starstruck nine-year-old boy could have on a thirty-three-year-old woman. He insisted he wanted to be on TV, and unlike the rest of the universe, little Eli Fichera hadn't seemed to grasp the concept that Jane's TV career was over. "Yes, I know it's February break. Very cool. Is that why you're calling me? Are you having fun?"

She paused, listening to a rush of almost-understandable chatter about Transformers and Xbox and police officers and guns and something important his mother had told him to tell her. "So, sweetheart? Is your mom around? Can you go get her for me?"

Jane heard the empty hiss of the open connection.

"Hey, Tuck?" Jane had thought of something else. "Did you tell Carlyn Beerman we were coming? When I was pumping gas?"

"Uh, yeah, I did," Tuck said around a bite of burrito. She chewed, then swallowed. "I said I was coming up from Boston and—"

"Did you tell her *I* was—Oh, hi, Eli." Jane needed a sip of coffee, and needed another hand to do it. She poked the cell onto speaker, and set it on the dashboard. Took a grateful gulp. "Is your mom coming to the phone?"

"Yes, but she says, did you leave your door open?" Eli's little voice piped through the speaker.

Jane looked at Tuck, who'd stopped mid-bite.

"Hey, Jane." Neena's voice was subdued, softer than usual.

Jane leaned forward to hear, clutching the corrugated cardboard sleeve around her coffee cup.

"I called the police," Neena went on, "because, listen, your apartment door is open. Wide open. I saw it when I went downstairs. The nine-one-one operator told me—"

"My apartment door was open?" Jane's voice came out a screech. Tuck put a reassuring hand on her arm.

"—told me not to go in, so I didn't, but the police are on the way now. I looked, though, honey, and it doesn't seem like anything's—"

"The police, mommy?" Jane could hear Eli's voice in the background.

"Hush, kiddo." Neena's voice turned away for a second, then back to Jane. "They're on the way, like I said, and from what I can see standing out here in the hall, there's no—"

"Neen? Open, like, *open*? What do you mean, open?" It wouldn't help to freak out. Maybe she'd spaced, and left her door open? Had Tuck forgotten to close it? Impossible. Tuck had gone out first, Jane locked the door behind them. They were an hour from Boston. She had to stay calm enough to drive back.

"Honey, yeah, it's as if you left it that way. There's no damage, it's just, open, and looking at it, it doesn't seem as if—"

"No. I mean, *no,* I closed my door, absolutely. Locked it." She remembered the key turning, the mechanism clicking, the always-stubborn key snagging in the old brass lock. "Tuck was there. I fed Coda, and—"

She stopped. Imagined her kitchen and the little cat and the open front door and the stairway and the outside and the snow and the street.

"Neen?" Jane choked out the word. "Are the police there yet? And—do you see Coda?"

37

"**Supe? It's Brogan**. We're at the—Yes, sir, I'll hold." Jake watched Photo Joe clicking his exterior shots as Nguyen dusted the Lexus for fingerprints. Dolly Richards had apparently given up, gone inside. That interview was still on the to-do list.

They were holding off with the yellow tape on the car for the time being, hoping this side of Margolin Street wasn't also actually a crime scene. The neighborhood was waking up, porch lights flicking off, doors opening. Curiosity would probably intensify once Dolly Richards hit the telephone.

Jake had to give the Supe an update. Problem was, he had zero, other than a lead on the ID of this victim. And that brought up more questions than it answered. Niall Brannigan, if that's who it turned out to be—dead. Lillian Finch, his employee—dead. Why had Brannigan come to her house last night?

Jake blew out a breath, the puff of vapor vanishing in the morning sun. The lawns along the street were glazed with a sheen of ice on top of the snow, the sun glinting from the pristine surfaces. When he was a kid, he used to try to catch the sparkles.

"Jake?" Kat McMahan had opened the Lexus's passenger door, and now touched a gloved finger to a spot below her own ear, shaking her head. "I checked for a neck pulse, got nothing. He's been dead for hours. Doornail. DeLuca confirms visually this is Niall Brannigan, the man you met. RIP."

"Cause?" Jake mentally crossed his fingers as he waited for the Supe. If Kat said, "Heart attack, no question about it," they could all go home.

"Still in question." Kat stuffed her hands into her parka pockets. "No obvious signs of trauma, no GSW, no blood, no weapon. No contusions to the head, as one would expect if this were a car accident. We'll run the enzymes for heart attack or stroke. The victim is approximately seventy years old, so that'd make sense. Body is cold to the touch, and rigor is present, but I can't get a more exact time of death until I check lividity. And I can't do that out here in the cold. Or while he's wearing clothes."

"So—"

"So, I'll take the final in situ photos. Arrange for transport. I'll let you know as soon as my report is—"

"Yes, sir, no problem, sir," Jake said into his cell. He gave the ME a thumbs-up. *Got it.* The Supe had someone with him, Jake could tell by the murmur of voices in the background. "Standing by."

" 'Preciate it, Detective. I know you've got a lot on your plate." The Supe's attitude always reminded him of some desperate CEO, trying to convince the rank and file that their budget-crisis work overload was actually an opportunity for "team playing." "Lucky cops have big plates. I'll be right with you."

And the line went empty again.

Jake rolled his eyes, knowing the Supe couldn't see him. Jake's plate now served up Niall Brannigan, cause of death unknown. Lillian Finch, cause of death unknown. Brianna Tillson, murdered by person or persons unknown. Curtis Ricker, suspect, probably dumping bleach on every flat surface of that ratty apartment and starting a bonfire of documents in his fireplace. Not that he had a fireplace. Still no warrant from Judge Gallagher.

And a missing baby.

Maybe.

Jake kicked a chunk of frozen slush, watched it melt into gray.

He'd stayed up way too late, combing through the few documents he'd gotten from Margaret Gunnison, looking for clues to Brianna Tillson's history, her foster children, and any indication of one more child living on Callaberry Street. But nothing. The documents verged on boilerplate.

"The missing baby," Jake muttered. As if there were such a creature. DeLuca sure didn't think so. But Jake couldn't shake the image of the empty white cradle stashed in a corner of that tiny bedroom. The little mattress even had sheets. Pale blue sheets with little pink—well, some kind of animals on them. They'd show up fine in the crime scene photos. Why would someone have a cradle, with sheets, if there was no baby? Also missing—all of Brianna Tillson's personal stuff. Purse, wallet, files. Did whoever killed her take it? If so, maybe they took the baby, too.

Or not. Lucky cops have big plates.

Jake looked at the still-silent cell phone, wondered if he should remind the Supe he was waiting. Listening hard, he could barely make out voices in the background. He'd been ordered to stand by. He was standing.

A siren screamed down the street, a gray-and-blue BPD Crown Vic screeching to a stop outside Lillian Finch's house, exhaust pluming from the rear.

"Who's—?"

"Holy crap. Frick and Frack." D was snapping his own photos of the Lexus.

Both front doors of the cruiser opened simultaneously.

"Gimme a break. Why do we always get the short straw?" D, clicking, kept his camera in front of his face.

"Straw?" Jake watched the cruiser, phone still to his ear. The car doors slammed. Two uniformed—*oh*. "Shit."

"Like I said." DeLuca cocked his head at the two officers. "Now we're in for some big fun."

Kurtz. She probably looked okay in a dress, but what Jane always said was true, no way a female cop could look good in BPD-issue navy pants, awkward oxford shoes, and boxy nylon jacket. Newbie Officer Kurtz had tucked her blond hair under her billed cap, per regulation. Weighed down by her chunky black utility belt, she waddled up the walkway to Lillian Finch's house. Her partner, Hennessey, who Jake had met on Callaberry Street, was twice her size, twice her age, and apparently half her IQ.

"Brogan?" Jake heard the superintendent come back on the line.

"Yessir." About time.

"Officers Kurtz and Hennessey will secure the scene until the ME is finished with the victim. We'll hold off calling this a homicide for now. Even so, I expect the reporters will show up. I've got no PR guy, some schedule snafu. So you can make that work, correct? Whatever media tries to get out of you, you say—"

"Nothing. I copy, sir." Jake watched Kurtz and Hennessey step over the crime scene tape, tramp up the walkway, check Lillian Finch's mailbox and the crime scene tape sealing the front door, then march in unison back toward their car. *Quite the team.* "When will we—?"

But the Supe had hung up.

"All quiet at the Finch house, Detectives," Hennessey's basso boomed across the street. "Sealed up tight as a—" The officer leaned down to Kurtz, whispered something Jake couldn't hear.

Kurtz elbowed her partner in the ribs, and seemed to

be giggling. Her hat tipped and rolled into the slush. Now they were both laughing.

Jake looked at DeLuca, shaking his head. "What a circ—"

"Like I said." DeLuca raised an eyebrow.

"Gag me." The ME appeared at DeLuca's side. She'd unzipped her parka, revealing a black Megadeth T-shirt.

DeLuca eyed her, approving. "Happily," he said.

Jane slammed the TT into third, hit the accelerator, and hoped no staties were staking out the eastbound Mass Pike with radar guns. "I'm so sorry, Tuck, but I can't—I have to go home. The police—"

It took all the willpower she had to focus on the road. The police. Were coming to her apartment. *Because her door was open.* She took a deep breath, almost forgot to let it out. "I have to. The police are . . . are going to want to . . . and the cat might be . . ."

It was no use trying to finish a sentence.

The signs on the highway pointed them back to Boston. Twenty-four miles, the green marker said. Jane was doing eighty. More. *Her door was open.* Who had done such a thing? If nothing was taken, then why?

"Jane, listen, let me drive. You're obviously—"

"No, Tuck, really." Jane waved off her suggestion. "Driving gives me something else to think about. The police are coming, they'll be there in a second. And it'll be fine. I mean, whatever happened, it's over? Right? And Neena will call me if they—I'm fine. *Ish.* Fine-*ish.* As fine as anyone could be."

"Which is not that fine."

Tuck had a point.

"No. Not that fine."

The bare trees and spindled light posts flashed by, a surprising glint of sunlight melting the thin layer of snow into a damp sheen on the pavement. Jane tried the radio, briefly, news, jazz, oldies. It all seemed like noise. Her thoughts were jumbled enough. There was no appropriate sound track for fear.

Tuck propped both feet against the dashboard, wrapped her arms around her knees. "Listen, Jane?"

"Yeah?"

"I know you said back there you were only trying to get away from the truck. Not that you thought anyone was trying to scare you. Personally. But here's the thing. First, the guy tailgates us within an inch of our lives. Yeah, okay, I could maybe buy that he's a jerk and you blew him off with your fancy driving. But now there's a break-in at your apartment? Again, sister. Is there something you'd like to tell me?"

Jane swallowed, and tried to look like she wasn't hiding something. She punched the radio again, stalling. There was nothing to hide, really. Or anything to tell. She'd gotten a threatening phone call. Tuck had probably gotten her share of calls like that, too. Jane had weaseled some probably confidential info about a murder victim from a DFS caseworker in a Celtics cap. Then someone in a Celtics cap had—

Was that something to tell?

Truth be told, she wasn't entirely sure about Tuck. Yes, she was curious about the Brannigan's mistake. If it *was* a mistake. Why would they send Tuck to the wrong mother? Jane could not resist a puzzle like that. And it wasn't as if she could go to her regular job today, anyway.

But being in the car together didn't mean she was required to tell Tuck everything. Or anything.

"Listen, Tuck. I'm as confused as you are. But now, I need to see my apartment. I need to know everything's okay. Then I'll be able to think."

A perky voice on the radio was apologizing. "Sorry

about that, folks, turns out the snow wasn't as bad as we'd predicted. The winds over the ocean changed to the . . ."

Another mile marker. Twenty miles to Boston.

"See? Almost there," Jane said. Maybe they should talk about something else. "You better call Carlyn Beerman."

"You think your break-in's a random thing?" Tuck slurped the last of her coffee, and shoved her jumbo cup into the holder beside her. "You hear about all these kids, breaking into homes for fun, or whatever. It's February break. Maybe it's some stupid prank."

Tears welled in Jane's eyes, briefly blurring the road ahead. Would she never get home? "Maybe. Neena said it didn't look like anything was disturbed, or taken. But the cat. If she got out, poor thing, she has no idea where to go."

"Don't think about it." Tuck patted Jane's arm, reassuring. "Neena knows, they'll probably call any minute, say they found her. We have to get you home."

"Shit," Jane said.

A black truck was behind them. No question. Right there, in the rearview. Jane's stomach twisted, and sweat prickled the back of her neck.

"Shit, shit, shit. Is that—Look behind us, Tuck. A black truck."

"Whoa." Tuck clicked off her seat belt and twisted in the seat to look, knocking her empty paper cup onto Jane's lap.

"Oh, sorry. Damn it." Tuck fussed with a paper napkin.

"Just. Look. At the *truck*." Jane's shoulders clenched, her eyes narrowing in anger. This was too much. She was calling the police. She was calling *everyone*. And she was not letting this story go. If someone cared this much, she was on to something. Whoever it was. Whatever it was. She had to get home, and then she had to get to Alex. And then she had to talk to Jake. Life was too short.

"What?" Jane said. Tuck had made a funny sound, a gasp or something. "*What?*"

"We're both losing it," Tuck said. "There are two girls in the truck, a license plate on the front, it's a Ford, it's totally different. Let's get you home, sister."

Sixteen miles to Boston. The rolling hills of suburban Newton were in front of them. Soon they'd see the architecturally preposterous hotel built on the highway overpass, then the snaking off-ramps to Newton Corner and Cambridge and the Charles River parks. Almost home.

With a whoosh of speed, the black truck passed them, rattling the Audi's windows. Just another random Boston driver, ignoring the speed limit. Unlike the truck that targeted them this morning. That one—Jane was no longer even trying to talk herself out of it—was not random. That guy was trying to scare her.

Why? That she did not know. But she was sure of who was driving. That was a slam dunk. Now she would prove it. Time to take control.

"Listen, Tuck," Jane said. "Remember, before, I wanted you to do me a favor?"

"Oh, right. What?"

Jane grabbed her cell phone, handed it across the seat.

"Punch in 'recent contacts.' See it says DFS?"

"Yeah. Who's DFS? You want me to call him?"

"Nope. Don't call from my phone. I really want to leave it open in case Neena calls. Just get the number."

Tuck thumbed in, following Jane's instructions, then scrolled through the contacts. "Okay, got it."

"Now, call from your phone. Okay? If they have caller ID it won't matter. It's a state office."

Tuck was already tapping in numbers. "What state office? It's ringing. Now what?"

"Ask for Finn Eberhardt," Jane said. "I want to find out if he's there. See what they say when you ask for him."

"Finn Eberhardt? Who's he?" Tuck had the cell phone pressed to her ear. "Oh, I get it. DFS. Family Services. Is it good if he's there, or good if he's not there? It's still ringing."

Jane imagined the voluptuous Vee, remembering her laissez-faire attitude toward her receptionist duties. "Yeah. I'm not surprised. Ask for him. If he answers, say oh, sorry, wrong number. I'll tell you about it after."

"Very myster—Oh, hello, may I speak to—"

She looked at Jane, grimacing, wriggled her fingers in a "give it to me again" gesture.

"Finn Eberhardt," Jane mouthed the name.

"Finn Eberhardt?" Tuck said to the operator.

Twelve miles to Boston. The signs pointed them to Fenway Park, then the new tunnel to the lofty Prudential Center and Boston Public Library. An electronic billboard flashed lighted block letters: SNOW EMERGENCY CANCELED.

Tuck punched her phone onto speaker. Jane heard the crackly buzz, then a voice.

"This is Finn Eberhardt."

Jane felt the warmth drain from her face. *What?* He was there? If Finn Eberhardt was at the Department of Family Services, in his office in Boston, he could not possibly have been in that Dodge truck on the Mass Pike. And could not have just been at her apartment. Could he? Had she been completely wrong? If so, who was in the truck?

Hang up! She pantomimed the action, as if Tuck held an old-fashioned receiver. Then she whispered, making sure Tuck would understand, "Hang up!"

Tuck clicked the button and stuffed her phone back into a pocket.

"What was that?" she said. "Finn-whoever answered. Is that good? Or bad?"

"I have to get home," Jane said. That was first on the agenda.

Then she would start demanding answers.

38

"Jake?"

"Yeah, D?" Jake looked up from his phone filing system, then went back to it. Photo Joe and Nguyen still puttered around the Lexus, measuring and marking tread marks. Kat had packed up and called for transport. Not a reporter in sight. Maybe, finally, things were going their way. Unless Jane showed up to cover the story again. That might be complicated. But not such a bad thing. Life was short. Maybe they should—He yanked himself back to the present.

The Brannigan scene was almost clear. Until there were cause-of-death updates on Lillian Finch and her boss, he could focus on the already-confirmed murder of Brianna Tillson. *That* case was bugging the hell out of him.

"Jake?" DeLuca said again. "We've got a situation."

"Yo, Jake?" Officer Hennessey came around from behind the Lexus, flipping through a grimy spiral notebook. "Supe's orders. He says Kurtz and I are supposed to—"

DeLuca interrupted. "Need a word in private, Jake."

Hennessey put up both hands in mock surrender, backing away. "Don't mind me," he said. "I'm sure you two detectives have big secret *detective* stuff to discuss."

"Stuff it, Hennessey," DeLuca said. "Jake?"

DeLuca's voice had an edge to it. Maybe he'd picked up some intel. They could use it.

"Just heard a call on the radio," DeLuca continued. "On the third channel. Response to a nine-one-one. They're sending two units to Corey Road. Three-forty-seven Corey Road."

Jake's blood froze. Three-forty-seven? *Jane's* apartment? Nine-one-one? What the hell for?"

"Detectives?" Kat McMahan trotted toward them, picking her way through the freezing slush, her boots crunching on the pavement. She paused, looked at DeLuca, then at Jake, then back at DeLuca. "Am I interrupting something?"

"Ah, Kat?" DeLuca wiped an invisible smudge from one sleeve. "Give us a sec."

"Will do. But I wanted to ask you, Jake." The ME smiled at D, but otherwise ignored him. "When you first saw Mr. Brannigan—"

"When I first saw Brannigan?" He could focus only half his brain on the body in the Lexus. The other half was on Corey Road. *Jane's apartment? Nine-one-one?* "I didn't know it was Brannigan."

The ME waved him off. "Right. Not the point. When you arrived, did you open the car door?"

"What? No. No one did. That I know of. Seems pretty obvious. Why?"

What was she getting at? He hadn't touched the car. Neither had Mrs. Richards. Any fingerprints would show instantly in the icy frost of the car's exterior. There were none. *Jane. He had to find out—*

"That's the dilemma." Kat McMahan tilted her head, staring at the Lexus. "Our victim was in his car. You say it's registered to Niall Brannigan, and we did find that name on the driver's license in his pocket. Prelim, my take on it, at least, seems to be a heart attack. So there's your ID, gentlemen. And a likely cause."

Jane. What was going on at her apartment? Jake drew the two-way from his back pocket, clicked on "send." "Brogan to Dispatch. Do you copy?"

"Jake?" The ME turned to him, frowning. "Are you with me here?"

"Copy, Detective," the radio crackled back.

"The Corey Road call. Can you give me a status?"

"Thanks, Kat," DeLuca stepped in front of Jake. "If it's natural causes, score one for the team. We're outta here. Hennessey and Kurtz can do the next-of-kin thing, Jake and I have some other fish to—"

She held up a hand, stopping D mid-sentence. "Thing is. There's an issue."

Jake clutched his two-way, straining to hear an answer in the staticky silence.

"Stand by one, Detective Brogan," dispatch said.

Jake had to leave. Check on Jane. *Now.* Niall Brannigan was dead, Kat McMahan's medical inquiry was under way, Kurtz and Hennessey would babysit. Some things were bigger than his police responsibility. His grandfather always told him, *Family first. You'll never regret the family time.* Now the advice from the past moved front and center. How could he have let her go?

"The issue being," the ME was saying, "our victim has no car keys."

"No keys?" Jake thought back. He hadn't tried the car door. "Not in the ignition?"

"Negative. We tried the glove compartment, see if there was a registration, some identification info. That was locked. So we went to the ignition to get the keys. But nothing. No keys in the ignition."

"In his pocket, then," DeLuca said. "Or the floor. You look there?"

The ME shot herself in the head with a forefinger. "Oh, no. We for*got*." She paused. "Of course, we did, Detective. Hennessey and Kurtz checked the entire car."

"Dispatch?" Jake tried the radio again.

"Stand by one, Detective," the radio voice crackled. "Units are still en route."

The radio went silent. Jake focused his attention back to the ME, thinking out loud. "So that means the vic got into his car without using the keys. And clearly didn't plan to drive anywhere. Because he didn't bring the keys."

"He could have been visiting," DeLuca said. "Left the car open, it's a nice enough neighborhood. Forgot something, came back to get it, opened the already unlocked door, sat down, had a heart attack. Bingo. In the car, dead, no keys."

"In some reality, yeah, I suppose." Jake played out D's scenario. "But no one's looking for him, you know?"

Jake's cell phone rang. He jumped. *Jane?* Maybe it was Jane, thank God, telling him she was okay. Man. She really got to him.

But the display showed "caller blocked." Still, it might be her. Who knows what phone she might be using.

"Brogan." He heard the hope in his own voice.

"Detective?"

Not Jane. *Damn.* Whoever it was, he didn't have time.

"Yes?" He tried to telegraph "leave me alone" into that one word.

"It's Bethany Sibbach," the voice said. "Phillip and Phoebe's—"

"Yes, Bethany," Jake said to the therapist. "Can you hold a second?"

"Sure, but—"

"D?" Jake turned to DeLuca. "I'm going to check on that *thing,* okay?"

"Ten-four, Jake. I'll follow up on the key situation. Keep me posted."

Jake trotted toward the cruiser, phone clamped to his ear.

"Detective Brogan? Are you there?" Bethany Sibbach's voice interrupted his thoughts.

"Sorry, yeah," he said. He'd head to Jane's, see what was up. Try to call her. As soon as Bethany got off the line.

"Thing is," the caseworker continued. "Phillip has said something that—"

Jake stopped, keys in hand.

"I'm listening," Jake said. "What did Phillip say?"

"Well, Phillip is finally napping now, but we were all on my living room floor, Phillip and Phoebe and I, and we had Phoebe's dolls out, and a little dollhouse my grandmother gave me as a child, lots of miniature doll furniture, a dresser, and a cradle, and, you know, I had them acting out a happy—"

"Heya, Jake." A voice beside him.

Jake turned. A camera flashed in his face.

Some photographer. Three cameras looped around his neck. A fourth pointed right at him. It flashed again.

"Bethany? Hold on one more second." He squinted at the man, put up a palm to protect his eyes from another flash. "Hey. Who the hell are you?"

"Hec Underhill from the *Register*." He held out the hand without the Nikon, keeping the camera in front of his face as he clicked the shutter. "Whatcha got? Our sources say there's another body."

Jake pointed to his cell. "Look. I'm on the phone. As you can see. You've got a big media pass on that lanyard, right? You should know the drill. See those two officers, up by the crime scene van? Ask for Hennessey. He's handling press."

"Gotcha." The photographer took off his cap, tipped it, then replaced it with the bill in the back as he headed toward the van.

"Go Celtics," Jake muttered after him. He *had* to get to Jane. "Bethany? Sorry."

"That's okay. But I think you should know. Phillip was putting one of the dolls into a little white wooden cradle, and burst into tears. He's not sleeping well, and the poor thing has been removed from the environment he's used to. Still, in my assessment, that reaction was not quite normal."

Jake aimed his keys at the cruiser door. Clicked. "But you told me 'said'—"

"Exactly, Jake. When I asked him, 'What's wrong, honey?' Phillip said, clear as day, he said, 'Baby. Where baby?'"

Jake stopped, hand poised on the door handle. "*Where baby?* Are you sure?"

"Where baby," she said. "I'm sure."

39

Kellianne's dad called this the Afterwards "office," even though it was only a corner of their old pine-paneled basement. Her mom had insisted on staying at the hospital with him, wouldn't be home until whenever. Kev and Keefer were somewhere, who knew. Kellianne had privacy. Sitting at the battered desk, she stared at her reflection in the computer monitor.

She could see her hair, still all sucky, her skin, still sucky, her T-shirt with the same logo and title as the one on the computer screen. She'd sent for the "Ladies' large short-sleeved black" a few weeks ago to see if the company she was interested in was a real place or a rip-off. She could risk ten bucks to find out.

A few days later, the T-shirt arrived. She'd been wearing it under her regular clothes so no one could see. She knew what it meant. It meant she could win.

Kellianne rested her cheeks on her fists and sounded out, silently, the name of the company she was about to e-mail. Mur-der-a-bi-li-a.

It was a funny name, but she'd typed *souveneers from murders* into her search thing, panicking she'd be stuck with a bunch of stuff she couldn't get rid of. It turned out to be "souvenirs," so she'd spelled it wrong, but the Internet found it. As she scrolled through page after online page, she realized she not only wouldn't be stuck, but that she was sitting on a gold mine.

Murderabilia. She whispered it, trying the word out loud. It seemed like there was a market for what she had. People were buying, like, the weirdest stuff. She leaned into the screen, clicking on the photos. That Unabomber guy's letters. A lock of Charles Manson's hair. Gross.

She looked at the teddy bears in the cardboard box at her feet. Next to them, the little rabbit bowl. Thing was, those didn't belong to the "murderers." What she had belonged to the *victims.* Would people buy *those* things?

She clicked through more photos. A drawing by the Son of Sam. A clown outfit worn by some guy in . . .

Shit, if people wanted stuff from murder cases, if they were that crazy sick, wouldn't they just as likely—*Souvenirs from murder victims,* she typed it right this time. "Victims" was the important part. She clicked. *She was right.*

"From the *New York Post,*" said the first article on the list. The headline was, Murder Victim Relics Suddenly Hot.

Then in little letters, "Survivors powerless to stop commerce in notorious . . ."

She clicked through, trying to get the gist of the article, skipping some of the long words and what looked like boring parts. "The more personal the better," someone said. "Despicable," someone else said. Her eyes skidded to a stop at the word: legal.

One forefinger hovering over the screen, she read hard to make sure she didn't miss anything. *In only eight states is the sale of murderabilia prohibited. And those are—*She kept reading the list of states, hoping. She could do it whichever way, but sure would be better if it were legal.

Massachusetts was not on the list.

The muscles in her back relaxed, and she looked down at the logo on her T-shirt again. Murderabilia. *Freakin' a.*

Besides the bears and the rabbit bowl, she'd taken a candlestick from the Callaberry Street apartment. Silver, probably, which might bring a lot of cash. From the Margolin Street house—which her brothers said the cops were calling a homicide—she'd selected a pale pink silk nightgown and a shiny golden compact with raised flowers on the outside. She'd also snatched a tiny silver-framed photo of what looked like the dead woman and some man. That "personal" gem had been in the bedroom drawer under the nightgown.

Kellianne pulled the framed photo out of the cardboard box, rubbing one finger across the bumpy dots on the silver frame. The guy with her must be the woman's father. He looked kinda familiar, but shit. He was old. All old people looked alike.

Putting the photo back in the box, she picked up another item she'd gotten last night. Keys with a fancy golden cross on the key chain. She'd taken off the keys, stuffed them under a couch cushion. But the golden cross was so pretty. She held it up to the dim glow of the ceiling light. Her good luck charm.

She saw a little smile reflected in the computer monitor. Well, why not smile? They'd heard nothing on the news about a dead guy in a car. They'd gone back in, gotten their stuff, and sealed some crime scene tape on the door like they'd been instructed.

She clicked to the Web site where she'd ordered the T-shirt.

NO questions asked, the red and black letters promised. She sure as hell hoped not. She reread the instructions on the company's home page. *Do you have items to sell? Click here to register!*

"Don't mind if I do," Kelliane told the screen. And she clicked.

* * *

"Go," Tuck said, unlatching her seat belt. "I'll lock up and bring you the—"

Jane was already out of her car. She'd used frantic seconds finding a parking place on Corey Road, even jumped the curb as she wedged her Audi into a too-small spot as close as she could get to her apartment. Half a block away. *Damn.*

"Thanks," Jane called over her shoulder. "I've got to—" She cut herself off, mid-sentence. It didn't matter. She had to get inside.

Mom's jewelry. Her silver. Her photos. Her computer. Her TV. What did people steal? Or were they searching for something else? Or hoping to encounter Jane herself?

Where was Coda?

A black-and-white Brookline Police cruiser, blue light whirling on the roof, seemed quickly abandoned, skewed half on the street, half on the sidewalk. A clump of people hovered on the sidewalk, watching, pointing, speculating. It all barely registered as Jane ran toward her front door. Eli, silhouetted in the open foyer entryway, waved at her, both spindly arms flailing in a too-big orange parka vest.

"They had guns out, Jane!" he called as she got closer. Eli's puppy-brown eyes were wider than she'd ever seen them, and he grabbed her hand, dragging her inside. "The police had guns and everything, and they told Mom and baby Sam and me to stay out here, and they went upstairs really, really fast, and I heard them yelling really loud, and then they let Mom and baby Sam go back inside, but not me, because they told me to—"

"They had guns?" It mustn't be anything too awful, Jane reassured herself, if Eli was still here.

"Jane, what on earth?" Mona Washburn came out of

her first-floor doorway, a smudge of white flour on her face, wiping her hands on her striped chef's apron.

"Sorry, Mo, I have no idea, I just got here." Already halfway up the first flight, Jane clutched the banister, hauling herself up, two steps at a time. Mona was obviously fine, too, cooking as usual, so it seemed like everything was—

"Guns?" she repeated.

Eli, two steps ahead of her, jabbed one forefinger upstairs. "Come *on*."

When she arrived at the first landing, a uniformed police officer blocked her way, all elbows and nose, one hand worrying the nightstick looped at her side, the other poised over her holstered gun.

"Ma'am? Are you Jane Ryland, the occupant of unit three?" The officer cocked her head toward the third floor, kept her hands at the ready. Not letting Jane pass. "May I see some identification, please?"

"This is *Jane*." Eli stomped one supersized running shoe on the carpeted step, and pointed at the cop. "Like I told you!"

"Yes, ah, officer, ah, thanks, Eli." Jane patted him on the shoulder, every fraying nerve in her body straining to get past this uniformed obstacle. *Fine time to think about security.* She scanned the officer's plastic name badge. "Officer Guerriero. Listen. I'm Jane Ryland, I have my ID right here, I'm trying to dig it out of my bag now, as you see. Can you at least tell me what's going on?"

"Ma'am?" Patricia Guerriero raised her chin. "We are still securing the scene, so if you would be so kind as to—"

"Jane!" Neena's head appeared over the wooden railing of the next floor up. Baby Sam's bright blue cap peeked out of the Snugli slung over his mother's shoulders. "Officer Guerriero, that's Jane, I can vouch, and your partner up here says it's all good, send her up. You recognize her from TV. Right? Jane. Ryland. You know. The reporter."

Officer Guerriero narrowed her eyes, wary, as if she thought Jane and Neena, and perhaps their nine-year-old accomplice, were trying to pull something sneaky on her.

"Here. See?" Jane waved her driver's license at the cop, hoping it would allow her to get by this gorgon and into her own damn apartment.

Guerriero studied her license as if there was going to be a test.

Maybe she *would* panic.

"Officer? Can you tell me? Did someone break into my apartment?"

"She's showing an ID, sir." Guerriero ignored Jane, talked into the cigarette-pack radio velcroed to her uniformed shoulder. "Appears in order."

Jane heard the crackling transmission from upstairs. In about ten seconds she was going to—

"Okay, ma'am. You're clear." Guerriero handed back her license and Jane grabbed it, already at full speed. Up the stairs, around the landing, past Neena, and up to the third floor.

Her door was wide open. Wide. Open.

She stood, paralyzed.

Eli grabbed her hand again, and Neena's arm went across her shoulders.

"You okay, honey?" Neena smelled of baby powder. Sam gurgled, kicked his tiny foot into her side.

"Not so much," Jane said.

Who'd been in her apartment? Why? Maybe was still inside, hiding. What if Jane had been home, instead of on that excursion with Tuck? Would the person have still come in?

"Miz Ryland?" The upstairs cop stood, arms crossed, in the center of the round oriental rug in her entryway. The top of his billed police hat almost grazed the dangling crystals of her mini-chandelier, and his size alone made Jane feel safer. He could crush the bad guy with one hammy fist.

If there *was* a bad guy.

"There's no intruder in your apartment, Miz Ryland. We've checked thoroughly, and nothing appears disturbed. Now. We'd like you to take a look around and see whether anything seems out of place, even whether there's something that's here now that wasn't when you—"

The cop's voice was velvet, soothing, as he went on to describe how he'd checked every closet, every room, every possible hiding place. But now, for some reason Jane's eyes smarted with tears. She was about to cry? Now? When this hunk of a cop was telling her it was okay?

"But, ma'am?" The officer adjusted the patent leather brim of his hat. "I need to ask you. When you left this morning? Are you certain you locked the door? If so, does anyone else have a key?"

40

At least no one would disturb her. Not with everything going on at the Brannigan this morning. Sitting at her desk, Ella thought yet again about what she planned to say, hoping-hoping-hoping that Jane Ryland would answer her phone at the *Register*. Of course it had been Jane at the Dunkin' Donuts. It seemed like she didn't want to be recognized, so Ella had played along. But it would be such a relief to tell. If Jane didn't answer, Ella would leave a message.

She felt the cell phone, cool against her cheek, and heard her own shallow breathing, her palm already damp with uncertainty.

The phone rang. And again. If Jane was there, if Jane wasn't there, either way would be fine. Listening to the silence, Ella let her gaze stray through the open inner office door, to what was, until yesterday, Lillian Finch's private office. Was it just yesterday? Ella herself had been in there Sunday, looking through those documents. And now . . .

Pull yourself together, Ella. You've done nothing wrong. You're doing your job. You're helping.

"Good afternoon, the *Register*," a voice said.

Afternoon already? How long had she been sitting

here? She asked for Jane, and heard a click and a buzz, like she was being transferred.

Maybe Ella should have said something at the Dunkin' Donuts, instead of pretending. Because who didn't know Jane Ryland? Ella knew the whole scoop. She'd been fired from Channel 11 for protecting a source and losing her TV station a million dollars. Something like that. Then it turned out Jane was in the right. Something like that. Then she'd read Jane's stories in the *Register* about that mess in the last election. And about the Bridge Killer.

First ring.

Anyone who'd gotten fired for protecting a source, well, that meant she was trustworthy. That's probably why Tucker Cameron trusted her. Now Ella would trust her. What other option did she have?

It felt like Lillian Finch was in the room. That faint fragrance of lilies of the valley she always wore, seemed like she could still smell it, just a whisper, just a hint. She could see the white roses on Lillian's desk browning around the edges, the rest were full and white and plump, just as if nothing had happened. But they'd die soon. Too.

Second ring. Jane must not be in her office. *Darn.* She swiveled in her desk chair, putting her back to the door, watching the tatted curtains puff gently in the heat coming through the latticed radiator cover. She had her thumb up to her mouth, realized she was chewing the edge of it. She took it out, surprised.

Third ring. She was doing the right thing, no question.

Mr. Brannigan was dead. Ms. Finch was dead. Lillian had made a bad mistake, an incomprehensible mistake, and now she was dead.

"This is Jane Ryland," the familiar voice said. Ella smiled, hearing it. Jane Ryland helped people. "Thank you for calling us with a news tip, and we're eager to hear your story. I'm away from my desk or on the other line right now so—"

Ella marshaled her thoughts, waiting for the beep.

"Um. Miss Ryland? Jane? This is Ella Gavin, I met you at the coffee shop with T—um, Miss Cameron? Of course I recognized you, but it seemed like you didn't want me to. Anyway . . ."

This was getting off on the wrong foot. She was babbling, but she had to keep going.

"Um, the reason I'm calling is because I'm concerned that, well, you know, what Miss Cameron was worried about, being the wrong girl, and yes, I guess I agree that seems like it's true."

There. She said it.

"And since it is, what has me concerned is . . ."

What if the tape runs out?

She left her phone number quickly, then went on. "Sorry, anyway, now that Mr. Brannigan is dead, you probably know that, and Ms. Finch, too, and if they *did* make a mistake with Miss Cameron, I'm worried that's why. That's why they're dead, I mean. Maybe. And now *I'm* involved, because Miss Cameron talked to me, and Miss Cameron is involved, because what if someone else knows there was a mistake, and—"

Oh. But Jane knew about it now, too. What if this message had put Jane in jeopardy? She gulped. She was trapped. Even if she hung up, the message would still be there. She paused, hearing her own indecision, wondering if there was some way to undo the message.

"Miss Gavin?" Munson. From the hallway. "You were instructed not to call anyone."

End of message, the recorded voice on the phone told her. She heard the click as the connection ended.

*   *   *

"Officer Guerriero? I'm Detective Jake Brogan." Jake tramped up the stairs to Jane's apartment, headed toward this obviously new-kid cop, holding his gold badge visible in his flip wallet like a shield. "I heard over the two-way you were in the neighborhood, thought I'd stop by to confirm everything was in order. SOP."

It wasn't standard operating procedure, of course, but he had rank, and this Guerriero newbie would have no idea. Maybe she'd be intimidated by his detective stature. Didn't matter. He just had to get past her and upstairs to Jane. And then back to Bethany and little Phillip.

Guerriero looked uncertain. So much for "intimidated."

"Ah, sir? I'd better . . ." She fingered the button on her shoulder radio, clearly weighing her duty with her knowledge of chain of command.

"Go ahead," Jake said. "Sure. By the way, has Miss Ryland returned?" He had to get upstairs. Make sure she was okay. And what he'd learned in the car on the way over was disturbing. One way or the other.

"Yessir, about twenty minutes ago," Guerriero told him. "Officer Wayland? I have a Detective—"

"Brogan." Jake finished her sentence, loud enough so Wayland could hear. Thank goodness, a familiar name. A cop with a brain. "Chris? It's me. Brogan."

"He's clear," came the voice over the radio.

By that time, Jake was already on the landing.

"Brogan." Jane heard his voice over Officer Wayland's radio. Jake. Here. How'd he know? Now she really would cry.

Footsteps on the stairs. Of course she couldn't let Wayland know there was anything between them. Even though there wasn't.

Luckily, Neena had taken Sam and Eli outside to look

for Coda. They'd met Jake, just that once, but once was enough to end the charade.

Jane had flown through the apartment, Officer Wayland behind her, checking every place she could think of. Mom's jewelry was in the second dresser drawer as always, two emergency hundred-dollar bills still safely under the scarves, Gramma's silver trays and candlestick shiny in the dining room breakfront. No cat.

"Did you see a cat? A kitten?" she'd asked.

"Like I said, ma'am. No. Sorry about that."

She'd gone into the study, Officer Wayland at her side, still half-expecting to see her computer ripped from the wall and everything in chaos. But no, there was her desk, and the computer monitor with all her yellow stickies on the edge of the screen, her lucky rocks and her ceramic jar of pencils and her photos of her parents, of Murrow, and giving her first Emmy acceptance speech. Her stack of notes and file folders on the Tillson case and research on the foster care system seemed untouched.

"Kitty, kitty?" she'd called. But no cat.

Now Jane sat on her leather couch, elbows on her knees, chin in her hands, staring. At the crystal vase on the coffee table, filled with her favorite red tulips. At the latest *New Yorker* she'd left open on the floor. At the black tips of her leather boots. The navy and crimson flowers of her rug.

Nothing was changed. But everything was changed. And nothing, as the officer kept asking, had been added. Nothing but her stuff, just as it always was. "No sign of forced entry," the cop kept saying.

"So, Miss Ryland."

She looked up. "Oh, sorry. I was trying to figure out—"

"I understand," the cop said. "But I've been in touch with headquarters, and they tell me . . ."

"Miss Ryland? Hey, Chris. We set here?"

Jake. *Jake.* Standing in her entryway. *How did he know?* All she wanted was to fall into his arms, and just, just stand there and let him hold her and smooth her hair and tell her everything was going to be okay because he would never leave. And tell her it was silly they'd even decided to be apart and to hell with his job, or with hers, or whoever's.

"Yes." She stood, pressed her lips together for a moment.

"Detective Brogan is here as backup, Miss Ryland," Wayland interrupted her. "He may ask you some questions. I assume you're willing to cooperate in case he feels this warrants further investigation. You up to speed, Detective? About the—"

"Yup. Got it," Jake said. He unzipped his leather jacket, then zipped it again.

What was he nervous about? Jane always teased him about his zipper habit. Maybe he was nervous about her. Or was something wrong?

"Bottom line, I think we're done here, Miss Ryland." Wayland was still talking. "If you feel comfortable with us heading out."

"I guess I do," Jane said. She looked at Jake, who had a funny look on his face. Well, so did she, probably. "Thank you."

"Here's my contact numbers," Wayland handed her a business card. "Call if you need anything."

He turned, took one step toward the door.

Jane could feel herself drawn toward Jake. They'd be alone in ten seconds. Alone. Together. She sighed. Except for Tuck, who was somewhere, and Neena, who would certainly come back to get the scoop, and Mona, who'd probably come up with food, as she always did.

Wayland pivoted, stood in front of the still-open door. Jane saw Jake take a step away from her.

"Ma'am?" Wayland took his hat off, looked at it,

then put it back on. "I know we all have busy lives. But next time? Make sure you lock the door."

"But I—" She had locked the door. *She had.*

"I'll handle it from here, Officer. Thanks." Jake nodded at his colleague. "You're clear."

Jane heard the door close. But all she saw was Jake.

41

"Are you sure you locked the door?" The cop question came out before he actually thought about it.

Jake saw her eyes well with tears. There was a look victims got—haunted and questioning, knowing they'd never feel completely safe again. He could try to protect her, physically, but the parasite fear was tougher to eradicate.

"Janey?" he whispered. "I'm so sorry. Are you okay?"

Jane had taken a step toward him, but after his first question she plopped back onto the leather couch, pushed all the way into the far corner, arms wrapped around her knees, booted feet on the cushions.

"Yeah, I'm okay."

Not true, Jake knew. Not true and not okay.

He sat next to her, eased her linked fingers apart. Pulled her close. Hell with it all.

"Jane, honey, I'm so sorry. I came as soon as I found out."

"How did you . . . ?"

"DeLuca heard a transmission on the radio. We were at the scene of a—" Of a what, Jake wasn't even sure yet. It didn't matter, anyway. Niall Brannigan's death was police business, not connected to Jane.

"What the hell, Jane?"

"The cat."

Her voice muffled into his shoulder, and he lifted her chin with one finger. Her eyelashes were wet, little dribbles of black stuff underneath, and there were lines around her eyes he'd never seen before. She was—wounded, and frightened.

"Cat?"

"I got a kitten. At least, a kitten got me. She arrived a couple days ago, a stray. Guess you didn't know." She shrugged. "I mean, how would you know?"

"You're such a softie," he said. "Always trying to make everyone's lives work. Even a stray."

"Yeah." She pursed her lips. Dismissive. "So much for that idea. Now she's gone. I *have* to find her. What if—"

He could tell she was trying to pull herself together. And he'd help her look for this cat. It was probably easier for her to focus on the missing pet than on what really happened.

"Jane? They'll find the cat, or the cat will come back. And I'll stay as long as I can. But I need to—"

"Jake. Listen. *I* need to find out who it was that got into my apartment. Aren't you going to take fingerprints or something? I mean there was obviously—and that Officer, Way-whatever his name is." She pulled a business card from the rear pocket of her jeans. "Wayland. Didn't seem he was terribly concerned. He was nice enough, and I know he didn't find any 'signs of forced entry,' as he said about a million times, but aren't there investigations that you guys are supposed to do to figure out if—and who—and what if they're—?"

She took a deep shuddering breath, closing her eyes and sitting up straight, untangling herself from him. "I mean, someone broke *in*to—"

"Honey?" It slipped out again, and he didn't correct himself. He took his arm from around her shoulders, and turned to face her. This was gonna be tough.

If the "honey" registered, Jane's face didn't show it. "What?"

"That threatening phone call you got? Involving Brianna Tillson. The one I was asking you about yesterday when you so conveniently had to get off the phone."

Jane's eyes widened. She looked at him from under those wet lashes, wary. "Why do you—"

He held up both palms. "You want to be coy? Or talk about it?"

She nodded, acquiescing. "Yeah. Fine. You heard from the *Register*. Alex Wyatt called Superintendent Rivera."

"Okay," Jake agreed. "And I cannot believe you didn't tell me. Anyway. So. Remember you were told there'd be someone watching your apartment? Doing surveillance?"

"That's what they said, but I never saw anyone."

Jake had to smile. "Well, that's why they call it surveillance. But in this case, there's a Boston cop who's got a brother or pal or something, a camera buff, apparently, who lives across the street from you. In that brownstone. I talked to them from the car, on the way over here. They told me after that threatening phone call you got, they'd set up a surveillance cam on the third floor, recording everything. You follow?"

Jane blinked, tilting her head, as if picturing it. "I was on camera?"

"Well, when you came and went, you were. So was anyone else who came and went."

Jake saw the light dawn.

"Oh, now I get it. Whoa. You don't *need* to investigate."

This was the first smile he'd seen since he arrived.

Jane clasped her hands under her chin as if she was praying for an answer. "So? Who was it? Who came in? Are they in custody?"

And here we go.

"Well, Janey, that's the thing," Jake said.

* * *

"The thing?" This was the first good news Jane'd heard in a long time. Jake had gone all cop on her, which, she supposed, was his job. Officer Wayland was solicitous enough, but he'd seemed distracted, not really focused on—well, her home invasion.

This must be why. They had a suspect. It would be pretty damn interesting to find out who. Couldn't be Finn Eberhardt, because he'd answered the phone when Tuck called DFS. Which meant she was wrong about that whole thing, but soon there'd be answers. Big answers. And she could go back to work and her life would be normal again.

"Jake? Thing about what?" He hadn't answered her, and he had that funny look on his face again.

He couldn't avoid it any longer. She would be so pissed. Or confused. And she'd never accept it. That's what Jake was worried about the most. He stood, adjusting his jacket, feeling the weight of the weapon under his shoulder. He'd kept his jacket on so his gun wasn't so obvious. But part of his job here was to be a cop. The Sig reminded him.

"Yeah, well. The surveillance guy has the video, and we could get it, if need be. We've been given parallel jurisdiction for your case, Superintendent Rivera talked to the Brookline brass after the *Register*'s call. Anyway. Bottom line, the camera has night vision, and they've gotten ID on everyone who came into the building."

"And?"

"And. They just talked to the surveillance guy, and he reports he saw you come home last night. Saw a thirty-ish woman, identified as Neena Fichera, the one I met the day—remember?"

Jane made the hurry-up sign with one hand. "Geez."

"Her son Eli, and the baby. He reports seeing the mail carrier, and a couple of tenants—they check out, including the guys from the back apartment one floor below you. Saw Tuck come in this morning. Saw your car leave."

"Yup yup, fine." Jane waved off his words. "Get to the good stuff."

"There is no . . . good stuff." Jake needed to handle this as if Jane were any other "victim." That's what he was trained for, and that's what he'd rely on. "Jane, according to the surveillance person, no stranger came into this building. No one. You, the Ficheras, the tenants, Tuck. That's all. You must have left your door unlocked. And it came open."

Jane stared at him. She looked at the ceiling, as if searching for answers. Stood, and took two steps to her bay window, pulling back the gauzy curtains and peering out to the street, curving her hands around her eyes to block the glare. Then, with both hands, she waved.

"Jane?"

"I'm just waving at the stupid asshole who thinks he can do surveillance by looking at the *front* of the apartment." She talked into the window, then whirled to him, hands on hips. "Brilliant. Even I, dumb girl who supposedly can't remember to lock her door, know it's pretty stupid to watch one fricking—to watch one side of a building. Cheap, yeah, oh-so high tech. Convenient. Fabulous. But there's a back door, right? Did your cut-rate police brain trust think of that?"

She put her hands over her face, so all he could see was the wave of her hair and tiny gold earrings, and the slim gold band she wore on her right hand, her mother's wedding ring, she'd told him. Her good luck talisman.

"I'm so sorry, Jake." She took her hands down from her eyes. "I don't mean to yell. But that's so dumb, and someone got in the *back* door, *duh,* and I just don't see how you can blame it on me. I mean, you saw Mona Washburn, right? She's home. How'd *she* get in? She's not on the big-time night-vision hot-shot video."

"Yeah, I know. But the back has a keypad that opens with a number pad code, correct?" He'd expected an explosion, and got one. Now the fireworks would dissipate, and Jane would see what had to be reality.

She was frowning, stretching the black wool of her sweater sleeve down over one hand. Not looking at him. Then she did. "Yeah. So?"

"Well. It activates every time the door is opened, and keeps a record of who entered. Don't need a surveillance cam for that. And it shows tenants only. Mona Washburn was the last to use it, around three A.M. She told Officer Wayland she'd stayed late to close her restaurant and didn't see anyone or anything unusual."

Jake's radio crackled. "Jake? DeLuca. You copy?"

"Copy." Jake talked into his shoulder radio, raising a hand to put Jane on hold.

"Got that warrant," DeLuca said. "For the Ricker house? Time to make his day, Jake. You clear to move?"

Nobody had broken into her apartment? Maybe nobody had really been following her in the truck?

Jane lowered herself to the couch, her mind racing, balancing, trying to juggle a couple of realities while Jake talked to his partner on his two-way. He'd looked so upset. No wonder. He had to tell her all this chaos, the cops and the "investigation" and the fear and the worry, was *her* fault.

A knock on her front door.

"See?" Jane pointed to the door, accusing. "How'd *that* person get in?"

She knew there was something else. Had to be. She

had not left the door unlocked. Impossible. One hundred percent impossible.

"Stand by, D," Jake said. Then, to her, "Maybe it's—"

By that time, Jane was at the door, checking the peephole.

"Who is it?" Jake said.

Jane fumbled with the lock, yanked open the door. Couldn't open it fast enough.

Tuck. Holding Coda.

Tuck handed her a squirming ball of fur and a jangling ring of keys. "Heard you're looking for a cat, ma'am." Tuck was doing her cop imitation. "And here's your keys."

Oh. She'd left her keys with Tuck when she parked. That's how Tuck had gotten in the front door. And she'd found—

Coda. Mewing and burrowing into her neck, the bottoms of her little paws damp and cold, her tail whipping back and forth. Jane stroked the trembling little body, now rattling with a fervent purr.

"Where was she?"

Tuck waved a vague hand. "You know. Cats. Some nice guy on the street was holding her, said he found her in the—she seems okay, you think?"

"Yes, oh, Tuck, thank you so much. Hey, you stupid cat. Where were you? I was so—oh, she's lost her collar, somehow. A red stretchy one. Come on in, Tuck."

Jane closed the door with one hip, still cuddling Coda, waved Tuck toward the living room. *Oh. Jake. Tuck. Too late now.*

Tuck shrugged. "Got caught on something, maybe."

"That's good news." Jake stood, gestured at the cat.

"Hey, Detective Brogan," Tuck said. "My, my. Fancy seeing *you* here." She paused, then picked up a photo of Jane's mother from the end table, examined it, put it back. "Did you guys not dust for fingerprints? Jane, are you cool with that? Even after the thing with the truck?"

"Jake? You copy?" His radio was crackling again. "We need to—"

"Stand by one, DeLuca." Jake looked at Tuck, then at Jane, then back at Tuck. Then back at her.

"Thing with the truck?" he asked. "Jane? What thing with what truck?"

42

Ella fumbled her phone closed. Stashed it. Collins Munson stood at her door. She felt a wave of rebellion. Or something. Maybe—the new Ella. Munson might be the head of History and Records, but he wasn't her boss. Even now that Mr. Brannigan was dead, and Ms. Finch dead, too. She'd had two bosses, now she had none.

Maybe she was tired, or maybe she was confused, or maybe she was just sick of it. Always Miss Deferential. Everything was different, now. She had information. Now she could be different, too. The new Ella.

Nothing and no one could intimidate her. If they thought so, they had the wrong girl. She tossed her head to prove it.

"Hello, Mr. Mun—Collins." If they were going to fire her, it didn't matter what she called him. If she was on the phone was none of his business. He wasn't the cops.

"I called a friend to cancel an engagement. What can I do for you?"

Munson's face changed, his furrowed forehead seemed to relax. He unbuttoned the gold embossed button on his navy blazer, shot his starched white cuffs. Ella saw a flash of cuff link. He'd been some sort of military person, Ella knew. Kept the haircut and the bearing.

"Well, Miss Gavin."

He paused, and Ella watched as he seemed to take in the room and the curtains and the fading roses in Ms. Finch's inner office. The documents were still under her desk, but Ella knew he couldn't see them.

"May I join you for a moment?"

Munson's voice was different, too. He seemed, well, nice. But Ella remained skeptical.

"Of course." She waved him to the damask chair and took the matching one beside him. If he was going to be cordial, she could be cordial. "How is Mrs. Brannigan?"

"She's fine. Thank you." Munson crossed one lanky gray flannel leg over the other. "It's difficult, for all of us. But there is a greater good in our work. Ms. Finch trusted you, and that trust is important to us. We'd like to make sure, in this time of transition, that you're still interested."

"In what?" *Wait*. The new Ella should be nicer. She smiled, softened her voice. "I mean, interested in what?"

Munson seemed to buy it. "In continuing to work here. I know Ms. Finch—God rest her soul, she's in a better place now—"

Ella nodded. That was true. She hoped.

"—not only trusted you. She confided in you. Correct? I'm sure it'll be a smooth transition if you agree."

"Agree?" The new Ella was confused.

"We can talk about it later, Ella, this is an emotional time. But we'd be very happy if you'd agree to stay, and—in an 'acting' capacity at first—take over Ms. Finch's duties. Then, perhaps, we can discuss a new salary."

What? Ella leaned into the rounded back of the club chair, curled her fingers around the puffy armrests.

"We all agree. You seem sincerely devoted to making the connections that have shaped the Brannigan's stellar reputation for reuniting families. That's the key to our current success, and our *continuing* success."

"It's, of course, I—" Ella couldn't compute this fast enough. Who's "we," she wondered. It didn't seem like the right thing to ask.

"It's settled, then." Munson stood. "We'll be in to clear out Ms. Finch's personal things. You should go home, take the rest of the day. Tomorrow we'll begin anew. Unless Ardith Brannigan decides to hold her husband's funeral tomorrow. Paying our respects comes first. Agreed?"

"I should clean out Lillian's desk." She stood and shook the hand he offered, not really clear what she was agreeing to. "I mean, I know where everything is."

"Not necessary." Munson buttoned his jacket, arranged his shoulders. "Very kind of you, good soldier, but unnecessary. My—Grace will handle it. Until tomorrow, then?"

Ella watched his navy blue back as he walked to the door, gave her a final nod, and left. She was alone. In her office. *Her very own office?* Would she soon have an assistant and someone bringing her white roses? Did Lillian Finch's tragic death mean *her* life would really change for the better?

She sank into the comforting upholstery. Other people called their mothers at times like this. Times where you didn't know exactly what to do, needed advice from someone you loved and trusted, someone you knew cared about you and loved you more than anyone or anything in the world. But Ella didn't have that.

She stared through the walnut paneling of her desk, imagining the stash of documents underneath it.

Collins Munson was making her the new Lillian Finch. Why?

Jane Ryland, she thought. *Please please please call me back.*

* * *

"No way. We can't go to Connecticut *now*." Jane shook her head, absolutely refusing. Tuck was crazy. Jake had rushed out after the call from DeLuca, telling her to file a police report about the truck, just in case. The cat had apparently decided to live under the couch and never come out. Jane peered into the darkness. Coda's green eyes were barely visible, the furry body annoyingly just out of reach. "Come on, cat."

Jane, on her knees, looked up at Tuck. She, at least, might be reasonable. "It's three in the afternoon, Tuck, it'll be dark in an hour."

"So? We can take my car, if that's what's worrying you." Tuck unlooped her orange scarf, then stretched her arms across the back of Jane's striped armchair. "We can leave yours in the front so they'll think you're home. And the cat'll come out when she's hungry."

"So *who'll* think I'm home? Who is 'they'?"

"Whoever. Whoever you're scared of. Whoever you still think chased us on the Mass Pike." She pointed at Jane. "Whoever you think broke into your apartment."

"Well, the cops seem to think there's no 'who.' They think the door 'came open' because I forgot to lock it. Which I most assuredly did not." Jane kept peering under the couch, the pooching belly of the upholstery blocking her view. "Still, I'm calling a locksmith. Changing the lock. *Cat. Come out.* I'm not kidding."

"Whatever," Tuck said. "Tomorrow, then?"

Jane couldn't decide whether she wanted Tuck to hurry up and leave so she could be alone, or wanted Tuck to stay so she wouldn't be alone. She almost laughed. Well, Mr. Surveillance across the street was on the job, of course. *That* made her feel so much better. She should text Jake and thank—

Huh. He never answered her text from yesterday, after he'd pantomimed *text me* at Maggie Gunnison's office. *Maggie Gunnison's office.*

That gave Jane an idea. But she couldn't act on it with Tuck around. "Sure. Tomorrow. Call me. Did you tell Carlyn you weren't coming?"

"Yeah, I did." Tuck used a forefinger to dab an invisible something from the glass coffee table. "Well, no answer, but I left a message. And I think tomorrow we should just go. Don't call in advance. Then she won't have time to, I don't know. Concoct a story."

"Whatever." Jane watched Tuck's finger. *Fingerprints.* If Tuck was worried about her identity, there was an easy way to find out. "Tuck? Listen. You know your file, your baby file?"

"My—?"

"Yes. File. The one Ella showed you. Did it have your baby footprint in it?"

"My—?"

"Your baby footprint. You know. The ones they take at the hospital. Sometimes it's on the birth certificate, sometimes it's on a separate document. Mom used to show me and Lissa our little footprints, all the time. She said that's how she'd prove we were hers, if anyone tried to take us away from her."

She saw Tuck's look.

"It was a game. A *game.* We loved it, and always told Mom we needed a copy of her footprint. In case they tried to take her away from *us.*" Jane paused for a fleeting second, flickered a glance upward. *Hi, Mom. Miss you.* "You had to be there. Anyway, your footprint. Was it in your file?"

Tuck considered, then shook her head. "No. No footprint."

"I wonder who has it, then," Jane said. "If there is one."

Jane's cell phone trilled. Coda streaked out from under the couch and hurtled down the hall.

"She hates the phone," Jane said. "I know the feeling." She checked for caller ID. Up popped the photo she'd taken a couple of months ago in the newsroom, right after her election story hit the front page. Wire-rimmed glasses, pencil behind his ear, paper cup of celebratory champagne, big smile.

"Shit. I forgot to call Alex back," Jane said. "So, ah, are you—"

"Outta here." Tuck jammed on her knit cap. "*Mañana*, sister. Road trip. I'll call you."

"Hi Alex," Jane said, waggling her fingers at Tuck as she opened the apartment door.

"Thank you," she mouthed. They could talk more tomorrow. Then, into the phone. "What's up?"

Walking down the hall toward her study, she absently pushed books back into place on the floor-to-ceiling shelves, listening to Alex's questions about her "break-in."

"Yes, I'm okay, thanks. The police didn't take fingerprints. Yes, I'm having the lock changed." She pulled out her desk chair and signed in to her computer with her free hand. The stack of notes from Maggie Gunnison lay right there on the desk. So did that Inspector General report Alex had given her from his couch filing system.

Alex was still talking, seemed to know the whole damned story about the open door. Not about the truck thing, though. Should she tell him? Maybe there was nothing to tell. "Yes, that's what the police think. But I *always* lock . . ."

She paused, listening, as Alex's concerned voice interrupted her.

"Sure. Yes, I understand. I'll lie low another day or two. If that's what you think is best."

Glass half full. Maybe being banished was a good thing. She could work on the Tillson story without having to actually produce any copy. She could still check her e-mail. And see if anyone called. And she needed to find Hec Underhill. He just might have a photo of Brianna Tillson's murderer.

A ball of fluff landed on her lap. "Where's your collar, cat?" Jane said. "Oh, nothing, Alex. Yeah. I'm fine. Does anyone else have my Tillson story? TV? Are the police naming her?"

She opened the IG report on her desk, turned the spiral-bound pages as Alex told her how the cops had slammed the lid on the Callaberry Street thing. Nothing coming out of HQ.

"Alex?" She stared at page 37, his voice blurring as she realized what she was reading. It might be nothing, but—"Oh, someone's at the door," she lied. "Might be the locksmith. Talk later, okay?"

She almost missed the off button as she tried to hang up without taking her eyes off the page. "Special Circumstances," the bolded chapter heading said.

> The inspector general analyzed the fifteen so-called "special criminal circumstance" cases handled by DFS in the previous three fiscal years. Research reveals the DFS has no established systems for custody or inquiry for the children who may have witnessed criminal activity. The inspector general recommends there be designated a qualified individual who . . .

Jane skipped the rest of the sentence, lured to the end by a footnote. The numbered footnote indicated, she knew, that the DFS had responded to the IG's recs and taken corrective action.

She flipped to page 71, and slid a finger to response #7:

> The DFS agrees with the IG's assessment, and as a result has appointed an on-call therapist-counselor, Bethany Sibbach, MSW/PhD. Dr. Sibbach is designated as "point of contact" for all children considered

witnesses or persons of interest in a criminal investiga-
tion connected with a fostering situation. Dr. Sibbach
is a registered and licensed . . .

"Bingo," Jane said. The cat looked up at her, blinked. "That's what I said, cat. Bingo. Paging Doctor Sibbach, right? Because she might not be happy about it, but the good doctor could have the scoop about Phillip and Phoebe. Then *I* will have the scoop, and we'll all live happily ever after."

The cat did not seem to care.

"Hel-lo, Google." Jane typed in Bethany Sibbach's name. "Show me the money."

43

"**Welcome. Look all** you want, *Officers.*" Curtis Ricker's insolent stance and leering sarcasm hardly conveyed welcome, but Jake knew it didn't matter how Ricker felt. They had a warrant allowing them to search every damn inch of this Allston duplex, Ricker's half of it at least, and they could also confiscate Ricker's drowned cell phone. If they could find it. After they'd finished griping about their backlog, barebones staff, and impossible workload, the geniuses in IT had admitted they could probably retrieve something.

"Thank you, Mr. Ricker." Jake matched his sarcasm and raised him one. "We appreciate your hospitality. But we have a warrant, and that means we don't need your permission. Usually we'd ask you to wait outside, but it's somewhat cold for that. So if you would just wait here in the living room with Officer Hennessey— Hennessey, you set?"

Hennessey managed to drag his attention from the screen of his cell phone and gestured toward the grubby couch, the Bluetooth in his ear hanging precariously. "Mr., ah, Ricker? Care to take a seat?"

"First, we'll need that cell phone," Jake said. Big smile. "The wet one. Please."

Ricker did not smile back.

"Not a frickin' chance." He leaned against the front door jamb, arms clamped in front of his chest. One leg of his jeans was tucked into his boot, the other wasn't. His plaid shirt flapped open, unbuttoned, over a once-white T-shirt, and a ring of keys dangled on a chain from a front belt loop. "I'm calling my lawyer. Right, fricking, now."

"Do that. But on what phone?" DeLuca was already pulling out a thin drawer in one of the end tables. He gave the knob a yank and the drawer slid all the way off the runners, spilling a clutter of pencil stubs and scraps of paper and match flaps onto the floor.

"Mr. Ricker?" Jake held out a hand, waiting.

"Oh, gee." DeLuca shook his head, full of the deepest woe. "Drawer's broken, I guess."

"I frickin' mean it." Ricker extended a middle finger for the briefest of seconds.

Jake decided to let that go. Sticks and stones.

"I'm calling my lawyer, now, so you have to—"

Jake interrupted him. "Like my partner said. Be our guest. But we are here pursuant to that warrant we showed you. Plain English? That trumps your lawyer. There's no more magic 'lawyer' word. We're legally sanctioned to search these premises, lawyer or no, and to confiscate—well, I'm sure you plan to read the document in question yourself."

"I can help you with the big words, if you want," DeLuca said.

"You're both complete a—"

"So we've often been told," Jake said, so agreeable. "However, the longer we stand here and chit-chat, the longer it's gonna take."

Ricker drew out a pack of Marlboro Reds, snapped one out with the side of his hand. Looked around, then picked up a matchbook from the floor, waved it at them. "You gonna 'confiscate' this? Is it legal if I smoke?"

"Knock yourself out." DeLuca was pawing through the scraps of paper now scattered on the rug. "Nothing here."

He reached for the drawer on the other side. "This one broken, too?"

Ricker's stream of smoke headed for the ceiling as Jake ran a flattened hand under the scarred dining room table. Lots of times people taped stuff there, thinking no one would ever check. He patted, feeling only splintery wood. Not this time.

One after the other, he turned over the dining room chairs, rickety, mismatched, wood, each with fabric stapled over its seat cushion. One after the other, a cushion fell out of place and tumbled to the floor, leaving an empty rectangle where the seat had been.

Would someone think to hide whatever it was that would connect him with Brianna Tillson—*birth certificates? money? the cell phone?*—in a seat cushion? Jake refused to focus on what haunted him. That his own shitty police work and that "prize patrol" visit had given Ricker enough time and warning to dump or stash anything he didn't want Jake and the cops to see. But maybe Ricker was arrogant enough to think he could get away with it.

They'd gotten the warrant, so might as well search. He'd skip the cushions for now. Come back if the rest of the house turned up nothing.

Closet. Jake turned the white plastic knob, pulled open the door. Two coats. *Pockets?* Nothing. Empty black metal hangers rattled against each other as Jake leaned in, aiming his flashlight at the wooden floor. Cleaner than he would have predicted, and deeper, but whatever. Ratty running shoes, an umbrella leaning in the corner. A lot of nothing.

Kitchen next. Jake opened a series of greasy-knobbed drawers, each haphazardly lined with tattered paper. It might have been bright green, say, ten years ago. Knives, forks, nothing under the liner. Next, junk drawer. Matches, corks, keys.

Keys.

Jake hooked a set of keys with one finger. It wasn't like there were gonna be fingerprints. Six keys, maybe seven. A silvery ring, no dangling tag to designate what any key opened. He'd wondered how the killer had gotten into Brianna Tillson's apartment. There had been no sign of forced entry. So whatever asshole killed Brianna might have used a key. And the same key to lock the door behind him.

Jake could see Ricker through the archway from the kitchen. He had that bunch of keys on his belt loop. These were other keys.

Seven keys. Looped through a steel ring attached to a thin square of aluminum. No logo, no decoration, no designation. Clearly not car keys, and not the flat ones, not for a drawer or jewelry box. Door keys, plain and simple.

Jake didn't need easy, of course. Problem was, "keys" weren't listed on Judge Gallagher's warrant. "Evidence in the killing of Brianna Tillson" was. He could argue they were a plain-sight exception to the search warrant—the perpetrator potentially used keys, here were keys. They hadn't, however, exactly been in plain sight. Jake marshaled his arguments. He'd opened the drawer pursuant to the warrant, which clearly allowed him to look for the cell phone. As a result, the keys were in plain sight. As long as the drawer was legally opened.

Iffy.

Very, very iffy.

And if any of these were the keys to Callaberry Street, and if they got thrown out because Jake had seized them illegally, he was screwed.

"What're these to, Mr. Ricker?" Jake held the key

ring between two fingers as he took the few steps back from the kitchen. Ricker, still lounging against the front door, tapped his cigarette ash into a can of A&W root beer. The room was so quiet, as Jake waited for the answer, that he heard the hiss of the ember hitting the liquid.

"No idea." Ricker didn't look up, swirled the can. "Never saw them before. That I can remember."

"Okay, no problem." Interesting response. "You're sure they're not yours?"

"Lawyer," Ricker said. "Right now."

Hennessey looked up from his phone screen, put a hand on the black plastic baton hooked to his belt. "Jake? You need me to—?"

"Mr. Ricker has a right to remain silent," Jake said. Good cop. "However. We do not need his permission to try these keys in his front door."

Which might actually be true.

"Jake?" DeLuca had taken the slipcovers off the couch cushions and held a limp piece of zippered corduroy. A rectangle of foam rubber lay at his feet. He cocked his head at the front door, cleared his throat. "Ya think . . ."

He paused, not finishing the question.

Jake could predict what DeLuca was thinking: *Plain sight? Scope of the warrant? Inadmissible evidence? You sure about this?*

As answer, Jake held up the keys. He was sure. As sure as anyone would be, faced with an uncooperative suspect and potential evidence in a murder case, his only weapon the power of a search warrant.

Which he hoped would cover his ass.

"Let's do this." Jake started toward the door. "We don't have all day."

* * *

Jane locked her door, *absolutely,* and started down the stairs to the street and her car. She'd read Coda the riot act about escaping, asked Neena to call a locksmith, and in one computer search and two phone calls had found Bethany Sibbach, who'd agreed to talk with her in person. "Off the record," naturally.

Feeling the chill of the gray afternoon, she tucked the tails of her plaid muffler into her black parka and patted her pockets. Gloves, where was her other glove? Damn. Had she left it in the car?

She paused on the front steps of her brownstone, looking up through the bare branches of the municipal maples that lined Corey Road. *False alarm,* the cops had insisted. Nicer to think so. Maybe. Still, was it better she was leaving?

Her shoulders sagged briefly. Was she afraid? No. *Yes.* No. *Of what?* And if she were, what should she do? Call the police? They'd think she was the girl who cried wolf.

Scanning the mid-century brick and brownstone buildings across the street, she wondered if the cop's brother or whatever he was with the surveillance camera was still on the lookout. Was he watching her right now? She raised both arms, waving, then pointed to her car. Half-serious.

"I'm leaving," she mouthed the words.

44

Jake took the seventh key from the front door. "Not this one, either, Mr. Ricker."

"So the hell what?" Curtis Ricker's contempt for the situation, for the cops, for Jake, apparently knew no bounds.

Jake couldn't care less. "You sure you can't tell me what door these keys *do* open?"

"I told you, I never saw them before."

"They're in your kitchen drawer," DeLuca said. "Sir. You don't open your kitchen drawer?"

"I never—that's—you can't just—"

"Inventory." Jake interrupted Ricker's bluster, signaling Hennessey, who unclicked the snaps of a hard-sided leather briefcase and pulled out a glassine bag and a legal pad.

"Yup." Hennessey patted his pockets, found a pen. Clicked it open. "All set. Item one?"

"Inventory item one, subsequent to the Ricker warrant, number thirteen dash nine-forty-four, at," Jake looked at his watch, "approximately three twenty-six P.M. Tuesday. One set of keys, one Schlage, one Yale, five blanks. One key ring, metal, no identification."

"That's the most idiotic—I'm gonna call—"

Jake ignored Ricker, who, judging by his sudden rigid

posture and deepening frown, seemed finally to realize this visit was not a game.

"Officer DeLuca, you'll stay here with Mr. Ricker. Officer Hennessey, you'll come with me. Officer DeLuca will take over the inventory."

This was a tough one. Jake'd rather have D with him when he tested the keys, but he sure as hell wasn't going to leave loose-cannon Hennessey here with the bad guy. They'd probably wind up in a contest to see which moron would convince the other to flee to Vegas. Hennessey would have to be his witness. Sad but necessary. "We'll return in approximately thirty minutes."

"Where're we—?" Hennessey couldn't have looked more befuddled.

How'd this guy make it, all these years?

By the time Jake got back from Callaberry Street, six more butts crowded Ricker's ashtray, and the suspect apparently hadn't moved from his post at the front door. DeLuca was counting a lineup of amber plastic prescription containers he'd arranged on the coffee table. A cast-iron frying pan was bagged on the couch. So was what looked like a bowling trophy and a stack of ratty-edged papers. No cell phone.

"Only took us two tries with the keys," Jake announced. "One opened the door to 56 Callaberry Street, and another the front door of apartment C. Why'd you have Brianna Tillson's keys, Mr. Ricker?"

"Are you fricking—" Ricker took two steps backward, toward the now-closed front door. DeLuca was at his side before the second step ended.

"You said you didn't remember when you'd last seen her," Jake said. "So why'd you have her keys?"

"Hey, I never . . . ow! *Shit.*"

He saw DeLuca unclick the cuffs, heard them ratchet over Ricker's scrawny wrists. Hennessey breathed through his mouth, slack-jawed, as if he'd never seen an arrest. Had Ricker been the one who called the Callaberry Street 911? Soon the voice-forensics guys would find that out.

Jake thought about Brianna Tillson's ragdoll body, her spotless kitchen, the awkwardly wrong splay of her long legs, and those bare feet, somehow all the more heartbreaking. ME Kat McMahan had confirmed her cause of death as blunt trauma. No accident. Murder. Jake was a murder cop. Times like this were what made him happy. Happy as you could be when an innocent person got bludgeoned to death with a frying pan.

What happened to set Ricker off like that? To murder that woman? With Phillip and Phoebe probably in the next room?

Those two kids—*maybe three, that was next on his list*—had lost another mother. He couldn't bring her back, no one could. But he'd made a promise to Brianna Tillson, as he did to all his victims. Right now, this minute, in this smoke-stained sorry excuse for an apartment, he got to keep that promise. Case closed.

"Curtis Ricker? You're under arrest for the murder of Brianna Tillson."

Jane clicked her remote, trotted the last few steps to her car door. Yes, fine, she was looking around to see if anyone was . . . *no*. No one was watching her; no one was even in the street, or in a car, or pretending to be casually walking down the sidewalk. She couldn't be spooked for the rest of her life.

She slammed the car door, slipped her keys into the ignition. Bethany Sibbach lived on Hinshaw Street, about twenty minutes away. She opened the center console, got out her GPS. It would be so much easier if there were a GPS for everything in life. A magic gizmo that would give you exact directions, alternate routes. So you could never be lost.

The Audi's engine hummed to life. She needed to find Hec Underhill. But first, Bethany Sibbach. It would be so rewarding to power back into the newsroom with a big scoop. Then, no way they could lay her off.

Jane glanced in her rearview. Nothing. No one. She was on the way to her story, and, she promised herself, leaving her fear behind. She was not, *not,* going to allow her own possibly overdramatizing brain to scare her with shadows of terrors that did not exist.

And there appeared the first good omen. She spotted it on the floor of the passenger side. Her missing glove.

"Thank you, universe," she said out loud. "About time."

Leaning across the center console, she stretched full out to reach, and patted her hand across the floor, blindly feeling for the glove. She scooped it up, then felt something . . . else? She stared, uncomprehendingly, at what items now lay in her hand. Her no-longer-missing black leather glove.

And a red stretchy cat collar.

Where baby? If little Phillip Lussier was actually re-membering, those two words were about to explode this whole case. If there was a baby, where was it? Jake had worked his share of juvenile crimes. Knew, bottom line, if a third child had been in the Callaberry Street apart-ment, only a few possibilities existed for where that baby was right now.

Dead, for one. If so, there'd be another murder charge in Curtis Ricker's rap sheet. And no jury would let the asshole off.

Jake opened the door of his cruiser, slid into the seat, adjusted the rearview mirror. Getting dark already. His shift ended at five, but there were no shifts in a murder case.

Thing was, there were other potential outcomes. The ones that also made his knuckles go white on the steering wheel and pushed his cop instincts into overdrive.

What if the baby were alive? Kidnapped? Sold? By who? And why?

Jake turned the key in the ignition, then paused, seeing his own frown in the rearview. "You watch too much TV," he said aloud.

He shifted into reverse, checked for street traffic as he backed out of Ricker's patched asphalt driveway, and considered his to-do list. Ricker was in custody. Check. Kat McMahan still hadn't filed her autopsy reports for Brannigan or Lillian Finch. Check.

For now, only one question remained. The person with the answer might be playing with a Batmobile at Bethany Sibbach's house.

Where baby?

"Not exactly what I expected." Jane smiled at Bethany. The DFS counselor said it was easier in person than on the phone, and invited Jane over. She'd set out a couple of ground rules: One, park in the back to let the snowplows clear the street. Two, that her wards, Phillip and Phoebe, were off limits. As was their history, their birth parents, and their murdered foster mother. Other than that, she'd be happy to discuss the state's foster care system to help Jane do a "compassionate and comprehensive" story.

Jane could handle ground rules. Ground rules always changed.

And now Phillip Lussier showed no inclination to leave Jane's lap. The little boy's Spider-Man sneakers were leaving damp footprints on her Levis. Kids liked her, she was used to that, but this show of affection was surprising. Phillip had dropped his chocolate chip cookie on the floor the moment he saw Jane. When she sat down on the couch, he climbed onto her lap without invitation.

Jane settled Phillip in, extricating one little foot from that tender place on top of her kneecap, seeing what looked like swipes of chocolate on his blue striped T-shirt and crumbs around his lips. Somehow Jane was his new best friend.

"First time he's smiled in—well, I can't remember a smile." Bethany tied the ends of her dangling cardigan into a loopy knot, then untied them. "Phoebe's napping, for now. These kids have been through a lot. I cannot predict how much the situation will affect—well, what can I do for you, Jane?"

Jane felt the tickle of Phillip's curls. He'd wrapped one hand around the turtleneck of her sweater, yanking it away from her face.

"Hey, sweetie," she said. "Should we . . ." She looked at Bethany, baffled, hoping for direction. "Read a book or something?"

"Book!" Phillip crowed. A smile wreathed his chocolaty face, and he bounced with excitement, a pudgy bobblehead. "Read book, Mama!"

"When will she be back?" Ella paced the length of her living room, clutching her cell phone to her ear as the receptionist at the *Register* made up a bunch of reasons why Jane Ryland wasn't available. "Well, is there someone who *would* know? Yes, I'll hold."

She paced the other way, seeing the color of the evening change as the streetlights popped on along her street. Someone had looped a string of valentine hearts on the building's front door, reminding Ella that the second worst holiday in the world—after New Year's Eve—was around the corner. She was nobody's valentine. As a kid, had she gotten valentines? Maybe in school. But Aunt Marion, as she'd been told to call the woman, hadn't been much for "Hallmark holidays." Or any holidays except the "real" ones, Christmas and Easter. Mother's Day they ignored.

"Yes?" Ella heard the connection change, but it was only someone telling her to hold again. It really sounded like the *Register*'s people were making up excuses for why Jane wasn't there. Or maybe today was simply a day off. But she had to talk to Jane. *Had to*.

"Okay, fine, I'll hold. She still works there, doesn't she? Would there be a better time for me to call?"

Did she want to leave a message? the receptionist asked.

Did she? She'd already left one on Jane's voice mail. Jane hadn't called her back.

Had she trusted the wrong person? She usually had good instincts about people. But reality—and relationships—weren't reliable. Ella prided herself on how she could predict which matches were going to thrive, and which ones might better have been forgotten. Maybe because of all that'd just happened, she was losing it.

"No, thanks," she replied. "I'll try later."

The receptionist was saying something more, but Ella hung up. Her kitchen table now held two stacks of pilfered folders. Tucker Cameron's. And some new ones.

Ella had come home early, as Collins Munson suggested. But she wasn't about to abandon Ms. Finch's office or all her personal stuff for that Grace to paw through. Not to mention the files.

Once they got hold of them, Ella realized, every bit of evidence of—whatever it was—could be gone. It was up to her to protect the history. Protect the sanctity of the

Brannigan families. That's when she realized what had been nagging her, almost tormenting her, ever since she'd begun to believe Carlyn Parker Beerman had been sent the wrong girl.

What if there were others?

Before she could change her mind, Ella had snatched the files for the last five Calls Ms. Finch had made. With the snap of rubber bands and the flap of manila folders, she'd stuffed them in her backpack and whisked them out of the building, right past Collins Munson's closed office door.

Tonight, right after her chicken potpie and Diet Pepsi, she would make a few . . . what would she call them? Follow-up calls. Just to see how things were going with the five new families.

After all, she was now the "acting" Lillian Finch. And she didn't need some reporter to help the new Ella find out what—she smiled—the *hell* was going on.

45

"Book, Mama! Phillip get!" Phillip leaped from Jane's lap and plowed himself into a pile of shiny picture books stacked on the floor by the end table. He grabbed a glossy turquoise-and-red cover and held it up, triumphant. "Dis one, Mama!"

Jane recognized *The Cat in the Hat.*

"Did he say . . . ?" Jane looked at Bethany, wondering if she'd heard properly. " . . . *Mama?* Did he mean me? Or does he call everyone—oof."

Phillip clambered back onto her lap and plastered his spine against Jane's chest, awkwardly propping the too-big book on his outstretched legs. His feet barely reached beyond Jane's knees, and the plaid laces of one of his rubber-soled shoes had come untied.

Bethany crossed her arms in front of her, watching the two of them on the couch. "I'm sorry, Jane. Yes, he did say 'Mama.' And no, I must tell you he's never said that word, not in the three days he's been with me. He has said— well, some other things. But I'm trying to assess what, if anything, he means. Possibly you look like his birth mother? Or wear her perfume? You don't look like Brianna Tillson. We may never know."

"Hey, Phillip." Jane cuddled him closer. *Poor thing.*

"Sure, we can read this. Okay?" She looked up as the boy pawed through the pages. "Bethany? You were saying?"

"Yes. Well. There is some discussion in the literature," Bethany, drawing out her words, seemed to be remembering, "that children who are too young to properly imprint, or who have been removed from their biological mother and put into other arrangements for care at what might be a vulnerable time in their emotional development, might possibly fail to adapt, and subsequently create the belief system that whatever woman is presented as a caregiver is, therefore, 'mother.' That the word represents more of a role, you see, rather than terminology signifying a specific, singular person. We call it role conflation."

"Mama, read book. Mama! Read book!" Phillip made himself heavy in her lap. Wiggling his insistence.

It was kind of adorable, really. Reassuring. That this tiny boy would see Jane as a mother. Oh, she'd felt the stirrings. Of course. Of the possibility that someday, with someone, there'd be a little person who was half her and half—whoever. Her own mother had always told her nothing was comparable to motherhood. But that was for someday. Here, Jane understood the sad reality. Probably the reason Phillip called her "mama" was that his own mother was dead.

Well, his foster mother, at least. Brianna Tillson. "Is Phillip's real mother alive?"

"Can't discuss that." Bethany stopped her, palms up. "Jane, he's had a tough time. I've been hoping upon hope—not very professionally said, I know—that he won't remember anything about what happened to him."

"Has he shown any signs of remembering?" She turned to the next page, saw a fishbowl balanced on a broomstick and a grinning cat. "It was too cold to go out, it was too wet to play," she read, pointing to each word as she spoke it.

Then she had another thought. "Did the police come to interview Phillip? Did he tell them anything?"

Bethany burst out laughing, then put a palm over her mouth. "This has quickly deteriorated, Jane, into a conversation far beyond the boundaries of—"

"Mama? Where baby?" The tiny voice came from Jane's lap. Phillip had pushed the book onto the floor and wrenched his body around to face her. Wide-eyed and entreating, the little boy was clearly waiting for an answer.

Jane frowned at Bethany, confused. "What baby? Does he mean Phoebe?"

"Phoebe sleep. Where *baby*?" Phillip's voice had the edge of a whine.

"That's right, she's taking a nap, honey," Jane said, smoothing his hair. "It's okay. Here, we can read again until she wakes up. Bethany? You were saying about the police?"

Bethany leaned down, handed her the book. "You know I can't—Oh. Now who is that?"

The doorbell rang, again, a cheery bing-bong.

"Excuse me." Bethany went to the front door, peered through the peephole. Then turned to Jane, one hand to her mouth. "I don't know quite how to handle this. It's the police. That detective, Jake Brogan. And you—well, you shouldn't be here."

46

The last time Jake looked at his alarm clock, the glowing green numbers said 2:47 A.M. He refused to look again. He stared at the ceiling, stretched out in bed, spy thriller on his chest, no idea what he'd read. He was doomed, as Jane always said. He'd longed to call her, but held off. Surveillance reported her situation as normal. She'd better have changed those locks.

It didn't make sense. The Jane he knew would not have left her door unlocked. He plopped the book onto the floor, turned over on his side, then tried the other side. He slept, right, every night? So why not tonight?

Nothing else made sense, either. The whole Bethany thing. When he'd arrived at her house, the social worker had been on the couch with Phillip, reading Dr. Seuss. No matter how they tried, cajoled, enticed, the boy would not say anything but "Batcar."

"Yes, Batcar," Jake had said, half-amused. At least the boy remembered him. *Poor kid*. But they got no further. He'd left Bethany—who seemed more flustered than usual, but maybe she was wiped out from dealing with two troubled children—with instructions to try to tape Phillip's words. He could put *her* on the stand, or before a judge, to report she'd heard the little boy refer to a baby. It'd be hearsay, of course. In court, some defense attorney would object the hell out of it.

And what if he'd been talking about his little sister, Phoebe? Jake had stayed for an hour, hung out watching Phillip and Phoebe power through Bethany's mac and cheese, but nothing. The boy said zippo. Which meant Jake was either nuts, or unlucky.

"Damn."

Diva, curled up on her special rug, opened her inquiring eyes to check on him, then closed them, keeping one paw on her stuffed frog.

Phillip Lussier wasn't the only thing keeping Jake awake. What if he'd arrested the wrong guy?

Jake went over it, yet again. Something snagged his brain, every time. For one, what motive would Curtis Ricker have for killing his ex-wife? Yes, he was a slug and a lowlife, but that didn't make him a murderer. What if Jake's drive to close the case had turned him into a narrow-minded hack?

Ricker's alibi was thin. He'd told Jake he was at Doyle's Bar. Impossible to confirm. But even more problematic, the kids, Phillip and Phoebe, weren't his. Maggie Gunnison's records substantiated that. So the whole "calling 911 to protect the children he cared about" theory made zero sense.

He'd had Officer Kurtz show Ricker's photo door-to-door on Callaberry, but she reported she'd come up dry. No one knew him, no one had ever seen him.

But. The keys. No reason for Ricker to have keys to Brianna's apartment unless he'd used them. The jerk had denied knowing anything about them. Not possible. Jake punched his pillow, tried to get comfortable.

Ricker was in the Suffolk County House of Correction, awaiting Wednesday's arraignment. Had Jake arrested an innocent man? Charged him with murder?

No. The keys were—the key. Jake sighed, turning over again. He had no one to talk to about this. DeLuca was probably off with Kat, enjoying double entendre pillow talk about blunt instruments.

"Shit." He said it out loud. This time Diva raised her head, floppy golden ears perked. Gave a questioning woof, and sat up. "No, not sit."

He sighed, staring at the green-lighted numerals on his alarm clock: 4:00 A.M. *Time to sleep.* But his brain would not shut off.

No one else lived at Ricker's apartment. So the keys could not belong to someone else. Unless someone else had access?

"Shit," Jake said again. This time, Diva bounced to her feet, picked up Frog, and deposited it on the edge of Jake's bed. "Good girl," he said. Poor dog was totally confused. She was probably as exhausted as he was, too.

He gave her a pat, then reached to his nightstand and clicked on his iPad. This was the stupidest idea ever. He could do this in the morning. *What the hell.* It was already morning.

He found the city of Boston Web site. Clicked on "Assessor's office." Then "property owner."

Typed in Ricker's address. *343 Edgeworth Street, Allston.*

Waited.

The screen dipped to black, then flashed into life.

Error 404, Server is unable to process your request.

Jake clicked off the tablet, resting it on his chest as he stared, once again, at the murky ceiling. *Of course.* Why did he think anything would work? Shadows slashed across the walls, headlights from an occasional car.

Grandpa Brogan always told him to trust his instincts. Did Jake even have the cop instinct? Sometimes it seemed he did, and was gratified by that. Even proud. Times like this, though, he wasn't so sure.

* * *

Jane stared at the ceiling, her downy white comforter pulled up to her chin. No way could she sleep. Had she ever lived through a weirder day? Tuck and the stupid truck, then her open apartment door. Jake's arrival. Phillip calling her Mama.

She closed her eyes, but that didn't work, and she stared at the white-painted ceiling again.

Why had Jake gone to see Bethany Sibbach? Bethany had been so nervous, upset that she'd been speaking to Jane without permission. There wasn't time for Jane to explain she and Jake were—whatever they were.

Jane punched her pillow, trying to get comfortable.

Bethany had grabbed Jane's parka and purse and shooed her into an upstairs study, with stern warnings to keep perfectly silent until Bethany came to get her. She'd tried like crazy to hear what the two were talking about in the living room, actually put her ear to the floor—you never know—but couldn't hear a thing. Trapped, she'd paged though about four *New Yorker*s and used up the battery on her iPhone catching up on e-mails. She couldn't risk the sound of voice mail. Her sister Lissa's wedding was looming, if you could call June "looming" in February. Liss was being relentless about making sure Jane would be there in time for the rehearsal, and get her dress altered, and find shoes, and was she bringing a date? Jane finished quietly tapping out her reassuring answer—except for the date part, for which there was nothing reassuring—just as the battery warning flashed.

Bethany had finally given the all-clear. Luckily, Jane had parked in the back, so Jake didn't see her car. But no matter how Jane pressed, Bethany had decided their "interview" was over. Spooked by Jake's arrival, she'd decided one close call was enough. She was done talking to Jane. About anything.

Jane punched the eiderdown again, stuck her bare feet out one side. Too hot. So much for her interview idea.

What was that?

She lay still, listening. Flat on her back. Was someone trying her front door?

She swung her feet to the floor, slid into her slippers, grabbed her cotton robe from the hook, and tiptoed down the hallway, yanking the terry belt closed and trying to decide whether to be angry or terrified. She paused, listening. Nothing.

Should she call 911?

Hawkeye, or whatever the cop's brother's name really was, was still supposedly monitoring her building from across the street. Or had the cops concluded she was a ditz who imagined catastrophes? And told him to forget about her?

Her front door. She listened. Nothing.

She checked in the peephole. Nothing. Left the chain on, clicked open the door. Peered through. Nothing. Opened the door. Nothing.

The hallway's wallpaper, tones of taupe stripes, glowed in the light of the fluted milk-glass sconces. Jane heard silence, only silence, not even a murmur from some insomniac's TV, or a gurgling dishwasher, or a midnight shower.

Flecks of sawdust from the locksmith's work sprinkled the hall's hardwood floor. Her new lock, shiny brass and solid, announced to all comers that changes had been made. Neena had left her three new keys with a note saying she'd kept the fourth for herself. So even if someone, whoever it might be, had made a copy of her other key—ridiculous, and unlikely, but still—they couldn't use it anymore.

Puffing out an annoyed breath, she closed the door, locked it, chained it. She held up three fingers, Girl Scout's promise: No more fear.

She was going. To. Sleep. No more fear.

Jane climbed back under the rumpled comforter, nestled into her pillow, closed her eyes.

Tomorrow, she and Tuck would go to Connecticut and see if they could figure out the connection between Carlyn Beerman and Tucker Cameron. If there was one.

Was Tuck her real daughter? Or the wrong girl?

47

Ella crunched the aluminum potpie pan into a shiny ball, tossed it into the wastebasket. It was late, now, really late. She'd been so eager to get some answers, she'd made all the phone calls first, then finally had dinner, poring over the family files and her notes again. She checked the clock above her toaster oven.

Almost three in the morning.

No wonder her brain was so fuzzy. She hadn't stayed up this late for—well, ever. But somewhere in her notes, somewhere in those talks with the newly minted families, there had to be the answer. She plopped into the one chair at the kitchen table. Maybe if she looked at the notes one more time. Tomorrow she'd be tired. It was already tomorrow.

Ella flipped to the next page of the yellow legal pad she'd brought home from the office.

First page were the notes on birth mother Margaret DaCosto. The DaCosto family was happy, content, even thrilled. Their "long-lost" daughter Leah—families always referred to them as lost, though "lost" was hardly what they were, since they'd been intentionally given up for adoption at birth—had become part of their lives. She'd moved into the DaCostos' home, and they were spending their days making up for lost time. Making amends.

Next page, Sarah Hoffner. She reluctantly described a more difficult transition. Krystyn Hoffner—who grew up as Helena—had arrived, and was a lovely young woman, but "never quite felt at home," Sarah said. They were in counseling. "Working it out."

Both families, though, were effusive about the Brannigan's supportive staff, especially mentioning Lillian Finch's tireless efforts to bring them together.

Ella had completely forgotten the families might bring up Lillian Finch. Or Mr. Brannigan. Should *she* be the one to tell them they were dead?

She'd fumbled for words when the question first came, finally deciding not to tell. If she *had* told, they might have called the Brannigan and mentioned that Ella had called. *That* would be difficult to explain.

Two families had not been home. The last call, though, was pretty interesting. Curious, even. The Lamonica family, in Brattleboro, Vermont. "We were just this week thinking of calling the Brannigan," Mrs. Lamonica told her.

Mrs. Lamonica explained her "long-lost" daughter Francesca, who grew up as Carol White, had gone to the family doctor after stepping on a nail and running a high fever. They'd done blood tests, checking for tetanus and other problems, and the lab results showed Carol had some blood work issues that perplexed the physician. Mrs. Lamonica herself didn't have those issues, so it was surprising her daughter would. Not impossible. Unlikely.

"So what did the doctor say about that?" Ella asked.

Mrs. Lamonica was silent for a moment, and Ella could hear muffled talking in the background.

"Sorry," the woman said, coming back on the line. "It's nothing, I'm sure. We're so happy, and Francesca—Carol—is perfect, she was only a newborn when I last saw her, and we're happy to be together. As a family. The doctor said she could be wrong, that the tests are—iffy."

A deep sigh. "But we wanted to check with Ms. Finch or her colleagues to see if there's anything we should know."

Ella had wrapped up the conversation with "it's late" and "of course" she'd have "someone from the Brannigan" call as soon as possible. She'd offered her private phone extension, reassuring Mrs. Lamonica that Ella would be her point person.

Whiskers jumped into her lap, jolting Ella back to the present.

"Was Carol White's birth name Francesca?" Ella asked her out loud. "Or who do you think she *really* is?"

Yes, this is Seller Heavy Metal, Kellianne answered, typing in the user name she'd chosen. Who'd be messaging on the Murderabilia system so late at night?

Buyer RedSky42 is typing popped onto her computer screen.

A customer. It *was. Already!* You were supposed to monitor your inbox for "transaction requests." Good thing she did.

The glow from Kellianne's monitor and the pinspot desk lamp gave her just enough light. Kev and Keefer were asleep, passed out, more likely, and her mom was staying over at the hospital again. No one would know what Kellianne was doing.

She'd posted her first "offerings," that's what the Web site called them, on the "to sell" page a few hours earlier. The teddy bears, the compact, the rabbit bowl, the nightgown. She'd had to fill out a bunch of personal stuff, too, and she made up most of it, hoping there'd be no way anyone would know, and when she clicked on "enter," it was all fine.

She'd chosen "Heavy Metal" when instructed to create a seller name. Made sense to use them, since you had to think people messing with this kind of stuff probably didn't want their personal info and the things they sold plastered all over who-knows-where. Payment and shipping were through a P.O. box in Idaho.

She'd clicked through a couple of other "to sell" items. A blouse with blood on it. A pillow with "peace" stitched into black velvet. What looked like a wedding ring.

Gross, gross, gross. People were totally sick. She pictured "RedSky42"—greasy hair, some skeevy guy, in a crappy apartment in some crappy city, getting his kicks touching stuff that once belonged to people who were dead. Murdered.

But who was she to judge? It was—what did they call it? Supply and demand. She had the supply. And the demand would bring her some bucks, and then her freedom.

Now, someone was contacting her. It was all going to work.

The message appeared: *Do you have the teddy bears?* Then it disappeared.

"Huh?" Kellianne whispered. What was this guy trying to pull?

Buyer RedSky42 is typing popped up again.

Kellianne waited. Then read the new message.

Not teddy bears. Compact. And the nightgown. How much will you take for them?

48

"**You ready? I** brought lattes. I must say, Jane, looks like you could use this." Tuck handed her a Starbucks venti, then gestured to the apartment stairs. "We taking your car or mine? I'm all gassed up, but fine with me if you want to drive."

Jane gestured her inside, taking a grateful sip. "Yeah, I'd rather drive. Thanks for this."

"You have a rough night?" Tuck, in black jeans, black parka vest, and buckled boots, looked her up and down. "How come you're not dressed yet? I thought we decided on eight. Unless you're planning to win over Carlyn Beerman with the terry cloth robe look. You're gonna be cold, though."

Jane backed into her entryway, almost tripping over Coda, who'd placed herself exactly where Jane's bare feet would step. "Come in, have a seat, watch out for the silly cat. Yeah, didn't get much sleep. I'll be ready in a sec. Just have to throw on my jeans. Did you call Carlyn?"

Tuck had plopped onto the couch, flapped open a *New Yorker*. Coda jumped up beside her, batting the edges of the cover. "Nope. Like I said yesterday. If I do, I'm gonna have to explain, and I don't want to explain on the phone. And if I say, 'I want to talk to you about something,' it'll freak her out."

"Maybe," Jane said. The whole thing reeked of wild geese, but it was better than staying home and watching out the window for imaginary intruders. Probably imaginary.

Tuck had been supportive yesterday when all hell broke loose, and even, somehow, retrieved Coda. Humoring her was the least she could do.

Jane took another sip of latte, heading down the hallway, then turned back. "Hey, Tuck?"

"Mmm?" Tuck, lounged against the couch cushions, didn't look up from the magazine.

"When you were in the car yesterday, did you see a red cat collar on the floor?"

"So that's that, at least. Case closed. Thanks, Kat." Jake handed the ME back her manila file folder and clicked open his BlackBerry, checking for messages. Coming to work on three—maybe two—hours of sleep was going to be a challenge. At least City Hall's property ownership Web site should be back up and running this morning. If not, he'd just use the phone, now that the rest of the city was also awake.

Jake was not looking forward to the Ricker murder arraignment, set for this afternoon's court session, provided some poor public defender had the bad luck to be appointed for him. But the news Kat McMahan just revealed to him about the Brannigan case could make his life one level less nuts.

The two stood outside the revolving glass door of Boston Police Headquarters, corner of Ruggles and Tremont Streets, under the ornate silver seal that reminded all visitors that Boston had needed cops since 1630. Kat's

ME van idled in the no-parking zone by the curb. Jake had parked his cruiser down in the motor pool, hoping someone would gas it up and maybe wash off some of the gritty road salt.

The Supe was expecting Jake at 8:35, no earlier, no later, according to the confirmation text that just arrived. Jake didn't look forward to reporting the Tillson arrest, which still twisted his gut when he thought about it. At least now he could mitigate with the good news—the cause of Niall Brannigan's death.

"You put it in writing yet?" Jake continued. "I didn't see the three-oh-three in the file. But great. Natural causes. Like I said. Case closed."

"Possibly," Kat said.

Jake looked up from his BlackBerry screen. "Huh? What do you mean, possibly?"

Two uniforms brushed by them, cursing the Celtics' latest defeat.

"They suck," one said.

"Give 'em a chance," the other said, disappearing through the revolving door.

"Then they'll suck worse," the first cop said to the glass as he pushed it.

"Two days ago," Kat shook her head, watching them. "That game was two days ago."

"Boston." Jake waved her off. "But Brannigan. You said it was a confirmed heart attack. Myocardial infarction. Natural causes."

Today Kat wore her white lab coat under a neon orange parka. Her black baseball cap asked DR. WHO?

She flapped her arms against her sides, puffed out a breath, and watched the vapor evaporate. "I love that. We don't have that in L.A. And yes, Detective, as I informed your friend DeLuca, Niall Brannigan died of a heart attack."

"So what's the problem?"

"Well." The medical examiner cleared her throat, and raised a finger. "One thing."

"I'm not kidding, it was on the floor, where your feet are now." Jane had argued over the cat collar, with Tuck, once again in the passenger seat, all the way to the Mass Pike entrance. "I suppose I could have dropped it when I took her to the vet the other day. Maybe Coda wasn't even wearing it when she got out. But I gotta tell you, Tuck."

She accelerated past the green light at the tolls, and yes, damn it, checked her rearview for the black truck. Which of course was not there.

"There's no way I can talk myself into that. The silly cat was wearing her collar when I left home yesterday morning. And I *locked* the stupid door. When I got back, the door was open and the cat was gone. And then, boom, I find the collar in the car. That—is freaky."

The light poles flashed by, just like yesterday. Today's adventure better have a more satisfactory ending.

"Yeah, got to admit." Tuck pulled down the sun visor. Jane looked over, saw her smoothing one eyebrow, frowning at her reflection.

"Tuck. Listen. The nasty phone call. The open door. The cat collar. I think I'd better call—" Jane paused. *Jake,* she had been about to say, tell him the whole thing and hope he didn't think she was a nut. But Tuck couldn't know that was an option. Come to think of it, it wasn't.

"Alex," Jane said out loud.

Damn. That reminded her she still hadn't gotten in touch with Hec. She really wanted to see his photos of the Callaberry Street neighbors. What if he'd deleted them? She'd pull into the first rest stop they saw. Call him.

"But you said Alex ordered you to stay away from the

Register, kiddo. Now you're 'away.'" Tuck took her paper cup of coffee from the console, toasted Jane. "And like you said, your place has a new lock. Only you have a key. I found the cat. That cop or whoever is watching your building. We're going to find the truth about Carlyn Beerman. So it all works out. Right?"

Tuck took a sip of coffee, leaned back in her seat, and propped her boots on the dashboard. "Right?"

Jane picked up her own coffee, watching the road in front of them. She wasn't quite sure of the answer.

49

"**What do you** mean, one thing?" Jake looked at his watch, impatient. He had seven minutes until his meeting with the Supe. Even if the elevator cooperated he'd need four minutes to get upstairs and another thirty seconds to walk the carpeted eighth-floor corridor to the corner office. That gave him two and a half minutes to hear what Kat had to say. So it better be good. And fast. "One thing about what?"

Kat took off a leather glove, clicked open her ME briefcase, took out a manila file.

"I read that," Jake said.

"Not this one." Kat opened the file.

Two minutes left. "So?"

"So," Kat said. "Yes, Mr. Brannigan had a heart attack. But—not in his car."

Jake blinked, mentally reviewing the scene. The man in the driver's seat he later learned was Brannigan, hands at his sides, head plonked on the steering wheel, seat belt on.

"Why do you think that?"

"I was there when Crime Scene opened the car door. You were off with—wherever you went."

"Yeah, and?" He'd gone to check on Jane. But that couldn't matter.

"When Crime Scene tried to open the car door, it opened."

"So?" *Ticktock*. Get to the point.

"So nothing. We figured maybe he hadn't locked it yet. But Jake, there were no keys. Not in the car, not anywhere."

"Yeah yeah, I know that. D and I discussed it on scene. Maybe he went to the car to get something. Maybe he left it unlocked."

Kat shrugged. "Could be. But Jake. Where are the keys now? Where was he going? Went to the car to get something to take *where*?"

Jake stared at her. He'd been so focused on Jane that he'd—

"What's more, I found mud and slush on the inside surfaces of his shoes. I mean . . ." Kat lifted one booted foot. Pointed to her instep with a pale manicured fingernail. "Right along here, and on both feet. And up the insides of his pants legs. The inside only. If you're walking, any wetness is going to accumulate on your whole foot, evenly distributed. So now, imagine how Brannigan's condition, the pattern of moisture on his pants and shoes, could have happened. See what I mean?"

She paused, waiting for him to answer.

Jake was going to be late to the meeting, but it wouldn't matter, because Kat's findings meant he'd screwed this one up. Royally. And it would only get worse from here on. The Jane thing. Exactly what they'd feared—the distraction—looked like it finally made him blow a case. If he'd stayed at the scene on Margolin Street, like he should have, he'd have focused on this. Figured it out. Instead he'd blown it.

"Jake?"

"Yeah. Kat. I hear you." He tilted one foot sideways, touching his instep to the ground. He tried doing it with his other foot at the same time. Couldn't. His knees knocked together, and he wouldn't have been able to stay upright to walk. He'd need—*Shit*. "The only way that could happen is if someone was holding Brannigan up. Supporting him. "Maybe he wasn't even dead."

"Yeah. It's possible he wasn't. Look."

Kat grabbed one of Jake's arms, draped it over her shoulder. They stood face to face. He, a good five inches taller, smelled vanilla and a whiff of roses in her faint perfume. "Now imagine someone else on your other side. Supporting you. Half-dragging you. Down a path or some such, to your car. To an observer, it might present as if you're drunk. But you're—woozy. Dying. What would happen to your feet?"

"This looks cozy." DeLuca's voice preceded him, coming through the revolving door before he did. "Should I give you two some privacy?"

"Damn, you caught us," Kat said. She stuck out her tongue at D. "But perfect timing, actually. Let Jake put his other arm around your shoulders. Then you can help me drag Jake to his car."

"Huh?" DeLuca took a step back. "What the hell?"

"Let's just say we're screwed." Jake looked at his watch. "And we're late for our meeting with the Supe. *Shit*. I should have gone to law school."

50

"Hector Underhill, please. Skim milk, please." Jane held her cell phone tight to her ear, talking to the *Register*'s receptionist and the barista behind the Lavazza counter at the same time. The turnpike rest stop smelled like fried everything with bleach on top. Glaring fluorescents colored it floor to ceiling in unnatural blue-white. Tuck headed for the twenty-four-hour mini-mart, insisting she needed to stock up on Swedish fish and corn nuts. *Disgusting*. Jane was sticking with lattes. Especially this morning, running on empty. Three hours of sleep. Four, max. "Yes, please, extra-large. Yes, I'll hold."

The *Register*'s annoying hold "entertainment" played a recording of the morning's headlines. "MBTA officials fear rate hikes as deficits mount" and "City Hall bigwigs charged with computer fraud in growing scandal." Wonder who'd scored the City Hall story? Some lucky duck certain to stay employed. Someone who wasn't banished.

"Also this morning, the *Register* reports police have made an arrest in the Sunday afternoon murder of a still-unidentified Callaberry Street resident. The woman was found dead in her kitchen on . . ."

"Ma'am?" The barista held out a steaming paper cup. Her fingernails were polished purple, and her black T-shirt was XS when it should have been M. "Ma'am?"

"One second," Jane mouthed. She held up a finger, pointed to her phone, wincing. She hated to be rude, but she needed to hear. "So sorry."

"Boston Police confirm the arrest of one Cur—," the recording continued.

"Ma'am? You'll need to take your drink, ma'am." The barista's voice grew louder, more insistent. Jane heard an elaborately weary sigh from the woman behind her in line.

"In other news," the recorded voice went on, "the Boston Celtics . . ."

A human voice interrupted. "Hector Underhill is on another call right now, would you like to leave a message? Or hold?"

"Thanks. I'll hold." Jamming the cell phone between her cheek and shoulder, Jane accepted the almost too-hot-to-hold latte, defeated. She grabbed two napkins, wrapping the brown paper layers around the steaming cup. Maybe the newsstand past the McDonald's still had this morning's paper? Still, reading it would only increase her depression. *The police made an arrest in Callaberry. She'd missed the whole thing.*

Shit.

She headed for the newsstand, phone clamped to her ear, waiting for Hec, stewing. This sucked. It blew her scoop on the Brianna Tillson reveal, since the moment they got to court the cops would provide the name of the victim. All would be public.

So much for that.

But. *On the other hand.*

Jane stopped. Stood up straight, realizing her new reality. A good reality. A flame-haired woman toting a matching puppy and trailing two flame-haired kids bumped her, jostling her latte.

"Sorry, honey." The woman gestured at her entourage in explanation. "Kids, you know?"

"Soda!" one child whined.

"Bafroom!" said the other.

Jane moved out of their way, slurping up the foam that had sloshed through the opening in the plastic lid. The hold recording began the news cycle again. Maybe this time she'd at least get the name of the suspect. See if it was someone she'd interviewed that day. *Where the heck was Hec?* She smiled. She must be even more tired than she thought.

Thing was. She took another sip. If they'd arrested the bad guy, then whoever was warning her to stay away from the story—that was over now. Wasn't it? The bad guy—whoever they'd arrested and she could find out by reading the paper—was surely the one who'd threatened her.

She nodded, agreeing with herself. That meant the murder suspect wouldn't be phoning her again, or tailgating her in a black pickup truck this morning, or breaking into her apartment. Yay, Jake.

But wait. Why hadn't Jake told her about the arrest? Okay, easy one. Maybe, when he was reassuring her that she was under surveillance, the arrest hadn't happened yet. She reached the newsstand. Wonder who'd written the story? If Hec *ever* came to the phone, he could give her the scoop.

"Hey, kiddo. Want a fish?" Tuck had her own cell phone in one hand. With the other she held out a cellophane bag of red gummies.

"Oh, hey, Tuck, no thanks, I—Oh. Hello? Hec? Yeah. It's Jane Ryland. I'm calling about the photos. The ones we took on Callaberry Street? I was thinking—"

And like that, poof, her great idea went down the drain. Even if Hec had the digital card with the photos taken during their door-to-door, it didn't matter. The police made an arrest. Every reporter on the planet would get shots of the suspect in a perp walk or the courtroom.

Tuck bit off a red tail, waved the rest of the gummy fish at her. "What's wrong, Jane?"

Jane held up a hand. Hec's voice in one ear, Tuck's in the other, and it all ran together in a big tangle of failure. The Tillson story was over. There wouldn't be any flashy Jane Ryland bylines. She might be safe at home, so that was a relief, but at the *Register* she was back to square one. That was not a good thing.

"Hec, never mind," Jane said. "Keep the pictures, though, okay? You never know when—"

She paused as Hec interrupted her. "Well, I'm actually in the fabulous Natick rest stop, on the Mass Pike. With—did you ever meet Tucker Cameron? We're driving out to Connecticut to—well, anyway. But about the Tillson case. Who'd the police arrest?"

"Jane?" Tuck was holding up her cell phone, shaking it back and forth. "Carlyn Beerman's at *home*. We should *go*. Jane? I don't like to interrupt, but—"

The flame-haired family exploded out of the bathroom door, the little girl wailing as her brother ran after the mop-tailed puppy that was now on the loose, snaking a pink leash across the rest stop's dingy floor, yapping.

"Grab her, Allan! Grab her!" the mother shrieked.

"Sorry, Hec, I didn't hear you." Jane gestured to Tuck with her latte, trying to telegraph *I can't hear both of you at the same time*.

"*Jane.*" Tuck held up her phone again, waving it at her.

Tuck's phone was turned off, the screen obviously black, so what was Jane supposed to see? Hec was saying he had no idea about the arrest, but Tuck was so insistent she could barely understand him.

"We have to go, Jane." Tuck stuffed the Swedish fish into her tote bag, then the phone. "Now."

"Hec? I have to call you back. If you get the scoop, call me. Thanks, dude." Jane clicked off, then trotted after Tuck, already headed for the door.

"What the hey, Tuck? I was on the phone."

"I'm really sorry." Tuck pushed through the glass door. "But I thought about what you said, about not knowing if she was home? Carlyn? So I called, and she answered."

"What'd you say?" Jane, pushing through behind Tuck, raised her voice to be heard. They headed to Jane's car.

"I hung up. But at least we know she's home now, so we should hurry."

Jane clicked open the car. "Hung up?"

"They told me she was my *mother*, you know?" Tuck looked at Jane over the roof of the Audi, then slid into the passenger seat.

"But you're pretty sure she isn't." Jane put on her seat belt, turned the ignition, shifted into reverse.

Tuck stared straight ahead. "Right. So now *I've* got to tell her. That I'm a *lie*. That what she was told is not true. I suddenly—couldn't do it. It didn't seem right."

Jane had to agree. "Yeah. I guess it's not something you could say over the phone from a turnpike rest stop."

"Exactly. I can't explain how happy she was to see me that first time. She said she'd thought about me every day. Missed me, every day. I kept envisioning her face, looking at me with that . . . love. So I just hung up." Tuck sighed. "So. *Drive*. Let's go. Do this. Get this the hell over with. Then we're going to find out exactly why this happened. To both of us."

51

Yes. She'd simply get in her car, and go.

Maybe.

Ella sat at her desk, her old desk, not ready to move her possessions into Lillian's quite yet. It was unnerving that Lillian's body was still at the Medical Examiner's. *Morgue.* Ella closed her eyes to make the thought go away. According to office scuttlebutt, the police hadn't decided if she'd committed suicide, or if her death was suspicious.

When Ella arrived at the Brannigan this morning, Wednesday, Lillian's desk had been cleaned out. Nothing on the top, nothing in the drawers. The desk surface, gleaming, held a faint fragrance of lemon oil. Ella had predicted they'd take everything, and they had. The roses. The photos.

Knowing Lillian was dead was hard enough to accept. Seeing her possessions gone made it final.

She'd never be invited to tea at Lillian's again. Never go inside that beautiful home. Wonder what would happen to all of Lillian's crystal and china? Her silver? She had no family Ella knew of.

She stirred her pink ceramic mug of English Breakfast, then dunked the tea bag up and down. Up and down. Deciding. Should she go?

Her computer monitor showed a map, a green line highlighting the suggested route from the Brannigan to Norrisville, Connecticut. A red teardrop labeled "destination" marked 4102 North Ritter Lane. Carlyn Beerman's house.

Driving time: two hours.

Collins Munson had offered her the day off, so if anyone asked she could say she came in and tried to work, but Munson was right, it was difficult and she needed more time. *Yes*. She'd go.

She hit "print," listened to the whir as the map emerged from the printer along the wall. It was just after nine. Maybe she should . . .

Ella eyed her desk phone, then the manila file open on her desk. She chewed her bottom lip, considering.

Before she could decide not to, she dialed, listened as the phone rang. The Brannigan's phones all had caller-ID blocked, of course, no problem there.

"Carlyn Beerman," a voice said.

The woman sounded annoyed. Snippy. Maybe Carlyn was having a bad day.

"Who *is* this?" the voice said. "Why do you keep calling me?"

"Oh." Ella had forgotten she was going to hang up. "Uh, wrong number."

She clicked the receiver back into place. The map lay in the printer bin. All she had to do was . . .

A knock at her door, and before she could say anything, it swung open. Grace O'Connor, dressed up in a black suit with a ruffled blouse, kept one hand on the doorknob.

"I saw you were here," she said. "I thought you might—"

Ella stood up so quickly her desk chair tipped backward. It paused a fraction of a second, then crashed onto the floor.

"Oh, gosh." Grace hurried across the room, helping Ella right it. "Are you okay?"

"Oh, sure, yes." Ella tried to think. "It always does that."

"Shall I get your printing?" Grace gestured a hand toward the printer.

"No, no, it's fine," Ella brushed past her, grabbed the map to Carlyn Beerman's home and folded it in half, hiding the directions. *Whew.* "You look nice."

"Well, the funeral. Mr. Brannigan's. That's why I came in. I thought you might need a ride." Grace eyed Ella's everyday skirt and cardigan, then pushed back the silky ruffle at her wrist and checked her watch. "Didn't anyone tell you? Ardith Brannigan set it for today. Ten thirty. At All Saints."

Ella slid two fingers along the fold of the map, then creased it again.

"I'm going to run home and change, that's what I planned," Ella lied. There would be no trip to Connecticut today. Her questions for Carlyn Beerman would have to wait. She smiled, trying to convey sorrow and authority. "I'll see you there."

"He wouldn't have been coming *here,* that's the one thing we know." Jake ran a finger down the strip of the yellow tape sealing the perimeter of Lillian Finch's front door. "Lillian Finch was dead, been dead for about two days when Niall Brannigan arrived. The back door's taped up now, too. So no way was he inside this house."

"True," DeLuca said. "Seems like."

Jake turned, looked out over the tree-lined Margolin Street, mostly empty front porches and empty driveways, each house with one blue and one green plastic trash bin wheeled to the sidewalk, waiting for the morning pickup. Each house with a shoveled front walk, concrete or flagstone or pavers, lined with browned grass and muddy flowerbeds. Was Niall Brannigan dragged down along one of them? Which one? "So. Police 101. His car was parked across the street. Who saw it?"

"The what's-her-name woman, funny hat, remember? Any leads there?"

Jake pulled out his BlackBerry, following DeLuca's gaze. "Dolly Richards. Hennessey and Kurtz say not. Their report says they hit every door half a block up, half a block back, and got zippo. According to their canvass yesterday P.M., no residents knew Niall Brannigan, no one's positive they'd ever seen his car here before. So if you believe the Kurtz and Hennessey version of the world, we're—"

"Screwed."

"Yeah." Jake ran the zipper of his jacket up and down, thinking. "The only logical reason Niall Brannigan would have come to Margolin Street is to see Lillian Finch— someone he knew wasn't home. And to go inside a place he couldn't possibly enter."

"Even if for some reason he had a key, right? The place is sealed."

Keys. Which only reminded Jake of the arrest of Curtis Ricker and the woodshed meeting in the Supe's office that morning. First Jake had to admit he was iffy on the Ricker arrest, not the best beginning to an already inauspicious morning. After that, the Supe read them the riot act about the Brannigan thing, wondering why he and D hadn't spotted the telltale mud pattern on the vic's pants. A damn good question, and Jake didn't exactly want to face the answer. What's more, the mud evidence turned a natural into a potential homicide, and made Jake's workload nearly impossible. Tillson. Finch. Brannigan. The baby. Even though no one else thought there was a baby.

And Jane.

Jake didn't need easy. But he wouldn't mind trying it about now.

"Yeah. The whole thing sucks." *Keys*. "Okay. The keys. Niall Brannigan didn't have any keys. No car keys, no house keys. Those keys are somewhere. Wherever he'd been. We have to canvass again."

D took out his spiral notebook, flipped to a new page. "I live for door to doors, you know that."

"You take this side, I'll take that side." Jake ignored D's sarcasm, pointing his BlackBerry toward the cul de sac, then toward the cross street. They had no time. "You got a photo? There's an hour before Brannigan's funeral. That's one hour to find out where the hell Niall Brannigan was going, and why. And some kind of a lead on who dragged him to his car."

"That's why we get the big police bucks," DeLuca said. "Just another morning in paradise, redoing what Frick and Frack allegedly did already. Followed by a funeral."

"Hang on." Jake scanned the case notes Kurtz and Hennessey compiled, searching for a question and answer he'd realized was not there.

"You got to be kidding me," Jake said. "Did those two bozos ever think to just ask Brannigan's wife where he was going?"

52

"Is Carlyn Beerman related to Snow White?" Jane buzzed down her window, looking at the shingled cottage with the white gingerbread shutters. She'd parked on the side of the winding road near the white-posted mailbox marked 4102 North Ritter Lane. A wreath of greenery entwined with tiny red berries decorated the bright yellow front door, and a redwood birdfeeder on a metal pole twittered with starlings and fluttering sparrows.

"I know. Kind of Disney," Tuck said. "She didn't seem so—whatever this is—when we met at that hotel. I'd pictured a condo. Maybe a cat. Oh. Not that there's anything wrong with that."

"*Thanks.* Least she's not, you know, the evil one. Not in a middle-of-nowhere Hallmark card like this. But there's no car in the driveway."

"So what? There's a garage."

"Hey." Jane pointed to one of the curtained front windows. "Curtain moved. Second from the left. Someone's inside."

As they watched, the curtain was pulled pack, and a woman's face, barely visible, peeked out.

"That's her." Tuck unsnapped her seat belt, clicked open the car door. "You ready? We're doing this."

* * *

"I don't care that your computer went down last night." Jake couldn't believe they were giving him such a hard time. "You're the assessor's office. I *did* mention this is Detective Brogan, Boston PD, correct? Happy to send a couple of uniforms over to pull the info, of course, but I figured you might prefer to do it this way. . . . Sure. Delighted to hold."

D had swerved the cruiser into a no-standing spot in front of All Saints Church, where Niall Brannigan's funeral was scheduled to begin in fifteen minutes. Their neighborhood canvass resulted in absolute zero. Lots of nobody-homes. Nobody admitted to recognizing Niall Brannigan. A few were maybes on the green car. "I might have seen it" was about as specific as anyone got. No times or dates.

According to Kurtz, who alleged she had asked but "forgot to write it down," Brannigan's wife, Ardith, had no idea why her husband would have been on Margolin Street Monday night.

"She told me her husband was always off somewhere, that he never told her where," Kurtz had reported when Jake called. "Said she'd 'given up' asking."

"You set?" DeLuca unclicked his seat belt, drained the last of his coffee, tossed the empty cup onto the floor of the backseat.

"I'm still on hold with City Hall," Jake said. "But what about the wife? Do we maybe like her for it? What she told Kurtz sounds like there was trouble in the Brannigan marriage. Right? 'Always off somewhere' and 'given up asking' is pretty much wife shorthand for a lying husband. Maybe Ardith killed Lillian."

DeLuca nodded, considering. "I hear ya."

"Okay. Say Brannigan is having an affair with Lillian Finch. The wife suspects."

"So Ardith kills Lillian. Then, after Brannigan himself has a fortuitous heart attack, somewhere, the wife drives her dead husband to the love shack and leaves the body. And takes his keys. And where does she go, then?" D spun out a theory. "Pretty elaborate. I've seen weirder, sure. Still. Unlikely."

"Yeah. But Brannigan had to be going there." Jake heard the sound change on the cell phone, and raised a palm to put D on hold. "Yes, I'll keep waiting. Okay, D, how about—what?"

"Well, maybe it's not suicide. Maybe Brannigan offed Lillian Finch. For some reason? Even—an affair gone sour." DeLuca pointed at Jake. "Hey. What if he was going to retrieve evidence? Then discovered the place was sealed, thwarting his plans, and then he had a heart attack."

"Thwarting," Jake said. "Good one. That works, except for the mud thing. And the missing key thing. Sure would be helpful to know how Lillian Finch died. Confirm it's a suicide or not. Can't you push your Kat on those tox screens?"

"She's not 'my' Kat," DeLuca said. "Tox screens take weeks, you know that."

"Okay, yes, I'm here," Jake told the voice on the phone. "And have been, for—Yes, I have a pen."

Jake listened as the clerk at City Hall read him the ownership information for 343 Edgeworth Street, Curtis Ricker's house.

"Well, now." Jake clicked off the phone. Things were looking up.

"Funeral's about to start." D opened his door, looked at Jake. "What?"

"D? Guess who owns the duplex Curtis Ricker's renting?"

"What is this, *Jeopardy!*?"

"Leonard Perl."

"Leonard—"

"Perl. The absentee landlord who also owns Brianna Tillson's building. The one who never called us back. The one from Fort Something, Florida, according to the crime scene cleanup—"

Jake stopped, mid-sentence. He stared out the windshield.

"Earth to Jake?"

"Hang on," Jake held up a palm. "Hang on. I've gotta think for a minute."

Jake watched the line of mourners, heads down, bundled in hats and scarves and heavy coats, filing along the sidewalk and up the broad front steps of All Saints. The winter sun glistened on the damp sidewalks and curbs, clumps of snow blowing down from tree branches once lined with white. All Saints' celebrated carillon invited the mourners to "Abide with Me."

A young woman, frizzy red hair, hunched into her coat and walking by herself. A tweed-coated tall guy in horn rims, escorting an elegant white-haired woman wrapped in a black fringed shawl and wearing a black veil. Could she be Ardith Brannigan, the wife? Jake didn't relish approaching her.

The parade of mourners blurred as Jake stared past it all, now almost unseeing, envisioning the kitchen floor of Callaberry Street, the voice in the hallway, the request for the Afterwards crew to start their crime scene cleanup. And the puzzle pieces fell into place.

"Close your door," Jake said. "Start the car. We're gonna miss this funeral. Because someone else is about to get—"

"Detective Brogan, this is base," a voice crackled over Jake's radio. "Do you copy? What's your twenty?"

"Copy." Jake looked at D, inquiring. D shrugged. "Twenty" was shorthand leftover from the old days of police ten codes. A new dispatcher would have said, *What's your location?* Jake imagined he could hear some kind of stress in dispatch's voice, though they were trained to hide it.

"Harrison Street, two blocks from HQ," Jake said.

"You're needed at this location, Detective," the dispatcher said. "Now."

"At Lillian Finch's house?" Ella struggled to understand what Wendy Nunziatta was telling her. Seated next to each other in one of All Saints' carved wooden pews, the two had piled their coats and scarves beside them. Ella had barely made it home in time, racing into the shower, throwing on a black dress with only a little bit of cat hair on it. She pulled her cardigan close. No one would care how she looked.

Wendy worked in Collins Munson's office at the Brannigan, and Ella was glad to have someone to sit with. Wendy was a yakker, kind of a gossip, everyone knew that, but in this case, what she was saying sounded interesting. In the front pew, Ardith Brannigan—Ella could see only the back of her black suit jacket, the black lace veil covering her silvery hair, and a white-gloved hand—accepted the condolences of a line of mourners.

Ella kept her voice low. Watched to make sure no one else was listening. "The police found Mr. Brannigan's body at *Ms. Finch's* house?"

"Yes." Wendy covered her mouth with one hand, and leaned in closer to Ella, whispering. "Well, not *in* her house, of course, it was all locked up by the cops. But he was in his car. Outside her house. Across the street. And now, according to—well, anyway—now, the police are trying to figure out why he was there."

"He was *there*, really?" Ella was having a hard time processing this. *Niall Brannigan at Lillian Finch's house?* She was *dead*. Ella murmured, so only Wendy could hear. "But he had a heart attack, right? Oh, sorry."

A couple Ella didn't recognize edged in front of them in the pew, the woman's paisley shawl dragging over Ella's lap. Ella scooched against the back of the pew, pressing her knees to one side, until the couple finally settled in their seats.

"Well, he was *there*. That's all I know. Can you believe it?" Wendy pulled a Kleenex from a little woven pouch, then unwrapped a yellow hard candy and popped it into her mouth. "So sad."

Ella thought about how devoted Ms. Finch was to Mr. Brannigan. But after she died, he'd asked for the records on her last round of calls. Why? Ella, of course, had never actually delivered them because of—what happened. What if Mr. B. *suspected* Ms. Finch was sending people the wrong children? And feared she was putting his agency in legal jeopardy?

Or, wait. Ella picked up a leather-bound prayer book from the back of the pew in front of her and pretended to study a random page. She'd pretty much convinced herself Lillian Finch had committed suicide after she realized she'd made a mistake. But what if *Mr. Brannigan* had been the one in the wrong? And Ms. Finch threatened to tell what he had done?

"Do they know how Ms. Finch died?" Ella had to ask.

"No." Wendy leaned in again, so close that Ella could smell butterscotch. "How weird is this, you know? Mr. Brannigan. Before that, just two days before, Ms. Finch. I actually think it's a little scary."

"Do you know if the police think they're . . ." Ella began.

"Shh." Wendy put a finger to her lips, frowning. "It's starting. Hey. Sit down. Where're you going?"

"I'll be right back." Ella put the prayer book on the pew to save her spot. She might regret this, but she might regret it more if she didn't. "I have to make a phone call."

53

"No, I've never seen *that*, either." Carlyn Beerman was staring at the bracelet Tuck dangled between them. They sat side by side on a flowery couch, Jane in the wing chair. "It has your name on it? Tucker? And you say it was with you? When you were—given up?"

Crackling logs in a redbrick fireplace turned the scene fairy-tale perfect, but Jane knew what Tuck had just revealed was hardly the stuff of happy endings. Carlyn's delighted greeting of Tuck, and her instant welcome to the sunlight-filled cottage, brought tears to Jane's eyes.

She should have stayed out of it. Why was she always so compelled to help?

"Yes. The bracelet and note were attached to my blanket. That's what my . . ." Tuck paused, and Jane could almost hear her selecting words. ". . . adoptive mother told me."

Jane cradled her hot tea—chamomile, in a chunky earthenware mug—wishing she could be anywhere but a chintz chair in the Connecticut countryside hearing someone's dreams get crushed. Carlyn had first been bewildered by the note Tuck described, and now the bracelet provided the *coup de grâce*.

"I see." Carlyn didn't reach for the bracelet, kept her hands folded in her lap. "You're sure."

Tuck slid it back into the velvet drawstring bag. Tied the braided cord. Zipped it into her tote. *Case closed.* "I'm sure."

Strange, watching the two of them, identical profiles, really, each with exactly the same arched eyebrows. Even the way they crossed their legs seemed similar, though Carlyn was all soft edges in a filmy lavender scarf and a crinkly ankle-length skirt, and Tuck her opposite in tight jeans tucked into sleek black boots. Carlyn's graying hair, short and spiky, might have once been as dark as Tuck's, even though Tuck's was now that funny auburn. They certainly *looked* related. On the other hand, Jane hadn't resembled her own mother at all.

"So that's why we're here, Carlyn." Tuck's voice wavered only a little. "The bracelet. And the note. I'm sorry to just show up. I didn't want to tell you over the phone because it seemed so—I don't know."

"You're sure."

Tuck nodded.

Carlyn dabbed under her eyes with a shredded Kleenex, then tucked the tissue into the ribbed wristband of her cornflower blue sweater. "How could that happen? It *seemed* right, when we met, didn't it?"

"I don't know," Tuck said. "I don't know *what's* right. Or how anything . . . seems. All I know is, I'm so sorry. I'm so very sorry."

The fire popped, a glowing ember hitting the woven metal fireplace screen. No one moved. Wishing she was invisible, or better yet, not there at all, Jane watched the two women, one younger, one twenty years older, who had been promised a miracle, then bitterly disappointed. Was there anything she should say? Or do?

Tuck broke the silence.

"But, actually, the reason I brought Jane is, I'm enraged. Aren't you? Carlyn? I waited all my life for this.

Then they called, and I came to meet you, and it was terrifying and then wonderful, and now, I mean, these are people's *lives* they're messing with. How could they—" Tuck's voice caught. She gulped, and tried again. "How can they *do* this?"

Carlyn reached over, touched Tuck's knee, then took her hand away. "Why do people do what they do? I was in love with a professor who never cared about me. I was eighteen. *Eighteen!* I had to give up my own child. I *never* wanted to. Now I'm almost fifty. For years, I battled regret. And anger. But you know? That's destructive. It steals your soul, honey. Incredibly disappointed? Yes. Disheartened? Yes. But enraged? After all this time? I'll have to—"

"Listen, Carlyn." Tuck kept talking. "Jane's a reporter for the Boston *Register* newspaper. I don't work there anymore, remember?"

"Of course, honey, but—"

"And I think if something went wrong with *us*—if the agency sent me to you incorrectly . . ."

Tuck paused, and an ember popped, filling the silence.

"I see. That it could have happened to other people, too." Carlyn finished Tuck's sentence, then turned to Jane, frowning. "Is that what you're suggesting? Jane? Have you ever heard of such a thing?"

Jane took a sip of tea, then set her mug on a raffia coaster. Shook her head. "I haven't," she said. "And it would be very difficult to find out. Some adoptions are 'open,' those wouldn't be the problem. It's the sealed ones, like yours and Tuck's, that'd be in question. But those closed adoptions are confidential, and private, and protected. We could never have access to those cases, unless someone complained. And even then it would have to be a public complaint, since if they simply contacted the Brannigan, no one but those involved would ever know. It would be in the agency's best interest to keep it quiet."

"Lawsuits, maybe?" Carlyn asked.

Jane held out both palms, agreeing. "Possibly. We can check. If you like. Of course, I'd predict if there were lawsuits, they'd be gagged by confidentiality agreements, maybe even completely sealed."

"But what they did is unacceptable." Tuck crossed her arms over her chest, matched Carlyn's frown. "We have to pursue it."

"Or not." Jane knew Tuck was hurting, but it should also be Carlyn's decision.

"Action is always more effective than anger." Carlyn stood, brushing down her skirt with the palms of both hands. "And I think . . . we're *required* to look into it. Not simply for our sake. For everyone's. Let me show you something."

Reaching under the coffee table, Carlyn pulled out a black portfolio, unzipped three sides. When she placed the folder flat on the table, Jane saw it was filled with papers, what looked like documents, and clippings. Carlyn selected a newspaper clipping attached to a pink piece of typing paper.

Jane recognized the typeface of the *Register*. And the tiny font size of the death notices.

Carlyn pointed one finger at a clipping. "The death notice of Lillian Finch. She's the one who called me about Audrey. Last Sunday, she died."

Jane nodded along with Tuck. "Yes, we know of her. I guess the police must still be investigating the cause of—or, wait. Is there something else about it?"

Carlyn didn't answer, but selected another clipping. "This is the death notice of Niall Brannigan. He was there when I dropped you—I mean, Audrey Rose—off that morning. He died on Monday night, apparently. His funeral is today, according to the—Honey, are you okay?"

Tuck was lowering herself to the couch, clutching the flowery armrest for balance. Jane sank back into the armchair, wondering if her face had turned as ashen as Tuck's.

"Niall—," Tuck whispered.

"Brannigan?" Jane heard the hollow sound of her own voice. Two people from the same agency, dead, in a matter of days? The two people connected to Tuck's case. "*Died?* Of what? Tuck, did Ella Gavin tell you that?"

"Ella Gavin?" Carlyn looked up from her documents. Jane could not read her expression.

"Ella? Gavin?" Carlyn closed the folder. "You know who Ella Gavin is?"

54

"You don't want to do this, Ricker." Jake kept his weapon trained at Curtis Ricker's head. He had to be ready to take the kill shot.

It had been three minutes since Jake arrived in the basement parking garage of Police HQ. The garage was a bitch of a place for this to happen. The dank shadows. The dripping pipes. The crammed-in cruisers and oil-slick floors. The suffocating smell of exhaust. The concrete walls that could ricochet a good shot into a catastrophe.

Not that this wasn't already a catastrophe.

The Supe had met Jake at HQ's front door when he and DeLuca arrived, ran them down the back stairs. "He's been holding her for ten minutes," the Supe said over his shoulder as they bounded down the concrete steps, all taking two at a time. "Desk guy didn't see them, you know how the cams are down there. This the collar you're having second thoughts about, Brogan? Seems guilty as hell to me. She was putting him into the transport van. Apparently the slimeball convinced her to loosen the damn handcuffs, and she—whatever."

"So what's the plan?" They'd clanged open the metal door to the parking garage.

"Plan? Hostage unit's en route. I'll bring 'em down.

But the slime's asking for *you*, Brogan. Says he wants *you* to see this. What a complete asshole. Get over there and make this go away."

Ricker stared daggers at Jake. He still wore the grimy jeans and faded plaid shirt he had had on when Jake arrested him. One aluminum handcuff dangled from his left wrist as his arm clenched Officer Jan Kurtz in a headlock. His right hand—the one with no handcuff—held her police-issue Glock against her temple. Though he was a full head taller, they stood ear to ear. His head almost touched hers.

Jake had no shot. Impossible.

Kurtz, tears streaming, was not doing well. Eyes red and swollen, nose running, black mascara dripping down her face. One boot was gone, and the tails of her blue uniform shirt pulled askew from her navy pants. At least she wasn't screaming.

"You're okay, Kurtz. You're doing fine." Jake needed to reassure her. Make her a real person to Ricker. He had to understand Kurtz was a human being, not a pawn. He had to let her go. Or he'd be dead.

D was backing him up, now behind him somewhere with the other cops ducked between cars. Waiting. But it was all Jake's show. And he knew it. *If he hadn't arrested Ricker, none of this would have happened. What if Ricker wasn't guilty, and now this was—*

Later. That was for later. Now, Jake needed to keep calm. Lower the energy. That was his only hope.

And Ricker's. And Jan Kurtz's.

"Screw you." Ricker half-dragged Kurtz toward the van, walking backward as the woman stumbled along with him. Her billed hat had landed in a puddle by a concrete post, and one lock of curly blond fell into her face.

Another step closer to the van. Another.

"She's got the keys, she's gonna drive me the hell

outta here," Ricker said. "You back the hell off. I didn't do anything. This is bogus."

In about four more steps, Jake figured, Kurtz would be at the van's open driver's side door. The multihinged mechanical garage door, Jake could see from a patch of daylight glistening on the damp concrete floor, was also open. What if—

"Don't even think about closing that frigging garage door." Ricker spit out the words.

"Ricker." Jake kept the weapon pointed at him. Kept his voice as calm as he could. Focused. "Where do you think this is gonna go, right? You've made a decision, now unmake it. Let her go, we can talk."

"Talk about what?" Ricker said. Two more steps.

Kurtz had pressed her lips together, the tears still coming. Jake saw her eyes close, then open, looking at Ricker in panic.

"Jan, stay strong. You're doing great." Jake nodded at her, as if he believed it. Actually she was, given the situation. She certainly realized she was a split second from . . . "Curtis, listen to me. Look at me. We can talk about it."

Jake knew Ricker could almost touch the van door. He made his arm into steel, his weapon an extension of his hand. The rest of the garage disappeared as Jake focused on one man. One moment. Waiting for his one chance.

"Last time we 'talked,' you arrested me for—who cares. We're done." Ricker yanked Kurtz another step toward the open van door. "We're outta here."

He'll have to put Kurtz inside. There'll be a moment when Ricker's alone. His plan isn't going to work. He'll see that. And that's when I'll take the shot.

"Let her go, and I'll drive you," Jake said. "This is between you and me, Ricker. She's a girl. You gonna take a girl? You don't need this. Let her go. *I'll* drive. I'll drive you right out of here. Then we can talk."

Ricker blinked. Jake saw the gun hand waver, just a fraction.

Almost enough.

"Ricker. This ain't gonna work. You can't get her into the car. You see that, right? You're done." Jake kept his weapon pointed at Ricker's center mass. Steady. If Ricker freaked, didn't mean Jake had to kill him. One more try. "Give her up. I'll protect you."

"Shit," Ricker said.

"Yeah," Jake said. Okay. This was going to be okay. Ricker was in deep trouble. But he wouldn't be dead. And they could go from there. "Good call, Curtis. Now let her go."

Jake saw Ricker's arm drop—and in that fraction of a second, Kurtz leaped away, rolled across the grimy concrete floor, and disappeared under a parked crime scene van.

At the same instant, a blast of light and sound. Ricker buckled to the floor, a burst of bright red blooming in his chest. Jake heard the clunk of skull on concrete. Saw the red spill onto the gray.

"What the *hell*?" Jake whirled, lowering his weapon. "Who the . . ."

Behind him, Hennessey, red-faced and breathing like he'd just had a heart attack, still clenched his gun, now pointed at nothing. Behind him, a dozen cops rose to watch, like startled prairie dogs popping from their holes.

"Son of a bitch had it coming." Hennessey's chest rose and fell. "He can't do that to my partner."

"Did you get the feeling Ella was going rogue? By calling you and arranging the meeting?" Carlyn Beerman stabbed the dwindling fire with a metal poker, then added another split log. She'd listened as Tuck and Jane

described their coffee shop discussion with Ella Gavin.
An ember cracked, then popped in a flash of orange.
Carlyn jumped back, then poked again. "Did you get the
impression the Brannigan people knew about it? Maybe
they sent her. To assess your reaction. See if you'd be
angry."

Jane shook her head, no, looked at Tuck for confirmation.

"Not at all," Tuck said. She pushed the sleeves of her
turtleneck up to her elbows, then pulled them down
again. "That's what was so . . . I don't know. She's a
mouse of a girl, and seemed devoted to the Brannigan.
But this was unauthorized. I thought, at least. She was
nervous. She flipped out over the bracelet. Right, Jane?"

"Well, yeah. I didn't stay the whole time, but when
Tuck showed the bracelet, she freaked. All I can say. She
had a whole pile of—Hey. Carlyn? Do you have a set of
documents from the Brannigan? Wait, though." Jane interrupted her own question. "Why'd you ask about Ella
Gavin in the first place?"

"She called me. Today. This morning." Carlyn looked
at a shiny brass clock on the end table. "Gosh, a couple
hours ago. She left a message."

"Really?" Had Ella discovered something on her
own? "So you know her? Did you keep the message?"

"Yes, but it won't matter." Carlyn set the metal fire
screen back into place. "And no, I don't know her. She
didn't say where she's calling from. Or anything about
the Brannigan. That's why I was so surprised when you
said her name."

"Can you play the message for us?" Jane had to interrupt. Lillian Finch was dead. Niall Brannigan was dead.
And clearly she and Tuck were right in the middle of
whatever it was. Carlyn, too.

Had Ella been calling to warn Carlyn? Or to threaten
her?

"On speaker? So we can all hear?" Tuck said.

"If you think it'll help. I suppose. Phone's in the kitchen." Carlyn pointed. "That way."

She led them through a chintz-draped dining room, billowing curtains, circular table covered in a muted scarlet cloth, a pot of spidery white chrysanthemums in the center. Into the kitchen, rubbed copper pans on cast-iron hooks, glass-fronted cabinets, seafoam green walls. In one corner, a bookshelf haphazardly stuffed with cookbooks, a to-do list tacked to a mini-bulletin board, and a tiny desk with a silver wall phone.

"Sit." Carlyn gestured Jane and Tuck toward wicker stools beside the counter. She punched some buttons on the phone. "I'd been getting strange hang-ups today. Annoying. Probably telemarketers."

Jane fired a look at Tuck behind Carlyn's back, *told you so*.

Tuck shrugged, waved her off.

"But this one, it didn't sound like a telemarketer call. Frankly, I didn't know what to make of it. And hadn't deleted it yet."

There was an amplified beep, then a whisper, and then a woman's voice.

"Mrs., um. Miss, Beerman? I'm so sorry to bother you, I, this is Ella Gavin? I'm at the, well, um. I wonder if we might—If you have a chance, could you—"

Jane strained toward the phone, struggling not only to hear, but to understand what Ella was trying to say. Jane's own phone rang, from somewhere deep in her tote bag, but she ignored it. Ella, her voice muffled and hesitant, seemed unable to finish a sentence. Jane thought she heard—music? And someone else's voice?

"Oh, I'm so sorry. Yes, I know it's starting. Mrs. Beerman, I guess this is not the time to—"

And then Ella hung up.

Carlyn punched a button on the phone console, and it

went silent. "So you see. Or—hear. That's why I probably looked like I'd seen a ghost when you mentioned the name," she said. "So she's from the Brannigan."

"Sounds like she wanted to tell you something," Jane said.

"Then didn't," Tuck said.

"It sounds as if she were interrupted." Carlyn leaned against the kitchen counter, eyelet lace curtains covering the window behind her. The window framed lofty pine trees piercing a cloudless blue sky. "She calls, then you two show up. Is there something you want to tell me?"

"Well, no. I mean, yes," Tuck said. "But it was just the—you know. Bracelet. So maybe that's what Ella Gavin was calling about, too. To tell you they sent the wrong girl."

"Or not." Carlyn unlooped her filmy scarf, draped it around her shoulders. "I still have difficulty believing that. Even though I know the truth."

"Question is, what did *she* know?" Tuck said. "Ella. And if it was all a mistake—which is really the only explanation, isn't it?—did she know why it happened?"

"And now," Jane said, "both people who brought you two together are dead." Jane had driven here with Tuck only to support her in this uncomfortable situation. Now, "uncomfortable" seemed an understatement. "I mean, were Brannigan and Finch allies? Or antagonists? Or is it all simply coincidence?"

Carlyn fussed with the scarf again, this time winding it around her neck, then tying the fringed ends. "Tuck? Should we join forces? See if we can get to the bottom of this? Your real birth mother is out there, somewhere."

Tuck nodded. "Yes, and I—"

"And my daughter, too." Carlyn went on. "Somewhere. Maybe waiting for me."

A flock of sparrows wheeled outside the kitchen window, fluttering the snow from the pine branches. In the silence, Jane couldn't think of what to say. Both women had such a loose end in their lives. A missing connection. *Mom,* she thought. *Now that you're gone, there's a hole in the fabric of the universe. But at least we had our lives together.*

"I may not be your mother, Tuck, but I can still be your friend," Carlyn was saying. "How about a little surprise visit to the Brannigan? Together? And let's just see who sent me the wrong girl."

"And why." Tuck nodded, almost smiling. "And yes. Together."

Another riff of marimbas came from Jane's tote bag. "Oh, sorry. I should probably take this call."

Maybe it was Alex. She'd been feeling guilty, away from the office. Even though Alex had sent her away, she didn't want him to think she was neglecting her job. Maybe he had a story assignment. Something she could be doing from home. *Ugh.* She should have thought of that.

But it wasn't his photo on the screen. "Blocked," it said.

"This is Jane." She smiled, held up a palm at Carlyn and Tuck. Silly to answer the phone, but there it was. She could feel her smile fade as she listened.

"What?" Tuck leaned toward her, frowning as she watched. "You look like you've seen a—"

"Kind of dumb for you to leave home again," the voice was saying. The same disturbing voice she'd heard two days ago on Cambridge Street after she'd left the Kinsale. Ominous. Hard. "Thought I made it clear you were to keep back from the Callaberry Street thing. Thought I told you I needed quiet. Okay, then, *Miss* Ryland. Are you all having fun out there in Connecticut? This is call number two."

Jane stared at the now-silent phone.

"Who was that?" Tuck asked.

"Jane, are you all right?" Carlyn crossed to her, put a hand on her arm.

"I don't know." Jane answered both questions at once. She clenched the phone, white-knuckled, staring at the blank screen. The cat collar in her car. Her open door. The noise in the night. The phone calls. *Jake*. She had to call Jake.

55

"Is this day almost over?"

Jake needed another coffee, a couple thousand aspirin, a beer. And a vacation. Instead, he and DeLuca once again trudged up the front path of 343B Edgeworth Street, where Curtis Ricker used to live, trying to clean up someone else's mess. Or maybe it was Jake's own mess. Jake arrested Ricker for murder, and less than twenty-four hours later, Ricker was dead. Jake couldn't shake the guilt.

"He must have done *something*, you know?" DeLuca crumpled his coffee cup, looked around as they walked, stuffed it into his jacket pocket. "An innocent guy doesn't do what he did. Set himself up to get shot."

He must have done something. Jake hated that. A cop's excuse for a bad collar. But in this case, he had to agree. Or was he rationalizing? Letting himself off the hook for what happened in the garage? Hennessey. What an asshole.

Kurtz had been given compassionate leave, and was already on her way to her mother's on the South Shore. Covered in grease and soggy with basement grit, she'd clamped on her filthy hat and insisted to the Supe that she was fine, all set to go back on duty. The Supe ordered the rookie home, accompanied by an officer from

Human Resources. They'd investigate her botched handling of the prisoner transport later.

Hennessey, all bluster and conquest, was in the hands of Internal Affairs. His weapon confiscated. His life on hold while IA investigated the shooting. "Moron deserved it," Hennessey'd bellowed as two blue-suited IAs escorted him from the basement. "It was righteous."

Curtis Ricker was in the morgue. But Kat McMahan didn't have to make any decisions about his cause of death. Ten cops had watched him die.

"Jake." DeLuca clamped a hand on Jake's shoulder, stopping him just before they got to the front steps. Withdrew it, as if caught in a too-emotional gesture.

Jake had to smile. D was a good guy. Trying to help.

"Yeah?"

"It wasn't your fault. Ricker. Hennessey lost it, no question, he'll fry. Deserves it. The asshole. But you held it together. You did good. Ricker'd grabbed Kurtz. That's a life sentence. He could have killed her. Would have. You saved her."

Jake saw it again, the moment Kurtz ducked and rolled, the flash of relief, *this worked*. And then, from behind him, the shot. He'd looked at his own weapon for a weird twist of a second, wondering, *Did I . . . ?* But he knew he hadn't. The whole thing should never have happened.

"I appreciate it, D. Thanks. Now let's see if we can find some next-of-kin information and get the hell out of here," Jake said. "The DA's deciding what to do about the Tillson murder case now that the guy we arrested for it is dead. We arrest someone else? Defense attorney'll have a field day. Talk about reasonable doubt. No way anyone'll be convicted of it. We better hope Ricker was guilty."

"Or that someone confesses," D said.

"Oh, yeah. That's gonna happen." This sucked beyond

belief. Jake hadn't been certain of Ricker's guilt. As it turned out, the arrest had been Ricker's death sentence. What's more, if the real killer—*the real killer?*—was still out there, he was gonna walk.

They climbed the front steps to the wooden porch. No one had moved the soggy phone books. Water-soaked newspapers in yellow plastic bags still lay scattered in wet patches across the double-wide porch, like someone had gone on vacation and forgotten to stop delivery. Two rusty rectangular mailboxes, lids open, were attached to the dirt-streaked siding.

"He's got mail," DeLuca said. "Huh. Some in the 'A' mailbox, too."

Jake shrugged, patted his pockets for the key to 343B. All of Ricker's effects were in lockup, so they'd signed out the key. They still didn't have the damn cell phone. Why had Ricker dunked it into the water? Not that it mattered at this point.

Jake slid the key into the front door, twisted it. D lagged behind.

"Ah," D said.

"What?" Jake paused in the open door. "Hey. You can't look at the mail, bro. It's a federal—"

DeLuca handed him a white envelope.

"So arrest me," D said. "But first, look at this. Electric bill. From the other side's mailbox. Not Ricker's."

"Even worse," Jake said.

"Jake." DeLuca gave him a full-out eye roll. "Look at the damn letter. The letter to the *empty* side of the house."

Jake took the envelope. *Whatever.* Addressed to— "Leonard Perl?"

"How about them apples," DeLuca said.

"So what? Maybe he gets the bills. He's the landlord. We know th—" Jake stopped. Held up a hand. "D. You hear that?"

He stared at the closed front door of the vacant apartment A. Looked at the open door of Ricker's unoccupied apartment B. Late afternoon in a seedy neighborhood, darkness just beginning to gather. Streetlights not on yet, evening gloom creeping into the day. Not a car on the street. Not a light in a neighboring window. Deserted.

"Hear what?"

"Shh. Listen."

The silence was so profound, the very air was buzzing with it. With Ricker gone, there was no more Allman Brothers, no more pounding bass guitars. Maybe Jake had been mistaken. Maybe the sound had come from a neighbor's radio. Or someone's TV. Now, there was quiet.

"Never m—" Jake took a step into the apartment. And then, he heard it again.

D's head came up, his eyes wide. "Shit."

Jake nodded, trying to keep his balance. His phone rang, the sharp trill breaking the silence. He slammed it off.

"It's a . . . ," DeLuca whispered.

"Baby." Jake pointed to the vacant apartment. "In there."

Dammit, Jake, where are you? Jane heard her call go to voice mail. What was she supposed to do now?

She propped her elbows on Carlyn's pristine kitchen counter, rested her head in her hands. Trying to think. *Another phone call.* "Tuck, tell Carlyn about it, okay? I have to decide what to do."

Jane vaguely heard Tuck's explanation—phone call, tailgating pickup truck, open apartment door, missing cat—watched Carlyn open the refrigerator, felt Tuck's hand on her back.

"You okay, Jane? That was Jake you just called, I hope," Tuck murmured.

There was no time to be coy. Jake was the police. And she needed the police. "Yeah. It went to voice mail."

Jane stared out the window. Not another house in sight. The rutted road, twisty and remote. Just three women in a little cottage. Had someone followed her here? Someone in a pickup truck?

Where were they waiting? And why?

56

Jake stared at the front door. Alvarez in Records had reported 343A as vacant, but Jake hadn't had time to check that. Perl owned this house, *and* the Callaberry triple-decker. Perl would have access. Perl would have keys. Maybe the ones Jake found in Ricker's kitchen drawer belonged to Perl. Maybe Ricker had been telling the truth? Maybe he'd kept the music loud to drown out the—

A lone car hissed by in the slush. The streetlights came on, buzzing gradually into a somber glow. A couple of porch lights clicked on across the street, probably on timers. February in Boston, afternoons almost telescoped into nonexistence.

"Let's check the side. Check the rear." Jake motioned for DeLuca to follow. In less than a minute they'd gotten the lay of the land. Side door, out to the driveway, locked. Fenced backyard, no rear exit.

Returning to the front porch, Jake took two steps, pulled open the screen to unit A, knocked on the scarred white paint of the front door. *Sounds hollow. That's good.*

"We're going in. Community safekeeping," Jake decided. "A baby crying from inside a supposedly vacant apartment? I don't think so. Meets the guidelines for me."

"Gotcha." DeLuca, behind him, had one hand on his weapon. "Lock looks pretty old, if it comes to that."

Jake banged on the door again, using the heel of his fist. He angled his body away, out of the line of fire. Just in case. They were in the right here. The community safekeeping rule let them enter without a warrant where they thought someone might be in danger. Ever since that grisly killing in Westchester, where police had waited for permission to check on the mother and baby—then found them murdered—cops had been given some leeway in potentially dicey situations. Leeway was exactly what they needed right now.

If he was wrong, the paperwork would be massive.

Jake's phone rang inside his pocket. Damn. Not now. It rang again. One hand by his weapon, one for the door. He let it go to voice mail. If it was HQ, they'd radio.

The baby cried again.

Jake checked the door's rusty hinges. The door opened in, away from them. *Good*. Small favors.

"You set?" Jake said. "On my three."

"You need to contact the police," Tuck was saying. "And Alex. I'm not kidding." She and Carlyn were making sandwiches, blotting pieces of romaine lettuce, adding mayonnaise. It smelled like tuna. Jane, perched on a wicker kitchen stool, pretended to listen.

She frowned, fussed with a ceramic pot of tarragon on the counter, running her hand along the feathery leaves. Contact the police? She couldn't even prove the call had happened. There'd be no record of it. Jane picked up her cell to check her call history. "Blocked call" was all it said.

Plus, even if the police could trace it using the SIM card, it would just go to a burner phone. The caller had made that clear the first time. There was no one to help her. She was at a dead end. She didn't like the sound of the word "dead."

"Jane?" Tuck, now holding a plate of whole-wheat triangles, interrupted her thoughts, gesturing toward the dining room. "You want a—?"

"Go ahead, you two," Jane said. "Be there in a minute."

She had to figure this out. Even dismissing the probably-nothing black pickup and the couldn't-have-happened break-in, the phone calls were indisputably real. Someone wanted her to stop—something.

But it couldn't be following up on Tillson. There'd already been an arrest for Brianna Tillson's murder. That case was closed. Everyone knew it. What else might someone think she was investigating?

She shifted on the stool, the ridges of wicker digging into her rear. If the caller wasn't warning her away from Brianna Tillson's killer, what *were* they warning her away from?

Who would think she was "poking around" in the Tillson case?

The Callaberry Street neighbors she and Hec interviewed, certainly. She flipped the collar of her black turtleneck up over her mouth, then flipped it down again. She could hear Tuck and Carlyn in the other room, talking in low voices.

Closing her eyes, Jane mentally replayed the phone call. And then again.

Well. *Odd*. The caller hadn't actually mentioned Brianna Tillson. He'd said, "Keep back from the Callaberry Street thing." The Callaberry Street thing? Was it something about Phillip and Phoebe?

Yanking open her tote bag, she scrabbled for a pencil and her notepad. She hooked her heels over the rungs of the stool and used the kitchen counter as a desk. Who would know she was asking about the children? Alex.

Jake. DeLuca. Hec Underhill. They didn't count. She twisted open the mechanical pencil. Who else?

Margaret Gunnison at DFS, she wrote. Then: in Anguilla. But not during the murder.

Finn Eberhardt. Then: in office so not driving pickup. Person at DFS Finn told??

Other caseworkers. *Whoever they were.*

Vee at the DFS reception desk. *Unlikely.*

Who else? Jane tapped her pencil on the Formica. Point, eraser. Point, eraser. Point—Oh.

Bethany Sibbach.

Jake had interviewed Bethany. *She had to talk to Jake.*

She put down her pad, hit redial on her cell. His voice mail again. *Damn.* She punched up the contact list. *Alex.* Tuck was right about that, too. She had to tell him about the call and discuss what to do. He was her editor. She needed him.

"Alex Wyatt." He answered on the first ring.

"Alex, it's Jane. I'm in . . ." *Damn.* She was losing it. She should have called home first. "Listen, Alex, sorry. I know this is strange, but can I call you right back?"

"Jane. *You* listen. I've been trying to reach you. Did you have your phone off? Where are you?"

She knew it. She should never have ignored her job. "Ah, well—"

"Jane? There's been a shooting at Boston police HQ. Like, two hours ago. Apparently it's bad. But all we can find out is it's something to do with Curtis Ricker."

"Who's that?" Was this someone Jane was supposed to know? Why did Alex's voice sound so strange?

"Curtis Ricker? You kidding me? The guy who was arrested for the Tillson murder. Don't you read the paper?"

Jane stood, slowly, then sat down again. Her pad tumbled to the floor, her pencil rolled after it. *Jake hadn't answered his phone.*

"Jake?" She cleared her throat. The word hadn't come out properly. She tried again. "Jake?"

"That's the thing," Alex said. "Police aren't confirming or denying. Not till a four o'clock news conference. We've got a reporter there. But right now? We don't know. I need you to call your cop sources and find out."

57

"Three!" With DeLuca holding open the screen storm door, Jake slammed his left heel at the wooden door, aiming to hit right beside the crummy-looking lock, the door's weakest spot. Shattered chips of white paint rained down. Jake could feel the wood begin to splinter and crack. Luckily old doors like this were hollow, and the dead bolt mechanisms cheap, this one probably extending only an inch into the flimsy doorframe. It could work.

He paused, taking a breath. He'd seen enough rookies dislocate their shoulders. Kicking was the only way to go, especially with an already-neglected door like this one.

"You got this, Harvard." D gave him a thumbs-up.

"Anyone in there with the baby, they're sure gonna know the cavalry is on the way."

"Well—"

Jake held up a palm. "Hang on. Listen. Let's see if anyone comes."

"Or goes." DeLuca gestured toward the driveway, watching for bad guys heading out the side door. "Nada. All clear."

"One more time," Jake said. "And we're in. You set?"

He gathered himself, grateful for his sturdy cop-issue boots. "Three!"

With a heave and a shouted "Police!" Jake's second kick splintered the thin veneer of the rickety door, the bar of the dead bolt breaking free from the doorjamb. Jake fell back with the force of his effort, almost landing in DeLuca's steadying arms.

The door—what was left of it—swung open.

Call her cop sources? Alex wanted her to call her cop sources? Jane's "cop sources" were Jake, and calling him was exactly what she'd already tried to do. And her sources—Jake—were not answering the phone. She'd told Alex she'd call him right back if she found anything. She dialed again. Voice mail. *Where was Jake?*

She called PR guy Tom O'Day at police HQ, nothing. Called Jake again. Nothing. It was two minutes to four, and she was about to lose it. Carlyn's little television worked fine, but she didn't have cable and they were out of the Boston viewing area. So no way could they watch a four o'clock news conference on Boston TV. No local TV stations around here had four o'clock newscasts. Jane could check the Web on her phone, of course. But it would take a little time for the news cyberjournalists to get the conference posted. She punched up another contact, hit "call." Neena's phone was ringing, and if *she* didn't ans—

"Neena. Oh, thank God. It's me. I'm down in Connecticut with Tuck. But is everything—Have you heard anything about—Listen, can you go check my front door?"

"What are you talking about?"

"Just—can you? I'll hang on while you look. And can you—" Well, she couldn't ask Neena to turn on her TV and look at her door at the same time. One thing at a time.

"On my way. Eli, you watch little Sam for two seconds, okay? I'll be right back. Okay, Jane. On the way. I'll look over the banister. What on earth, Jane?"

"I got another phone call. Like the other one. They didn't say anything about—But you know, I just want to make sure—I put a tiny piece of paper in the door. If everything seems okay, can you see if—"

She couldn't manage to finish a sentence. There were too many questions.

"Well, isn't the guy across the street still watching out for—Okay, I'm here. Looking over the railing. Hang on. Nope, nothing. Hang on, going down. Nope. Fine. Door locked, all good. And yup. I see the paper. I'll leave it. But don't you—"

"Oh, thank goodness." It was troubling, though. Both calls had come in when she was not home. Did the caller know that?

"Jane? Don't you think you should call the police?"

"One more thing, I know this seems strange." Jane ignored the question, couldn't believe she was doing this, but she had to know about Jake first. "Are you going back upstairs now?"

"Jane? Shouldn't you call Jake? Isn't it about time you—"

"That's exactly what this is about," Jane interrupted. "Are you upstairs?"

"Hang on, opening the door. Yes, I'm back in our apartment. Hey Eli, I'm here."

"Turn on the TV. Channel Eleven."

"Jane?"

"Please."

Jane heard the sound of a door closing, Sam babbling, Neena babbling back at her son. Eli's voice. A pause.

"Okay, TV's on and—Oh."

"What? Is it the news?"

"Yeah, it's a live shot from police headquarters, reporter is saying, hang on, it's on mute."

"Neena." Jane was dying. In one second, she'd know. And if Jake *was* okay, she promised, *promised,* they'd never be apart again. If she had to give up her job, fine. Whatever. If the universe would only make him safe, she'd agree to—

If that's what Jake wanted, of course. All that mattered was that he wasn't dead.

"Jane?"

Jane touched her chest with the flat of one hand, certain she'd feel the pounding of her heart. She remembered to breathe.

"Yeah?"

"Yeah, okay," Neena said. "There was a shooting . . . um, at police headquarters. I'm just looking at the readout thing on the screen now. Apparently the guy they arrested in the Brianna Tillson murder was holding a police officer hostage."

"*Who?*" It was Jake. Of course it was Jake, since he'd probably arrested this Ricker person.

"Ahhh . . . a rookie? The caption says. No name. Seems like it's a woman."

Jane steadied herself on the kitchen counter. *Thank you.*

"And apparently—hang on. Another police officer offered to take her place, and then—oh."

Jane sat down. She couldn't feel her feet. She couldn't feel her hands. This was unbearable. "Oh, what?"

"He was shot. And killed."

"*Who?*"

"That Curtis Ricker. The suspect. A cop shot Curtis Ricker to death, and now the incident is being investigated."

"Anything about Jake? Do you see Jake at the news conference?"

"Nope."

"Nope what?"

"He's not in the background, I don't see him. And they're not—hang on, stop talking, let me listen."

Tuck, with Carlyn behind her, appeared at the kitchen door.

"Jane, what's up with you?" Tuck held out a hand, reached out to her. "What on earth—are you crying?"

Jane touched her own cheek. She was.

Jake stood in the twilight of the entryway of 343A Edgeworth Street, listening. Beside him, DeLuca, weapon pointed dead ahead, took a step into the apartment. Stillness surrounded them, so intense Jake thought he could hear the buzz of electrical current. *Huh.* That electric bill. Addressed to Leonard Perl. The landlord who'd never returned their calls. The one who lived in Florida.

D raised a questioning eyebrow, gestured with the Sig. *Upstairs?*

Jake frowned, held up a hand at D, *hang on.* There was no more crying. But he had not been wrong. He hadn't. His brain clicked into fast-forward, considering all the possibilities. Was someone with the baby? Quieting it? How? No one would leave an infant alone. Right? Who was in this house? Whoever it was certainly heard them break in, but hadn't run away. How would that person figure this was going to play out? *Maybe time for backup.*

Inventory. A lamp on each of the entryway side tables, both off. Jake touched one tabletop with a finger. No dust. Living room—dark couch, two chairs, curtains drawn. No photos, no stuff. No magazines or mail. The layout of the place was the mirror image of Ricker's next door, so Jake knew the kitchen was ahead, the bathroom around the corner. Hall closet, just like Ricker's. The stairway up. Two bedrooms upstairs.

Jake pointed to the kitchen, pointed up the staircase. Waggled a hand back and forth. *Which?*

D touched a forefinger to his radio. *Backup?*

58

Like it was her fault no one had died?

Absurd. Kellianne's favorite new word. Kev and Keefer were all bummed, they'd been hoping for some new job, but their guy hadn't called. Didn't mean they had to be so crappy to *her*. They were home in their living room, watching TV, of course, holding their cell phones like some kind of life preservers.

Kellianne tilted back in the red plastic kitchen chair, took a sip of Diet Dr Pepper. Afterwards hadn't gotten a job for the last twenty-four hours, and the boys were, like, oh my God, we'll never make quota. They didn't want to tell her dad.

She was worried about her dad, too, of course. But she didn't give a care about their absurd quotas. She'd be gone, soon enough.

Plus, it was good they didn't have a job today. She needed to hit the post office, check her box. Maybe she'd have actual money. She couldn't believe how awesome much RedSky had agreed to pay for the compact and nightgown. She needed to check her secret e-mail for offers on her other items.

So what if they didn't have a job this second? People would keep dying. You could count on it. And that meant she would never run out of opportunities. People might not be dying fast enough for her creepo brothers, but they were dying fast enough for her. *Supply and demand*.

She tossed the soda can into the trash, tucked her T-shirt into her jeans. It was four-ish, according to the sometimes-right clock on the stove, so the P.O. would still be open.

She grabbed her parka and headed for the living room. The TV was blaring, as usual. The news.

"Guys?" She called to their backs. "I'm going to the drugstore. Gotta get some—" She pretended to blush, even though they weren't looking at her. "You know. Stuff."

"Holy freaking asshole shit." Kev leaped to his feet, his back now blocking the TV screen. "You have got to be kidding me. You hear that?"

"Huh?" Keefer took a tug from his Michelob. "What the hell's up with you?"

"Holy crap. You hear that?" Kev aimed the remote at the cable box, clicking the volume button with his thumb. The woman's voice, that news reporter from Channel 11, blared through the room.

Kellianne took a couple steps back, clamping her hands over her ears. "You want me to hear something?" she yelled. "Turn down the damn TV."

"Shut up," Kev shouted. Eyes still glued to the screen, he waved her away. "I gotta listen to this."

Kellianne, hands to her ears, came around the couch, stood next to her brother. She could almost feel the fear coming from him. The blonde was talking about a shooting? At Boston Police headquarters. Why would he care about that?

The picture changed to a car crash somewhere. Kev popped the audio to mute.

"We're screwed," Kevin said. He plopped down on the couch, planting both feet on the coffee table, knocking over his beer. The empty bottle rolled to the rug, then under the table. No one moved to pick it up.

"How come?" Kellianne was seriously baffled.

"Yeah." Keefer poked his brother in the thigh. "How come?"

"Because, you incredible morons, does the name Richard Hennessey sound familiar?"

It did, in fact. Kellianne totally knew him. "He's the cop who—"

"Exactamundo," Kevin said. He threw the remote across the room. It landed with a thud on Dad's empty recliner, and then slid to the floor. "Like I said. Ska-rooed."

Jake pointed to his own chest, then up the stairs at 343A Edgeworth Street. *I'll go first.*

D nodded.

One step. The riser under the thin pile of the once-blue runner creaked under his weight. Jake held up a hand. *Wait.* Another step. *Wait.*

Nothing. Not a sound. Jake cocked his head toward the top of the stairs. *Let's go.*

They took the stairs, Jake two at a time, reached the top landing. Without hesitation, Jake planted himself in the open doorway of the room he'd mentally labeled bedroom one, the one on the left. Surveyed the place. Two windows facing front, bed with pillows and bedspread, dresser, nothing on top, closet open, empty.

If anyone's up here, they're either hiding or in the other room. And the baby is silent. I hope that doesn't mean someone silenced it.

"Clear," Jake mouthed the word as he turned to De-Luca. But D was already in stance in the other bedroom doorway.

"Clear," DeLuca turned. A strange look on his face. "But check this out, Brogan."

Jake trotted across the hall, shouldered in front of his partner. In bedroom two—a white wooden crib. Complete with a bouncy mobile, a polka-dot mattress cover, a pink rabbit in the corner. Beside the crib, a rocking chair. On the floor, face up and eyes wide-open in surprise, a plush teddy bear in a yellow-striped T-shirt.

The bear. *The bear.* Just like the bears he'd seen in the Callaberry apartment. They had the crime scene photos to prove it.

He gave DeLuca a look. *What the?* He examined the seat cushion on the rocking chair. Dented. Put his hand on the backrest. Warm. Pointed his weapon at the bedroom closet. Gestured to D. *I'll do it.*

In one motion he yanked open the closet door, pointed his weapon dead ahead. Inside the closet—nothing.

"Shit," Jake whispered. He lowered his weapon, trying to figure out where the sound had come from. "You heard it, didn't you? The baby? And that's like the bears from Callaberry Street, remember?"

D nodded, his head on a swivel, looking to see what they'd missed. But there was nothing to miss.

"Someone's been here," Jake whispered. "Now they're gone. We know this place. It's the mirror image of Ricker's. So where the hell did they—?"

Jake stopped, mid-sentence, replaying his search of Ricker's apartment. Living room. Dining room. Kitchen. Hallway. Stairs. He put a finger to his lips, took a step toward the door.

"D," he said, keeping his voice low. "Downstairs. Follow me."

59

Jake still hadn't returned her call. But it was okay. It was the bad guy who'd gotten shot, Neena said. A woman cop, safe now, taken hostage. Jane flipped the station on her car radio. That's what the news reported, too. *Not Jake. Not her Jake.*

Now she had to see him. Meet him wherever he said, even for a moment. She had to touch his face. Make sure he was not hurt. Make sure he understood. Life was short. This proved it.

The traffic on Route 84 North plowed through the rush-hour slush, Jane watching aggressively impatient drivers weave lane to lane, honking, only to wind up trapped in another slow-moving line of traffic.

Carlyn had invited Tuck to stay for a day or two, saying she'd drive her back to Boston. When Jane left, the two women sat side by side on the couch, shoulders touching, poring over the Brannigan paperwork. Even if they weren't mother and daughter, they'd certainly each found a new friend.

Jane took a sip of her drive-through latte, even though she'd regret the caffeine later, and felt for one of the wax-paper-wrapped tuna sandwiches Carlyn insisted on sending with her. One thing kept pushing to the top of her mind. *Timing.*

The first time she'd gotten a phone call, she was on a sidewalk in downtown Boston. She'd already talked with Maggie Gunnison at DFS, then weaseled the "Brianna Tillson" name from Finn. She took a bite of tuna. After that, the black pickup followed her on the highway. The open door. The cat. The collar. All those times, she wasn't home.

Then this last call. She was in Connecticut. Again, not home.

How would someone know that?

The streetlights lining 84 North blurred the highway in front of her. Jane blinked, quickly, refocusing her eyes on the road and pleading with her brain to recapture a wisp of a thought. She punched off the radio. She needed quiet.

The mile markers ticked by slowly, headlights glaring from the oncoming cars, the daylight-bright spots of a highway crew blocking one whole lane. Jane sat in the stalled traffic, uncaring, needing the time. Rewinding the last couple of days, frame by frame.

Someone was watching her?

Yes.

Of course they were.

But it had been presented to her as a *good* thing. The brother-or-whatever of the cop. The "camera buff." The surveillance guy. He knew where she lived, and when she came and went. It was how the cops proved nothing happened. That there'd been no break-in. That she had it all wrong. That the unlocked door was *her* fault.

But now she saw it from the other point of view.

Only one person knew exactly when she was home and when she wasn't. The surveillance guy.

"Ha!" Jane punched a fist in the air. She put her hand back on the wheel, gripping it tight as she tried to figure out the rest of the story. Exactly who was the watcher in the window? Why was he doing this? Who else was involved?

She had to get home.

But wait. If the surveillance guy was more threat than protector—was *home* where she should go?

Ella Gavin sat in the driver's seat of her car. The evening darkness surrounded her, the streetlights pooling amber puddles along Margolin Street. What if she was parked right where Mr. Brannigan had been Monday night? She couldn't bear to think about it.

She shivered, even though she'd raised the heat to high. Would some neighborhood-watch type be suspicious of her car? Indoor lights edged front windows, up one side of the street, down the other, but otherwise no signs of life. Was this a bad idea?

It was her only idea.

She'd considered it all through Mr. Brannigan's funeral service, which seemed to go on forever. Music and hymns, a too-long homily, an endless procession of relatives and acquaintances stepping to the podium, saying how wonderful Mr. Brannigan had been.

She'd also thought about Lillian Finch, still in the morgue as police continued their investigation. Either way, murder or suicide, soon she'd have to go to Lillian's funeral, and that would be even sadder. She'd never forget the anguished look on Ardith Brannigan's face as the widow left All Saints, leaning on Collins Munson as he escorted her up the chrysanthemum-draped aisle and past the solemn faces of the mourners.

Ella had planned to go home after the command-performance reception in the church fellowship room. Mrs. Brannigan had been red-eyed, stoic, as the receiving line filed past, Ella desperate to think what to say to her, coming up with only a weak "I'm so sorry." Would Ardith be taking over for her—*dead*—husband? If so, the whole Carlyn Beerman problem was about to get bigger. Would *Ella* have to tell Mrs. Brannigan?

She'd kept thinking about it, worrying as she sipped a glass of rosé wine and ate a napkin-full of round lemon cookies. No one came to talk to her. Just as well. She had to think.

If the Brannigan agency got in trouble, Ella would lose her job. That wasn't fair. But if something was going on, it had to stop. She took another bite of cookie. Maybe she was the only one who could stop it.

If she had to, she had to.

So now what? If proof existed that Lillian sent families the wrong children, it sure wasn't in Lillian's office anymore. Before Munson's crew came sweeping through, she'd confirmed nothing there proved anything. Had Lillian taken the incriminating papers to her house?

That's why Ella was here tonight. That's why she hadn't gone home.

She flipped on her windshield wipers. Turned up the defroster as the windows fogged and the outside world disappeared. They were predicting snow. She hated to drive in snow. Maybe she should come tomorrow instead.

Yes. She shifted into drive. *No.* She shifted back into park. The most important thing was to protect the Brannigan—no, the most important thing was to protect the families. She couldn't imagine how Ms. Cameron felt, thinking she was meeting her birth mother, only to find . . . well, Ella would not have been able to bear the disappointment. And what if the same thing happened with other Brannigan cases? Her entire adult life had been spent bringing families together. She couldn't have it tainted with something as terrible as this.

She'd been *planning* to call Carlyn Beerman about the paperwork proving her daughter had not been dropped off with a bracelet and a note. Paperwork that Carlyn, as birth mother, would have. Then, phone in hand, Ella had panicked. What if Carlyn *sued* the Brannigan? Made huge trouble? Ella needed advice.

But first she needed information.

And she had a key, so it wasn't trespassing. Besides, how could you trespass on a dead person?

Ella pulled a pink leather pouch from her tote bag. Unzipped it. Inside, a white enamel lily topped the keys on a gold-linked chain. Lillian had laughed when she entrusted them to Ella. "In case I get locked out," she'd said. "Then I won't have to call an expensive locksmith to let me in."

A few fat snowflakes plunked onto her windshield. The metronome beat of the wipers slashed them away.

Ella stared at Lillian's keys, wondering if she was up to this.

60

This was such a long shot. Jake led DeLuca back down the stairway of 343A Edgeworth. Weapons stowed but available, the two moved quickly and silently. This long shot seemed like the only answer, and if he was wrong, he was wrong.

Mirror image.

Jake pointed to the first-floor closet under the stairwell, then pointed to himself. *I'll go.*

DeLuca gave him a questioning look. *Huh?*

Jake took the last three steps toward the wooden closet door, turned the knob, pulled it open. Stepped inside. Dark. Smelled wood, and dust, and musty disuse. Empty. No fuzzy woolen silhouettes of coats, no clacking metal hangers, nothing. He could touch each side of the closet if he stretched out his arms. He took a step inside. Another. Like Ricker's closet on the other side, it was deeper than he'd imagined. And dark.

Too risky to click on the overheard light.

He held out an arm until his fingertips touched the back wall.

He sensed DeLuca close behind. Heard him breathing. With the palm of his left hand, Jake felt along the left edge of the closet's back wall, barely touching it, almost closing his eyes with the effort to find something that seemed out of place, different. But there was nothing. Maybe he was wrong.

Wishing for the light, he turned slightly, felt along the right edge of the wall. There it was. A hinge. A foot or two beneath that, another hinge.

"This opens." Jake barely whispered the words, demonstrating with one hand. "Into Ricker's side of the house."

DeLuca nodded, touched a hand to his weapon.

Jake patted again along the left side, feeling for a knob, a hook, a gizmo of some kind that would allow him to open the back of the closet—and enter the other side of the duplex.

Nothing. *Nothing.*

There had been someone upstairs. Unless Jake was massively, impossibly mistaken, there had been a baby. Now, no one. And no one had left the house.

Only one other possibility.

Jake's eyes had adjusted enough in the closet gloom to see the almost-amused look on his partner's face. Jake pointed to his weapon, drew it, motioned to D to do the same.

He reached out his left hand, flat, and pushed as hard as he could.

The back of the closet swung open.

"Did either of you morons leave anything at Callaberry Street? Are we clean out of there? What about Margolin Street? Are we clear?" Kev paced back and forth in front of the TV, raking his hands through his hair and looking totally freaked out. The news was now showing some huge fire in a forest somewhere, Utah or Arizona. "We have signed contracts, right, Keef? Both places? I told you to get them."

Keefer shook his head. "Not for Margolin Street yet. We went in on Hennessey's go, but we're waiting for next of kin. Hennessey was s'posed to call us, like, to-day." He shrugged, waved his beer at the TV. "Guess that's not in the cards now. Bummer."

"Shit," Kev said.

"What's the big whoop?" Kellianne couldn't figure out why Kev was so nervous. Yeah, it was true the cop who'd been the shooter was the one who'd hooked Afterwards up with the jobs. But that wasn't on paper anywhere, just a "business proposition." She'd learned that only when Dad got sick.

"Hennessey will call you as soon as he hears of a possible," Dad had instructed the three of them from his hospital sickbed—once the hovering nurse left and Mom went down to the caf for coffees. "He'll contact you by phone. If it's his case, get to the scene, find him, and he'll give you keys or point you to whoever's got them. If not, you'll work it out with him. Either way, you make copies, you get the keys back to him. The death family—if there is a family—will think the cops sent you, that it's part of the deal, and who's gonna tell them otherwise? They have no idea they're supposed to hire the cleanup crew. How would they? They're always upset, and don't care who's getting rid of the crap in their house."

"How about the other cops?" Kev had asked.

"They'll think the family called. Each one thinks the other did it. Nobody cares. There's a dead person. That's all they're worrying about. That and the smell of death. So get in early, get what you can, and assess. Make sure there's insurance."

Had they been doing something she didn't know about? she'd wondered. Pretty funny, considering now they didn't know what *she* was doing.

"What's he get out of it?" Kev had asked that day. "The cop?"

"That's between us." Her father said it was all off the books, and probably not strictly illegal. "Just do it."

Far as Kellianne could see, it'd worked fine.

"Okay, we gotta take care of this." Kev aimed the remote at the front door, as if he could open it that way. "We gotta go back to Margolin Street. I mean, like, now."

"But Kev. We can't." Keefer's voice always sounded whiny. "That's where the guy had the heart attack. If the cops knew we were there, they'd put two and two together."

"Shit." The remote dropped to his side. "But what're we gonna do, bro, UN-clean? We took up all the rugs. And . . ." Kev flashed his brother some kind of a look. "You know. The bathroom."

"I told you," Kellianne said. They were idiots. "I frigging told you. That was the world's dumbest idea, dragging that guy out. Now they're gonna know we were there, and figure out how he got into his stupid car, and you're gonna be in the electric chair. I sure didn't have anything to do with it. But you two morons are gonna fry."

They all stopped talking. The only sound was the TV anchorwoman, yammering about how many acres of land went up in flames somewhere a million miles away.

"Holy freaking Christ," Kevin said. "What're we gonna do?"

Keefer pointed to the TV with his beer bottle. "Well," he said, "I might have an idea."

61

"I thought you** were in Anguilla." Jake blurted the first thing that came to his mind, not exactly by-the-book cop talk, but seeing the woman in Ricker's ratty armchair pushed protocol straight out of his head. He'd stepped through the back of the closet, pushed through the two coats on Ricker's side, and opened the closet door right into Ricker's hallway. Instantly had a clear view of the living room. And a clear view of Margaret Gunnison.

Last he'd seen of the DFS caseworker, she was fast-talking through their interview about the kids in the Tillson murder because she was headed for Logan airport. Off to the Caribbean for a week. Only two days had gone by. She wasn't tan.

"I only—" Margaret Gunnison pulled a swaddled bundle in a blue-striped flannel blanket closer to her chest. A molded plastic car seat decorated with pink Scottie dogs sat on the couch beside a zipped diaper bag. "You can't—"

Jake saw a pink knit cap peeking out from the flannel, a tiny pink nose, and tiny closed eyes. Tried to read the expression on Gunnison's face. Panic? Fear? Anger?

He cocked his head at D, who'd stepped from the closet behind him. *Stand down,* Jake signaled, as he lowered his own weapon, but didn't holster it. This situation—whatever it was—wouldn't be solved with guns. He hoped.

"Who's that?" DeLuca scanned the room, got the picture.

"You remember Margaret Gunnison, the deputy commissioner of the DFS," Jake said. "Maggie, you remember my partner, Detective DeLuca. Maggie? Who's that in your arms? Is that Phillip and Phoebe's . . . ," he was guessing now, ". . . sister?"

No answer. Okay, then.

"Is anyone upstairs, Maggie?" That'd be the big hitch. A woman and a baby in a supposedly empty apartment escaping into the home of a now-dead murder suspect, that was trouble enough. But if she had an accomplice hiding upstairs, that'd be a different story. What the hell was the deal? Was Maggie protecting this infant? Or kidnapping it? Was someone listening to everything they said?

Jake kept his voice calm. "We can talk. You can keep holding the baby. But only if we're alone."

Her eyes didn't flicker to upstairs, a good sign. She adjusted the bundle in her arms, pulled at the seam of the blanket. A tear rolled down her cheek. She swiped it away with a finger.

"You want me to check upstairs, Jake?" DeLuca, voice barely audible, still had his weapon out.

Jake raised a finger. *Wait one.*

"We're alone," she whispered.

"Okay, Maggie. I'm trusting you. What's the baby's name?" Jake needed to get into Maggie's head about this. Figure out what she thought about this child. So far, he had no idea if Maggie was a wacko who might use the child as a bargaining chip. Or a hostage. That damn car seat and diaper bag bugged him. Where was she planning to take the baby? When? Why? One wrong word, one misstep or miscalculation, and this whole thing would go up in flames.

"Her name is Diane Marie Weaver." Maggie looked down at the baby, fussed with the blanket, tucking it under her feet again. "Her mother's dead, but she *must* have wished her daughter to be happy. She must have. And since baby Diane Marie has no other relatives—her father's unknown—I'm helping her."

"So . . ." Jake had to tread carefully here. "*You're* not her mother?"

Maggie looked up at him, half-smiling as if that were the silliest question ever. "Oh, no," she said. "Of course not."

"Okay, Maggie, help me now," Jake said. "You were on the other side of the duplex, right? With baby Diane Marie? You heard us come in? And you ran to this side of the house so we wouldn't find you?"

Maggie nodded, silent.

"Is my partner going to be okay if he goes up there? There's no one there? I'm trusting you, Maggie. Yes?"

"It's only us," she whispered.

Jake cocked his head at DeLuca. "Okay. Check it out. Be careful."

What did she do before cell phones? By the second ring, Jane had grabbed hers by feel from her tote bag as she braked to a semistop in the slow-moving Fast Lane of the Mass Turnpike, rush hour in full swing. *Was it Jake?* She inventoried herself, just in case. Black turtleneck, clean. Good jeans, her good flat boots. Hair, okay. Makeup, fixable.

"This is—," she began. Fingers crossed.

"It's me," Tuck said. "Ella called. She wanted *you,* said she knew all along it was you at the Dunkin's. So much for *that* idea. But she said she had to talk to you, wouldn't tell me what it was about, so I gave her your cell, I hope that's okay, and she—"

Jane's call waiting beeped in, interrupting Tuck's light-speed recitation.

"Tuck? Call you back." She *had* to see if it was Jake. Punching the phone onto speaker, she inched through the tolls toward Boston. "This is Jane."

"Miss Ryland? I'm so sorry to call. It's Ella. Ella Gavin. Ella from—"

"Yes, Ella, I know." Jane was going to kill Tuck.

"Okay. Good. Like I told Miss Cameron, I recognized you at the coffee shop. It didn't seem like you wanted me to, but everyone knows you. How you protect your sources, no matter what. How trustworthy you are. That's why I'm calling. It has to be confidential."

"Well, thank you, Ella." Jane wondered where the hell this was going. *Why does everyone ask for confidential?* "Of course. Confidential. What can I do for you?"

"Have you not picked up your messages at work?" Ella said. "I left you one two days ago telling you about Mr. Brannigan."

"Really?" There had been nothing on Jane's phone, so—*oh*. The operator had probably sent Ella to the "Jane" line, the voice-mail limbo where stressed-out receptionists dumped what they decided were nuisance calls. Which interns answered. Sometimes.

"I bet you got the tip line," Jane said. "I apologize. That's—anyway. But I know about Mr. Brannigan, and I'm so sorry for your loss."

"Listen, Miss Ryland?"

"Jane." She was past exit 14 now. Almost home.

"Jane. Okay. Ah, I'd get in trouble if anyone knew I— Well, listen. I have the paperwork that proves Miss Cameron is not really Audrey Rose Beerman. The original intake documents for baby Beerman don't show a bracelet or note. Mrs. Beerman would have them, too, to compare. But thing is, I called some other families who were reunited with their birth children by Lillian, and it seems like . . ." Her voice trailed off, almost buried in the roar of a thundering sixteen-wheeler.

"Ella? Are you there?"

"Well, I think—I think they could have been sent the wrong children, too."

"What?" Jane tried to process this. "Why would anyone—"

"I'm outside Lillian Finch's house right now," Ella interrupted, talking even faster. "With a key she gave me. There was nothing in her office that proved anything. So I think the proof must be in her house."

Was this flake planning to go *inside*? Into the home of a possible murder victim? Jane tried to concentrate on the road, on the increasing sputter of snow, and on how to keep Ella from making the dumbest move imaginable.

"Ella? I'm so glad you called. Very wise of you. We can talk. But listen, don't do that. Don't go inside. I know you have a key, and I know she gave it to you." No harm in letting Ella think she believed it. "Let me ask you. Is there crime scene tape on the door? That would mean the house is sealed, and there's no way for you to go inside. It would be illegal."

Silence. The traffic was molasses, headlights and streetlights struggling to illuminate the way.

"I can't tell about any tape from here," Ella said. "There's trees. I'm across the street, in my car, and it's kind of snowing. I've been sitting here kind of a long time. But I don't care. I'm going in."

Jane hit her forehead with the heel of her hand. *Colossally dumb.* Insane. But it wasn't Jane's responsibility to—Fine. "Ella? You called to ask me what to do, right?"

"Right. But now I've decided. On my own. I'm not leaving. I'm going in." Her voice sounded taut, almost petulant. Or determined. "With you, or without you. It's my responsibility. There are families who think they—"

"Ella? Ella? Okay. Stay there. But do *not* go inside. Wait for me." If she could stall this girl, she could convince her to drop this ridiculous idea. "It'll take me a little while to get there, the snow's getting worse out here. But I'll come, we'll talk. But only if you promise."

Silence.

"Ella?" She imagined Ella breaking through the crime scene tape, the police finding out—*Jake!*—and poor Ella would wind up needing a very good lawyer. Jane was going to *kill* Tuck.

"I promise," Ella whispered. "But hurry."

62

The baby's eyes fluttered. Maggie was beginning to fidget on the couch. Jake needed to decide what to do. Now.

"Maggie? Is Diane Marie supposed to be in foster care?" Another thought. "Was she Brianna's foster child?"

Maybe this was the wrong baby. Maybe not the one from Callaberry Street.

"There are so many unloved children." Maggie looked down at the infant in her arms, her eyes softening. "It's not their fault, and there's no way the system can save them all. I'm supposed to send them to new homes, but how can I be sure they'll thrive and flourish? They . . . so often don't. It began to feel like we could never do enough."

DeLuca returned. "Clear."

"Watch the front," Jake said. Why hadn't Maggie just run out when she heard them come in? Probably figured they'd never find the connecting door. Safer to stay put. "Did you call anyone, Maggie?"

"No," she whispered.

"Gotcha, Jake. I'm on it," DeLuca said.

For now, at least, they were alone. Unless Maggie actually did have reinforcements on the way, no one would get hurt. And possibly he'd get some answers. Jake briefly envisioned the front door he'd smashed through outside.

Apparently no neighbors had noticed. You'd think someone would have called 911 by now.

Called 911. The blood drained from Jake's face. He felt his skin go cold.

"Where were you last Sunday afternoon?" Jake asked.

"What do you mean?"

"Do you know Brianna Tillson?" He paused. "Let me put it another way. How do you know Brianna Tillson?"

"I don't—"

"Be very careful, now, Maggie. I know you're a good person. Doing what you think is right. But whatever it is—is over. You know that, don't you? Little Diane Marie is counting on you to protect her. Relying on you. You're all she has. *You,* Maggie. Her only hope."

Jake could hear the baby breathing, a little snuffly sound.

"I just went to the drugstore," Maggie said.

"Drugstore?" Did his words not register with her? *The drugstore?*

"I asked Brianna to come over and babysit at Callaberry Street, only for that one hour. No one really lives there, you know. Like, over there."

She pointed toward the other side of the Edgeworth duplex. Then put her hand back on the baby's flannel, twisting her fingers into the fabric.

Jake took out his cell. *Here we go.* "I'm recording this, okay, Maggie?" Risky to interrupt. But if she agreed, it could be kickass evidence.

Maggie nodded.

"Okay?" Jake had to get her to say it out loud, so it was on the recording. In Massachusetts, the law prohibited secretly recording audio, even by cops. Jake couldn't risk losing this potential evidence.

"Okay, you can record," Maggie said.

"So you were saying about no one living there. In Brianna's apartment."

"It wasn't Brianna's. Len just uses his vacant apartments as, I don't know, way stations. Anyway, Len wasn't *supposed* to come to pick up baby Diane until later that evening. Brianna didn't know, of course. She was a registered foster mother, so she sometimes filled in as a babysitter if we needed help. She was good with kids. I was supposed to be there, watching the kids until Len came, but I *had* to get my stuff for Anguilla. You know? I couldn't take them with me."

She stopped, then started again. "I was only gone for an hour. An *hour.*"

Jake thought back, thought of the fragrance in the kitchen. He'd thought it was cleaning solution. But it was really—"Sunscreen," he said. "You went to get sunscreen."

"Yeah. But the bottle cracked open when I threw the drugstore bag. After I saw what Len had done. It was horrible. So horrible."

Jake watched her face as she remembered. Decided to let her fill the silence. Let her explain what this was all about. Once they started, the ones who felt guilty always kept talking. They'd held it in for so long, sometimes getting to tell was their only solace.

Maggie took a deep breath, her arms tightening around the baby. "Len told me Brianna had tried to keep Diane from him. Said she didn't believe it was . . . arranged, and she thought he was trying to steal the baby. Hurt her. A four-month-old baby! She threatened to call the cops. She died, protecting Diane."

Jake stared at her, imagining the scene. Brianna, somehow in the wrong place at the wrong time. About the rest, he still had no idea. But he'd act as if he did. "So Brianna didn't know about your plan." *Whatever it was.*

"No. Of course not. I tried to see if she was still alive, you know? But it was . . . too late. And Len was bleeding, too. Phillip and Phoebe, they were asleep, with their teddies, in the other room. They were all set with their new family, and I was going to stay over with them, drop them off the next morning on my way to the airport. But Len had arranged for Diane's potential new parents to meet her that afternoon. At the lawyer's. He had come to get her. But he was early. And—"

"Diane's new foster family, you mean?"

"Oh, no. No. Not foster family."

Her expression said—*don't you get it?* And no, he didn't. "Then—?"

"Adoption. Private adoption," Maggie said. "I mean, it all takes *so long.* The red tape is horrendous for foster care, and adoption is even worse, and there are so many foster kids, and so many files, no one can possibly keep track of them all. No one's counting. No one but me. All I had to do was find kids with no relatives, fix the paperwork, and poof. One at a time, I saved them. One at a time, they disappeared from the nightmare. And they lived happily ever after. As they should."

"So you were taking kids *out* of the foster system and—"

"For their own good! Len arranged it all. And it worked perfectly, every time. Until Brianna. He said she was freaking out, that she grabbed a pan from the stove to keep him away from Diane. Keep him from taking her. There was nothing he could do, Len said. He had to grab the other pan. And . . ." Her voice trailed off.

"Leonard Perl," Jake said. The landlord. The landlord here, and on Callaberry Street. No wonder he hadn't answered their phone calls to Florida. He'd been right here in Boston. "Leonard Perl. Correct?"

"Yes," Maggie whispered. "Finn's uncle. Well, foster uncle. So then we—"

"Called nine-one-one," Jake said. *Finn? Who was that?* Maggie nodded. "Yes. We had to get out, of course.

But we knew police would come, and they'd make sure Phillip and Phoebe were taken care of. Len's lawyer told *their* new parents some story, the kids' birth mother reneged, claimed parental rights or something. It happens. We knew they'd be returned to the system, poor things. All I had to do was quickly restore their records, you know? Those were the files I gave you. But at least we saved the baby. I gave up my vacation to stay with her. Her adoption arrangement is almost final."

"Brianna's purse." Jake understood now. Why there'd been no stuff. Brianna Tillson didn't live there. Neither did Maggie. "You took that, too."

Maggie nodded.

"Yes?" Jake remembered the recording. "I need you to say it."

"The purse. Yes." A tear trickled down Maggie's face. She made no gesture to wipe it away, and it landed on the baby's fuzzy blanket. "She lived alone. Wasn't fostering a child. There was no one to miss her."

Jake paused, watching this poor misguided woman. Seeing how she cradled that little girl. The baby she had stolen from the system—and how many others?—convinced she was doing a good deed. Convinced she was saving lives.

Not what the law would call it. The law would call it falsifying official records and abducting children from the legal protection of state custody.

"Margaret Gunnison, it is now seven thirty-two P.M. on Wednesday. You're under arrest for the kidnapping of Diane Marie Weaver, for the attempted kidnapping of Phillip and Phoebe Lussier, and for being accessory to the murder of Brianna Tillson. You have the right to remain—"

"Will you take care of Diane?" Maggie said. She stood, touching the baby's wisp of colorless hair with a finger, then leaned down and kissed Diane on the forehead. She handed Jake the pink bundle, not trying to hide the quiet tears now coursing down her cheeks. "Will you? Nothing that's happened is her fault. There's a loving family still waiting for her. You can't keep her from that. You *can't*."

63

Ella clicked off her phone, regretting, instantly, her promise to Jane Ryland. She felt the muscles in her back go stiff, the ones in her neck, too. Her car was impossible. With the heat on it was too hot. With the heat off it was too cold. She'd finally decided to take steps. Important steps, on her own, but then she'd blown it by calling Jane.

She banged her hands against the steering wheel. The horn gave a little beep. She jumped, stomach clenching, and waited in the heart-pounding silence to see if any lights went on in the homes nearby.

Nothing.

Snowflakes sparkled through the streetlights, blowing almost sideways at times, hypnotic and relentless. The weather was about to get hideous, dark and hideous, but maybe that would make her plan easier. Because she was going in.

She was.

She felt the hard edges of Lillian's keys in her hand. If she didn't do this now, she'd lose her nerve. She'd get in, look quickly, get out. How would she know where to look? Lillian's office, certainly. She'd been there before. Not like she was invading anyone's privacy. Not like

Lillian was going to catch her. She laughed out loud, then clapped a hand over her mouth.

Calm down. Okay. It would be okay.

If all went well, by the time Jane arrived, she'd be out and back in her car. It would all be over and all would be fine and she could show Jane what she'd found. If she found anything.

She was going in.

She was.

Maybe.

"I already said, I'll tell you when we get there." Kev was being horrible. Bossy. Kept refusing to tell her what he was going to do. Kellianne, relegated to the backseat of the Afterwards van a-*gain*, yanked her seat belt over the front of her puffer jacket. *Hate* this. But know-it-all Kev ordered her to stay home, and she had to prove he wasn't the boss of her. So here she was.

Only fifteen minutes to Margolin Street, usually. When the weather wasn't this crappy. *Hmm.* Maybe she should snake a couple more items. Since the TV said their cop guy was, like, out of commission, who knew when her next opportunity would be?

She braced herself against the headrest as Kev ignored a stop sign and barely missed a guy in a Jeep. The radio was blaring. The boys whispered as they smoked a blunt in the front seat, but she wasn't about to ask for a hit. Not while she needed her brain to figure this out. She hadn't put two and two together before, but now she could do the math. The cop plus the shooting equaled shit for Kellianne. Would her supply and demand dry up?

So, okay. She'd held off on the valuable stuff before, but this time she wouldn't hesitate. Who cared about a dead person?

She smiled, thinking of something funny. She was always cleaning up after dead people, right? Now she would just clean up.

They were passing downtown, the familiar jaggedy skyline almost blotted out by the snow. The row of weather lights on the top of the Hancock Building flashed blue, which meant snow. *Duh.* The van turned toward Margolin Street.

What were Kev and Keefer gonna do? Probably make sure all their equipment was out of there. She knew they'd left disinfectant and alcohol and cleaning supplies. While they did whatever, she'd find what she was looking for, and get out. They never made her a part of anything, and this time she was happy about that. *Morons.* When it was over, she'd be another step closer to getting out for good.

Life was short.

Was that Jane? *Already?* A block away, headlights flashed in Ella's rearview mirror. She'd never asked her what kind of car Jane drove, so silly of her. Already three had whooshed by, and each time Ella almost jumped out of her skin. If Jane arrived too soon, she'd never make it inside and out in time.

But she wasn't quite ready.

"It's okay," she reassured herself out loud. "This is a public street. You're allowed here."

She turned off the engine, just in case. Stayed in the dark.

The headlights came closer. Closer. They lit up her car interior with their cold blue beams. She flopped onto the passenger seat, staying out of view. *It's weirder if someone sees you lying on the seat. Sit up!*

When she did, she saw the car—a van, really, a grayish van, drive slowly past Lillian's house.

Relief. *See? It's not even—*

But the van backed up. Parked. Almost in front of

Lillian's. Was it Jane? Now everything was ruined, because if Jane didn't want her to go in, well, how would she convince her she *had* to? She was doing her job, she really was. If Jane didn't like it she could just leave.

It wasn't Jane.

The doors of the van had opened, and two men got out, smoking, wearing baseball caps. Then another door slid open and another person got out. Ella squinted through the murky night. A woman? A woman.

Ella sat back, flipped down her sun visor to block their view of her, just in case. Lillian's porch light had clicked on. Ella narrowed her eyes, used a finger to make a slice of clear on the foggy side window to watch.

This was confusing. If people knew Lillian was dead, maybe they were trying to break into her house? But not in the middle of the—well, it was eight o'clock. What kind of stupid burglar, three burglars, would walk right up a front path?

She watched, transfixed, as they approached the house. Should she call the police? *Holy God.* Then how would she explain why *she* was there? Maybe not say who she was? Well, that might work. She reached for her cell phone. Then stopped.

They might have a perfect right to be there. Then where would she be? It would be so embarrassing. But not if her call were anonymous. She put her hand on the phone again. Took it off. Why could she never decide what to do?

Now they were—

She risked buzzing down her window, a tiny bit. They were across the street, couldn't possibly see *her*. Plus, they were busy at the door. Now, with the porch light on, she could see there *was* crime tape.

They were—*How could they do that?*

* * *

"Just cut through it. Don't you have your knife?" Kev sucked down the last of the joint, tossed the roach aside, and waved to Keefer.

Keefer pulled out his Swiss Army, flipped it open, and poked the point into where the space should be between the door and the jamb thing. The blade snagged on the triple thickness of the sealing tape and almost flipped closed on his gloved finger.

"Gimme that, you moron." Kev shouldered in front of him, picked at one edge of the tape with the knifepoint. He found a loose strip and gave it a yank. It ripped down in one motion, pulling the other layers with it. "Wah-LA. As they say in France."

In a few seconds, Kev had crunched up the yellow tape and tossed the sticky ball behind a snow-blanketed shrub. "So much for that," he said.

"But Kev, now the police are gonna—" Kellianne didn't get this. Not at all. "Wouldn't it be better to have it look like no one'd been here? I mean, leave it on?"

"Won't matter, Miss Princess," Kev said. "Now if you'll do me the supreme favor of shutting up, we'll be in, be out, be gone. Our problems will be over."

They were morons. But who cared about their plans? She had her own.

Kev unlocked the door, and Kellianne was the last one in. The foyer light was still on, the rest of the house in gloomy darkness. It still smelled like their cleaning stuff, no question, and she didn't know what Kev planned to do about that. She clicked the door closed, then called after her dumb brothers heading toward the kitchen.

"I have to use the bathroom," she said.

"Knock yourself out," Kev called over his shoulder. "But don't take too long."

What was so funny about that? Kellianne heard their laughter as she made her way to her treasure.

* * *

Oh, she was so dumb. Of course. She should have thought of this. Ella watched the three police officers on the porch, since that's who they must be, plainclothes officers, with that gray van their unmarked car. Because who else would take down the crime scene tape?

Ella nodded, agreeing with herself, and counting her blessings. This was a sign it would all work. The more she thought about it, the more wonderful it was. The police had taken down the tape, meaning the house wasn't a sealed crime scene anymore. Meaning she could easily and legally go inside.

Ella smiled for the first time in a long while. She settled back into the driver's seat, drawing her coat around her in the chill.

The police had closed the door behind them. They were probably checking that everything was okay, which it certainly was, then they would leave.

Then she was absolutely definitely going in.

She would only have to be out before Jane arrived. Things were going nicely. All would be fine.

64

This had to be a first. It was for him, at least. Jake had gathered up a squirming baby Diane, strapped her into her car seat, and fastened the whole thing into the back of his cruiser. There she sat, eyes closed, tiny fingers curled into fists, looking like the smallest suspect ever in Boston Police custody. She'd zonked out the minute the engine started. It broke his heart to see her sleep this profoundly, unaware of the furor around her and no idea how her little life had changed so many others.

You'll take care of her, Maggie Gunnison had pleaded with him as DeLuca led her away in the arriving BPD van. Jake assured her he would. But what could he do? Baby Diane would go back into foster care. There was no other way. Soon, DeLuca would get the scoop about the lawyer and the whole scheme, whatever it was. They'd find Leonard Perl.

Jake stopped at the light on Wiscasset Street, checked the backseat, carefully hit the gas again. How long had it been going on? How many children had Maggie erased from the system? They'd investigate, see how many families were involved. Discover how many parents would get a life-changing phone call.

Diane made a whimpery noise as the cruiser took the

turn onto Hinshaw Street. Jake caught her pink reflection in his rearview. Asleep again. *A bad dream? You have no idea, baby girl.*

What bugged the hell out of him? Maggie was right, in an impossible way. Diane would probably be better off with the family who'd arranged for the illegal adoption. Problem was, they'd arranged to adopt a kidnapped child.

He punched up his cell. Bethany Sibbach answered before the end of the first ring.

"I see you," she said.

Jake saw a curtain in her front bay window pull aside, a warm glow from the living room lights behind Bethany's silhouette. From inside, she raised a hand in salute. "I'll be right out to help," she said into the phone.

"She's asleep," Jake said. He parked, then twisted around to look through the meshed metal barrier. Diane's head lolled to one side, her fists open. The floppy ears of her pink stuffed rabbit peeked out from under the blanket.

"No problem," Bethany said.

A porch light flipped on, and Jake saw Bethany's front door open.

"Dispatch to Detective Brogan," the voice cracked over his radio.

Damn. He checked to see if the staticky communication had awakened the baby. As a babysitter he stunk, but Diane Marie would be in Bethany's hands in a minute. Margaret Gunnison—who, if all went as hoped, was currently at HQ spilling the whole deal to DeLuca and a stenographer—had insisted she'd never heard of Bethany Sibbach. So Jake decided there was no risk in turning the baby over to her. He had to identify Diane and confirm she'd been in the Callaberry apartment, the infant Gunnison and Perl kidnapped from state custody. Would little Phillip recognize her? Would the word of a toddler be ruled credible? He did not want to put Phillip on the stand.

"This is Brogan, I copy," Jake said. Bethany was hurrying down her front walk, wrapped in a fluttering plaid shawl, carrying a white blanket.

"We have your BOLO on Leonard Perl, Detective," dispatch said. Jake had called in the lookout so cops could start tracking down the asshole. If he was still in Boston. "Airlines report no one using that name through Logan. Planes are delayed anyway, Detective, no one coming or going. No one at the bus or train station has a record of the name. We're efforting a photo from the Florida registry."

"I copy." There was no reason for Perl to run, since he'd have no idea they had Gunnison. Or baby Diane. No idea they'd be on his trail. Unless he'd heard about Ricker's death and feared the cops would make the landlord-tenant connection.

Bethany arrived at the cruiser as Jake climbed out and opened the back door.

"Thanks, Dr. Sibbach. Like I told you, this is a new one. But this little girl . . ." He unclicked the pink webbing and scooped the blanketed infant into his arms. Diane squirmed, then settled, screwing up her eyes as if to cry, then deciding against it. ". . . might be the answer to Phillip's question."

Bethany accepted the blanketed bundle, draping her shawl around both of them, tucking it across the child. It had started to snow, a few gentle flakes. "Where baby, you mean," she whispered.

Jake nodded. "Is he awake?"

"He might be. Poor thing. It'd be better if he slept through the night, though."

Jake grabbed the car seat, closed the cruiser door, as softly as he could. He caught up with Bethany as she neared the front door. His cell phone rang.

Damn. "I'll be right there," he stage-whispered at Bethany, and put the car seat on the steps in the shelter of the front porch. "Don't let Phillip see the baby until I get there." That was a moment he had to witness first-hand.

"Brogan," he answered.

"News," DeLuca said.

"You find Perl? Maggie Gunnison give you the scoop on his whereabouts?" Nine o'clock. Jake was starving, freezing, and about to conduct a witness identification session with a toddler. It was time for some good news.

"Nope. But this just in. Kat McMahon is calling a cause on Lillian Finch. She's about to submit, but she told me—"

"Did she now?"

"Homicide." D ignored Jake's sarcasm. "By person or persons unknown. Somebody killed Lillian Finch. Jake?"

"Yeah?"

"You think it was Perl? For some reason?"

Jake needed to get inside. See if Phillip would react to the baby in some way, a way credible enough for Perl to fold when confronted with it. And with Maggie's confession.

But why would Perl have killed Lillian Finch? He should check Finch's house. He could let little Phillip sleep now, and come back first thing in the morning.

"You're thinking the adoption thing connects them?" Jake said. "Well, Perl had to be in Boston on Sunday to kill Brianna Tillson. Lillian Finch was probably killed that same day, so he'd have been available. He can't know we've got Maggie Gunnison, so maybe he's still in town. That's the problem. We have no idea of his agenda."

"Brilliant, Watson," DeLuca said. "But where the hell is he?"

"I'll just take a fast look at Finch's house." Jake hoped

it was the right decision. "Maybe there's something Hennessey and Kurtz missed."

"Listen, Harvard? Go home. Maggie Gunnison's contemplating her future in a cozy jail cell. We'll start on her again tomorrow. Finch's house ain't gonna vanish overnight. It's after nine o'clock. You've been on more than twelve hours. Go home."

Jake looked at Bethany's front door. Phillip and Phoebe were asleep inside. Bethany could call him before they woke up so he'd be there for Phillip's first moment with the baby. Maybe now he could call Jane. Make sure she was safe. Even get a large pepperoni and some wine and see if she'd like to—

"In my dreams." Jake clicked open his car door. "Assuming Hennessey left the access keys in the usual spot, it won't take long. I'll let you know what I find."

Finally. Traffic had been hellish, the forecast of bad weather inspiring Boston's already unpredictable drivers into speeding like maniacs or hugging the slow lane. Tuck had called, saying she and Carlyn were having popcorn and watching a movie, and they'd be in touch.

Jane made the turn onto Margolin Street. Most driveways were empty, garage doors closed. Every Bostonian knew this was a night to keep your car inside. She squinted through the dark and mist, scanning under porch lights for house numbers. *Almost there.*

A blue Accord was parked up the street. Ella? Pulling closer, she could see the empty front seat. And a bumper sticker announcing I HEART ADOPTION.

"Stupid!" Jane said out loud. If Ella had gone inside . . .

The 411 operator had told her Lillian Finch's address was 27 Margolin. No car in that driveway. Porch light on, and some interior lights. No crime scene tape. Maybe the cops had taken it down.

Where the hell was Ella?

She eased into the parking spot behind what must be Ella's car, grabbed her cell phone, punched in the number. A van was parked way up Margolin, but otherwise the street was deserted. That's because the smart people were inside.

The phone rang, and rang again, and then went to voice mail.

"This is Ella Gavin. I'm sorry I can't . . ."

Jane clonked her head against the back of her seat as the phone message ran out. She ignored the beep, hung up. *Now what?*

Then she saw the smoke.

65

"Why did we come back here, a-*gain*?" Kellianne wanted to go home. It was starting to snow a little, freezing, and the new 'bilia she'd snagged was burning a hole in her tote bag. After the boys finished inside, cleaning or whatever, they'd packed up the empty plastic containers, one of the solvent buckets, and the smaller drop cloth, and shoved it all into the back of the van. They'd started for home, driven a few blocks, yammering the whole way, and Kellianne figured they were out of there. Then Kev doubled back, and now, for some stupid reason, they were parked up the street from that woman's house.

"Are you listening to me? Yoo-hoo, in the front seat?"

"Stuff it, little girl." Kev didn't even turn around. "We don't have to tell you a thing."

"Yeah." Keefer didn't look at her, either. "Just shut up and think about—"

"She doesn't think," Kev said. "Doesn't know the meaning of the word."

They were staring out the windshield. Laughing. At her.

So dumb. And so wrong. She did *too* think. Right now she was thinking she needed to get home and look at her stuff. She sure couldn't do it in the backseat of the stupid van, even though her brothers were glued to the window. Looking at what?

"You see anything?" Keefer said.

"Nope." Kev buzzed down his window, stuck his nose out, and sniffed.

Maybe he was trying to catch a clean breath. The car was so hazy with weed and chemicals it was making her high just sitting there. She thought again about the contents of her tote bag. This time she hadn't held back. It was kind of—stealing. She didn't like the word. But again. If family members hadn't come to take the stuff, maybe no one wanted it. She bet no one even knew what the dead woman had in her bedroom drawers, so it wouldn't be missed. Yes. She was right. It was all fine.

A couple of pearl necklaces, a silver bracelet, some earrings—old lady clip-ons, but who cared—and a semi-cool gold chain. She glanced at the two doofus boys, but they were still focused front, so she rummaged into the bag and pulled out the chain. Yanking her parka open, she fastened the clasp around her neck, then patted it into place, feeling the weight of the metal through her T-shirt. She didn't have to sell everything. She'd put the gold cross she'd taken from the old guy's keys on this chain. It was okay for her to have nice things. About time, too.

"Can't smell anything, either," Kev said, closing his window. "Should be soon, though."

"*What* should be soon? What are we doing? I'm not kidding, you guys are the weirdest . . ."

And then she looked up and saw—was it smoke?

Not in Lillian's desk. Not in the files. *Darn.* Ella slid the second file cabinet drawer back into place and surveyed Lillian's tiny home office, hands on hips. Walnut-stained bookshelves, desk, rolling swivel chair, tweed love seat, rectangular coffee table covered with a flowery cloth, canvas magazine rack. No windows.

Lucky the living room light had been on, and back here, the office light, too. At first she'd worried, but then decided maybe the police didn't want burglars to believe the house was vacant. Made sense.

She'd been here a couple of times, but never thought about where Lillian might hide something. She sniffed, trying to ignore the funny smell. Ella's eyes were smarting a little, maybe because she was so nervous. Every second it seemed like she heard a weird noise. But that couldn't be. She was alone.

Which reminded her. Jane would be arriving soon. She had to hurry. She could call Jane and find out *how* soon, she supposed. But she'd left her phone in the car. Maybe use Lillian's? If it hadn't been disconnected? She picked up the receiver of the black desk phone. No dial tone. Jane's number was in her cell, anyway, not in her head. Better to just hurry.

She wrinkled her nose. Musty or something. Well, the house had been closed since . . . oh. Ella's arms went goose bumps. Was this what death smelled like? Was she smelling *death*?

Her eyes widened. Heart raced. It felt like the walls of the little office were closing in on her. She should go. Leave. *Now*. Nothing was worth—But then, no. *No*. This was her only chance, maybe, to find the proof that the Brannigan was sending families the wrong children. Lillian always kept every document. She'd told Ella that from day one. Since there was nothing incriminating in Lillian's office at the Brannigan, whatever she'd kept must be here.

Or in a safe deposit box, or in a safe, or somewhere else completely, Ella's common sense yelled at her. *Or perhaps you're looking for something that doesn't exist.*

She refused to accept that. Because the thing that

brought her here—all those files she looked at Sunday night about the Beerman baby, and the other most recent calls—Hoffner, Lamonica, DaCosto—everything had *looked* normal. No secret scribbles or special codes, no yellow stickies or funny numbers. Nothing that would indicate those reunited families were different from any others.

I've looked at these from top to bottom, from head to toe, she'd complained out loud to Whiskers. That's what did it.

Head to toe.

It wasn't about what was in the files. It was about what *wasn't* in them.

That's what she was looking for.

Was it really smoke? Jane rolled down her car window, leaning out through the half-rain half-snow that slickened the streets and would threaten power lines if the temperature kept falling. She thought she'd seen the slightest of wisps, snaking from the basement window on the side of Lillian's house. Now it was gone. Maybe it was from neighborhood fireplaces. Or the wind.

She buzzed up the window, looked at the glowing numbers on her dashboard. Nine thirty. It had taken her frustratingly long to get here in the maddening traffic. Ella promised to wait. Clearly she hadn't. Now she wasn't answering her phone.

Nine thirty-one. Now what? There was no police tape, but no matter. If Ella was inside, that was something Jane would *not* get involved in. Ella Gavin, a grown-up, could make her own decisions. If she'd illegally entered a crime scene, that decision was a stupid one.

Jane blew out a breath, calculating.

If Ella was in the Finch house, it was so absurd that—
Damn. Jane turned off the engine, and opened the door

into the night before she could change her mind. She'd knock on the door, see if Ella was there, and drag the idiot woman out of the house before she could do anything dumb. Well, dumber.

Jane checked both ways as she crossed Margolin Street. Unnecessary. There was no traffic. Just more sleet. She wrapped her muffler closer. Got angrier with every stride. She should be home, with a glass of wine. And possibly, Jake, planning their future, not goose-chasing this *delusional* person who imagined she'd find *proof* that an adoption agency was sending birth parents the wrong children. She would *definitely* kill Tuck.

Thing was. It would make a hell of a story. If she could nail it tonight, get whatever Ella was searching for, she could bang out such a blockbuster she'd be on the front page for weeks. Her job would be safe and everyone would live happily ever after.

She marched up the front walk, head down against the bluster, in the lee of the big shrubs, practicing what she'd say to Ella. Get out, let's leave, let's meet with my city editor, decide what to do. In a reasonable way. A legal way. Let's make sure you aren't arrested for trespassing and burglary.

At the front door, she knocked. Again. Nothing. She rang the doorbell, but didn't hear a chime echoing from inside. Broken? She knocked again. No answer.

Maybe Ella wasn't inside after all.

She turned, ready to bail. Happy to bail. Relieved.

She could talk to Ella in the morning.

The smell was getting worse, and it seemed like the room was . . . well, Ella's knees felt a little shaky. No wonder she was nervous. She kept hearing funny noises. It had to be the wind, though. Tree branches hitting the roof.

Ella lowered herself to the love seat, taking deep calming breaths. She'd rest, only for a moment. She felt a little sleepy, probably nerves. Leaning back on the cushion, she stretched full length, trying to slide her feet under the coffee table, but instead, they hit something solid. *Huh*. The table was more like a . . . She leaned forward, lifting the heavy cloth that draped over . . . something.

A trunk. Under the fabric, the table was really a trunk. Like those steamer trunks she'd seen in old movies. She picked up the fabric by the hem, and saw the trunk's two metal clasps, each with a loop for a padlock. But no locks held them in place.

Her eyes were beginning to water a bit. She was doing her best not to think what death smelled like, or how long Lillian's body had lain, undiscovered, in the bedroom right next door. She had decided to do this, and she was going to do it.

Ella stood, pulled at the cloth cover, tossed it aside. Lillian wasn't there to make sure everything stayed exactly in place.

Using both hands, Ella flapped open the clasps and lifted the lid. It creaked up on expanding metal hinges, and when she pushed it to the limit, it stayed in place with a click.

She stared at what she saw inside, almost afraid to reach out her hand to touch it.

The lid slammed closed. Ella jumped back, terrified at the sound.

"Ow!" she yelled, though she wasn't hurt. She held a hand to her pounding heart. Tried to smile. "Pull yourself together, Ella."

She creaked open the top again, this time holding it in place with one hand while she stared at the contents.

It was not packed with clothes, or old blankets, or battered photo albums. No family heirlooms, no souvenirs or memorabilia. On the bottom of the trunk, a spindly metal file holder, matching the empty one she'd seen on Lillian's desk. But this one wasn't empty.

One after the other, manila folders, labeled, lined up—alphabetically, she instantly noticed—in a row. A dozen, maybe more. Each folder marked in Lillian's precise handwriting on a stick-on label.

The label on the first file folder said BEERMAN.

Ella, on her knees, still holding up the trunk lid with one hand, reached in to pull out the folder.

If she was right? Everything would change.

66

"**Check. It. Out.**" Keefer's whispery voice had that stoned sound. Kellianne could always tell when he was high. Instead of passing the joint to Kev, he gestured with it, out the windshield. "Freakin' a. It's working. All we have to do is wait."

"No shit," Kev said. "But what if—"

"I took the batteries out," Keefer said. "So the alarms won't go off. Cut the phone. And it's getting snowy, no one can see out their windows. Till it's too late."

Kellianne leaned forward, her arms on the padded back of the front seat, talking around the headrests. "If you guys don't tell me what's going on, I'm gonna call the cops myself. Rat you out. I can do it, you know."

It probably wasn't the smartest thing to say. The boys weren't that much fun when they were high, and sometimes even got mad. And kind of ugly. "Ha ha, only kidding," she said. "But really, I mean—"

"Little sister," Kev interrupted. "We are the problem solvers. How do we keep five-oh from connecting us with the geezer in the Lexus? We gotta make sure they don't know we were in the dead woman's house. And how do we do that?"

Kev sucked on the joint again, then handed it to Keefer

with a nod. "Go ahead, say it, bro." He choked out the words to keep the smoke down.

"We get rid of the house," Keefer said.

Kellianne blinked, trying to follow Keefer's pointing finger. It was hard to see the house. Snow was falling and there were trees and shadows everywhere and a huge shrub right in their way. All she could see was the backs of their heads, the fogged-up windshield, the dark outline of the shrub, and snow.

Kellianne was so confused. "You can't even see the house."

"We're watching for the—never mind," Kev said. "Shut the hell up and go back to your coloring books."

Kellianne tried to see what they were seeing, but the whole van was smoky inside. Whatever.

Jane made it halfway down the path, heading back toward her car. Stopped behind the huge bayberry bush, protected from the icing night and the bitter sting of cold. Something smelled funny. She glanced across the street, looking for chimneys, thinking maybe there were fires in fireplaces.

She turned, sniffing again, and listened hard, trying to untangle the soft whistle of the wind and the hiss of the falling sleet from whatever had stopped her.

She should try Ella one more time. Jane reached into her parka pocket for her phone, but it slipped out of her gloved hand and onto the snow-slick flagstone path.

"Damn." As she turned to scoop up the phone, she heard the sound of shattering glass. Glass? It wasn't the phone screen, it was much louder than that. She turned, following the sound. The side of the house. The basement window. Smoke. Pouring from the blown-out casement. *Smoke.*

She grabbed her phone, yanked off her glove, punched 911, wiping with a finger to keep the snow off the screen. She stuffed the glove into a pocket. Her hand was already freezing.

"Nine-one-one, what's your emergency?"

Jane calmed her voice. She'd done dozens of stories about frantic 911 callers who delayed emergency response by incomprehensible terrified babble, talking too fast or leaving out facts.

"There's a fire," she said. "At twenty-seven Margolin Street."

"Are you in Boston, ma'am? Fire?"

"Yes, fire." It was all Jane could do not to shriek. She'd said *fire*, what was unclear about that? Oh, she was using her cell phone. The dispatcher had no idea where she was calling from. "Yes, Boston. A window's blown out."

"Are you outside, ma'am?"

"Yes, yes, I'm outside, but—"

"Is everyone else outside, ma'am?"

"Are you sending the fire truck?" Jane was losing it, fast. This was taking forever and she couldn't figure out why the dispatcher sounded confused. There was nothing confusing. "It's a *fire*!"

Jane turned back to the front door, clamping the phone to her cheek. The door might simply be open. She'd never tried the lock, but only knocked and tried the bell, assuming that Ella would have answered if inside. But what if something was wrong inside? Maybe Jane should have called 911 sooner.

And hoped they wouldn't think it was Jane-who-cried-wolf.

"Ma'am? Repeating the address, that's twenty-seven Margolin, Boston, correct? We've got some power lines down and—Hold on please. Don't hang up." Jane heard the dispatcher's voice connecting with someone, probably alerting the fire department. Jane strained to hear as she banged on the door again.

"Ella! *Ella!*" She touched the doorknob. Cold, even through her glove she could feel it was cold. She turned it. It opened.

"Ma'am? I have equipment on the way. Again, confirming it's Boston, twenty-seven Margolin Street."

"Yes, yes," Jane said. *How many times did she have to*—"A white house, red brick trim, driveway, white front door. I don't know if anyone is still inside. They might be. Should I go look?"

"No, ma'am," the dispatcher's voice was louder now. Insistent. "No. Please walk away from the building. As quickly as you can. Now."

Jane stood on the porch, looking through the open door. She saw the living room. All looked fine.

"Ma'am?" The dispatcher's voice cracked through. "Do you understand?"

"Reports of smoke showing at two-seven Margolin," the deep voice of the BPD dispatcher bristled over the two-way in Jake's cruiser. "Any available units are requested to . . ."

Jake stared at the blinking lights of his dashboard radio for an instant. Had he misunderstood? That's where he'd been heading.

"Repeating, any available units to two-seven Margolin Street. Reports of smoke showing at a structure. All units fire and police, all units near and clear, please report. We have a caller on hold, awaiting . . ."

Shit. Jake flipped up his wig-wags, switched on the siren, hit the gas.

"Brogan responding to the available-units call," he said into the radio. "ETA is in one minute."

"Copy that, Detective. One minute."

He felt his tires fishtail on the slick pavement, eased them straight again, powered through a red light, and banged the final turn toward Lillian Finch's house. *Shit.* Maybe Perl had gotten there first.

Or maybe someone had gotten to Perl. If it was Perl.

Ella lifted the rack of files from the trunk, set the wire file holder on the braided rug, let the trunk lid thud close. Sitting cross-legged on the floor, she stared at what was in the first manila folder she'd opened. The one marked BEERMAN.

A footprint. A photocopy, embossed with a notary seal. She ran her fingers over the raised letters. Woodmere Beach Hospital. The birthdate was—Ella quickly calculated—twenty-eight years ago. And it was marked BABY GIRL BEERMAN.

A tiny infant footprint, the incontrovertible evidence of identity. This was either Tucker Cameron's footprint, or it wasn't. Every folder she'd taken from Lillian's desk Sunday night had been missing that one critical piece of paper. Ella had put those folders safely away, hiding them in her apartment.

Had Lillian taken the footprints out on purpose? Or had someone else removed the footprints—and Lillian found out? Found them?

Was Lillian saving the footprints that proved birth parents had been sent the wrong children? Why?

The rack also held files labeled HOFFNER. LAMONICA. DACOSTO. The very families she'd contacted.

And a dozen more. Were they all the wrong children?

What was that noise? Ella lifted her head. Scanned the room. Sniffed again.

Now she could see it. She wasn't imagining it. *That's* what she'd smelled. Not death. But smoke. *Smoke.* And now it was seeping into the windowless room. Wisps of gray curled through each metal vent lining one side of the room. And on the other side. Every one. No question. It stung her eyes. Filled her nose. *Smoke.*

Fire.

"Ma'am?" the dispatcher's voice buzzed into Jane's ear. "Are you away from the house? We need you to move away. Right now. Let us take care of this, ma'am. There are units en route. Please confirm you are away from the building."

Jane stood in the doorway. She was brave, sometimes, but going into a burning building was—well, she'd done enough news stories to know what could happen. Sure there were sometimes those "hero" sound bites after. But not always.

The front door stood open now, no smoke in the entryway. Curvy wooden table under a framed mirror, circular rug. No smoke. Jane saw lights on in the living room and the back of the house. No smoke inside. Not that she could see. Maybe the fire was a little one, just in the basement. Maybe she should—

"Ella!"

"Ma'am?" The dispatcher's voice. "I'm ordering you to—"

"Ella!" She screamed now. Ella's car was still empty, that woman was somewhere, and if not inside this house, where? This had been Ella's destination, she'd made that clear, and Jane had told her to wait. But Ella had obviously ignored her.

Damn it, damn it, *damn* it.

She took a step inside.

67

"Jane!" Jake raced up the front walk, jacket flapping, his cruiser's wig-wags bluing the snowflakes and siren wailing. Jane's car sat across the street, behind a blue Accord. He'd instantly seen both were unoccupied.

What the hell was Jane doing here?

He saw the open doorway. Her unmistakable silhouette in the dim light from the home's interior. Smoke puffed from an obviously broken basement window. The street seemed deserted, except for a light-colored van up the block. Half his brain noticed the van pull away.

"Jane! Stop!"

He reached the door, ran inside, grabbed her by the shoulder, yanked her toward him.

Was she crying? Her hair was coated with a melting layer of sleet, drops of water lining her face. She wore only one glove.

"Jane, what the hell are you doing?" He pulled her out the front door, feeling her stumble and shake him off, then stop resisting. "There's a god damn fire."

"I think there's someone in there!" She pointed toward the house as he pulled her down the path to the sidewalk. "Ella Gavin. From the Brannigan. She told me she needed to get something of Lillian Finch's. That Lillian had given her keys. I told her not to, but—"

Jane gulped, hands on knees, catching her breath. "So I had to—"

"You were going *in*?" Jake grabbed his radio, raising his voice over the siren. "Dispatch, this is Brogan at twenty-seven Margolin. Reporting an emergency. Confirm smoke is showing from basement window. Reports of a person or persons who may be trapped inside. Please advise of your ETA."

He pulled Jane behind his cruiser, clutching her hand, snow swirling around them. "You're completely crazy. Listen. Get across the street. Behind your car. Stay there. Stay *down*. Hear me?"

He turned her to face him, needing to let her know this was serious. Dangerous. She was crazy, his Janey, thinking she could go into a burning house.

He was going to kill her.

But first he had to go in. Try to save whoever was in there. "Do not go near that place. Engines are on the way, the fire isn't even—"

There was a sound. A whoosh. A flash.

Jane ducked into Jake's shoulder, shielding her eyes. Ella was inside. Jane knew she was, had to be, and it seemed she'd been inside way too long, and the fire department hadn't even arrived, and someone needed to—

"Down!" Jake pulled her close, held her hard, his breath warm against her ear. Smoke plumed from the house. "Get *down*!" She'd never heard his voice like this. He clicked his radio.

"Dispatch? You copy?"

Jake yanked her, so hard her knees buckled and she grabbed his car door handle to stay standing. He was trying to protect her, she understood, but Ella was in there. Inside. Someone had to save her. Someone had to help.

"Jake! We have to—"

"I *know*, Janey. Dispatch, this is Brogan. Requesting all available fire and rescue units." To Jane. "I'm going in. But it's—All units. You copy?"

Orange flames licked from the basement window, and then another sound, another whoosh, and another window exploded with black smoke, flames following the darkness out of the shattered glass.

"Go, go, *go*!" Keefer yelled, one fist pumping the air as Kellianne's head slammed into the seatback. Kevin must have floored it. The van lurched forward, sliding on the slick street, tires slipping in the slush, Kev ignoring the stop sign again and hitting the gas, careening onto Mass Ave.

Looking out the back window as Kev hit full speed ahead, Kellianne had seen the fire. So that's what they were doing.

"You *set*—"

"The house was empty, right? But full of our stuff. Only Hennessey knew we were there, right, and not like he's gonna rat us out. Get him in as much trouble as us. So, *adiós*, house. We started in the basement. One match to that disinfectant stuff alone's enough to—hey—whoa, watch it, bro! That's a goddamn bus!"

Kev yanked the wheel and slammed on brakes, as a T bus turned a corner right into them. The van lurched to the right, up the curb onto the sidewalk. Kellianne clutched the side strap with one hand, her tote bag to her chest with the other, closed her eyes, felt the van bump back on the street. She risked opening her eyes, but couldn't let go of the strap. They were fine. Driving again. *Holy shit.*

To cover up what they did when that old guy died, her stupid brothers had set the whole freaking house on fire.

The tote bag of 'bilia seemed to get heavier on her lap.

No one would connect them to that house, right? There'd been no contract, no formal business deal except with the Hennessey cop, and Kev was right, *he* sure wasn't gonna rat. Their cleaning supplies would burn up in the fire.

She guessed that was the whole point.

The streets of Boston whizzed by, snow splatting on the windshield. Kevin finally keeping to the speed limit. The fire was way behind them, out of their lives. Who'd ever blame *them* for it?

She nodded, grudgingly giving her brothers some props. This could work.

68

Plumes of white steam hissed from the remains of 27 Margolin Street. Snaking canvas fire hoses connected hydrants up the sidewalk and across the street. Neighbors clustered on the sidewalk, faces bundled against the cold, shielding their eyes from the glaring daylight-bright spots the firefighters switched on to help them in the darkness.

Jane could no longer feel her feet, but could not bear to wait in the car. She stood with the others, behind the firefighter lines, watching, mesmerized, as the water froze almost as quickly as it hit what was left of the roof and puffed white into the dark night. The snow had stopped, but the temperature had plummeted, Jane could tell by her fingers and tingling face. Firefighters, some with icicles on their helmets, stood red-faced and determined, rooted, aiming their powerful hoses.

"Losing battle," Jane heard one guy mutter. "The place went up like a—"

"Miss Ryland? Jane?" The incident commander touched her coat sleeve. Jane recognized Sergeant Monahan from her general assignment reporter days. Her heart clenched. This was going to be about Ella. It could not be good. And it was her fault. Jane's own fault.

She'd watched, tears streaming down her face, as a

canvas-clad firefighter emerged from the still-black smoke, emerged from where the front door used to be, carrying a blanket-draped—well, a person. Jane saw feet poking from under the edge of whatever covered it. Had to be Ella. Ella's body. Motionless. The firefighter had not been running. Might Jane have been able to save her?

Jane lunged forward, toward the figures silhouetted in the flames, but Jake had held her back, one hand wrapped around her arm, his body pressed against her back. Stronger than she was.

"Honey, Janey, stop. There's nothing you can do. Nothing you could have done. Just—let's see what happened."

"But I could have . . . should have . . ."

"No. You shouldn't have," Jake said. "Trying to help is one thing. Being an idiot is another."

"But what if—"

"There's no 'what if,' " Jake told her. "There's what is. And *that* we don't know yet."

The commander was saying something. She had to focus.

"Ma'am? Jane?"

Jane turned. The air still reeked of fire and smoke, the choking darkness blanketing the night. Jane could taste it, and could smell nothing else.

"She's asking for you," the sergeant said. "She's getting oxygen, she shouldn't remove the mask. We're transporting her any second. But she was trying to tell us something, pretty upset, so we gave her paper. She wrote 'find Jane Ryland.' And here you are."

Monahan touched his mustache with the tip of a finger. "Is there something you'd like to tell us? You have ID on her? Could she have set this fire? This one's clearly suspicious. Arson's on the way."

"Huh?" Jane tried to sort this out. Of course the

firefighters couldn't know who Ella was. How could they? "Her name is Ella Gavin. She works at—She's a friend of the person who—She's asking for *me*? I'm sure she couldn't have—wouldn't have—She'll be okay?"

"She'd covered herself with a thick tablecloth of some kind," Monahan told her. The glare from the emergency lights made elongated shadows on the snow and slickening ice as Jane and Monahan picked their way toward the ambulance, stepping over an obstacle course of engorged canvas hoses.

"She was trying to carry a bunch of papers, something like that, but O'Toole says they dropped as he carried her out." He gestured at the smoky destruction. "Hope they weren't important."

"Hello, Detective Brogan, I remember you. Do you remember me?"

Jake felt a tug on his sleeve as he watched Jane follow Monahan toward Ella Gavin. He knew how Jane felt. He, too, had stood there, helpless and surprised, as freaking Hennessey shot Curtis Ricker. Barely a moment had gone by since the shooting when he hadn't wondered—*Might I have prevented it? Was there something I could have done?* To hear Jane express the same wish and know she felt exactly the same remorse made him care about her even more. If that was possible. Such a genuinely good—

"Detective?" The tug grew more insistent. "Remember?"

He turned. In the bright circle of the street light, wearing a white crocheted hat and too much rouge, stood— Dorothy. Debbie. "Dolly," he said. "Dolly . . . Richards."

"Yes, exactly, Detective Brogan." Dolly poked his arm with a finger. "I told you something was going on here, didn't I? *Now* don't you agree? Don't you suspect it might be those people in the van?"

"People in the van?" Jake's peripheral memory dragged up the image of a gray van driving away from the fire when he'd been focused on yanking Jane out of the burning house. He turned to Mrs. Richards with narrowed eyes. "What van, ma'am?"

"Ella?" Jane's whisper was almost more to herself than to the blanketed form on the gurney. Ella's face was covered with a plastic oxygen mask, her body silvered with a space-blanket throw. Her eyes were closed. *Was she—?*

"Ma'am?" The EMT beside the gurney, brush-cut and zipped into a parka yellow-stenciled DONALD CANNON, stepped between them. "We're transporting her now. Please contact Mass General for more information. She's on oh-two, she cannot take off that mask to talk to you."

On oxygen. Ella was breathing. Jane looked at Monahan, pleading for intervention. "Will she be okay?" *Tell me she'll be okay.*

"Don, this is Jane Ryland." Monahan stepped up, showed the EMT the handwritten paper. "The person your patient was asking for."

Cannon frowned, shook his head. "Negative. She cannot talk. Let her see you're here, Miss Ryland. Then we're going."

Jane took one step toward the gurney, fearing what was under that blanket, fearing the future, knowing she might have made a difference, and didn't. *Didn't.*

A movement under the blanket, and Ella's right hand came out, gestured Jane toward her.

"Go ahead," Cannon said. "Thirty seconds."

Ella made a motion like *writing*.

Cannon handed Ella a mechanical pencil, then pulled

a tiny pad from a pocket in his coveralls and held it in front of her, not touching the blanket. The three of them watched, Jane holding her breath, as Ella scrawled something, then something else.

"Pocket?" Jane leaned in to the paper. "Cat?"

The pencil moved again. "Feed?" Jane read.

"There's something in your pocket, and you want me to feed your cat?" Jane struggled to keep herself from crying and laughing at the same time. "Are your keys in your pocket? Blink twice for yes."

Ella did. Then pantomimed *write* again.

"I'm sorry," the EMT said. "No more. The sooner we get her out of here, the sooner she'll recover. Say your good-byes."

The EMT had said "recover." That was a good sign.

"Cannon, let's do this," Monahan said. "Get her keys. And whatever. Quickly."

"Yessir." Using two fingers, the EMT lifted the silver blanket, inch by inch. Then turned to Jane, holding a keychain in one hand. A folded piece of paper in the other.

"Is this what you want me to have?" Jane leaned in, close as she could.

Ella's eyes widened, blinked twice, then closed.

"What *van*?" The woman shot Jake a withering look, right out of grade-school detention. "The van I told you about before. They've been here a couple times now. Looked to me like some kind of cleanup crew, you know? Carrying in buckets and mops, carrying out big green trash bags of—whatever. It reminded me of that movie, where the girls come and clean up after murders and things? I thought that's who these people were. That's why they had those rolls of yellow tape. But they wouldn't come after dark, would they, Detective?"

Afterwards? Was here? He'd keyed in on them outside the funeral, but had been crazed with the Ricker thing since then. Afterwards was the crime scene cleanup crew who'd interrupted Kat McMahon's examination of Brianna Tillson.

They'd been called to Callaberry Street. That must have been okayed by landlord Leonard Perl. And they'd been here. *Who okayed that?* This was Finch's house. She owned it, not Perl. Jake had checked with Alvarez in Records. Finch lived alone.

So. Brianna Tillson—murdered. Lillian Finch's death—ruled a homicide. Niall Brannigan's death outside Finch's house—suspicious. The glue that held all three together was Afterwards. And, possibly, the elusive Leonard Perl.

"Did you see any of the people from the van, Mrs. Richards?"

"Dolly, I told you. There were two at least, maybe three. I can't be sure." She gestured toward the house with her mitten. "You think the fire is out? Who was the body that firefighter was carrying? How do you think the fire started? The van people could have done it."

Mrs. Richards paused her monologue and nodded, apparently approving of her own detective skills. "They sure could've."

Jake had to agree. They sure could've.

He reached for his cell, ready to alert DeLuca to accompany him on a come-to-Jesus visit to the now-unsuspecting folks at Afterwards. Folks who would not be so happy when he interrogated them about their role in the death of Niall Brannigan. And their certain knowledge of the whereabouts of Leonard Perl.

He hit DeLuca on speed dial. Then Jake hit "end call." Shit. How many gray vans were there in Boston? No way to prove whose van had been on Margolin Street. Any evidence of their "cleanup" was a smoking mass of embers and debris. Some defense attorney would rip them to shreds.

"Ma'am?" Maybe she could ID one of them. Something. Anything.

"Look at that Jane Ryland," Mrs. Richards was saying. "So pretty. I'd recognize her anywhere. What's she doing here, a story for TV? That's her little black car, must be."

"Yes it's . . ." Jake watched Mrs. Richards take out a little pink spiral notebook, a ballpoint pen dangling from the spiral.

She clicked open the pen and began to write. "Is that a three or an eight, Detective? My eyes aren't what they used to be."

"A three or an—on Jane's license plate?" Jake was confused. "Why would you be writing that down?"

"Like I told you the other day." Mrs. Richard puffed out an exasperated breath. "I always take license plates. Always. Even yours. It started when some neighbors were bringing in all kinds of unsavory types. Then it got to be kind of a habit. Tell you a secret, I use the numbers to play the lottery." She smiled up at him. "Silly, I know. But very lucky."

Jake was almost afraid to ask. Might *he* get lucky? "Mrs. Richards?"

"Dolly," she said.

"Dolly. Let me ask you." He eyed her notebook. "Do you keep track of the dates? Did you write down the license number of the gray van?"

69

"I *hate* search warrants."

Jake had to smile as DeLuca's voice came over the cruiser's speaker.

"No reason to wait to get those assholes. Crime scene cleanup, my ass. They're the freaking criminals."

"Yup, D. They're in on something. And they sure as hell know where Leonard Perl is. But Supe insists we get a warrant before we hit them up. Judge Gallagher's been sent the request affidavit. Hey. It's law and order, right? We're the law. We need her order."

Jake checked his rearview, made sure Jane was following him. It was after midnight. She'd looked zonked and scared and exhausted, but she'd insisted on driving home herself. He shook his head, keeping an eye on her headlights. They'd compromised that she'd follow him, he'd see her safely inside. He held up a hand. Jane waved back. She was so . . .

"Talk about law and order."

Even over the speaker, D's voice oozed disdain.

"What about it?" Jake turned onto Beacon Street, Janey right behind him. The snow was over, but the streets were still slick.

"Well, the bad news is our Maggie Gunnison lawyered up. Guess she realized she was in deep shit. Kidnapping and murder being your basic life-in-prison deal," De-Luca said. "So we're hearing zip from her. She's currently residing in the luxurious confines of the Suffolk lockup, probably calculating her options."

"Which may include offering up the whereabouts of Leonard Perl," Jake said. "Speaking of which, you ever get that Florida DMV photo?"

"You're livin' right," DeLuca said. "It's a fax, if you can believe it. Stone age. The quality's not that great. But I'll e-mail it to your cell. You never know."

Jane pulled into a place in front of her building, behind the spot where Jake had just turned off the engine of his cruiser. She saw his interior lights blink on, saw his door open. So he was getting out, not just waiting for her to come to his window to say good-bye. Would he want to stay over? Would she want him to?

She clicked open her car door and got out, grateful to be home, grateful to be safe, grateful that Ella would live, would even be okay. She wished she could be mad at her.

Ella's keys weighed heavy in her pocket. Tomorrow morning, she'd go feed the cat. Tomorrow morning, she'd try to figure out what to do with the piece of paper Ella had given her. The sky was brightening, the moon a fading memory in the dark blue sky. It was already morning.

Headlights glared around the corner, then stopped at the stop sign up the block.

"Hey, Officer." Jane met Jake halfway on the sidewalk. Then took a step closer. "I'm good. I'm fine. Thanks for, ah, babysitting me. Always good to have a cop around."

"Your tax dollars at work." Jake glanced at her front door. Took a step closer to her. "Your tax dollars also allow me to see you inside. If you so desire. It's our after-hours special."

They stood, less than arm's length away. Jane felt his force field, drawing her, in the murky light from the streetlights, and the thin whisper of the wind, and the gray clouds separating to show a glimmer of the winter stars. *Jake.* She remembered his touch, the urgency in his voice as he'd grabbed her from the fire. Why couldn't she fall into his arms, grateful, needing him, giving in, forgetting all the rules of the world and caring about only their own rules? "Jake, I—"

Did they have to be careful, even *here?* Was the watcher in the brownstone seeing the two of them? What if he was the one who—She was too exhausted to think about it. About anything but Jake.

"You—we—" Jane took another step closer, reached out her hand, dared to brush an imaginary snowflake from Jake's jacket. Maybe now they could—His phone beeped, and she warmed with reassurance when he ignored it. "It's been quite a day."

She heard a car's engine shift, and looked up to see the headlights at the stop sign move closer.

"Yeah, it has. Quite a day. And now we both smell like fire."

Jake had to leave, needed to leave, couldn't possibly leave. He should be at Bethany Sibbach's house at the crack of dawn, before Phillip got a look at baby Diane, and there was no way he could make it through another day on no sleep. Today'd been tough enough. *Putting it mildly.* Dolly Richards' license plate list—including the gray van's—were safely in his notes. But Jane. She'd been through so much. He didn't even know why Ella had called her. "You were nuts to go into a burning building, hon—Jane."

"You went in, too, you know." Jane's voice was a whisper. Her touch lingered on his jacket. "To get *me.*

So you're just as nuts. But I keep thinking what might have happened if you hadn't."

Headlights pulled into a parking space in front of the brownstone across the street. Jane pointed to the car.

"Your hot-shot surveillance guy's probably seeing him, you know," she whispered. "And, more importantly, he's seeing us. Don't want him to report you, right? You here with me in the middle of the night. Standing like this. How'd you explain that?"

"Police business, ma'am." Jake looped her arm through his, pulling her even closer. "All on the up and up. In fact, I won't have done my duty until I go upstairs, check your whole apartment. Maybe—stay awhile. Make sure nothing untoward happens. Make sure you're safe. Doing my sworn duty."

Jane smiled that smile up at him. He could feel the weight of her body against his. He was exhausted, she was, too. If he went inside, they'd probably fall asleep instantly. Very romantic.

"Hec." She was looking over his shoulder now, and her face had changed.

"Heck what?" *Heck?*

"No. H-e-c. Underhill. The *Register* freelancer. Getting out of that car across the street. In front of surveillance-guy's building," Jane said, her voice low. She shrugged. "Alex told me he lived in my neigh—"

"What?" Jake turned, following her gaze as she paused, mid-sentence. She was staring at the man across the street.

He felt her hand clutch his arm.

"Jake?" she whispered. "If you want to do your sworn duty, come with me."

70

She was right.

Had to be. Where had Hec Underhill been all those times she tried to find him? "He's always out," the guy in the photo lab kept telling her. Hec obviously knew she was working on the Callaberry Street story. He'd known exactly which house Brianna Tillson's body was in. Knew she was looking for pictures of the bad guy. Knew she'd been banished from the paper. He had her cell phone number and could easily have made the threatening calls. And she herself had told him she was going to Connecticut with Tuck. But *why* would—

"Hec!" Jane kept her voice cheery, waving, as she and Jake approached. He had those cameras strung around his neck. Keys in his hand. She needed to see where he lived. See if he had a camera pointed at her windows. Problem was, Jake still thought Hec was a good guy, working with the cops, and there was no time now to explain her theory. She'd play it by ear.

Hec turned, standing by his car, out of the glow of streetlight. A dark shadow. But Jane recognized him easily enough. She heard Jake's phone beep again, and this time he took it out of his pocket.

"Hey, Hec," Jane began. "What brings you here this time of night? Big story?"

* * *

Message from DeLuca. "Photo," the subject line said. Photo? Must be the picture of Leonard Perl, finally, from the Florida Department of Motor Vehicles. Jake opened it with one thumb. Hec Underhill was a new freelance *Register* photog, he remembered. And hadn't he just seen him at—where was it?

Those cameras around his neck. Right. The pushy guy who'd shown up at Lillian Finch's right after they'd found Brannigan. Jake had been on his way to Jane's supposed break-in. He'd directed the guy to Hennessey. Forgotten about him. *What's to remember?*

Jane was already chatting with Underhill. They were colleagues, of course. Jake checked his phone, where the faxed, then e-mailed, photo from DeLuca was slowly downloading.

Keeping half an eye on Jane, he looked at the emerging photo of Leonard Perl.

Then at Hec Underhill.

Then at the photo.

Same person.

Why was Jake staring at his cell phone? Jane had to keep up the chitchat with Hec until Jake joined her. Hec was blathering about some news story he'd been shooting, complaining again about his imminent retirement and his crap assignments.

Jane nodded, pretending to be fascinated. If Hec was the surveillance guy, he could have broken into her apartment, somehow. He wouldn't tape *himself*! He could have even watched, among the bystanders, as she raced into her building the morning of the break-in.

A break-in that *had* happened.

Hec was even wearing a Celtics hat. But he couldn't have been the guy in the black pickup, because he'd talked to her on the phone from the *Register. Damn.* What was taking Jake so long?

"Yeah, but you know, the news must go on." Jane decided to risk it. "In fact, did you hear there was a break-in at my apartment?"

"Yeah. I live right there." Hec pointed to the brown-stone. "Police have any idea who did it?"

Gotcha, Jane thought. She was tempted to say yes, just to see what he'd do, but gestured toward his apartment instead. "Oh, interesting. Did you see the cops from your apartment that morning?"

"Hey, Jane." Jake stepped up to them, close, almost putting himself between her and Hec. He was holding his cell phone with one hand, with the other adjusting something under his jacket.

"Hey, Jake," she said, moving aside. "Hec Underhill, do you know Detective Jake Brogan? Jake, this is—"

"We met at Margolin Street, if I'm not mistaken. Hold this for a second, Jane, okay?" Jake gave her his cell and stuck out a hand to shake Hec's.

Why would he give her his phone? She glanced at the screen. It had gone to black.

"Hec Underhill?"

Jake had not let go of Hec's hand. And with the other he was bringing out—what?

Underhill tried to pull his hand away. That wasn't gonna happen.

"Hec Underhill?" Jake said again. He flipped open his handcuffs, snapped the first side over Underhill's left wrist, then with one motion turned him and clicked the other so Underhill's hands were cuffed behind his back. His cameras still hung over his chest. "Or should I say—Leonard Perl? You're under arrest for the murder of Brianna Tillson. We know about Maggie Gunnison. We know about the baby. We know about Finn. And Ricker."

Which wasn't exactly 100 percent true, but there was time to find out.

"You have the right to remain silent. Anything you say—"

"I demand a lawyer," Perl interrupted.

"Brilliant," Jake said. This explained why Perl had never answered their calls to Florida when they'd tried to contact him. He'd been here in Boston. Killing Brianna Tillson. "And if your lawyer forgets to tell you, I'm pretty sure kidnapping and murder are both life-sentence felonies. After I finish informing you of your rights, feel free to use the phone downtown. Your tax-payer dollars at work."

Leonard Perl? The landlord? Hec? As Jane worked to put the puzzle pieces together, Jake was finishing his recitation of the Miranda rights. But Perl lived in Florida, didn't he? Absentee landlord. This was Hec Underhill. *The phone?* She punched the button. Up popped what looked like a driver's license photo. Florida DMV. Leonard Perl's name.

But it was a picture of Hec Underhill.

Holy sh—And what did Jake mean by kidnapping? And Jake said Finn. Did he mean Finn Eberhardt? Before Jake took the guy away—whoever he was—she had a few questions of her own.

"Jake, I bet Hec's the surveillance guy. Perl, I mean. Right? He didn't report *himself* to the police, see? When he got into my apartment? Probably simply turned off the camera or something. He knew I was looking into

Callaberry, and Brianna Tillson's death. He's the one who called me, Jake! The nasty calls. *Hey.* Were you in my building last night, too?"

"Lawyer," Underhill-Perl said. "And just so you know, Miss Hotshot, the *Register's* about to lay off a bunch of people. You heard it here first."

What a skeeve. She handed Jake his phone. Then understood the final puzzle piece. Underhill—or, Perl— knew what kind of car she drove.

"Hec? You took my *CAT?* Are you kidding me? You're the guy who handed her to Tuck. And then put her collar in my car." *Total skeeve.* "Tuck had left the car open, right?"

"Good luck finding a new job," Perl said. "And don't get old. No one hires you if you're old."

"Nice guy." Jake guided Perl toward his cruiser, talking over his shoulder at her. "Call me, Jane. Sorry we had to cut this short."

"Hey. Wait." Jane trotted after him, already composing the story in her head. The arrest of Tillson's killer? A *Register* freelancer? The paper's lawyers were going to explode. But she had the headline.

No longer tired, she pulled out her phone, ready to speed-dial Alex and fill him in. So much for her terror of layoffs. This was a big fat story. Who cared how late it was.

"Jake? I need a statement. Did you say 'kidnapping'? And Maggie Gunnison? From DFS? What's this all about? Sounds like a huge story."

"Ah, maybe so. But not written by you, Janey girl." Jake stuffed Perl into the backseat of his cruiser, slammed the door. Touched her on the nose with one finger. "Because unless he decides to confess, you'll have to testify at this asshole's trial."

* * *

"Dispatch, this is Brogan."

Jake shifted into drive as the radio crackled to life. Perl slouched in the backseat, in the same spot where baby Diane Marie had slept only a few hours before. Perl was more the type. "I am en route with a suspect in custody, per the BOLO on Leonard Perl. You can cancel that BOLO, dispatch, as of . . ." Jake checked the dashboard readout. "Two-oh-five A.M."

He needed to call DeLuca. Imagined where he might be. Poor guy wasn't getting much Kat McMahan time. But he'd want to hear about this. He punched in the speed dial as dispatch responded.

"Copy that, Detective. We'll make HQ aware."

"Jake?" DeLuca's phone voice sounded groggy. "Where are you, for crap's sake?"

"With Leonard Perl, on the way to HQ," Jake said. "I'm about to tell him what we know about Maggie Gunnison and baby Diane Marie. Maybe he'll give up Finn. Before Finn gives *him* up."

Jake checked his rearview, gave Perl a cheery wave, hoping he was taking it all in. *Whoever Finn was,* Jake didn't say.

"So. D. If you're not—otherwise occupied—thought you might like to join us downtown."

71

Jane stared out her living room window, looking through the gray morning light toward the building where she'd been told the surveillance guy lived. The police department's "camera buff." *Right.* Hec Underhill. Leonard Perl. Now—as she'd heard during the arrest—in custody for the murder of Brianna Tillson. A murder he hadn't wanted Jane to care so much about. *Why had he killed her? Jake said—kidnapping?*

She'd barely been able to sleep, her brain too full of Perl and Ella and the smell of fire. She'd e-mailed Alex to pitch the story, whatever they could confirm via police protocol, but he hadn't responded yet. There was plenty of time, especially since her byline couldn't be on the story. Jake was right about that. The conflict of interest was enormous. Which totally sucked.

Especially if the *Register* was laying off people. Like Hec—or actually, Perl—had said.

Coda jumped onto the windowsill, getting between her and the view. She scooped her up and carried her down the hall to the study.

Hec—well, Perl—had taken the cat. So disgusting. So brazen. So nice that he was in custody. And so satisfying that she hadn't been wrong. Jake had texted that Hec— she still thought of him that way—had admitted picking her lock and later rattling her door, just to scare her. The cops owed her big. *Girl who cried wolf, my ass.* "I don't think so, cat."

Coda writhed to the floor, scampered away.

It was easier to think about how right she'd been than about Ella Gavin, now in Mass General's ICU. Jake would probably inform the Brannigan people about her, but Jane would have to tell Tuck. And Carlyn. Before they heard about it on the news. What would she to say to them, anyway?

She plopped, exhausted, into her swivel chair, then looked for the millionth time at the tattered piece of paper she'd left on her desk, smoothing out the crumples yet again, smelling the remnants of the smoke that clung to it.

A footprint. A baby's footprint.

Certified by the hospital as an official copy and marked BABY GIRL BEERMAN, this one piece of paper Ella saved from the fire provided the incontrovertible evidence that could reveal Tuck's identity.

The person whose foot matched this decades-old print was unquestionably Audrey Rose Beerman. Was that Tuck?

The moment Jane told someone about it, the moment Jane set the wheels in motion, two lives—at least—would be forever changed. And there'd be no way to stop it.

But this is what Tuck asked her to do. A young woman had almost died to help Tuck find the answer.

Jane reached for the phone. Then stopped, hand in mid-air.

Was it too early? She checked her computer monitor—still before eight in the morning. Too early. She wasn't stalling. But no need to terrify anyone with an early morning call. She took her hand away, rested her chin on her fists, stared at the inky footprint.

Thinking of her drive with Tuck to see Carlyn. And

that person in the black truck who'd terrified them on the highway.

Jake had mentioned "Finn." There could be another Finn, of course, but Jake's Finn was involved with Perl. Maybe she should give Mr. F. Eberhardt a call at DFS.

Hmm.

Were the DFS people—Maggie Gunnison—aware of Perl's arrest yet? Even if Jane couldn't write the story, she could help out the reporter who did by digging up a reaction quote. Any brownie points she could get with Alex were a good thing.

It took only a second to get connected. Eight o'clock. She imagined Vee enthroned at the reception desk. "Maggie Gunnison, please."

"She's not . . . available," Vee said.

Probably too early. Or—of course, she was still on vacation, in Anguilla. She'd missed everything. "Okay, then, may I speak to Finn Eberhardt?"

"He's in today, but out of the office, on the road, ma'am," Vee said. "He's probably driving right now. I can patch you through to his cell phone."

Before Jane could reply, she heard a click and a buzz—exactly like she had in the car when she'd asked Tuck to check that Finn couldn't be tailgating them. The same noises she'd heard when Tuck placed their test call to DFS.

"Finn Eberhardt," the voice came back.

"Curtis Ricker. What an asshole." DeLuca, in the passenger seat of Jake's cruiser, was already on his third cup of coffee. From the looks of him, he'd had about as rough a night as Jake. Turned out DeLuca hadn't been with Kat McMahan, but hearing a crack-of-dawn confession from a terrified, hysterical Maggie Gunnison. "They're all assholes."

"So you told her Ricker was dead? Why?" Jake stopped at the light, a search warrant safely in his pocket. He and DeLuca were about to kick some bad guy ass, if he did say so himself. About time. According to Maggie Gunnison, Ricker had been in on the kidnapping scheme. Though it didn't excuse Hennessey's disastrous action, at least Jake's arrest of the creep was righteous.

More good news—since Perl was now in custody, it didn't matter whether little Phillip identified baby Diane. He'd be safe with Bethany till this all played out. Things were looking up.

"Why *not* tell her?" DeLuca shrugged. "Filled her in on the Perl arrest, too. I went to her cell, told her—'You don't have to say a thing, just thought you'd like to know.' Yadda yadda. She flipped out. Couldn't spill the beans fast enough. Said she didn't need a lawyer."

"You got her on tape? Saying that?"

"Oh, duh, no, shoulda thought of that. Mercy me, if only you'd been there."

"Screw you." Everybody was a comedian.

"No, thanks," D said. He took a slug of coffee, put it back in the cup holder. "So. That guy Finn that Perl was talking about? Works at DFS with Maggie. He's Perl's nephew. He's in the dark about the arrest, of course, so we'll pay Mr. Eberhardt a nice visit. If we can get him to talk voluntarily, we won't have to read him his rights."

"You're a credit to the force, D," Jake said. "Did Gunnison explain the Ricker connection?"

"Yup. Ricker was Perl's—like, apartment manager. Watched over the places where they did the 'kid exchanges,' that's what they called it. Knew all about it. Maggie'd yank the children from the system, always on a weekend. She'd babysit until Perl picked them up."

Jake thought back. "Remember when we asked if he had 'dependents'? On Prize Patrol day? He kinda hesitated, remember? Man. It was because there *were* kids depending on him. Just not his own."

"Asshole. Like I said. Anyway, this Maggie Gunnison. Turns out she had no idea Perl was cashing in. That he was getting money for arranging the adoptions. I informed our clueless Maggie that he was not Lord Bountiful. That Crime Scene had easily found the bank records in Perl's apartment, the kickbacks from the adoption lawyer. We're talking like, megabucks. That's what really did it. She's gonna testify. Slam dunk. Yay for the good guys."

Jake considered this as he checked the house numbers on the cookie-cutter Cape Cods lining the neighborhood. Lots of "for sale" signs. Sagging shutters and rusting cars. Grim. Even the melting layer of snow was grubby. "She was doing it out of some misguided good intentions? Thought she was helping kids go to better homes?"

DeLuca pointed at a maybe-white house. "That's it. Forty-three Bronwell Street. Up the block. Yup. That's how Uncle Lennie Perl and nephew Eberhardt convinced her to help them. 'You have the power to make a better life for the kids.' She said she couldn't come up with a reason why it wasn't a good thing."

"The old 'kidnapping is against the law' didn't occur to her, apparently. You ready?" Jake parked the cruiser half a block away. It was unmarked, but scumbags could always sniff out cops. Only the good guys were easier to fool.

They walked up three concrete steps to a sagging wooden porch, saw the aluminum mailbox gaping open, hanging by one nail.

"Don't even think about it," Jake muttered.

"Gimme a break." DeLuca kept his voice low, too. "You knocking?"

"Backup's nearby if we need 'em. Here we go." Jake banged on the door. "I hear a TV inside. They're home. This is gonna be interesting."

* * *

"Get the door," Kev yelled. As usual, he didn't move from his spot on the couch. The creeps were glued to some guy on TV who was eating raw bugs or something, completely gross. She'd headed for the kitchen, where there was real food. Calories didn't count this early in the day.

Kellianne twisted open the plastic milk bottle. Sniffed. Winced. *Yuck.* "I'm in the kitchen, moron," she yelled, dumping the milk into the sink. "Get off your ass for once." That part she said only to herself.

She turned on the water, looked for a cleanish glass. It would be great if Mom was home more. She was always at the hospital, where things weren't looking good for Dad, least that's what she'd heard her mother say to someone on the phone. Mom hadn't talked to the three of them much at all. There was some commotion in the living room, probably on TV. Who'd be knocking on their door? It was only like nine in the morning.

But maybe it was a special delivery? Her money from RedSky? *Shit!* She should've answered the door. If the boys got hold of it they'd demand to know what it was and she'd be—

She ran down the hall, toward the noise, trying to think of how she was gonna explain this.

Who was that?

She skidded to a halt at the edge of the living room. Kev and Keefer were with two guys, a tall guy and a cuter one, both wearing leather jackets. They looked familiar, but she couldn't place them. The cute one was showing Kev a piece of paper.

"You a Sessions?" the tall one said to her.

"I'm—" Kellianne pursed her lips, thinking hard. Who were these guys?

"Don't you say a word." Kev pointed to her. His ears

were turning red and she could see he was fuming. Keefer's fists were clenching and unclenching.

This was not the mailman.

"I'm Detective Jake Brogan, Boston PD," the cute one said. "This is my partner, Detective Paul DeLuca. I gather you're Kevin, Keefer, and Kellianne? We've got a search warrant for the residence of Kent R. Sessions and the offices of Afterwards Cleaning, Inc., including any and all items belonging to Lillian Finch, Niall Brannigan, and Brianna Tillson. So now I'm going to ask all of you to—"

"I demand a lawyer." Kev yelled it at the top of his lungs, though someone had put the TV on mute and there was no problem hearing.

"Lot of that going around," the DeLuca guy said. "Jake, if you'd care to explain to Mr. Sessions that we don't give a crap if he wants a lawyer. He's not under arrest. We're executing a search warrant, whether he yells about it or not."

Search warrant? For what?

"Search warrant for what?" If no one was gonna stand up for them, she'd better. The cute one—Brogan, did he say?—was still holding the paper up for Kev to read.

"At least one of you has a brain," DeLuca said.

Ha, Kellianne thought.

Then she thought about what was under her bed. On her computer. She remembered the chain with the cross around her neck. *Shit.* If they found that? But wait. It wasn't illegal to sell murderabilia. Let these cops look wherever they wanted. She had nothing to hide. Only her brothers did. *The old guy and the fire.* No way the cops could get *her* for those things. She'd been forced. *Yes.* Forced to do what they said.

"'For what' is precisely what I'm in the process of explaining to your—brother?" Brogan answered her.

She nodded silently, trying to look like she was scared of her brother. Might as well.

"By the way. Anyone care to tell us where you three were last night?" Brogan said.

"Here," Kev said.

"Yeah," Kellianne said. *Were the cops on to them? They couldn't be. This was just fishing.*

"We were here the whole time," Kev said.

"The whole time of what?" DeLuca asked.

"You were all home. Okay." Brogan was interrupting him. "So let's have the three of you sit right there on that lovely couch, and Detective DeLuca will stand by while I do some checking. We have backup on the way. It shouldn't take long."

72

Why hadn't Alex called back or e-mailed? Jane checked her watch. Nine A.M. He should be at the *Register* by now, she thought, stepping inside the black-and-white tiled foyer of Ella's apartment building. The address had been a cinch to find on Google.

She sniffed, wrinkled her nose. Oatmeal. Coffee. Wet wool. A row of louvered metal mailboxes labeled "G" through "8" lined one wall. "G" had a stick-on label saying Gavin. Okay, then.

Which key for the inner door? Jane guessed right, the door opened easily, and she took a short flight of stairs down to the door marked G. She listened, half-worried it'd be the wrong apartment and she'd get yelled at—or shot—by some trigger-happy terrified resident. Jane smiled, shaking her head. She was tired. She'd finish here, call Alex again, maybe even risk going to the paper.

Wait a minute. What risk?

She paused, holding the key, motionless, in the silence of the hallway. The bad guy was arrested. She stood a little straighter, smiling. No longer anything to be afraid of. Go in, feed the cat, get out. Get back to real life.

The lock clicked open. Jane heard a thump and a rustle, then one inquiring meow. A ball of white fluff padded toward her—stopped—then skittered away, streaking underneath a glass coffee table and flattening itself under a plaid couch.

"I'm okay, cat," Jane said. "Chill. Ella says hi. She'll be home soon. I'm just going to feed you."

The cat did not come out.

Jane headed toward the kitchen, keeping her parka on. An insistent red light flashed on Ella's phone, but Jane ignored it. In, then out. She'd open cabinets till she found the food. And she'd leave extra water.

Guessing again, Jane pulled the white ceramic knob of the cabinet nearest the refrigerator. A tattered Target bag tumbled to the floor.

Damn. No cat food.

She reached down to stuff the bag back into place. It looked like the one Ella carried at Dunkin's Monday morning, the one she'd guarded so vigilantly. Jane looked inside. Files.

She dumped the manila folders onto the kitchen table. Beerman. *Tuck's file?* She examined the others, fast as she could. Lamonica. Hoffner. DaCosto. Who were those people?

She unsnapped her parka, draped it over the metal chair, and sat. *Just for a minute.* Opened the Beerman file. A yellow sticky on the inside had a penciled notation: *No footprint?*

Lamonica. The same notation, the same handwriting. Over and over.

She tried to make herself close the files and leave. This was—private stuff. Another yellow sticky caught her attention.

What was that? A noise.

She jumped up, almost toppling the files. Then burst out laughing. The cat had padded into the kitchen and was now nudging Jane's leg with her nose.

"I know you're hungry, cat." Jane reached to pet her as she sat down at the table again. "But I need to look at one thing."

Which one of the Sessions was the weak link? They needed only to get one to confess and rat the others out. Jake couldn't decide which sad sack looked most unhappy. The three lumped on the couch, two of them—the big shot with the muscles and the sidekick with the ratty mustache—staring straight ahead. The sister was intent on her hair, biting off the ends one strand at a time.

"Before I execute the warrant," Jake said, "let me offer you an option. We're gonna find something. I have no doubt of that."

"Pssss," one of the three muttered.

"Sorry? I missed that," Jake said.

"Piss off," DeLuca said.

"Oh, gotcha," Jake said. "Like I was saying. If any of you would like to simply tell us what's going on—about Niall Brannigan, and Margolin Street, and whatever you have going with Leonard Perl, who is now in custody, you might like to know—" Jake paused, checking for reactions. Got none. "It's gonna go a lot easier. First to talk is the first to walk."

DeLuca nodded. "And the other two are suckers."

"Any takers?" Jake held up a palm. "You don't have to say anything now. Just stand up and come with me. Show me where to look."

"So you've got to come, Tuck, soon as you can." Jane hadn't budged from Ella's kitchen table, although the files she'd been reading for the past half hour made no sense at all. The cat was now purring on her lap. "Like I said, Ella gave me a footprint. Now all her other files are marked as 'no footprints.' Last Sunday you asked me to help you figure out if you were the wrong girl, and I think the answer's here. But the only people who can decipher these files are at the Brannigan. I say—get back to Boston, and let's go. Let's go ask them."

As Tuck protested, Jane eased the cat to the floor and filled up an extra bowl of water. What was Tuck's problem? She thought of Ella. What she'd sacrificed.

"Listen. Tuck. *You* started it. Come, or don't. I'm going to the Brannigan. I'm going to find out what's going on. With you, or without you."

Jake would have bet on the wiseass sidekick, but Kellianne was his second choice. She stood, slowly, eyeing her brothers, then tossing her unfortunate hair. Jake kept thinking about how she bit off the ends. Why would anyone do that?

"Yes, Kellianne?" Jake said.

"And we have a winner," DeLuca said.

"Hey, bitch, what do you think you're doing?" The one called Keefer tried to stand up, but the Kevin guy yanked him back to the couch.

"Rat blood." Kevin took a swig of whatever was in his mug, then raised it at her. "Rat blood in her veins. Screw you, sister. We know what's under your bed."

"Hey, you moron," Kellianne said. "*I'm* the one who—"

"Screw you. Not anymore," Kev said. "Do it, Detectives. Look under her bed."

This was going nicely.

"Kellianne?" Jake said.

"Yeah, well, you should look in their backpacks. See the scrips they swiped from every house we've done." The girl planted her fists on her hips, stuck out her tongue at her brothers. "They get in early, take the good stuff from the medicine cabinets before anyone notices. They think I don't know. Well, think again."

She plopped back down on the couch.

"Hey, you can't—" Kevin stood, glowering at her.

"What're you trying to—?" Keefer got up and shouldered in front of him, interrupting.

Jake shot them a look. *Make my day.* They stopped. Closed their mouths.

"Family Feud," DeLuca said.

"My favorite show," Jake said.

It took Jake less than two minutes to find the brothers' stash of prescription drugs, a ratty brown paper bag crammed with amber plastic containers, contents all still conveniently labeled. Oxycodone. Percocet. Oxycontin. Vicodin. Dilaudid.

All labeled with *other* people's names.

"You're all three under arrest for the illegal possession of class B narcotics." Jake returned to the living room, holding up the bag. "Oh, and larceny. And suspicion of arson, since there are several bottles here labeled 'Lillian Finch.' Seems to me you'd have to be in that house to have swiped those. Did you know there was a woman inside during the fire? That's gonna present another legal problem for you."

"Screw you," Kevin said.

"So you keep saying," Jake said. "But wait. There's more. Let me mention you're also being charged with manslaughter in the death of Niall Brannigan. He had a heart attack, the medical examiner says. But she will testify someone dragged him—still alive—to his car. And there he died."

"Yes. Yes. *They* carried him out." Kellianne stood, raising her hand, like a little kid trying to get the teacher to call on her. "The old guy. They made me help them. And that's all I'm saying until I get a deal."

"Shut *up*," Kevin said. He yanked her back down to the couch.

"Smartest thing you've said today, Mr. Sessions," Jake said. "D, wanna take over from here? This is quite the drugstore our friends have accumulated. They've really—how shall I put it? Cleaned up."

"They're gonna love you at Cedar Junction," DeLuca said. "Maximum security prisons always need experienced cleanup crews."

As DeLuca read the three their rights, Jake headed for the back of the house. He guessed Kellianne's bedroom was the one with the pink walls and the flowered bedspread. Lifting the edge of the spread, he felt around underneath the bed.

And pulled out a zipped tote bag.

73

"Well, who *is* on the city desk, then?" Jane checked her gas gauge as she started the engine. The *Register* receptionist was giving her a hard time. "Ginnie? It's me, Jane Ryland. I need to talk to whoever's making up the front page. I have the lede. But it's like no one cares."

Jane punched her phone onto speaker as Ginnie answered. ". . . take a message, that's what I've been told," she said. "I don't know what else to tell you."

"Hang on, my call waiting is beeping in," Jane said. "Maybe it's Alex."

"Yeah," Ginnie said. "Maybe." And she hung up.

"I'm on the way." Tuck didn't bother with hello. "But it'll take us at least ninety minutes. Can you wait?"

Us? Interesting. That meant Carlyn was coming, too. Although how else would Tuck get there? Jane made the turn onto Route 128, the eight-lane highway that looped around the city. To get to the Brannigan was a huge pain.

"I'll try," Jane said. "But if anyone's there, ah, I don't know. I may have to go in myself. The Brannigan people are the only ones who have the answers."

* * *

"The Brannigan people are the only ones who have the answers." Jake pointed to the framed photo DeLuca was examining as Jake drove them across town. Jake had found it in Kellianne's macabre tote bag of treasures.

Backup had finally arrived to cart off the handcuffed and cursing Sessions trio to lockup. Desperate for leniency, Kevin had ratted out Hennessey as their conduit and Internal Affairs was already into the cop's records for evidence of kickbacks.

"Lillian Finch and Niall Brannigan, huh?" Jake considered the couple in the photo. "That's a cozy little snapshot. Now they're both very dead. Apparently Ardith Brannigan has taken over the reins at the agency. Very interesting."

"And very guilty. Woman scorned, huh?" DeLuca held up the photo.

"Maybe." They were only a few blocks from the Brannigan. Something he'd seen nagged at him.

D interrupted his thoughts. "Friggin' Sessions."

"Yeah. My favorite part was when Kellianne tried to explain how selling—what'd she call it? Murderabilia? Wasn't illegal."

"The look on her face when *you* explained how selling stolen property *is* illegal?" DeLuca put the photo back into the bag. "Worth the price of admission."

"Now we can give Phillip and Phoebe back their teddy bears, at least." Jake sneaked the cruiser through a just-changing yellow light. "Whenever the district attorney is done with them."

He needed to call Bethany, too, check on those kids. And the baby. The brick edifice of the Brannigan appeared as Jake turned onto the tree-lined side street. Perfectly pruned evergreen shrubs, shaped without one stray branch, lined the flagstone path to the front door.

"So. Alvarez called undercover this morning, pretending to be a worried mother. Confirmed Ardith Brannigan is here. You ready for this? Think we can nail her for killing Lillian Finch?"

"Hell hath no fury," DeLuca said. "And the killer could have been a woman, all right. Kat says it looks like Lillian Finch got a plastic bag over the head after a dose of sleeping pills. Then the pillows were taped around her head. No muss, no fuss. Female style."

"It's a wonder any pills were left for the Sessions to swipe." Jake pointed left. "Let's park over there. On the side street. No need to give them a heads-up, right?"

One good thing about reporting for a newspaper. You didn't need anything but a pencil and paper. You could do it with nothing more than a reliable memory.

Jane turned onto Linden Street, resisting the caffeine temptation of the Lotsa Latte on the corner. In the old days—less than six months ago—she'd have had to call Channel 11 and beg for a camera guy. Now she had only to tell the city desk where she was going. If anyone cared. Which, this morning, no one seemed to. Budget cuts, probably.

And there was the Brannigan, in all its austerely pruned glory. The Web site had listed the public's opening time at ten, but Jane's "Sorry, wrong number" test call revealed someone was already there.

She puffed out a breath, slowed her car to a crawl, deciding. Tuck and Carlyn had not yet arrived, nor called her back. Should she wait?

She'd wait.

Ten more minutes. She drove past the Brannigan, turned right. So no one noticed her, she'd go once around the block. Maybe twice.

On the other hand, having a camera guy with her made forays like this a bit safer. Hard to beat up a re-porter when someone with a video camera was getting it all on tape. Hard to refute a lie you'd told while the camera was rolling.

Past the Brannigan again. One more time. Jane took out her cell, deciding to put it someplace more accessible than the black hole of her tote bag. She could shoot video with it, too, if need be.

Damn.

Her cell was less than half-charged. She pulled to the curb, grabbed her plug from the center console. Jammed it into the thing on the dashboard. Why hadn't Alex called back? She sat at the wheel, engine idling. Seeing reality.

She was going to be laid off. That was why he hadn't called. Why Ginnie had acted so weird. Why the desk hadn't responded. They couldn't. If they talked to her, they'd have to say something, so it was easier to ignore her. Put her off. Until the axe fell.

She rested her forehead on the steering wheel. She envisioned her future unfolding and it was not pretty. Her father would be so disappointed. Again. She'd have to slink home to Oak Park, a failure, live in the shadow of her perfect sister, a pitiful minion at Lissa's wedding. A failure at TV. A failure at newspapers. A single woman with a cat.

Mom, she thought. I'm glad you're not here to see this.

No. She sat up, shaking a finger at herself. No one had fired her. As far as she knew, really knew, nothing had changed. Onward to her story. If she was getting kicked out of the *Register,* she'd go out with a bang.

Once more around the block. Then she was going in.

74

"I apologize, Detectives, for the disarray." Ardith Brannigan, dressed for success in a dark suit and pearls, gestured at nothing. Jake and D now stood side by side in
front of the widow's desk, a sleek slab of glass set on
elaborate wrought-iron pedestals. Already she'd changed
all the furniture, Jake noticed. No more club chairs and
tweed. Now it was all sleek black leather, heavy brass. A
black monolith of a couch with chrome armrests. What
was it, two days since the funeral?

"We're on a bit of a skeleton crew right now, reorga-
nizing, of course, after . . ." She paused again, dabbed
her eyes with a handkerchief.

Grief 101, Jake thought, then tried to stay objective.
He heard DeLuca clear his throat. He was feeling the
same way, Jake could tell.

"We're here about your employee Ella Gavin?" Jake
decided to keep it vague, see how this woman reacted.

"What did she do?" Ardith Brannigan's eyes narrowed. She no longer seemed on the verge of tears. She
sat in her black swivel chair and tapped a chunky black
pen against the desk, her pearl bracelets clacking. Hearing the sound, she stopped. Blinked at them.

"Do?" DeLuca asked.

"Have you heard from her today?" Jake asked. This woman was nervous. Guilty. *About something.*

Ardith blinked again, several times. "Well, I'm sure we have. . . ." Her voice trailed off. "We asked our staff to stay home today, so I assume . . ."

Jake waited, silent, watching this woman's mind work. Maybe realizing she'd jumped to an ungracious conclusion.

"Would you like me to check?" She raised both palms, questioning. "Detectives, is she all right?"

"Yes, she's fine," Jake lied. "Let me ask you—how well did you know Lillian Finch?"

"Yeah, Mrs. Brannigan?" DeLuca broke in, flipping open his notebook. "I'll take it from here."

Bad cop. Right on cue. Jake gave him the floor.

"Can you please account for your whereabouts last Sunday? Did you go to Lillian Finch's home?" DeLuca was being a hardass. "Your memory should be pretty clear on that, it was only five days ago. Sorry to bring it up—but it was the day before your husband died."

"She was with me," said a voice at the door.

Jane had driven around the block four times. Still no Tuck, even though there'd been plenty of time for her to get here. And, a little worrisome, there'd been something in Tuck's voice, some hesitancy. For some reason she wasn't hot on coming.

"I'm done," Jane said out loud. She drove into the parking lot, plenty of spaces, only one other car. *Five more minutes.* She'd sit in the car for five minutes. Look at the files again. Continue not-worrying about her job.

Then—Tuck or no Tuck—she was going in.

* * *

That's the guy. The thing Jake had been trying to remember. Old-school tie, tortoiseshell glasses, nose in the air. Hard-edge. The one he'd seen outside All Saints, his arm around an elegant woman in mourning. Mrs. Brannigan, he now knew. Squiring the widow to her own husband's funeral.

"She was with you." Jake repeated the man's statement. "All day Sunday? And night?"

"And you are?" DeLuca put in.

"Collins Munson." The man closed the office door behind him.

"Mr. Munson is the—," Ardith interrupted, fluttered a hand, no wedding ring, Jake noticed. "—director of History and Records for the Brannigan. He's a longtime and valued—"

"We'll take it from here," DeLuca said.

"I heard you asking about Ella Gavin," Munson said. "I attempted to call her this morning, but no answer at her apartment. So I'm afraid I have no answers for you. Happy to give you her address. If you need to contact her? For some reason?"

Jake ignored his offer. Munson didn't seem to know of Ella's situation. The cops had kept her name out of the news coverage. "So I'm sure you heard Detective DeLuca here ask if Mrs. Brannigan was at Lillian Finch's home. If you were together, were you 'together' at Lillian Finch's home?"

"Why would we be at Lillian Finch's home?" Munson took a step closer to Ardith, then another. "We were here at the Brannigan, working on a case. Which case was it, Ardith? Our cars were parked here, all day. Although we have no parking lot surveillance video, I fear."

"Well, that's no problem, of course, Mr. Munson," Jake said. Big smile. "I'm sure we'll be able to confirm through the building's pass card reader. Correct?"

Munson flickered a glance at Ardith Brannigan, whose

hands had curled into fists. "I'm sure I have no idea," Munson said. "Sometimes it doesn't work. It's new."

"Technology, huh?" Jake stayed pleasant. He was the good cop this time. But about to go bad.

He tapped his cell phone, pulling up photos, found the one he'd snapped of a guy in a Newbury Street cafe he'd thought was Harry Belafonte. It wasn't. "Do you recognize this man?"

He held the phone toward Munson, who lifted his glasses to peer at it. Jake glanced at DeLuca, who'd looked at it, and now was frowning. It was DeLuca who'd confirmed it wasn't Harry Belafonte.

"I'm afraid not," Munson said.

"Mrs. Brannigan?"

She moved closer to Munson, took her turn examining the little screen.

"I'm afraid not," she said.

"I see," Jake put his phone away. "That's the cab driver who brought you to Lillian Finch's home Sunday afternoon. That's why we don't need nonexistent surveillance video of your cars in the parking lot. And we don't really need you to recognize the man in the photo. Because *he* recognized *you*. One of the neighbors keeps track of every license plate that goes by. She got the number of your cab. She didn't see *you,* since you cleverly got out up the street, behind that big evergreen. And it was snowing, I'm sure you remember. But well—you can figure out the rest. An absolute and unmistakable identification."

Munson wrapped his arm around Ardith, who moved into the circle of his embrace. "Preposterous." Munson flipped one hand, dismissive. "Our cab driver was a—"

He stopped.

"Don't say a word, Ardith," he said.

75

Jane walked through the parking lot, up the evergreen-trimmed length of winding sidewalk, then turned onto the manicured flagstone path. Looked for a doorbell, saw only an electronic entry thing. Maybe she needed a pass card? But the door opened with a turn of the polished brass knob.

The more Jane thought about it, the more it was better to do this alone. She'd figure out whoever was in charge and simply lay her cards on the table. The files, that is. They were safely in her tote bag, with the smoke-stenched footprint. Tuck was a no-show. Fine.

She pushed the door the rest of the way open, heard it huff over the thick pile of the interior carpeting. Took a step inside, pushed the heavy door closed behind her.

Strange. Jane expected a bustling office, or at least some sense of activity. But what looked like a reception desk—with a phone console and a guest book and a crystal vase of fiery chrysanthemums—was unstaffed. A long carpeted hallway stretched in front of her. She took in the glass-windowed doors, an occasional chair, and on one wall, a floor-to-ceiling gallery of framed photos.

Jane stood on the entryway's circular oriental rug, alone, in the silence. The phone jangled. She stepped back, expecting someone to come answer it. It rang again, and again, and again. Then stopped. No one appeared.

Jane frowned, calculating. The front door had been unlocked, so the place was open. Only that one Mercedes in the lot, though. Still, it was Thursday, a weekday, and now past ten o'clock in the morning. So, open.

And hey. She'd knocked on doors before, looking for answers. She could knock on a few again. Since the place was open, someone had to be here. She headed down the hall, unzipping her black wool jacket, stuffing her gloves in her pocket. A light was on in the office at the end. She could see it through the window of the closed door.

All good.

Was Tucker Cameron the wrong girl? Jane was about to find out.

"So why were you at Lillian Finch's house?" Jake asked.

Munson's face had turned to stone, but Ardith Brannigan's seemed about to crumble. Dolly Richards had indeed gotten the cab's license number, but Alvarez in Records had reported the real cab driver could only describe a man and a woman, bundled in mufflers and winter coats, silent behind the cab's thick plastic barrier. And he'd dropped them off on a side street. So score this one for Jake.

DeLuca pulled the framed photo from his inside jacket pocket, showed it to the unhappy couple. "Was *this* the motive? Jealousy? Revenge? Mrs. Brannigan? That your husband was—sleeping with—Lillian Finch?"

"What?" Ardith Brannigan paled, her eyes widening as one hand flew to her mouth.

"I said, not another word, Ardith." Munson kept one arm around her, his hand clamped to her shoulder.

With the other he reached into the pocket of his tweed jacket. Took out a gun. And rested it on Ardith's right temple.

Jake and DeLuca went for their weapons at exactly the same time. *Shit.*

"Gentlemen, I wouldn't do that," Munson said. "You're going to let us go. If you touch your weapons, I'll shoot her. If you interfere, I'll shoot her. If you follow us, I'll shoot her. I'm sure you can tell I'm dead serious."

Great. There were people in that office. Jane could tell as she walked closer to it. The wooden door had a four-part glass insert, and though the glass was frosted and faceted, it showed signs of people inside. Even down the hall, she could see colors moving, and indistinct shapes. Three people, maybe. Four.

Someone in there would know something. All she had to do was knock.

"Collins." Ardith Brannigan's voice was a whisper. She was looking at something over Jake's shoulder, it seemed, but Jake couldn't risk turning around.

He'd mentally raced through all the possibilities and the result was zero. Munson had Ardith at gunpoint, both standing behind a huge glass desk. No way for him or D to get close. In time, at least.

"How do you plan to—" The guy was nuts. Jake could almost smell the crazy.

"Shut up." Munson moved his gun. Jake saw the woman wince as he pushed it against her forehead. "You two. On the couch."

"Mrs. Brannigan, we can help you," Jake said. Calm. Compassionate. *Rule one. Keep the victim on your side.*

"You can see this is a doomed proposition. You can see how much Mr. Munson cares about you. He's decided to use you as a hostage."

"True love," DeLuca said.

"DO it!" Munson yelled.

Jake perched on the edge of the black leather and aluminum couch. D beside him. Ready to move the instant there was a chance.

"Lillian was going to ruin the Brannigan," the woman said. She was still looking over Jake's shoulder, not at him. Not at Munson. "Collins told me she'd—"

"Shut. Up." Munson pointed at DeLuca. "You. Put the cuffs on your friend. Cuff him to the armrest. Both hands. *Do* it."

Shit. "Munson. Look. There's no way—"

"DO it!" Munson yelled.

He didn't want to break concentration on Munson to look at DeLuca, but he knew his partner was making the same calculations.

Munson, Ardith, desk, gun.

Whoa. It sounded like they were having some hell of a meeting. Fine, she'd knock, they'd stop yelling. Jane couldn't really hear all they were saying, but if they were in a meeting, they were in a meeting. People yelled in meetings, no biggie. It wasn't like it was life or death.

She rapped the wooden door, once. No answer.

Again.

"We're busy!" someone yelled.

Well, that was pleasant. Must be some meeting.

"We're busy!" Munson yelled again, without taking his eyes off the officers.

D unsnapped his cuffs. Flipped one over Jake's wrist,

then the other, then around the metal armrest. There was no way to communicate, but Jake knew he was assessing how to fake it. Fool the moron into thinking he was cuffed. Whoever was outside the door—he hoped they left. Fast. If they didn't, they were certain to be in the line of fire. *Do not endanger additional victims.*

"Stand back." Munson pointed DeLuca away, then walked Ardith, gun to head, closer to them. One step at a time. Jake calculated as the man approached. Not close enough. *Assess risk-benefit. Do not take unnecessary chances.*

"Show me. Show me the cuffs."

Jake did. *Damn it.*

"Now. Take his gun and radio." He pointed to a file cabinet across the room. "Put them in that drawer."

"Screw you," DeLuca muttered. "You're only making this wor—"

"No, sir," Jake said. *Never give up your weapon.* "That's not how this is gonna work."

Okey dokey, then, Jane thought. Guess they don't want to be interrupted. She moved away from the door and took a few steps down the hall, zipping up her jacket and fingering her cell phone. She should call Tuck. And Alex again. Unlikely anyone would bother her in the hall. Plus, she needed to get answers. These people had them. Maybe she could sit in one of those chairs in the hallway, stall until the meeting was over. They'd never know she was the one who'd knocked.

"You want to *see* how this is going to work?" Munson clasped Ardith closer. His voice was a hiss, a whisper. "I don't want to shoot her. Or you. But you know I will."

Jake and DeLuca exchanged glances. *Protect the*

hostage. D took Jake's gun, then his radio, and put them into the drawer.

Ardith was crying now, silently, shaking.

"Now you, Detective," Munson said. "Your equipment, too. Into the drawer."

"You can't shoot both of us," Jake said.

"Watch me," Munson said.

76

"Hang on, D. Wait. Don't do it." Jake knew D couldn't draw fast enough to shoot Munson before the prick killed Ardith. In any event, D couldn't risk the shot. But some innocent person was outside the door. Cuffed to the couch, Jake's only play was to try to reason with the guy.

He kept his voice low. "Munson. What if my partner refuses? You think you can shoot all of us?"

Silence.

Maybe this would work. "You shoot Mrs. Brannigan, we'll witness a cold-blooded murder. Detective DeLuca will blast out your knee. And you'll be in Cedar Junction till the next millennium. Is that your final decision?"

Jane looked at the door again. Listened. Didn't seem like anyone was yelling anymore, right? Good. Maybe she should try one more time.

A good reporter never gives up.

If they yelled at her this time, she'd leave. They'd never know who it was, so what did it matter? And if they let her in, she could apologize. Everyone hates reporters anyway.

She knocked again.

* * *

"*Go away,*" Jake yelled. Damn it. If he warned whoever it was to call the police, Munson would shoot. If he said *come in,* he was inviting another potential victim. "This is the police! Go away!"

Ardith jumped at his voice, clamped her lips together, her mouth a white line.

Munson smiled. "Excellent choice, Detective," he whispered.

Munson, Ardith, desk, DeLuca's gun. And no more time.

Whoa. That was *Jake.* Jake's voice. What the hell was he doing in there?

Jane stepped back from the door, edging up the hall. He didn't know it was *her,* that was certain. She paused halfway down the hall. Took out her phone. Should she call the police? Jake *was* the police.

She stood in the empty hallway. In. Or out? Out. Took two steps away, headed for her car. Stopped. Was Jake in trouble? What the holy hell was going on?

Should she call 911? Jane ran a few steps, on tiptoe, then opened an office door. And say what? The police needed help?

Damn it. Sometimes they do.

Munson dragged Ardith to the door, peered though the frosted window. "Okay, they're gone. Hallway's empty. Didn't we tell everyone to stay home today, dear Ardith? They should have followed instructions." He yanked the woman close to him again. "We'll give them a moment to drive away."

"You're hurting me," she said.

"Shut up," Munson said. "My final decision? Into that drawer, Detective. Your gun and radio. Over to the couch."

Jake watched D calculate. There was one possibility. D had to draw his weapon to put it into the drawer. But with Munson's .38 plastered to Ardith's head, there was simply no option. D, shaking his head, apparently coming to the same conclusion, put his weapon and radio in the drawer.

Jake flashed on Hennessey. Almost wished the guy were here to blast this asshole to hell. But no one was around to save his butt this time. And Ardith Brannigan— was she in on Lillian Finch's murder?—was good as dead.

"Mrs. Brannigan, you don't think this man is going to let you live, do you?" Jake began.

"If you know something he wants kept secret?" De-Luca said. "Tell us. Then we'll all know. Then you won't be the only one."

Munson slammed the file drawer shut with an elbow. Ardith Brannigan winced, stumbled, regained her balance.

"Now, Detective DeLuca? You are going to escort us out of here. Walk us to the parking lot. And wave good-bye."

"Not a—"

"Or wave good-bye to this fine lady right now, if that's your decision," Munson said, returning to the door. "Sorry, dear."

He clicked open the knob.

Jane closed door of the empty office behind her, gritting her teeth at the squeak of a hinge, the scrape of the door over the carpeting. The room was dark, no windows. An outer office, judging by the club chairs and couch.

Trying not to breathe, she pressed her face close to the mottled glass, tried to see into the corridor.

Yes. Someone might be coming out of that room across the hall. She could make out shapes close to the window, moving.

Would it be Jake? What was he doing in there?

The yelling she'd heard. *Do it. Shut up. Do it.* Hadn't been Jake's voice. Something was very wrong.

Brannigan was dead, Lillian Finch was dead. There'd been a horrible fire at Lillian's house. Ella had been inside. Was Jake here about that? Why?

She grabbed her cell to call 911. *No.* If she talked, even a whisper, she might be heard. She stabbed the off button. And the dispatcher couldn't trace a cell call. She squinted, surveying the murky room. No phone. *Damn it.* Jane couldn't call for help without being discovered.

She'd have to hide. She had to wait.

She also had to see.

Jane clicked the door open. The tiniest bit. And plastered herself to the wall.

DeLuca didn't have a chance. He must know it. Jake watched Munson open the office door, wave DeLuca toward it. As soon as they arrived in the parking lot, Munson would shoot him. Or maybe he'd drive him somewhere, shoot him there. Away from the Brannigan, away from his marked territory and away from any connections. There was no way he could leave DeLuca alive.

Munson had made a smart move, taking their weapons. Splitting them up. Now Jake was powerless. Both wrists were cuffed to a fricking couch, his weapon stashed in a drawer across the room. He couldn't reach the phone on the desk. Sure, someone would find him here. Eventually. He'd be able to testify about what he'd seen. But Munson—about to walk out the door—would be long gone.

And D would be dead.

"DeLuca," Jake said.

"I know," D said.

77

Jane couldn't move. Couldn't risk it. From her place against the wall—light switch stabbing her in the back through her jacket—her line of sight was a narrow sliver.

She couldn't see the office door across the carpeted hall. She'd have to listen for the click of the latch. Listen for footsteps.

When whoever it was got close enough to her, she'd have them in view. Briefly. Long enough to know the score. If it was Jake and all was well, she'd stay hidden, and he'd never know she was there. Nor would anyone else.

In that case, she'd leave, come back later. Make an appointment. All by the book.

Her eyes hurt from having to look sideways. Her neck was complaining. But she couldn't risk a move.

Footsteps. A door closing.

They were coming.

Should he yell? Try to move the couch? Somehow yank the couch across the carpet to the drawer where the guns were? With both hands handcuffed? *That'd never work*. Incredible that he had his damn handcuff keys, the spare ones, tucked in his wallet. Fat lot of good that'd do now.

Supe was going to kill him. And—it crossed Jake's mind—maybe he deserved it. His partner was about to be murdered. An innocent person was being abducted, maybe killed, too.

He'd blown it.

"Still time to change your so-called mind, Munson."

Paul DeLuca's voice? Jane was sure she was right. Munson must be Collins Munson, the Brannigan hot-shot Ella had mentioned. His name was all over the files she'd found in Ella's kitchen. Was he the one sending the wrong children? Had Jake and DeLuca found out about it? That's why they were here?

Damn it. She still couldn't see them.

Then she could.

Three people, DeLuca, certainly, who seemed to be walking slowly in front of—a man in a tweed jacket. And a woman. Crying? Yes. The woman—who was she?—was crying.

Holy shit. Jane clutched her phone. The man—Munson? Had a gun to the woman's head. Why was DeLuca walking with them?

Where was Jake?

No gunfire. No screams. No commotion. So Jake wasn't shot. Was he—well, where the hell *was* he? And why? He'd told her to stay away. Not that he knew it was her.

Now here was DeLuca, walking with a guy carrying a gun. Why wasn't Paul doing anything to stop that man?

If Jake was okay, why wasn't *he* doing something to stop him?

Was DeLuca—in on this? *DeLuca?*

She took a step forward, on tiptoe, holding her breath. Watched the trio stride down the hall. The woman tripped in her patent leather heels. The tall man's arm clamped around her, pulled her back into place. *The gun.*

As Jane peered after them, baffled, terrified, and completely unsure, DeLuca turned his head for a brief glance back at the office they'd all just left.

Jane had never seen such a look of anguish.

All his fault.

Ricker, dead, because of him. And now, DeLuca was in deep shit, and Ardith Brannigan, and it was his fault again. Jake tried to stand, thrashing, yanking the idiot cuffs and the idiot couch, which didn't move an inch.

"Damn it!" he yelled. "Damn it! Damn it!"

He closed his eyes, briefly, in disdain. *Save your breath,* he thought. Maybe no one would ever come uncuff him. Maybe that would be better.

That was Jake! Jake's voice. He was yelling. He wasn't dead. Jane took a chance, swiveled, peered down the hallway. The front door was closing. She saw a flash of daylight, then three silhouettes, then the front door swinging closed.

She raced to the end of the hall, tote bag slamming against her back, tripping, stumbling, almost falling in her frantic haste to get to Jake.

Wait. She stopped, bending almost double with her sudden decision. What if someone else was in that room?

She could hear only the sound of her own breathing.

If she went in, she might be in trouble. If she didn't, Jake might be in trouble. If she did, they might *both* be in trouble.

"Jake!" she yelled. Fine, it might be the exactly wrong thing to do, let whoever was in there with Jake know she was there but—she dialed 911 as she ran to the office.

"Nine-one-one, what's your emergency?"

Yeah. That was the question.

78

"**Operator, I'm at** the—at one-twenty-five Linden Street. *Jake!*"

"Jane!" His voice was loud, and strong. "It's okay, get *in* here!"

She grabbed the doorknob, twisted it, pushed. Jake was on the couch. No one else in the room.

"Ma'am?" the dispatcher's voice crackled through her cell phone. "What's your emergency?"

"Jake! What—?"

"In my pocket, Jane." Jake held up both hands. He was cuffed to the arm of the couch? "My wallet, back pocket. The key."

"Ma'am, you've got to tell me—"

She dropped her tote bag to the floor, raced to him.

"All units," Jake yelled. "This is Jake Brogan. Officer down. Officer down. Jane, let me talk."

She held the phone against his cheek as he twisted onto his stomach, letting her lift his leather jacket and grab his wallet from the back pocket of his jeans.

"In here?" She punched the phone on speaker, then flipped open the wallet, looking for—and there it was, a tiny silver key tucked into a credit card slot. She held it between two fingers. "This?"

"At one-twenty-five Linden, Forest Hills, officer down, officer in trouble, all units, all units, you copy, dispatch?" Jake sat up, cocked his head toward the handcuffs. "Do it, Jane. Hurry."

He could have kissed the hell out of her, but he didn't have time. Jake yanked his wrist out of one of the cuffs, then the other, clicked them back on his belt and threw himself across the room. Slammed open the file drawer. Grabbed his weapon, tucked D's into the small of his back.

"Yes, sir, we copy. Dispatch out." The phone went silent.

"Stay in here. Do *not* come out." Jake said. *The radios*. He tossed one to Jane, put the other in his jacket pocket. "I've got backup on the way. I'll call you when—"

He yanked back the curtains, looked out the window. Past the low hedge and the stand of hemlocks to the parking lot. Only two cars. One was Jane's. The other a Mercedes. No Munson yet. They had to be taking Munson's car. This was the only parking lot.

He twisted the latch, pushed open the window, then clicked up the storm window.

"What are you—who was—?"

"Tell you later. Close the window after me. Stay *here*." Would he have time to stop them? Would D and that asshole still be in the parking lot? Would Ardith Brannigan be alive? Would D?

She had no idea what was going on. None.

"Jake!"

But he was out the window. The curtains fell back into place.

"Be careful!" she said.

He was gone. Moving the curtains, she slid the storm back down, then clicked the frame shut as Jake had instructed. She looked outside. Couldn't see him.

"Be careful," she whispered.

79

The damn trees were in the way, his line of sight obstructed. Well, good. That meant they couldn't see him, either. All he had now, besides the Sig, was the element of surprise. And he had that only once.

Jake ducked low, running, following the line of thick shrubbery to its end. A strip of lawn, then the big hemlocks, then the parking lot pavement. He could see the three of them now, walking, arriving at the edge of the parking lot. They couldn't see him. Nor would Munson be looking.

He took a breath, darted to the stand of hemlocks lining the parking lot. The three were headed for the dark blue Mercedes. Munson behind, holding his weapon on D and Ardith. At least she wasn't clamped to him anymore. Still, if either of them tried to run, Munson could shoot in an instant. Both of them.

Jake's window of opportunity would be tiny. Minuscule. Probably impossible.

What was his responsibility here? Save the victim? Even if she was accomplice to a murder? She was innocent until proven guilty.

Or save his partner?

How could anyone make that decision?

Jake had confidence in his marksmanship—but a

one-shot deal at a moving car with two innocent people and one asshole? Even at short range, no way. He couldn't let them get into the car.

It was down to timing. And luck. So far today, neither had been that great for Jake.

The three were getting closer to Munson's car.

Backup was on the way. Jake listened for sirens. Nothing.

She had to see. Jane pulled back the curtain as she'd watched Jake do. She listened for sirens, squinting as if that could make her hearing more acute. Nothing.

Out in the parking lot—at the far end—she could just make out the people she'd seen in the hall. DeLuca— what did that mean? The woman. The man with the gun. Munson. Did he still have the gun? It was too far away to tell.

She didn't see Jake. The trees were in the way.

Jake had thrown her a police radio. What was she supposed to do with that?

A sound. *Damn.* Her phone. She put down the radio, hit the green button on her cell. *Was it Jake?* It couldn't be. She looked out the window, crouching below the sill, just in case, so she couldn't be seen.

"Jane. Tuck. Sorry about the delay. We had to get my car. We're almost there. Almost at the Brannigan. Wait for us, okay? Lots to tell."

"Tuck—wait—don't—"

"We're in traffic, kiddo. Gotta go. See you in five. Maybe sooner."

She hung up. *Tuck.* She'd call her back. Stop her.

Out the window. Nothing. Damn the trees.

She hadn't realized she was holding her breath. She was terrified, trapped. And had no idea who the good guys were.

* * *

One chance. And it was now. He was behind a bush. Five steps away.

"DeLuca!" Jake aimed at Munson, fired.

Missed.

A gunshot. *It was.* Jane peered over the windowsill. Could not see a thing. Tears came to her eyes. *Jake.*

Munson turned, fired back.

DeLuca grabbed Ardith, twisting her away, yanked her into cover behind the car.

"Down!"

"No!" she cried.

Jake flattened himself against the wet grass, fired again. Munson clutched his leg. Screamed. Fell to the concrete.

Jake flew the five steps to the parking lot, kicked Munson's weapon away from him.

It skittered across the parking lot, spiraling over the snow-slicked pavement.

Jake jabbed a knee into the middle of Munson's back, grabbed one hand, then the other. Clamped them together with the same handcuffs he'd worn minutes earlier. He hoped the concrete was hard and cold and wet and filthy.

"You okay, D?" Jake called. "Collins Munson, you're under arrest for the murder of Lillian Finch."

"Now I am." DeLuca brushed the grit from his legs as he ushered Ardith upright from her cover. He took out his own cuffs and pulled Ardith Brannigan's hands behind her back. "Ardith Brannigan, you're under arrest as an accessory to murder."

"But I didn't—he only—I never—it was *his* idea to kill her," Ardith sputtered, twisting against the restraints. "Lillian had discovered the footprints. She was about to—"

"Shut up, Ardith," Munson's voice came from beneath Jake.

"Such a happy couple," DeLuca said.

"We'd be pleased to hear your story, Mrs. Brannigan. Might cut a decade or so off your sentence." Jake couldn't help but adjust his knee. Munson cursed, his cheek crushed against the pavement. "Oh sorry, Munson."

He thought about yanking Munson to his feet, then heard the sirens. Fine. He could stay like this for two minutes more. About time Jake had the upper hand. "You have the right to remain silent. . . ."

It was the most fun he'd had all day. The sirens drew closer as he finished the Miranda.

"Hear that?" Jake said. "Say your good-byes. You two are done."

"This is going be some freakin' police report," DeLuca said. "Jake, how'd you get—?"

"Long story," Jake said.

80

"You sure you're okay? Both of you?"

Jane handed DeLuca his radio, and looked Jake up and down in the Brannigan parking lot. A squadron of cop cars had swooped in, sirens wailing. Jake explained that Ardith Brannigan was on her way downtown and Collins Munson en route to a hospital.

Funny that the sky was so blue. Funny that the cold sun was glowing in the winter sky. Funny that a couple of sparrows flittered into the warmth of the evergreens. Like nothing bizarre had happened. Jane looped her arm through Jake's, ignoring DeLuca's knowing smile. He was a pal. She couldn't believe she'd suspected him, even briefly.

"Our Jake here's the hero of the day, Jane," DeLuca said. "I'm fine. The good news? I heard Ardith Brannigan start talking the moment she hit the backseat of the cruiser. Her lawyer's gonna be pissed, but that's not our problem. Apparently Lillian Finch discovered some footprint scheme Munson was using to—" He shook his head. "Must have been a big deal. Anyway, I'll give you two a moment. I'm going inside to make the necessary phone calls."

"Kat," Jake said.

DeLuca looked at the pavement, then nodded. "Yeah.

And then I'll inform the Supe you're on your way to fill him in on what happened."

"That's what *I'm* trying to figure out." Jane almost stamped her foot in impatience as D walked away. "Ardith talked about footprints?"

Jake gave her arm a squeeze, then stepped away from her. "Jane? What do *you* know about them? That's the question."

"Remember the fire?" Jane said.

Jake rolled his eyes. Jane always had to tell every detail. There was no such thing as long-story-short with her. He loved her for it.

"Okay, fine. You remember. Anyway, Ella gave me a piece of paper, apparently one of the things she found in Lillian Finch's house before—" She paused. "Okay, fine, fast forward. It's a footprint. They were—"

"They?" Jake said.

"You want me to tell you this?"

Jake shrugged. Her ears were turning red and her hair was tousled and she'd run out without gloves. He wished he could grab her hands, grab all of her. Maybe he was simply feeling relieved. And alive. "Sorry."

"Anyway, someone—now I guess it was Munson, or Ardith and Munson—was taking the footprints, the baby footprints, out of adoption files," Jane said. "I can't figure out why, except that's the only thing in the documents that would absolutely clinch the identities of the children. Chief Monahan told me Ella was trying to carry out a pile of documents, but they all burned in the fire. Except this one."

She zipped open her tote bag.

* * *

And stopped, mid-zip. Jane looked up as she heard the beep-beep of a car's horn, the crunch of tires on the salted pavement. A black SUV rounded the corner into the parking lot.

"*What now?*" Jake's hand hovered over his gun.

"Don't worry." Jane knew that car.

"Huh?" Jake said.

"It's Tuck," Jane said. "She's how this whole thing started. Anyway. Look at this paper."

Baby Girl Beerman. Jake read the typed description on the creased and wrinkled paper Jane handed him. It smelled like fire. A tiny baby footprint, impossibly small. So what?

He looked up as Tuck slammed the car door. A woman he didn't recognize was getting out of the passenger seat.

"Hey, comrades," Tuck called. "What're you all doing here?

By the time Jane neared the end of the story, her hands were frozen and her ears would never be the same. She tried to tell the whole story, fast as she could, since they were still out in the parking lot.

"So if this is your footprint, Tuck," Jane said, "you really are baby girl Beerman. If it isn't—well, that's why we came to see you, Carlyn."

She handed the paper to Tuck and Carlyn. They examined it together, shoulders touching. Judging by their expressions, the two women didn't seem to understand.

"Get what I'm saying?" Jane said. "If this footprint *doesn't* match, that proves Tuck is the wrong girl."

* * *

"The wrong girl?" After hearing Jane's explanation, Jake worried about fingerprints on the document, about Ella Gavin's potential testimony, about the documents destroyed in the fire, and how to link it all to their growing case against Munson and possibly Ardith Brannigan. Was it fraud? Deception? *The wrong girl?*

"Tuck? We can take a print of your foot downtown," Jake said. "Take it to our lab."

"Great," Jane said. "Can we do it today? Tuck? What's wrong?"

She'd have thought Tuck would be eager to take Jake up on his offer. Carlyn, too. The footprint could instantly answer the questions that plagued Tuck. But Tuck had a funny look on her face.

Carlyn, holding the footprint, had a funny look, too.

Maybe Jane couldn't fully understand the depth of the emotions. The past and the future. Right here, right now. Revealed.

"I'm sorry." Was she being insensitive? Disrespectful? So interested in the story that she'd lost sight of the real people involved? "Do you two want to talk privately? Without—" She waved a hand at Jake, and the parking lot, at the Brannigan's brick walls. "All this?"

"Jane, we're so grateful," Carlyn began.

Tuck had pulled the charm bracelet from her pocket.

"Jane? My mother—my adoptive mother—is dying. You know that. The nurse called this morning. To let my mother say—well, I'm flying down there tonight."

"I'm so sorry." No wonder Tuck's voice had sounded strange.

Tuck held up the bracelet. Carlyn moved behind her, draped an arm across her shoulders. "She told me that *she'd* made this bracelet. *She'd* written the note. To prevent me from finding my birth mother. Remember I told you she'd hate that I was looking? So this morning she said . . ."

Jane watched Tuck struggle for words. Her eyes welled with tears and Carlyn comforted her.

"Go ahead, honey," Carlyn said. "We understand she did it out of love, sweetheart. Out of thinking you'd be happier."

Tuck took a deep breath. "She said she couldn't face me, but had to tell me the truth. Let go of the guilt. All these years, she wanted me to feel loved by *her*. That she was my only 'real' mother. That she and Dad were my real family. She knew if anyone tried to say otherwise, I'd use the bracelet and note to prove they were wrong."

"Which she almost did. Right, honey?" Carlyn handed the footprint back to Jane. "But that's why we don't need the footprint, Jane. I'm so happy to introduce you to—"

"Audrey Rose Beerman." Tuck blinked away the tears. The bracelet twinkled in the milky sun. "The *right* girl. The rightest girl in the world."

81

Jane stabbed the elevator button, again and again. If the *Register* people didn't fix this, she was going to—Damn. No time.

She yanked open the stairwell door, raced up the three flights, down the hall, and toward Alex's office. She stood in the hallway, catching her breath.

Scrabbling her hair into place and clutching Ella's bag of documents—Alex was gonna love the footprint thing—she headed toward his office, marshaling her pitch. She'd have the scoop on the arrest for the Lillian Finch murder. No conflict of interest there. They couldn't lay her off now.

A flutter in her chest as she approached Alex's office. *Calm down, Jane.*

She would dig up the whole deal on what happened at the Brannigan, too. The Tuck thing—well, that was a happy ending. Happy-*ish*. But what documents had burned in the fire? Had other families been sent the wrong children? It could be a huge story. But she'd need time to research it. And write it. She'd need a job to make that happen.

Alex was there, she saw him through the window in his jeans and starched oxford shirt, standing behind his desk, sorting manila folders. Not on the phone.

She knocked, twice, didn't wait for an okay.

"Alex, listen to this!" She was smiling, big time, but hey, this was a big scoop. "I've got a *hell* of a story."

Alex did not return her smile.

"Yeah, Jane." He gestured her toward the couch. Which was empty. No piles of files, no documents, no clutter. Just couch.

"Sit down, okay?" he said.

Her face went cold. Her heart weighed a million pounds. *The layoffs.* What Hec—whoever—had warned her about. This was it. She was being laid off.

"What, Alex?" She stayed in the doorway, struggled to hide her emotions.

"You know we've had some . . . difficulties, here at the *Register,*" Alex said. "I wanted to tell you face-to-face. That's why I haven't been answering your calls. Really. Please sit."

Jane lowered herself to the couch, then stood again.

"Am I—," she began. She could take it. "Just tell me."

"You're fine," Alex said. "The fifth floor is impressed. You're tough, and determined, and a real team player. Now that Leonard Perl's arrested—the whole Hec Underhill thing—you're clear to come back."

"So why did—?"

"It's me they're letting go, Jane. Someone had to take the hit for hiring Hec. And that was me."

Jane sat down. Stared at her knees for a silent moment.

"I'm so sorry." She wasn't fired. It was Alex. That's why no one had told her.

"I'll be fine, Jane. I've got a lead on a new job in Washington, D.C. Your pal Amy still there? Maybe we can all have dinner. Sometime. Now that I'm not . . . your boss anymore."

"But that's so unfair." Getting blamed for something he couldn't have known. He'd gotten her this job. Backed her. Trusted her. Now he was leaving.

"Life's not fair. It's only short." Finally he smiled. "My last day isn't until tomorrow. Tell me about your story."

Jake would never feel comfortable holding an infant. Little Diane had a death grip on his forefinger. Her tiny fingers barely made it around. He shifted on Bethany's living room couch, worrying.

"You're a natural," Bethany Sibbach said. "Look how she's cuddling into you. You ever thought about having kids, Detective?"

He had, of course. And someday, maybe soon, he'd want to talk about it, with Jane. But it was this little girl whose future he was interested in now. He'd promised Maggie Gunnison he'd make sure Diane Marie was taken care of. He'd been haunted by that. Now they were onto the whole scheme, and the DA had taken over.

But why should the baby be an innocent victim? He'd called Bethany to see if there was anything he could do. Instead of answering, she'd asked him to come over.

"Me and kids? That's a story for another day," Jake said. "But this particular kid—"

"—is staying with me," Bethany said. "We knew her birth mother is deceased, and her father—unknown. So. I wanted to tell you in person. I got the okay from the DFS director. She pulled some strings. Special circumstances. Paperwork's making its way through the system. She'll be Diane Marie Sibbach. I'll be her mom."

Bethany tickled the little girl gently under her chin, scooped her out of Jake's arms. "Right, sweetie? Right?"

"Phillip and Phoebe?" Jake asked. They were both upstairs, naptime. Bethany told him Phillip *had* seemed to recognize Diane, but wasn't particularly interested.

"Off the record? We have a wonderful family all set to adopt them." Bethany's eyes were on Diane, swaddled in pink fleece, only her pudgy face showing. "I'll keep special watch on them, extra close. We can't control everyone's lives, Detective. In foster care families, as in any family, we can't make certain everything works out for every child. All we can do is love them. And do our best."

82

"I promise," **Jane** said. Her fingers itched to push the green play button, but this was Jake's show. He'd sent his assistant on an errand so they could be alone in his office at police HQ. Jane had banged out an exclusive front-pager for this morning's paper about the Munson and Brannigan arrests, but she knew there was more to the story. She was about to see it.

"You cannot say I showed you this," Jake said. "It's strictly background. We're on to this case because of you. I owe you. Not because it's you, Janey. It's only fair. And the Supe is aware. But if you reveal—"

"I promise." Jake had Collins Munson's confession on video. And she was about to see it.

"This is conference room B. Munson's in a folding chair at the table. My back's to the camera. The woman's his lawyer," Jake said. "She objected, but after an overnight in a Suffolk County jail cell, probably contemplating life without parole, Munson insisted. I have to admit, Jane, his defense is a new one. I forwarded the tape to the relevant part."

"*Let me. See. The video,*" Jane pleaded. *Geez.*

Jake hit the green button.

"So how many were there, Mr. Munson?" Jake's voice came over the tinny speakers.

"Have you heard any complaints?" Munson said.

"That's not what I'm asking," Jake said. "You took the footprints out of the files so the probative evidence was gone. Ms. Finch found out, obtained copies from hospitals, and threatened to expose you. So you killed her."

"Has anyone called to say they're unhappy?" Munson took a pocket square from his jacket, polished his glasses, examined the lenses in the fluorescent lights. He wore a tweed jacket and gray slacks. No tie or belt.

Jake made a mark on his legal pad. "Mr. Munson, your role was to reunite, on request, birth parents with the children they'd put up for adoption. But you were sending—just anyone?"

Munson flipped a palm, derisive. "Of course not. When there was a true match, marvelous. That's our goal, after all. But for many of our clients, the birth mothers were—shall we say—uninterested. Or dead. I've handled these cases for many years, hundreds of them. Thousands. Many of these connections could never be made. Then I thought, if we matched basic characteristics, eye color and age and such, how would they know?"

Jane couldn't help it. She pushed stop. "How would they *know*?"

"Yeah," Jake said. "He realized—well, listen. We don't have much time."

He pushed play.

"How would they know?" Jake asked on the tape.

"Precisely," Munson said. "The children were infants when they were left at the Brannigan. No memories, no history, no idea of their origin. The birth parents, too, had seen their child only briefly. If at all. How would they know what they'd look like as adults? I mean, who would ask for a DNA test? When the agency offers you your *child*? Your *mother*? We simply took the outliers, often the ones whose birth parents were deceased, or where the child was deceased, and put them together. It was all they ever wanted. To be a family. We could give it to them."

"We?" Jake said.

"'We,' the Brannigan," Munson said. "But *I* put the families together. *I* created them. I *was* the Brannigan. No matter what that pompous ass Niall thought. Or Lillian, who was about to ruin it all."

Jane pushed pause. The screen froze.

"You didn't tell him about Ella, right?" she asked. "That she figured it out? Because—"

"Jane," Jake said. "Gimme a break."

He pushed play.

"So let me get this straight," Jake said on the video. "Every time—"

"Of course not," Munson said. "Of course not *every* time. Sometimes, the request came in and the family was available and it all fit together without my . . . help. Sometimes, however, we had to give Mother Nature a little nudge."

"Did they pay you?"

No answer.

"Munson?"

A woman's voice came from off camera. "Collins, you agreed."

"Of course they paid me," Munson said. "I would explain they had a difficult case. The Brannigan simply did not have the resources to do extensive research in the whereabouts of birth parents who did not want to be found. Or children who did not want to be found. I explained I knew a top-notch investigator who could help them. Separately. For a fee. Of *course* they paid. They'd pay anything."

"Who was that investigator?" Jake asked.

Munson stared at the camera, his disdain apparent. "Detective. There was no investigator. I took their money. I chose a family. *Et voilà.*"

Jane pushed pause. "Holy—"

"Yeah. It's almost over." Jake pushed play.

"So as I asked, Mr. Munson," Jake said on the tape. "How many times? And you'll need to provide the records of the instances where you sent—"

"You really want that, Detective?" Munson asked. "All those happy families we created. You think it's best to ruin their lives?"

Jane pushed stop. The screen went black.

"Yeah, you know? Tuck thought she was the wrong girl because of the bracelet. But she was the right girl, in the end. And they're so happy. But this means there are other adults out there, living with people they've been deceived into believing are their families."

Jake shook his head. "I know. It's sick, really. We're trying to figure out what's illegal about it."

"Can you just leave them? With the people they love?" Jane sat in one of Jake's office chairs, leaned back, stared at the ceiling. *Medical histories. Genetics. Inheritance. Truth.* Would she want to know?

"All those families," she said. "It puts their whole lives into question."

She clacked the chair upright again. "What are you going to do?"

EPILOGUE

Jane propped her feet on the low wooden coffee table in Jake's living room. Took a sip of her wine, leaned back into the couch cushions. Jake's feet were next to hers. Their socks touched. This was perfect. But she couldn't allow herself to get used to it.

Diva had flattened her golden retriever self on the floor against the couch, stretched out, from nose to plumy tail, under their legs.

"Diva would probably eat Coda," Jane said. "No way that'd work."

"We could figure it out." Jake took a swig of his beer.

They sat in silence, listening to the evening street sounds, a car or two, the buzz of an airplane.

"Ella's gonna be okay," Jake said. "She's talking—well, writing—the District Attorney. They'll decide what to do about the Brannigan 'families.' Good thing *we* don't have to. You know Ella said—wrote—that Munson had offered to find Ella her birth mother. Imagine if they had? And gave her an impostor family?"

"It's incredibly sad," Jane said. She'd been promised the scoop on the Brannigan story. Alex had insisted she send it to him in Washington. His office was empty now. There was already buzz about the new city editor. "People.

Families, you know. Everyone's is crazy, some of the time at least. But still—"

She touched Jake's toe with hers. Thought about her mom, and her father, and home. Thought about families. Maybe she *should* go visit. Her father meant well. He just wasn't good at showing it. People weren't perfect. Life was short.

"—that's all this whole Brannigan thing was about, you know? Families. People would do anything to find theirs. So Munson took their money, and sold them one. Sold them a family. He actually believed he was doing a good thing?"

"Yeah, so he insists," Jake said. "Not killing Lillian, of course. Or taking Ardith. But by then he was trapped. Maggie Gunnison thought she was helping, too. No good deed, you know? The DA is considering probation for her, though, now that she's promised to help untangle that paperwork."

"Leonard Perl," Jane said. "What a complete slime. Stealing kids and selling them. Using Maggie. Profiting from desperation."

"Yup. There the DA's going for the max. Even though Perl ratted out poor Finn, who is now a very unhappy camper. It *was* him who was tailgating you, Jane."

"Yeah, I figured that."

"And turns out fricking Hennessey set up Perl as your surveillance guy. Jerk."

Jane took another sip of wine, remembering. "Happy to hear he's toast," she said. "But Jake?"

"Yeah?"

"Remember in the elevator? At Maggie Gunnison's that day?"

"Sure."

"When you got into the elevator, you acted like—" Jane demonstrated with her thumbs. "Were you saying 'text me'?"

"Yeah. I was."

"I did, you know, but you never answered."

"I was a little busy." Jake took a swig of beer. "I wondered if you'd remember."

"Well?" Jane said. "I do. What was it about?"

Silence.

"Jake?"

"I was thinking about . . . going undercover," he said. "You and me. Someplace where no one knows us. Somewhere we don't have to hide. Just . . . hang out. Be together. See what happens."

Jane looked into the red of her wine, not sure whether to laugh, or cry. Or both.

"You *know* what'll happen," Jane said.

"Yup," Jake said. "I do."

ACKNOWLEDGMENTS

Unending gratitude to:

Kristin Sevick, my brilliant, hilarious, and gracious editor. Thank you. The remarkable team at Forge Books: the incomparable Linda Quinton, indefatigable Alexis Saarela, and Seth Lerner for the very cool cover. Copy editor Julie Gutin, who not only saved me from continuity disaster but found one hilarious error that would have had readers calling me at home. Bess Cozby, who, so cordially, keeps all the trains running on time. Talia Scherer, so talented, and so passionate about libraries. Brian Heller, genius, and my champion. The tireless and fabulous Bob Werner. The inspirational Tom Doherty, who makes it all happen. What a terrifically smart and unfailingly supportive team. I am so thrilled to be part of it.

Lisa Gallagher, a wow of an agent. A goddess. A treasure. Without you, none of this would have . . . well, you know.

Francesca Coltrera, the astonishingly skilled independent editor, who lets me believe all the good ideas are mine. Editor Chris Roerden, whose talent and skill and commitment made such a difference. Editor Ramona De-Felice Long, whose keen eye sees everything. Even the stuff I tried to finesse. You are all so incredibly talented.

I am lucky to know you—and even luckier to work with you.

The artistry and savvy of Madeira James, Charlie Anctil, Jen Forbus, Nancy Berland, and Mary Zanor. The expertise, guidance, and friendship of Dr. D. P. Lyle and Lee Lofland. And the wizardry of MJ Rose and Carol Fitzgerald.

The inspiration of Krista Bogetich, Mary Jane Clark, Tess Gerritsen, Mary Higgins Clark, Carla Neggers, and Robert B. and Joan Parker.

Sue Grafton. And Lisa Scottoline. And Lee Child. Your incredible generosity will be paid forward.

My dear posse at Sisters in Crime, the board, and the Guppies. Thank you. And at Mystery Writers of America, the MWA-U team: Reed Farrel Coleman, Jessie Lourey, Dan Hale, and Margery Flax.

My amazing blog sisters. At Jungle Red Writers: Julia Spencer-Fleming, Hallie Ephron, Rosemary Harris, Roberta Isleib/Lucy Burdette, Jan Brogan, Deborah Crombie, and Rhys Bowen. At Femmes Fatales: Charlaine Harris, Dana Cameron, Kris Neri, Mary Saums, Toni Kelner, Elaine Viets, Dean James, Catriona McPherson, and Donna Andrews. And Nancy Martin. And Katherine Hall Page.

The amazing Elijah T. Shapiro and Jill McNeil for brilliant ideas.

My dear friends Mary Schwager and Amy Isaac and my darling sister Nancy Landman.

Dad—who loves every moment of this. (Mom—Missing you.)

And Jonathan, of course, who never complained about all the carry-out salmon.

Many of the character names in the book—you know who you are and I won't spoil the magic by telling—are the result of incredible generosity of those who donated to charity auctions. It was such fun to swipe your names, and I hope you enjoy your alter egos.

I've tweaked local geography a bit to protect the innocent. And I love readers who look at the acknowledgments. Thanks to you all.

http://www.HankPhillippiRyan.com
http://www.JungleRedWriters.com
http://www.FemmesFatales.typepad.com

Turn the page for a preview of

TRUTH
BE TOLD

HANK PHILLIPPI RYAN

Available in October 2014 from
Tom Doherty Associates

1

"I know it's legal. But it's terrible." Jane Ryland winced as the Sandovals' wooden bed frame hit the tall grass in the overgrown front yard and shattered into three jagged pieces. "The cops throwing someone's stuff out the window. Might as well be Dickens, you know? Eviction? There's got to be a better way."

Terrible facts. Great pictures. *A perfect newspaper story*. She turned to T.J. "You getting this?"

T.J. didn't take his eye from the viewfinder. "Rolling and recording," he said.

A blue-shirted Suffolk County sheriff's deputy—sleeves rolled up, buzz cut—appeared at the open window, took a swig from a plastic bottle. He shaded his eyes with one hand.

"First floor, all clear," he called. Two uniforms comparing paperwork on the gravel driveway gave him a thumbs-up. The Boston cops were detailed in, they'd explained to Jane, in case there were protesters. But no pickets or housing activists had appeared. Not even a curious neighbor. The deputy twisted the cap on the bottle, tossed away the empty with a flip of his gloved hand. The clear plastic bounced on top of a brittle hedge, then disappeared into the browning grass.

"Oops," he said. "I'm headed for the back."

"That's harsh," T.J. muttered.

"You got it, though, right?" Jane knew it was a "moment" for her story, revealing the deputy's cavalier behavior while the Sandovals—she looked around, making sure the family hadn't shown up—were off searching for a new place to live. The feds kept reporting the housing crisis was over. Tell that to the now-homeless Sandovals, crammed, temporarily they hoped, into a relative's spare bedroom. Their modest ranch home in this cookie-cutter neighborhood was now an REO—real estate owned by Atlantic & Anchor Bank. The metal sign on the scrabby lawn said "foreclosed" in yellow block letters. Under the provisions of the Massachusetts Housing Court, the deputies were now in charge.

"Hey! Television! You can't shoot here. It's private property."

Jane felt a hand clamp onto her bare arm. She twisted away, annoyed. Of course they could shoot.

"Excuse me?" She eyed the guy's three-piece pinstripe suit, ridiculous on a day like today. He must be melting. Still, being hot didn't give him the right to be wrong. "We're on the public sidewalk. We can shoot whatever we can see and hear."

Jane stashed her notebook into her totebag, then held out a hand, conciliatory. Maybe he knew something. "And not television. Newspaper. The new online edition. I'm Jane Ryland, from the *Register*."

She paused. Lawyer, banker, bean counter, she predicted. For A & A Bank? Or the Sandovals? The Sandovals had already told her, on camera, how Elliot Sandoval had lost his construction job, and they were struggling on pregnant MaryLou's day care salary. Struggling and failing.

"I don't care who you are." The man crossed his arms over his chest, a chunky watch glinting, tortoiseshell sunglasses hiding his expression. "This is none of your business. You don't tell your friend to shut off that camera, I'm telling the cops to stop you."

You kidding me? "Feel free, Mr.—?" Jane took her hand away. Felt a trickle of sweat down her back. Boston was baking in the throes of an unexpected May heat wave. Everyone was cranky. It was almost too hot to argue. "You'll find we're within our rights."

The guy pulled out a phone. All she needed. And stupid, because the cops were right there. T.J. kept shooting, good for him. Brand new at the Boston *Register*, videographer T.J. Foy was hire number one in the paper's fledgling online video news department. Jane was the first—and so far, only—reporter assigned.

"It's a chance to show off your years of TV experience," the *Register*'s new city editor had explained. Pretending Jane had a choice. "Make it work."

Pleasing the new boss was never a bad thing, and truth be told, Jane could use a little employment security. She still suffered pangs from her unfair firing from Channel 11 last year, but at least it didn't haunt her every day. This was her new normal, especially now that newspapering was more like TV. "Multimedia," her new editor called it.

"We're doing a story on the housing crisis." Jane smiled, trying again. "Remember the teenager who got killed last week on Springvale Street? Emily-Sue Ordway? Fell from a window, trying to get back into her parents' foreclosed home? We're trying to show—it's not about the houses so much as it is the people."

"'The people' should pay their mortgage." The man pointed to the clapboard two-story with his cell phone. "Then 'the cops' wouldn't have to 'remove' their possessions."

Okay, so not a lawyer for the Sandovals. But at least this jerk wasn't dialing.

"Are you with A & A? With the bank?" Might as well be direct.

"That's not any of—"

"Vitucci! Callum!" The deputy appeared in the open front door, one hand on each side of the doorjamb as if to keep himself upright. He held the screen door open with his foot. His smirk had vanished. The two cops on the driveway alerted, inquiring.

"Huh? What's up?" one asked.

"You getting this?" Jane whispered. She didn't want to ruin T.J.'s audio with her voice, but something was happening. Something the eviction squad hadn't expected.

"Second floor." The deputy pulled a radio from his belt pouch. Looked at it. Looked back at the cops. His shoulders sagged. "Better get in here."